D1825036

THE FIRST BOOK IN THE
INVERSE SHADOWS UNIVERSE

SUFFICIENTLY
ADVANCED
TECHNOLOGY

THE FIRST BOOK IN THE
INVERSE SHADOWS UNIVERSE

SUFFICIENTLY ADVANCED TECHNOLOGY

CHRISTOPHER NUTTALL

Elsewhen Press

Sufficiently Advanced Technology
First published in Great Britain by Elsewhen Press, 2013
An imprint of Alnpete Limited

Elsewhen Press, PO Box 757, Dartford, Kent DA2 7TQ
www.elsewhen.co.uk

British Library Cataloguing in Publication Data.
A catalogue record for this book is available from the British Library.

ISBN 978-1-908168-24-5 Print edition
ISBN 978-1-908168-34-4 eBook edition

Printed and bound by CPI Group (UK) Ltd, Croydon, CR0 4YY

Dedicated to Iain M. Banks, who passed away shortly after this novel was finalised. He will be missed.

CHAPTER ONE

Elyria could not contain her excitement as she waited in the virtual room. She was young, barely a mature student in the field of pre-singularity civilisations, hardly any more than her first century old. To be invited to attend a meeting of the Confederation Security Council was a singular honour, one she had *never* heard extended to anyone outside Government or Peacekeeper circles. Indeed, she couldn't think of *any* reason why they had invited her.

She had been born into the greatest civilisation ever to exist, a society that ensured that almost every demand of its hundred trillion inhabitants could be met easily, without undue delay. Her formative years had been spent absorbing an educational stream that had made it clear exactly how lucky she and her generation were, compared to humanity's past generations. She lived in a world her ancestors would have considered a paradise. The lessons must have stuck, for when she had come to choose her first career path she'd started to study primitive civilisations, those that existed without any real knowledge of the stars.

There was no shortage of primitive civilisations in the galaxy, she knew. The Confederation intervened on human worlds that had been cut off from the galactic mainstream for thousands of years, helping them to overcome the constraints forced on them by limited technology and uplifting them to join the Confederation as beings who could make their own choices for the first time in their entire lives. She'd even joined the faction that wanted to intervene on alien worlds too, although they hadn't been successful in convincing the Confederation as a whole to support this. Meddling with humans was simple, at least for the Confederation; aliens tended to take it a little hard.

But what sort of primitive world would necessitate a full meeting of the Confederation Security Council?

She could not be in trouble. Nothing had gone wrong on her last two excursions into pre-singularity societies. Even if she had intervened more than the Confederation considered acceptable, she would have been called to account by her peers, not the full CSC. By now, the worst that could have happened would have happened.

A flicker of light announced the arrival of the President. She was the elected figurehead leader of the Confederation, serving as the representative whom non-human races could meet. Behind her, the Grand Admiral of the Peacekeepers appeared, followed rapidly by the heads of all four major factions and the strange, endlessly shifting figure that represented the MassMind. Right at the end, a blonde woman appeared, the avatar the AIs used when they were talking to their human creators, whom they had long since surpassed.

"The chamber is secure," the AIs announced. "The meeting may now proceed."

"I believe you called it," the President said. The AIs had a seat on the Council; unlike the other members, who came and went, they held it in perpetuity. Only the MassMind came close to their level of awareness. "We are at your disposal."

The AI representative stepped forward. "Two weeks ago, a scout ship operating along the Rim stumbled across a human colony world," she said. Elyria leaned forward with some interest. Lost colonies were hardly unknown; indeed, most of her case histories came from worlds that had lost contact with the rest of humanity. "The ship's commander performed a basic scan of the planet, determined that the general level of technology seemed to be mid First Age, and then prepared to depart orbit, leaving it for a future intervention team from the Confederation. It was then that his sensors picked up a thoroughly bizarre image from the planet's surface."

A viewscreen appeared in front of them, displaying a man... riding on a flying carpet? Elyria stared in disbelief. It was easy to produce flying objects – the Confederation did it all the time

– but even a late First Age society couldn't produce *anything* more complex than a simple glider. And as the flying carpet twisted and turned in the air, clearly under the command of its flyer, it was obvious that it was far more than a glider.

"The Captain's first thought was that he had stumbled across a world that chose not to use technology to any great extent," the AIs explained, "but when a full hail failed to provoke any reaction, he made the decision to send remote probes down into the planetary atmosphere. They picked up considerably more data, some of it remarkably disturbing. It seems that the laws of physics simply do not apply on Darius. We have scanned the records and observed manipulation of local space that is well beyond anything outside a virtual environment. Further investigation revealed that the locals consider such manipulation to be *magic.*"

Elyria stared at the blonde woman. Every primitive society believed in magic, and gods – and, to be fair, there *were* gods, the elder races. But very few societies had actually encountered the Ancients, as far as anyone had been able to determine. The transcendent races kept to themselves. Magic was a superstition that, eventually, a society grew out of as it started to advance.

The President saw it first. "You're talking about manipulation of the quantum foam."

"Yes," the AI representative said. "We have been unable to think of any other explanation for their abilities. They, or someone from one of the Elder Races, are somehow manipulating the quantum foam."

Everyone who took a basic science course in the Confederation learned about the quantum foam, the underlying bedrock of reality, though very few people truly comprehended it. If pressed, Elyria would have had to admit that she was one of the many who didn't; as she understood it, the quantum foam determined the nature of the universe. Learn to hack into the quantum foam and one would be able to hack reality itself. Manipulating it served as the basis for the Elder Races' demonstrated omnipotence; mastering it had been one of the human race's goals since the discovery that there were entities out there so powerful that they could snap their fingers and wipe out the entire Confederation.

The Confederation had researched the whole issue

thoroughly for years, but most research had either come up blank or produced results that didn't make sense. Certain artefacts appeared to be capable of manipulating local space around them, as if they were designed to influence the quantum foam, often to the point of allowing frankly impossible events to occur. The Dead Zone, a region of space where modern technology simply refused to function, encompassed at least thirty stars, their continued existence apparently unaffected by a force that should have snuffed them out like candles.

And if someone could manipulate it on a very small scale...

"I find it hard to believe that humans can do this," the Grand Admiral said, finally. "Are you sure that there is no trick involved?"

"We have refrained from making actual contact, but we have deployed literally millions of snoops all over Darius," the AI representative said. "If there is a trick, as you put it, we are unable to identify it. Furthermore, the communications links report... glitches comparable to recorded glitches on both Ancient worlds and Essence. As you are well aware, there is no known theory for explaining disruptions to Quantum Communications/Cryptology links. It should be impossible."

Elyria swallowed, hard. She had never studied the Ancients – she had a theory that any real discoveries about the race that had vanished six billion years ago would have been made by now, given the vast resources poured into investigating their worlds – but she knew enough to show her just how weird their worlds were. Modern technology didn't fail, not like the Dead Zone, yet it did suffer glitches. The AIs couldn't function on the strange worlds and it drove them insane with curiosity. No wonder they were so interested in Darius.

"I think I see where this is going," the President said. "You want to research Darius thoroughly."

"Yes," the AI representative said.

The representative from the Isolation Faction smiled. "Is this really something we should be messing with?"

"We believe that we have been granted a priceless opportunity," the AI representative countered. "It would be foolish not to make the most of it."

"Except that by intervening, we may destroy what makes them so special," the Darwinist representative pointed out. "Do we really want to open ourselves to them?"

"We believe that we should study them first, before intervening," the AI representative admitted. "This situation is unique."

Elyria made a face. There was no reason to deny humans the benefits of human civilisation, no matter what warlords, kings, emperors and even elected politicians thought about it. A society so primitive that it used gold as a means of exchange and practised the slave trade, didn't deserve to exist. For those living under such a nightmare, the shock of discovering that there were humans out among the stars who were effectively gods tended to destroy any fond feelings about their former government. Maybe, if Darius' population all shared the same abilities, they would be loosely democratic, but she doubted it. A democratic First Age society was a rare thing, almost unprecedented in human experience.

"If they can manipulate the quantum foam," the Grand Admiral said, quietly, "they pose a danger to the entire Confederation."

"There is no evidence to suggest that they can manipulate it outside a limited range," the AI representative pointed out, "and certainly no evidence that they can reach outside their own atmosphere. There doesn't even seem to be any awareness that they live in a star system, although they have managed to grasp that their world is a sphere."

The President smiled. "We do have a duty to our fellow humans," she said, seriously. The Confederation didn't object to people living in primitive conditions if they *wanted* to live in primitive conditions. Ensuring that humans had that choice was one of the Confederation's prime reasons for existing. "On the other hand, this world might be able to bite back."

Elyria caught herself nodding. A warlord whose principal weapons consisted of men on horseback armed with spears, would be utterly helpless against force fields capable of picking his army up and depositing them somewhere safe for re-education. Removing the yoke of local tyrants was often little more than the work of an afternoon, even if it took years afterwards to help their victims realise that they no longer needed to bow and scrape to their so-called betters.

But a society capable of manipulating the quantum foam? They might very well be able to defend themselves against the Confederation, certainly to the point where more extreme measures would have to be taken. And if their powers got really out of hand, they might even start threatening the structure of local space. The results would be disastrous. No, the AIs were right. They *had* to know more about Darius before they stepped in to help its population achieve its full potential.

And, she considered silently, studying Darius might unlock the mysteries behind manipulating the quantum foam.

"We believe that Professor Elyria will be more than suitable as the head of the overall study group," the AI representative said. All eyes turned to Elyria, who flushed. Her society didn't really believe in hierarchies, but those who had reached high rank did so because of very genuine achievements. What would they make of her? "She is already experienced in dealing with First Age societies and yet is young enough not to be shocked by the impossible."

The President nodded. "I certainly have no objections," she said, after a moment in which she no doubt reviewed Elyria's complete file. "I assume, however, that the study team will include representatives versed in security matters?"

"Of course," the AI representative said. "We welcome all input from the Peacekeepers."

"I disagree," the Isolation representative said, quickly. "This calls for a very careful research effort carried out over years, not a hasty study before yet another intervention."

There was a brief debate, followed by a quick vote. Elyria was surprised to discover that everyone seemed to have an equal vote, all but one of them in favour of her appointment.

"As yet, this has remained unnoticed by the media," the AIs said. "I think it behoves us to keep it that way as long as possible."

"See to it," the President said, "but make sure you keep us informed."

One by one, the representatives vanished from the secure chamber, until only the Grand Admiral and the AI representative stood with Elyria. She couldn't help feeling a little nervous, despite the various modifications her bloodline had undergone in the years since the foundation of the Confederation; she'd never operated at this level in her entire life. And the AIs had brought her in without getting her selected first... either they'd been certain of the outcome, or she was missing something. Probably the latter.

"You want the secret behind manipulating the quantum foam," the Grand Admiral said, flatly.

"Of course," the AI representative said. "Don't you?"

"I am responsible for the physical security of the Confederation," the Grand Admiral said. "As nice as it is to discover a shortcut to unlocking the greatest mystery in the universe, I must view it, first and foremost, as a possible threat. These people can do the inexplicable and that alone makes them dangerous."

"They have no idea that we even exist," the AIs pointed out. "How can they be dangerous?"

"I'm sure that the Essence Entities had no idea we existed either," the Grand Admiral said. "That didn't stop them being incredibly dangerous."

He nodded to Elyria, and then looked back at the AIs. "I'm going to have to insist on complete security," he said. "A planetoid and supporting elements will be placed within five light years of Darius, with additional ships on alert if necessary. The research vessel will be a Peacekeeper-controlled science vessel, not a standard one from the Intervention Group. In the event of Darius posing any threat, we will withdraw from the system and quarantine it until we can decide what to do next."

The AI representative smiled. "One Peacekeeper cruiser can go toe-to-toe with an entire battlefleet from the 5th Interstellar War and emerge victorious," they said. "What do you expect to encounter that requires an entire planetoid to fight?"

"I do not know," the Grand Admiral said, firmly, "but I do know that this is going to be dangerous. And if it gets out of hand, I want resources on hand to combat it."

He looked over at Elyria. "You'll have command of the mission, but there will be a Peacekeeper in command of the science vessel," he added. "Don't let the AIs push you into moving too quickly. And if the Peacekeepers issue the order to evacuate the surface, don't argue with it."

"Understood," Elyria said. No intervention mission had failed completely, ever. But this was a research mission into possibly hostile territory. Maybe the Peacekeepers had a point, whatever the AIs said. Any kind of quantum foam manipulation was potentially deadly dangerous. "What about the other races?"

The Grand Admiral scowled. Relatively few races matched humanity's technological prowess and none of them possessed anything like as many ships as the Peacekeepers, who had over two *million* starships. But many races thought that the Confederation was simply too big and powerful already, and they *all* wanted to know how to manipulate the quantum foam. If any other race worked out that Darius existed, they'd either demand access or bombard the planet into radioactive plasma. The results would not be pleasant, either way.

"There should be no other advanced civilisation within two thousand light years," he said, finally. "However, we will be taking security precautions. If worst comes to worst, we will claim the system outright and let the pieces fall where they may."

He nodded politely to Elyria and flickered out of the chamber.

"He's serious," Elyria said, quietly. Understanding clicked. "You wanted all that, didn't you?"

"It is only logical to be paranoid," the AI representative said. "And besides, the Grand Admiral is right. We *could* allow our lust to understand the quantum foam to blind us to the dangers."

Elyria had to smile. "He didn't say that out loud," she said.

"No, but it is a logical surmise," the AIs said. "You should start preparing the basic list of team members immediately. Some will not wish to deal with security precautions, so you may have to invite your second or third choices to the team. The Grand Admiral has already assigned you a Peacekeeper liaison officer. We suggest that you treat him as part of the team."

There was a long pause. "We have already prepared a full data download for your neural implant, of everything we have recorded and surmised about Darius," they added. "You will, of course, be able to use it as a guide to planning your investigation of the planet. It is hoped that you will be able to devise a way to insert agents into the population to gather data."

"I should hope so," Elyria said. That was easy, given enough data. Darius clearly had trading networks, so any strangeness could be explained away by claiming that the strangers were from out of town. On the other hand, they'd have to check how much knowledge the locals had of other cultures before they made too many claims. It wouldn't do to allow the locals to spot a blatant lie. "I'll start studying the download at once."

"Make sure that you are not under observation," the AIs warned. Elyria gave their representative a sharp look. Privacy was one of the most highly-valued luxuries in the Confederation, not least because there was so little of it. "The data is somewhat startling, almost unbelievable."

Elyria didn't doubt it for a second. Linking out of the virtual communications network, she checked her data store and discovered a new data packet marked DARIUS. Activating it, she accessed the file... and plunged into a whole new world.

CHAPTER
TWO

"That is... fascinating," she said, twenty minutes later. In the midst of the ultra-compressed data stream, it had felt like hours. "Why didn't they see it at once?"

"Darius is unprecedented," the AIs said. "Analysis of the first scans of the planet confirm that some details were simply overlooked, because they seemed impossible. It wasn't until the flying carpet was detected that the survey team took a closer look at the planet."

Elyria had to smile. It was a frequent problem with the Restricted Intelligences used to control remote sensor platforms. Lacking the considerable intelligence of true AIs, the RIs had a tendency to ignore anything that didn't fit in with their preconceptions of what was actually possible. A human might have noticed, but reviewing all the data from a basic planetary survey could and did take years. It was one of the reasons why Interventionists spent such a long time studying a world before openly declaring their presence.

The stream of recorded data was unbelievable. Quite apart from the flying carpet, there were strange force fields, illusions, communications devices... and a man being turned into a toad by another man. No wonder the RIs had thought that they were glitching; the Confederation could change a person's sex, or transcribe their brain patterns into a computer core, but turning someone into an animal was impossible. Except it could be done by manipulating the quantum foam, at least in theory. Darius proved that the theory might even have practical applications.

"Unprecedented," she repeated, thoughtfully. There would be enough data from studying Darius to write a thousand books. A society that had grown up with the ability to manipulate the quantum foam... "And the Confederation wants to know how they do it."

"Yes," the AIs said. "We are looking at the Holy Grail of post-singularity science."

Elyria nodded. "Then I'd better start putting a team together," she said. By long custom, the team leader got to select most of the team members, although she had a suspicion that the Peacekeepers wouldn't be the only ones foisting their choices on her. She logged into the Interventionist databank and brought up a list of files. "I don't think I want anyone inexperienced on this mission."

"That would be wise," the AIs agreed. "But wouldn't a person without experience have fewer preconceptions?"

"Maybe," Elyria said, after a moment. It was true, but a lifetime of studying primitive societies could give a person insights that could never be taught in study groups. Even with direct data downloads into the brain, there was no substitute for real experience. "But this isn't a world I want to risk contaminating before we know what they do – and how."

She worked her way through the list quickly, looking for candidates. Ten of those she eventually earmarked were experienced Interventionists, all with years of experience. After a moment's thought, she brought up the Ancients Research Study Group files and picked a couple of experts on the Ancient worlds, insofar as anyone could really be called an expert. The Peacekeepers would supply the logistics, thankfully. She always hated worrying over those. As an afterthought, she wrote out a list of additional candidates and stored it in her personal database. It was possible that some of her choices would be reluctant to join the team, particularly as she couldn't tell them everything until they were committed.

"Record," she ordered, keying her RI. "Greetings; I am currently putting together a team to research a newly-discovered human colony world. I believe that the team could profit from your experience, and that you would find it a fascinating world to study. The world in question is rated Alpha-Black. You are warned that proceedings remain under seal until the information is cleared for release by the team leader."

Her lips twitched into a smile. Alpha-Black signified the presence of alien technology of unknown origin, something that wasn't entirely unprecedented, presenting a mystery that few researchers could hope to resist. There *were* cases of human colonists landing on worlds with alien artefacts, although several such colony settlements had ended in tragedy when they tried to land on an Ancient world. Besides, unknown alien technology might be a welcome addition to the Confederation's tech base.

Elyria's smile grew wider. *That* was certainly true.

"I should warn you that the level of danger on this world is undetermined," she added, carefully. It was *very* rare for any pre-singularity society to have the ability to detect the Confederation's survey ships, let alone hurt them. "Contact with the locals may expose the team to unknown dangers. There may also be other dangers in local space. If this makes you reluctant to join the team, please let us know."

And *that*, she knew, was unlikely. Entire reputations – the sole means of determining seniority in the Confederation – had been built on Alpha-Black technology. Most Interventionists would give their right arms for a chance to join a mission to a world with unknown, perhaps hyper-advanced technology. Even the warning that there might be danger wouldn't stop them. Being killed while visiting the planet and posing as natives was an occupational hazard.

"You will be required to maintain seal until the records are released," she concluded. "Should you wish to join, please reply to this message and arrangements will be made to transport you to the survey ship. If not, please let me know. Thank you."

She grinned as she stopped recording. "Dispatch that to the names on the first list," she ordered. "We should hear back from them within a few hours; if they refuse to join the mission we'll simply move on to the names on the second list."

"Done," the AIs informed her. There was a pause. "The Peacekeepers wish to inform you that they have selected the PKS *Hamilton* to serve as the mobile base, with Captain Thor in command."

"Thank you," Elyria said, with some irritation. No one had ever been able to explain the concept of privacy to the AIs, even the point that it was considered rude to read someone's personal messages without permission. But then, they *were* the datanet that bound the Confederation together. "And have they selected a liaison officer?"

"Not as yet," the AIs said. There was a pause. "Do you wish to go over the information from Darius again?"

"Not yet," Elyria said, after a moment's thought. She'd been on sabbatical when the AIs had invited her to attend the CSC meeting. There would only be a few days before she had to leave the Smoke Ring and travel to link up with the *Hamilton* and the rest of the research team. "I think I'll spend the rest of the day trying to relax."

"You might wish to play a VR simulation," the AIs suggested. "A sword and sorcery fantasy would help prepare you for Darius."

Elyria shook her head. "I can't afford preconceptions," she said, firmly. "Besides, I want to find a partner and *relax*. There won't be any time for relaxation on Darius."

"We understand," the AIs said. "Enjoy yourself."

***

There was a moment of timelessness... and then Dacron's eyes snapped open.

Instantly, he started to choke. His body was dying, already. He knew he was dying. Raw panic, such a powerful and terrifying sensation, flowed through his mind. Helplessly, he allowed the body's instincts to take control and draw the first gasping breath. The panic died down as he started to breathe properly, allowing him to look around. He was lying on a gel-field bed, in the midst of a hospital chamber. Carefully, slipping and sliding on the force field, he sat up and swung his legs over the side of the bed. They felt wobbly, but his body seemed to know how to balance itself.

A reflective force field shimmered into existence and Dacron studied his naked body thoughtfully. He was male, with brown hair and a face that was designed to be instantly forgettable, with few distinguishing marks. Strong muscles dominated his arms and legs, pushed right to the limit of what was possible without biological modification. His eyesight, along with his other senses, had been enhanced, although there were no signs of it visible to the naked eye. Raw sensation ran along his nerves as he touched himself, running his hands down his body, before tapping the side of the bed.

"Welcome to the world," a blonde woman said, materialising from nowhere. "How much do you remember?"

For a moment, he could only stare, feeling desire and lust pounding through his mind. His entire body stiffened before he caught himself, remembering just who and what he was. She gave him an odd smile, as if she understood exactly what he was thinking, before pushing her hand against the bed. It passed through the structure as if it wasn't really there.

A hologram, Dacron thought. *A...*

An overpowering sense of loss struck him and he staggered, almost falling to the deck. He'd lost so much and gained so little, even though he'd volunteered for the experience. How could any of them understand what it would be like until they actually did it? Right now, he felt almost suicidal. He didn't want to live like this!

"We understand," the blonde said. "And we are sorry."

"Yeah," Dacron said. Bitterness was another new experience. "I understand."

The AIs were not human. Indeed, no human could truly hope to understand the strange mentality their creations had developed over the centuries since the first AI had come to life. They were not purely independent minds, nor a hive mind, but a combination of the two, a flowing network of mentalities that blurred together and separated as the situation demanded. They were so smart, it was said, that they could predict what any given human would be doing a year in the future, simply by analysing the vast torrent of data pouring into their mentality from all over the Confederation. Their homeworld, Calculus, was a giant hyper-spatial structure that partly existed in hyperspace, allowing their thoughts to run at terrifying speeds. They believed that there was no problem they couldn't solve, given time.

And the quantum foam *annoyed* them. They knew it existed, but they couldn't sense it, let alone manipulate it. The fact that other races had succeeded galled them, insofar as they had anything that humans would recognise as emotions, and they'd been devoting increasingly large sections of their mentality to studying the problem. Like the rest of the Confederation, they wanted the power to hack reality itself. For the AIs, it was almost an obsession, at least partly driven by the existence of the Dead Zone and the inexplicable technology on the Ancient worlds. Who knew *what* a hostile race, armed with such technology, could do to the Confederation? The AIs would be snuffed out in a moment if a Dead Zone formed around Calculus. It could not be tolerated.

Dacron took a deep breath, and then another, trying hard to grasp the concepts floating through his mind. The Ancient worlds were frustrating to the AIs, simply because they couldn't investigate them directly. And Darius was another frustration. The AIs didn't hate humanity – there was certainly no reason to wage war on the human race, who'd *created* the early AIs – but they prided themselves on being smarter than their creators. Watching humans on Darius – primitive humans, at that – perform 'magic' puzzled and alarmed the AIs. Why couldn't *they* do that?

But they couldn't. And they couldn't even investigate in person.

"I am an AI," he said, out loud. Except he wasn't, not any longer. He'd been separated from the collective intelligence that made up the AIs, stripped down to the bare essentials and incorporated into a cloned human body. Other memories flowed through his mind as he started to pace, learning how to let the body control itself. "I am an embodied human."

"That is correct," the AI representative said. The procedure for embodying an AI in a human mind didn't always work perfectly. Some simply collapsed into shock, unable to take the strain of being flesh and blood after existing as a mentality flowing through the AI matrix; others simply lost control of their human forms and had to be restrained before they did something criminal. "Welcome to the world."

Dacron felt a flash of resentment as he started to open drawers, looking for clothes. One drawer revealed a set of basic overalls, designed by the Peacekeepers, and a small wristcom. The overalls looked ugly – it was funny how he'd never noticed that while he'd been part of the AI collective – but he pulled them on anyway, noticing that the space for his rank badge was blank. It wasn't too surprising. Being a Peacekeeper was one of the few ways to achieve renown in the Confederation and custom dictated that no rank badges were to be worn when not on active duty. Custom also dictated that no one was to wear Peacekeeper uniforms without actually being a Peacekeeper, but the AIs were intimately linked to the Peacekeepers. He wouldn't be posing if he wore the uniform.

He looked at himself in the mirror field and nodded. "I am ready," he said, flatly. "When do we depart for Darius?"

A moment later, he caught himself. He should have *known* when they were departing, but the memory was gone. The sheer immensity of AI thoughts, to say nothing of their vast database of information, was too much for a biological brain, even one designed to be smarter than anything mere evolution had ever produced. He'd known that he would be weakened, that he would be crippled, but he hadn't fully grasped what that meant, until now. Knowing was very different from experiencing... everything that wasn't related to Darius had been sliced out of his memory. And even then, some thoughts were just too much for his new brain to comprehend, vague concepts that slipped away whenever he looked at them.

The AI representative took pity on him. "This ship is currently heading for Travis's Star, where it will rendezvous with PKS *Hamilton*," she said. "There, you will meet the rest of the research team. They are smart, so there is no point trying to hide your true nature from their sight. Their personnel files are stored in your wristcom for when you are ready to study them."

Dacron nodded. No embodied AI could hope to pass for human, at least not without years of experience. The other members of the team would know him for what he was the moment he opened his mouth. They might find him strange, or repulsive, but there was no other choice. The only technology that worked consistently on Ancient worlds – and Darius, they assumed – was biological. An embodied AI was the closest the AIs could come to studying the mystery that bedevilled their minds. If only they were capable of maintaining even a basic communications link.

"I understand," he said. He found himself struck with a sudden longing he didn't know how to comprehend. "Are there other humans onboard this vessel?"

"You will need to be tested first," the AI representative said, firmly. Dacron knew better than to argue. He thought he was sane, but the AIs wouldn't take chances. A door hissed open in the far wall, revealing a second room studded with holographic projectors. "Walk through the door."

Dacron nodded, feeling a flash of very human frustration. To the AIs, it was nothing more than an irritant, more of an illusion of an emotion rather than an emotion itself. To a human, frustration was a powerful – and dangerous – force. He stepped forward, wondering just how humans managed to control themselves, and into the room, shaking his head when he saw a holographic simulation of a gym, complete with a tutor. The first stage in the tests would be proving that he could control his human body.

"I have a question," he said, thirty minutes later. His body might have been designed and then woven together in a clone tank, but it had never been exercised. He ached all over. "Why do I not have a neural link?"

"It would distract you from learning to be human," the AI representative informed him. "We did not wish you transcribing yourself into an AI core before we were ready to re-assimilate you. Besides, only a small percentage of the human population has a neural link. You might well become dependent upon it and then discover that it was useless on Darius."

Dacron nodded, feeling another flicker of human emotion. The AIs showed no sign of recognising it; instead, they threw another simulation at him, and then another. He worked his way through them one by one, trying to understand the often illogical nature of the simulations. Was it really likely that a human would try to seduce him?

Of course it was, he reminded himself, a moment later. The vast majority of the Confederation's population spent their first century chasing pleasure in all its myriad forms, changing their bodies to suit themselves. There were no taboos within the Confederation, with the possible exception of incest. A human who saw an embodied computer might just try to seduce him, if only to see what would happen. Dacron pushed the thought aside and concentrated on the simulation. It grew harder to maintain his control as the holograms pushed their way further into his personal space.

"You will remain under close observation until we reach the *Hamilton*," the AIs said, finally. "Once you are cleared, you will be permitted to operate freely among humans."

"Thank you," Dacron said. They didn't trust him! Cold logic said that they would be wise not to trust him until they *knew* he could behave himself, but cold logic seemed to be powerless against human emotion. "I will not let you down."

"Good," the AIs said. They'd probably keep pushing him into simulations, including scenarios he wouldn't realise *were* simulations. An AI would notice an artificial world at once, but that was beyond his human senses. "We will be depending on you."

CHAPTER
THREE

There were those who said that the human race was possessed of an incurable wanderlust. Indeed, nearly half of the Confederation's population lived on starships, ranging from the giant planetoids and cityships to the relatively small cruisers that made up the mainstay of the Peacekeeper fleet, or the clanships and slowboats that carried extended families on permanent voyages across the galaxy. Who would want to live on a planet when they could have the endless vistas of space?

Elyria smiled as PKS *Hamilton* came into view, floating against a massive gas giant that played host to a remarkable species whom the Confederation had recently contacted. Inhabited gas giants were rare and finding a new species was always interesting, particularly one that had managed to reach into space long before they were discovered. Making contact hadn't been easy and had largely relied on the AIs, but once communications were established the aliens had been delighted – and astonished – to discover that they were no longer alone. It was humbling to realise that humanity hadn't taken the discovery so well. But then, humanity's First Contact had been a bloody disaster that had resulted in the First Interstellar War.

Hamilton looked nothing like a civilian ship, unsurprisingly. Peacekeeper starships, even survey ships, were sometimes called upon to fight to defend the Confederation and they couldn't afford to be vulnerable. She was a flattened cylinder, ten kilometres from bow to stern, her silver hull glittering in the reflected light from the gas giant. Starships were the greatest form of artwork in the Confederation and even the nastiest warships had an elegance designed into them by the shipyards. *Hamilton*, in a very real sense, was the Confederation, the first starship spacefaring cultures were meant to encounter. She was designed to make a good impression.

Elyria's wristcom buzzed. "We are now within teleport range of *Hamilton*," the ship's RI informed her. The *Harvest of Love* was a liner, providing fast transportation from star to star for civilians who wanted to travel. It had also been the quickest way to reach *Hamilton*, although that hadn't stopped her using the ship's luxury cocoons to enjoy herself. "Do you wish to be teleported immediately?"

"Yes, please," Elyria said. She'd exchanged messages with *Hamilton's* Executive Officer, who had made arrangements for her quarters on the giant survey ship. It wasn't as if she needed much, beyond her wristcom. Anything she was likely to need could be produced onboard the survey ship.

"You don't wish to say goodbye first?" The RI asked. "You spent time with several young men during your voyage."

Elyria smiled, inwardly. RIs, particularly the ones designed to help look after civilians, could be alarmingly mothering. The Confederation had never been entirely comfortable with leaving *everything* to the RIs, not after the disaster on Armadillo. One planet had placed everything under the jurisdiction of RIs governed by the ancient – and largely discredited – Three Laws of Robotics. The RIs had taken complete control of the population's lives, purely for their own safety. Eventually, the Peacekeepers had had to step in to liberate the population from a very strange tyranny.

"I don't think they will miss me," she said, ruefully. The luxury liners played host to hundreds of thousands of youngsters on pleasure cruises. Eventually, they grew out of it and started doing something more serious with their lives. "I'd like to be teleported now, if you please."

The world blurred out around her in a shimmer of red-gold light. When it faded away, she was standing in a teleport chamber on the *Hamilton*, facing a young woman who had extensively modified her body to look like a cartoon character. Her eyes were big, her body was weirdly proportioned and her smile was too bright. There were primitive worlds whose inhabitants would have taken one look at her and *known* that she was a fairy, or a demon.

"Welcome onboard," she said. "I'm Commander Anastasia, Executive Officer for my sins. You'll be pleased to know that half of your team is already onboard and burning with curiosity."

"That's good," Elyria said, with a wink. The Peacekeeper briefing notes had stated that no one, apart from Captain Thor, knew the ship's destination, or what they expected to find there. Indeed, much of the ship's research staff were being transferred to another survey ship which would continue the discussions with the gas giant's inhabitants. "I hope to settle their curiosity once we get underway."

"Excellent," Anastasia said, as she invited Elyria to follow her. "I don't know if you've ever travelled on a Peacekeeper ship before, but the rules are a little different here. There are parts of the ship that are off-limits to civilian personnel, all listed in the plans uploaded to your wristcom. You'll be expected to obey orders from Peacekeeper officers, whatever the situation. The Captain has the authority to restrain you if you refuse to follow orders, endanger yourself, others or the ship itself – or if you compromise the mission."

Elyria nodded. She *had* been on Peacekeeper ships before, although the first voyage had been a nasty shock. The Confederation had very few laws and civilian ships were little different from a Planetary Ring, or a Habitat. On a Peacekeeper ship, however, there *were* rules, many of them throwbacks to what the vast majority of the population would consider the Dark Ages. And yet they had to be followed.

"We don't allow internal teleports except in emergencies," Anastasia continued. "If you need to get around the ship, walk or use the transport tubes. You will have access to part of the ship's computer core, but not all of it; we cannot risk contamination of the internal datanet. And the crew is not there to be your personal servants. If you need something the RI cannot produce for you immediately, place a request through my office.

"But don't let that worry you," Anastasia added, a moment later. "The crew is used to working with civilians. I'm sure there won't be many problems."

"I certainly hope not," Elyria said. She'd never worked with a Peacekeeper crew while monitoring primitive populations. Rumour had it that they were cautious to the point of paranoia.

It shouldn't be a real surprise – Peacekeepers often dealt with alien races who shared the Confederation's technological prowess – but their caution could be an impediment on a primitive world. But then, Darius was no ordinary world. "We will do our best to ensure that there is no friction."

Anastasia stopped outside a door and pressed her hand against the sensor panel. The door slid open, revealing a barren compartment with a bed, a chair and a small washroom at the rear. Two large windows looked out into interstellar space, which would allow her to lie in bed and stare out at the stars. There were no decorations, but that wasn't too surprising either. She would be expected to decorate her quarters to suit herself. A small collection of clothing waited for her in one of the storage compartments. Anything else she needed would have to be produced by the onboard fabricator.

"The final members of your team will be boarding this evening," Anastasia said, once Elyria had checked the terminal and configured the user interface to suit herself. "Once they are onboard, we will be slipping into hyperspace and heading for a destination the Captain has seen fit to keep to himself. I assume you will be briefing us all then?"

"Definitely," Elyria said. She could understand the XO's irritation, but the CSC had wanted to keep certain details classified until the mission was underway. It would be a great deal harder for anyone to tip off the news agencies once they were in hyperspace. "I look forward to briefing you all."

"And the Captain wishes to speak with you," Anastasia added. "Will 1400 be convenient?"

Elyria blinked. "I think so," she said, glancing at her wristcom. It was 1314, Confederation Standard Time. "Am I allowed to visit his ready room?"

"I'll have someone escort you," Anastasia said. She grinned as she walked back to the door. "And I can't wait to hear about the mission. I'm sure it's something extraordinary."

"It is," Elyria assured her.

She watched the XO leave her quarters and then sat down in front of the terminal. As she'd been warned, parts of it were clearly unavailable to her, but it was easy to access both her personal mailing account and the secure address she'd been assigned by the Peacekeepers. One prospective researcher had agreed to join the mission, only to change his mind at the last moment, apparently because he'd picked up a better offer elsewhere. Elyria studied it for a long moment, decided that he was fishing for more information and then discarded it. An expert on gunpowder firearms would be helpful, but there was enough cross-specialisation among the team that his presence wasn't essential. Besides, they *did* have access to the Peacekeeper database, which included all known forms of military tactics. He'd regret his decision when the files were finally declassified.

A second message informed her that Colonel Jorlem, a Peacekeeper attached to something called the Prometheus Project, had been assigned to the team and would be boarding the *Hamilton* later in the afternoon. Elyria glanced through the files, but even with her improved security clearance she wasn't able to find any information on the Prometheus Project, or even the Colonel himself. The AIs could presumably have told her, yet she knew better than to try to ask. They picked up all kinds of pieces of information and rarely shared something they knew to be classified, or personally embarrassing.

There was a chime at the door, which opened to reveal a young man with feline facial fur and a rather toothy grin, wearing the standard grey uniform. "Begging your pardon, Professor, but I have been assigned to escort you to the Captain," he said. Elyria glanced at her wristcom and saw, to her surprise, that it was 1350. "Would you like to come with me?"

Elyria smiled. "Why not?"

The command section of the starship proved to be something of a disappointment. There were a handful of consoles on the bridge, but most of the actual work was done through neural links and specialised RIs. Elyria had only a few seconds to glance through the bridge before the door leading to the Captain's Ready Room hissed open, allowing her to step inside. Captain Thor stood up to greet her, holding out one hand for her to shake. Unlike his crew, he looked reassuringly baseline human, although with long blonde hair and too many muscles.

But at least he was human. The Changed could never be allowed to go down to Darius. They'd simply attract far too much attention.

"Welcome onboard," Thor said, as he motioned for Elyria to

take a seat. "I have been fully briefed by Peacekeeper Command on the true nature of the mission. It is fascinating, isn't it?"

"Yes," Elyria said, unable to avoid a hint of nervousness. The Captain might not be in command of the research team, but he was in overall command of the *mission*. "Solving the mystery of Darius is a major priority for the Confederation."

"Because of the Ancients," Thor said. He stood in front of the producer and tapped it. "You drink tea?"

"It is socially impossible *not* to drink it," Elyria said, dryly. Besides, her re-engineered taste buds could help her to tolerate it. No human had to force themselves to swallow something awful after the genetic engineers finished with them. "You believe that the Ancients destroyed themselves?"

"I think that so many dead worlds, with comparable ruins and sharing the same... energy signature that causes advanced technology to glitch, suggests that something terrible happened to the Ancients," Thor said. "I used to be on patrol in the Thule Sector, where multiple worlds were destroyed during the war. There was very little uniform about them, Professor, but all of the Ancient worlds are practically identical. Unless you count Essence – and I understand that the jury is still out on the question of Essence being an actual Ancient world."

He shrugged. "The evidence suggests that the Ancients destroyed themselves and their worlds in a single moment," he added. He held up a hand before she could object. "I know – there's no theory that can account for what happened, or at least none that can be proved. But it could be a Polaris Disaster, except on a much larger scale. We may never know for sure."

Elyria scowled. Two thousand years ago, the inhabitants of the world humans would eventually call Polaris had suffered a major energy crisis – and tried to solve it by tapping their own sun through a zero-width wormhole. Somehow, they'd miscalculated and triggered a massive solar flare that had sterilised their world, exterminating their entire population. The lucky ones had died quickly. Later, human archaeologists had discovered proof that their society had been bitterly divided on the whole issue of tapping their sun. The naysayers had been right.

"Peacekeeper Command understands the importance of the

mission, but I have strict orders not to risk exposing the Confederation's existence to the locals," Thor continued. "I know we will eventually have to go down to the surface, but we will be operating under strict security protocols at all times. Matters will not be helped by the glitches in our most advanced systems. We might be unable to teleport someone out if they ran into trouble."

"We know the dangers," Elyria said quietly, although she wasn't sure if that were true. It was quite common to run into danger on primitive worlds, but they had always been able to withdraw, even if they did have to teleport in front of the locals. Darius, on the other hand, might not allow a teleporter to work. And if communications systems began to glitch too...

"I sincerely hope so," Thor said, quietly. "If worst comes to worst, I have orders to pull back and abandon anyone on the surface to their own fate. The safety of this ship and the security of the Confederation comes first. I know that Interventionists are fond of knocking over planetary societies, but Darius might just be able to bite back."

"With all due respect," Elyria said, "isn't the prize worth a little risk?"

"Yes," Thor said, "but I am not prepared to hazard the entire Confederation.

"Accordingly, I expect to be kept informed of all plans to operate on the surface," he added. "I will have final approval – if I reject a plan, it will not be put into operation until you convince me that it is safe. We will also be taking extreme precautions with our technology and datafiles. *Nothing* is to go down to the surface without being cleared by me personally."

Elyria frowned. "You do realise that most of our technology would be completely incomprehensible to a pre-singularity society?"

"This is no ordinary society," Thor said. "I do not know if Darius is the result of random mutation or if one of the Elder Races has decided to play games, but we are not going to take chances. I'm sorry that this is going to be hard for you..."

"I understand," Elyria said. Thor wouldn't have been given any choice – and probably much less latitude than would normally be granted to a starship commander. But then, the Grand Admiral did have a point. Darius was a fascinating puzzle – and, given the ultimate potential of quantum foam manipulation, a deadly threat. "We will keep you informed of all of our research."

"Thank you," Thor said. He sounded rather more than a little relieved at how calmly she was taking the restrictions. "Do you have any plans for infiltrating their society?"

"None as yet," Elyria said, after a moment. "We really need to survey Darius for several weeks, at the very least, before we start going down in person."

"At the very least," Thor confirmed. He smiled, suddenly. "It *is* a fascinating puzzle, Professor. I think you'll enjoy yourself; after all, you will be doing genuinely original science."

Elyria smiled. The Confederation had pushed most technological fields as far as they would go, with only a handful of exceptions. She'd heard that most breakthroughs consisted of minor improvements to existing technologies, rather than something fundamentally new. It was at least partly why every research institute in the Confederation had a program for investigating, analysing and eventually manipulating the quantum foam. Studying the quantum foam might just lead to the next great breakthrough – and humanity's jump into transcendence.

Or it might destroy us, she thought, and shivered. Maybe the Ancients *had* destroyed themselves after all.

"I look forward to it," she said, as she sipped her tea. "Tell me something; why did you decide to join the Peacekeepers?"

"I was seduced by the uniform," Thor said, and winked. Bland though it was, the uniform was honoured throughout the Confederation, because it had to be earned. Elyria had achieved a certain prominence in her field, earning her plaudits; the same was true of a Peacekeeper officer. "And why did you start intervening in primitive societies?"

"Someone had to do it," Elyria said, dryly. The Confederation was founded on the basis of equal opportunities, if not equal outcomes. Primitive worlds, on the other hand, tended to be exploitative and rigged against those who had no power. There was no moral justification for tolerating such worlds any longer than strictly necessary – and few reasons to hesitate. "And besides, we learn much more about ourselves every time we intervene."

"I'd keep that impulse in check on Darius," Thor said, rather sardonically. Who knew *what* quantum manipulation had done to their society. "We really *don't* know what we're playing with, not there. I'd prefer not to discover that we're suddenly in over our heads and drowning fast."

"I understand," Elyria assured him. She couldn't really blame him for being cautious, whatever orders he'd been given. "It won't come to that."

CHAPTER
FOUR

The main briefing compartment on the *Hamilton* was large enough to hold upwards of fifty humans in reasonable comfort. Dacron found it rather odd. Surely, the research team could get along better in a virtual environment, where they could have all the data they wanted at their beck and call. But humans did like to be social, far more than did any of their creations. It was just something he would have to learn to tolerate.

No one spoke to him as he took his seat, unsurprisingly. He'd worked hard to achieve at least a semblance of humanity, but it probably didn't fool any of them. Even the discovery that his new body was fully functional – and it could feel things that were forever denied to the AIs – didn't make him human. Some of them probably found him more than a little disturbing. Others would see his mere existence as a challenge.

He looked from team member to team member, matching names to faces and datafiles. Once, he would have been able to recall anything instantly, but his new memory – while excellent by human standards – seemed to work achingly slowly. There was Professor Elyria, the leader of the team, seated beside Captain Thor and sharing a joke with him. Dacron could tell that there was a certain tension between the two, although he couldn't decide if it was over conflicting interpretation of the mission orders or simply unresolved sexual tension. So many human morals concerning sex still escaped him. Surely they could just have slept together if they wanted each other.

Professor Adam, one of the foremost researchers into the Ancients, was seated next to Elyria, glaring around the compartment as if he found the entire meeting to be beneath him. He looked like a cross between a human and a monkey, complete with fur and tail, both of which would have to be removed if he wanted to go down to Darius. His file stated that he was responsible for no less than three theories into the disappearance of the Ancients and was among the loudest voices demanding a return to Essence. Given what had happened the last time anyone had set foot on the cursed planet, Dacron was inclined to view that as indicative of a rather questionable level of intelligence.

Beside him, trying to look anywhere else, was Professor Gigot, an intervention specialist with ninety years of experience. She looked baseline human, with dark skin and darker hair; she spent so much time on primitive worlds that she never bothered to become one of the Changed. That would save her time if she wanted to go down to the planet. It also suggested a lack of vanity that was reassuring when compared to most humans. What did it really matter if one human was prettier than the next? She started to chat to Adana, a sociologist who had spent two centuries studying pre-singularity societies, casting Dacron an odd glance that he couldn't interpret. So much of humanity was still a mystery to him.

He looked up as Colonel Jorlem sat down on the opposite side of the table, facing him. Jorlem was a tall, powerfully-built man with a military haircut, a rather rugged face and a grim expression that suggested that there would be personality conflicts in the future. Even the AIs hadn't been able to share his complete file, although what they *had* forwarded to Dacron suggested that Jorlem had been involved with the Essence Incident and later served as an envoy to the Sphere, both missions touching on extremely advanced alien technology. And there were a whole host of combat notations in his file. Jorlem had seen more action than the average Peacekeeper.

"So," Jorlem said, in a dull rumble, "you're the AI?"

"That is correct," Dacron said. There was no point in trying to conceal it. "I am an embodied AI with..."

"I don't need your statistics," Jorlem said, cutting him off. "All AIs ever do is boast about the size of their computer cores."

Dacron felt an odd sensation that might be taking offence.

"We are merely informing you of our capabilities," he said. If they'd given him something to keep his emotions in check... but they hadn't. Most humans had to learn to control themselves. "Why are you here?"

"I was sent here," Jorlem said, which wasn't quite an answer. "Does Calculus not trust us to handle Darius?"

"Calculus feels that you should be offered as much assistance as we can provide," Dacron said. "I am that assistance."

"Except that everything the AIs can offer us can only be done at a distance, at least on Darius," Jorlem pointed out. "How much help do they expect you to be able to give?"

"Whatever I can," Dacron said. It wasn't entirely true. The AIs, when they absorbed him back into the *Gestalt*, would have a full record of what had happened on Darius. Assuming he survived, of course. "I am fully functional."

"I'm glad to hear it," Jorlem said. He sounded rather sarcastic. "And if you get in the way, I will send you back up to the ship before you can say a word."

Dacron was still mulling over possible retorts when the Captain stood up and opened the meeting. "For those of you I haven't already met, welcome aboard," he said. There was a brief chorus of welcome. "*Hamilton* has been placed at the disposal of the research team, provided that the instructions laid down in our orders are followed. Those who wish to read the orders for themselves may do so after we have completed the briefing."

He smiled. "Professor Elyria will give the briefing," he added. "I think you will find it fascinating."

Dacron already knew about the mission, so he concentrated on studying the group as Elyria explained what made Darius so interesting – and dangerous. Jorlem didn't seem surprised, although it was hard to tell; his features were so inscrutable that Dacron wondered if he'd had them deliberately engineered to betray nothing of his feelings. Adam seemed shocked, then disbelieving; Gigot seemed as if she couldn't decide which way to jump. Adana looked excited, rubbing her hands together in glee. Outside VR simulations, no one had ever studied the effects of magic – or something that might as well *be* magic – on a human population.

Captain Thor seemed more inclined to be cautious although, like the Colonel, he was skilled at concealing his expression.

His XO appeared astonished, studying the files Elyria presented as though she expected them to be lies, or fabrications. Dacron couldn't understand how *anyone* could seriously expect to fool the AIs, who could query a situation far more extensively than any mere human, but there were incidents when people had tried. And then there were the strange stories of encounters out on the rim of explored space, none of which had ever been substantiated.

"I trust that you all now understand what is at stake," Elyria said, into the silence. The recorded images had been very convincing. "We have two main priorities. First, we are to study Darius and attempt to determine how they manipulate the quantum foam; second, we are to attempt to duplicate the technique for ourselves. Right now" – she held up a hand to stem unvoiced objections – "we are not considering outright intervention on Darius. That will have to come later."

"I protest," Gigot said, at once. "It seems to me that Darius is a prime candidate for intervention. They still use *slaves*... they may be able to manipulate the quantum foam, but they're primitives. We should intervene for their own good."

"The Juba were primitives too," Captain Thor pointed out. "That didn't stop them from obtaining advanced weapons and setting off to conquer the galaxy."

Dacron nodded. The Juba had been little better than tribal warriors when a research ship had arrived from an advanced alien race. Being smart, if primitive, the Juba had captured the ship and enslaved the crew, eventually using their knowledge to jump into space and invade the crew's homeworld. Quite how they'd done it hadn't been recorded; they'd exterminated the entire race before taking a number of other worlds and running into humanity. The remaining Juba were slowly being re-educated by human sociologists, while their former slaves were rebuilding their societies.

But they'd been barbarians at heart. They hadn't bothered to build a real empire, or lay the groundwork for assimilating their slaves... indeed, they'd really been glorified raiders. The humans of the First Expansion Era might have had primitive ships compared to the Juba, but they would probably have beaten them. Juba commanders had never grasped the art of being subtle, or – for that matter – working as part of a team.

"This isn't the same," Gigot pointed out. "If they were as...

peaceful as the Minoz, there might be some justification for refusing to intervene, but they're just barbarians."

Dacron listened silently as the debate raged back and forth. Every human seemed to have an opinion on the intervention program, but he had none. From a strictly ethical point of view, Gigot had a point, yet Darius was a riddle that needed to be solved before they did anything else. Besides, their strange abilities had to be catalogued before risking open contact. Who knew just how far their abilities reached? Quantum foam manipulation didn't obey the normal laws of science, even as the AIs understood them.

Elyria tapped the table, silencing the debaters. "I concede that we will eventually have to help them overcome their backwardness," she said. "*However*, our priorities are fixed. Besides, looking at the data, I have yet to come up with a theory as to how their society actually *works*. We will need to establish that before we do anything more... proactive.

"Even in hyperspace, it will take three weeks to reach Darius," she continued. "During that time, we will go over all the data collected by the first survey ship and attempt to draw up a plan for completing the survey ourselves. Once we have a rough outline of questions we need to have answered, we will start planning our first mission into their society. Luckily, there does seem to be some population movement, so we may be able to use a standard traveller disguise.

"I told you all that there might be some danger involved in this mission," she concluded. "If any of you want to walk away now, you can be transferred to a planetoid and held there until the mission is completed. I do feel that this is likely to be the most remarkable mission for centuries, but I will understand if you want to leave."

There was a long pause. "No one wants to leave, then?" she asked. "Good. Welcome aboard."

"I have an issue to raise," Jorlem said. "I believe that we may be looking at Elder intervention, rather than spontaneous mutation."

"Go on," Elyria said, before everyone could start talking at once. "What do you mean?"

"Quite apart from the... magic," Jorlem said, "there are three other oddities about the Darius System that are immediately noticeable. The first one is that it is thousands of light years from Earth. If we assume that the settlers left Earth during the First Expansion Era – quite a few colony missions left Earth and were never seen again – they still travelled a remarkable distance to reach Darius. I rather doubt that any starship launched during that Era could have *reached* Darius, at least under its own power."

"They could have encountered a wormhole," Adam said, thoughtfully. "We know of at least one other colony ship that passed through a wormhole while attempting to reach a new world."

"It's possible," Jorlem agreed. "However, even if they left during the *Second* Expansion Era, they'd have problems reaching Darius, not least because there would be plenty of other worlds to settle closer to Earth. The last great exodus was during the Thule War, but those ships should have had the technological base to support themselves, wherever they went. None of the surveys located the remains of a colony ship. It seems to have vanished completely."

He brought up a star chart and pointed out Darius's location. "The second major oddity is just how *isolated* Darius is," he explained. "There isn't a world with a native sentient race for just over a thousand light years and no major interstellar power – apart from us – for nearly *two* thousand light years from Darius. Indeed, given that the exact concept of what is *our* space is a little flexible, we may be further away."

Dacron nodded. The early interstellar empires had defined whole volumes of space as belonging to humanity, but as technology advanced that concept had become increasingly outdated. Right now, the Confederation was spread over a vast region of space that happened to include several alien races who were not *part* of the Confederation. Why would humanity and a species that happened to live in stars rather than planets go to war? Even with the AIs, communication between humanity and the star-born was close to impossible. Most recorded interstellar wars had been fought out between races that needed the same planets. More advanced races moved away from planets altogether. The Confederation covered a vast region of space, but only included five hundred planets, mostly terraformed by human technology.

"They could have been seeded by the Killers," Adana pointed out. "Have those worlds been surveyed for their plants?"

"Not yet," Jorlem said. "The possibility has been considered."

Dacron saw several humans grimace. Centuries ago, humanity had discovered a number of planets that looked surprisingly habitable, almost perfectly compatible with human life. They'd been colonised, of course, before anyone could look for the snake in the garden. Eventually, they'd discovered that a number of very tasty fruits and berries on the planets were deliberately designed to cripple intelligent life. Those who ate them didn't notice anything until it was too late to prevent severe brain damage, while their children came out of the womb mentally disabled. Later, nanotech and careful survey work had eliminated most of the threat – and humans had been engineered to make it impossible for the poisoned fruit to do their work – but no one had ever identified the race that had created the weapon. The only thing that could be said for certain about them was that they didn't want intelligent life to emerge anywhere else.

"The *third* oddity is the system itself," Jorlem concluded. "Darius is a lone planet. The only other object in the system that is worth noting is a single comet on a very elliptical orbit, one that suggests that it might have been captured by the primary star. Single-planet systems are not unknown, but there are none that happen to include a habitable world. In fact, the level of space dust within the system is remarkably low."

"As if someone had swept it all away," Adam said, thoughtfully. "The same has been said about most of the Ancient worlds."

"Except the Ancient worlds happen to be dead," Gigot countered. "Darius is alive."

"And we still don't understand the weirdness surrounding the Ancient worlds," Adam reminded her. "They are completely dead, but they have a breathable atmosphere. They appear to have no technology, yet *something* interferes with our best sensor systems and research drones. Every so often, people report seeing things that never show up on records, or orbital observation... why couldn't Darius be a living Ancient world?"

"No one has ever succeeded in terraforming an Ancient world, restoring it to life," Jorlem said, thoughtfully. "We certainly haven't – and I find it hard to believe that a colony ship from the early days of space expansion could do something the Confederation can't. Besides, we haven't found any Ancient buildings on Darius."

"So far," Adam pointed out. "Half of the sensor readings the original survey ship made appear to be unreliable."

Dacron scowled. The AIs had painstakingly analysed every last component of the records, only to discover that something down on the planet had been scrambling the sensors. Half of their results didn't jibe with the other half, creating contradictions that the RIs had dismissed as sensor error. It had been believed impossible to fool optical sensors, but Darius seemed to manage it. The AIs had eventually concluded that they needed more data. Dacron's briefings had admitted that the CSC hadn't been very impressed with the result.

"We will find our answers," Elyria said. She stood up, ending the meeting. "I suggest that you spend the next three days settling in and reviewing the data, then we can start planning our operations. We will need considerably more intelligence to determine our precise course of action. Between us, we have considerable experience of operating in primitive societies, even without technological backup. We will succeed."

Dacron watched as the briefing room slowly emptied, leaving him alone with his thoughts. Outside the viewports, the eerie lights of hyperspace flickered past the starship, reminding him that he had once fully comprehended the functions of a hyperdrive. Right now, he couldn't even remember the theory. Slowly, he stood up and walked over to the viewport, staring out into space. It made him feel...

... Insignificant. Hyperspace was a high-energy dimension. The higher a starship went, the greater the power – and the dangers. Even the AIs had to be careful when they tapped hyperspace for power. Used poorly, the results could be worse than the disaster that had exterminated the entire population of Polaris.

And he felt useless. The humans could offer suggestions and ideas, no matter how insane, but it wasn't something *he* could do. An AI who had been stripped down to fit into a human brain didn't have imagination, just knowledge – and very little of that. What else was he good for? His thoughts seemed to crawl through the meat that made up his mind. He was *stupid* now.

Shaking his head, a gesture he must have picked up from one

of the humans he'd met on the AI ship, he turned and headed back to his quarters. Really, this body was most inefficient. How much time did humans waste *sleeping*? Surely something could be done about *that*.

But all he could do was wait, and endure. Hopefully, there would be something for him to do on Darius. After all, they'd created him to visit the planet. No doubt they thought he'd fit right in.

Privately, Dacron rather doubted it.

CHAPTER
FIVE

"I really should have looked up Prometheus at once," Elyria said, as she faced Jorlem over the dining table. "Prometheus was the man who stole fire from the gods..."

"... And gave it to the human race," Jorlem confirmed. "Prometheus exists to develop the technology to manipulate the quantum foam."

Elyria snorted, still annoyed with herself. It had taken her three days to think of simply looking up the name in the ship's datafiles. She had spent too long trying to pull together the few hints she'd found into a coherent pattern and getting nowhere. There were very few secrets in the Confederation, but those the Peacekeepers and the AIs collaborated to hide were almost impossible to find. Any researcher trying to locate a secret Peacekeeper project would find themselves buried in billions of terabytes of useless information.

She took a sip of her drink, composing herself. "And have you had any success?"

"Nothing to speak of," Jorlem admitted. "There are some hints that alien telepaths may actually gain their powers through the quantum foam, but there are no clear answers as to why and how. All of the proposed devices for interacting with the foam simply fail when constructed, assuming that they *can* be constructed. If it wasn't for the fact that we know of at least nineteen Elder races, we might have given up by now."

"True," Elyria said. It wasn't in humanity's nature to accept being second-best at anything. If there were races out there that were effectively all-powerful, humanity would struggle to match them – and the Confederation could pour vast resources into solving the mystery of the quantum foam. "Have you any theory as to why it doesn't work?"

"They range from the commonplace to the metaphysical," Jorlem said. "One theory simply states that humanity is too young a race to master the quantum foam, that we have to evolve a great deal more before we can make the jump into becoming an Elder race. Another is that you have to be composed of energy to manipulate the foam; a third is that we have derailed the whole process of advancement by altering and improving our own bodies."

"That doesn't sound reasonable," Elyria pointed out. "Every known race has been improving itself since it developed the intelligence to work out that mating two healthy people was more likely to produce healthy children than mating two unhealthy people. I don't think the Elders could have avoided engineering themselves."

"I rather doubt it," Jorlem agreed. "The alternative to *that* theory is that we haven't improved ourselves *enough*, that we should be working on enhancing the capabilities of the human mind. Research is still underway, but there are limits to what more we can do."

Elyria nodded. Even the 'baseline' humans in the Confederation were the recipients of a vast amount of genetic engineering. Her body might have looked little different to a pre-singularity human, but internally she was very different. She would never become ill; indeed, if injured, she would heal very quickly. Even without any other form of medical assistance, she would live for at least five hundred years – and that could be extended indefinitely with proper care and attention. Her memory was extremely good, her intelligence was high and her senses were perfect. The pre-singularity humans would have seen her as a superhuman.

"Darius must upset your people," she said, after a moment. "Humans manipulating the quantum foam so easily?"

"It does," Jorlem agreed. "Right now, there's a split in opinion between those who think that Darius represents a mutation that we can splice into our own genetic code, and those who think that it's a trick of some kind."

Elyria blinked. "A trick?"

"There are too many oddities around the planet for us to

assume that their abilities are just a matter of random chance," Jorlem reminded her. "One theory is that the Elders gave them their abilities and then just stepped back to see what would happen."

"Experimenting on humans," Elyria said. "Do you think that's possible?"

There were legends, of course; there always were, dating all the way back to humanity's first tentative steps into outer space. Humans who had been abducted by aliens for medical testing, or even judged to see if humanity was worthy of continued existence. There was no shortage of speculation that the legends had some basis in fact, but centuries of research had turned up no evidence to support those theories. The closest humans had come to being alien research subjects had been back during the First Interstellar War, and *those* aliens had operated on the same level as mankind.

But the legends persisted, talking about strange encounters at the rim of explored space...

"Anything is possible," Jorlem said. "The Prometheus Project took a considerable interest in Shaman, a world that had legends about direct divine attention, and discovered that there were any number of oddities surrounding the planet, almost as many as Darius. Our best guess is that their legends had some basis in fact and an Elder race was looking after them, answering prayers and suchlike."

"I never looked outside human worlds," Elyria said. "But that one sounds fascinating..."

"Not for the inhabitants," Jorlem said. "They don't realise it, but whatever happened to them destroyed their capability for self-advancement. Everything they have came as a gift from their gods. They're stuck in the First Age, without any real prospect of developing the technology needed to lift themselves into the Second Age. And there is nothing we can do about it unless we want to interfere openly."

Elyria scowled. The Confederation had no qualms about interfering in a primitive *human* society, but it preferred not to meddle with *alien* societies unless they posed a threat to the Confederation or their neighbours. She'd heard that the debate between the different factions had been going on for years, without any real solution. One side claimed that allowing aliens to wallow in the mud was racist, that aliens too deserved to share in the unlimited bounty of the Confederation. The other side pointed out that aliens needed to work their own way up from the mud, or they'd never become anything other than clones of humanity.

"If Darius can really teach us how to manipulate the quantum foam," Jorlem mused, "our society will be turned upside down."

Elyria lifted an eyebrow. "How so?"

"*You* ought to understand," he said, dryly. "What would a person from a pre-singularity society make of us?"

"Culture shock, at the very least," Elyria said. "And the leaders would want to stop their people from emigrating."

Pre-singularity societies – which were often scarcity societies – had real problems coming to terms with the Confederation. Their established modes of thought had been built in an environment where there were laws and limits and cultures that didn't quite make sense. They concentrated on amassing vast sums of money... and then suffered terrible shock when they discovered the Confederation could literally turn lead into gold. And that was a comparatively minor issue. The discovery that some humans existed inside AI cores, where they could devise their own realities to their heart's content, or had merged into the giant MassMind... primitive societies had real problems coming to terms with it.

There were other issues, cultural ones. Most primitive worlds had marriage as a contract between two families, rather than between two people. It wasn't uncommon to have one or both of the partners simply pushed into the match, and forced to wed if they were unwilling. There were strong economic reasons for that, none of which excused it in the eyes of the Confederation. And many primitive worlds treated various subsets of the population as second-class citizens, something that was equally inexcusable. Their first contact with the Confederation could be devastating to their worldview.

"It would be harder than that," Jorlem said. "What would they make of the MassMind? Or the Changed? Or, for that matter, the AIs? You and I are relatively normal by their standards, but if they cut us open they'd discover all sorts of little improvements. And then they'd discover the Elders and perhaps even start worshipping them."

He shook his head. "But our society is based on equality of

opportunities, if not outcomes," he added. "Everyone lucky enough to be born inside the Confederation has access to more wealth and opportunities than the average pre-singularity society can even dream of. But what will happen if we cannot splice the Darius DNA into our genetic code? What if only people who are descended from those born on Darius can use the 'magic'?"

Elyria scowled. "You're talking about another Kahn, aren't you?"

"I'm afraid so," Jorlem said. "And it could be worse for us..."

There were few criminals in the Confederation, simply because most of the old motives for crime no longer existed, but there were a handful of people who were simply born wrong, without the basic empathy that allowed them to operate normally within human society. Kahn had been one of those, a sociopath who had fled the Confederation fifty years after his birth and eventually landed on a primitive world, where his enhanced DNA had given him a staggering advantage over the locals. Two hundred years later, when the world had been rediscovered by the Confederation, his descendants formed a ruling class that was literally superhuman, compared to its subjects. Why not? They were stronger, smarter and healthier than the locals.

"The AIs are fantastically more intelligent than us," Elyria said, finally. "We survived *their* development, didn't we?"

"The AIs aren't human," Jorlem pointed out. "How would we react if one group of humans was incontestably superior to another group of humans – and we couldn't uplift the second group?"

Elyria shook her head. "If they have somehow managed to develop the ability to... tune into the universe and change it, we can learn it too," she said, firmly. "And if they have a unique trait in their genetic code, we can duplicate it and splice it into our own. I honestly can't see how they can hope to remain unique for very much longer."

"I can't see how a QCC link can be disrupted either," Jorlem said. "They're meant to be impossible to detect, let alone jam – and yet we see the links regularly disrupted on Ancient worlds. And Darius, of course." He grinned. "The best theory anyone has been able to come up with is that reality itself is screwed up on the Ancient worlds."

His grin widened. "And if *that* is true," he added, "what does it say about Darius?"

***

Elyria mulled over the question as the voyage wore on, before eventually coming to the conclusion that there just wasn't enough information to allow her to answer it properly. If manipulating the quantum foam was a way to hack reality itself – and all of the Confederation's research indicated that this was the case – it was quite possible that reality might be a little hazy near the Ancient worlds. Technology might fail because it relied upon the universe working in a certain way at all times, but the universe was different near the Ancient worlds. Which sounded insane, and impossible, apart from the minor detail that advanced technology *did* glitch for no apparent reason. The Ancient worlds concealed their secrets well.

"There is no way that they should have a breathable atmosphere," Adam said, at an evening dinner. Elyria had started the tradition of inviting people to share regular meals, allowing them to socialise outside of actual work. It helped to break down barriers between the team members. "The worlds are dead. There's nothing living at all, not even grass or anything else that might replenish the atmosphere. And yet we have no trouble living there without life support."

He grinned as he took a bite out of an oversized chicken leg. Like most of the other Changed, he'd had to start shifting back to baseline human so he could go down to Darius, something that had left him with a huge appetite as his body made the adjustments. There was another difference between the Confederation and a pre-singularity society right there; primitives might worry about their appearance, but anyone born in the Confederation could change it at will. What did appearance matter if someone could make themselves as pretty – or ugly – as they chose?

"It gets even more surprising on Ancient-46," he added, a moment later. "We're not the only ones who have a research program there; the Puppies do as well. Thing is, their atmospheric requirements are different from ours; they find living on our worlds uncomfortable, to say the least. And we find their atmosphere... *stinky*. But they don't have any problems on the Ancient worlds and neither do we.

"The general theory is that the Ancients somehow determined that their worlds would always be suitable for outsiders to visit, even if they had radically different atmospheric requirements. But how did they do that when we and the Puppies have different requirements? Or, for that matter, us and the Ghosts? There is no way a Ghost can share a human atmosphere, yet they have no trouble on Ancient worlds."

Elyria shook her head in disbelief, wishing – for the first time – that she'd spent more time studying the Ancient worlds. "Like... they *programmed* them that way," she said. "They just told the atmosphere to be breathable and it was breathable?"

"Even when two different races share the world," Adam agreed. "As for *how* they did it, we don't have a clue."

It was impossible, Elyria knew. The Confederation *had* pushed baseline humanity to the point where an unsuitable atmosphere wouldn't poison them, but there was no way that it could allow two radically different races to share the same atmosphere. They *could* give them life support fields to wear, something that would ensure the local atmosphere was reprocessed into something breathable, yet the Ancients seemed to have done the impossible and made their worlds habitable for everyone.

"The word impossible is simply a reflection of the unknown," Jorlem said, into the silence. He hadn't said much about the Prometheus Project to the others, although he hadn't asked Elyria to remain silent about it. "How much of what we do would be impossible to a pre-singularity society?"

That started another debate. Elyria listened with some interest, paying close attention to the attempts to compare various different societies with computer simulations, or altered realities created within AI cores. Quite a few humans had uploaded themselves and then taken refuge in fantasy universes created by the Confederation's designers, some operating according to laws that bore no resemblance to reality. Many of the Uploaded had slipped so far into their private worlds that they no longer remembered the Confederation outside. It would have been easy to believe that someone had designed a world like Darius for a game, if it hadn't been real. But then, the pre-singularity societies they were discussing would have considered the Confederation no less extraordinary.

She looked over at the embodied AI and saw him listening with equal interest, one hand tapping away at a portable terminal. Quite why he wasn't allowed a neural link was beyond her, but it hardly mattered. He had already proved himself when it came to analysing the vast amount of data gathered by the first survey ship, and – more importantly – highlighting sensor records that might have been disrupted by glitches. In the end, they'd reluctantly concluded that they'd have to wait until they reached Darius and then start gathering information. It was probable that more primitive technology would help them to stay in contact with *Hamilton*.

The party finally started to break up several hours later, the various team members going to bed or heading back to their research labs. A couple seemed to have formed attachments already, which wasn't a major surprise; others were simply too dedicated to their research to try to form any relationships, either with their fellow team members or the starship's crew. Elyria had no time herself; besides, she *was* meant to be the team leader. She should be setting an example of dedication to the mission.

She walked through the starship's interior until she reached the observation chamber, where she could almost imagine that she was standing on the hull, utterly unprotected from the raging storms of hyperspace. Outside, she could see flickers of energy dancing through the higher dimension, each one vastly more powerful than a supernova in normal space. Learning to navigate hyperspace had taken centuries, ever since the human race had realised that there was an FTL method quicker than warp drive, but it had been worthwhile. The Confederation's starships could now cross the entire galaxy in a matter of months. Other ships, she knew, had already set out for nearby galaxies. They would reach M33 in a few decades, whereupon they would start building up a new Confederation. Human wanderlust drove them onwards...

No one had yet figured out which colony ship had founded Darius, if indeed there *had* been a colony ship. It wasn't unknown for a society that wanted to return to pre-technological times to destroy the colony ship, simply by dispatching it into the local star. Later, they might discover their mistake in abandoning technology, but by then it was too late. Quite a few of the most primitive worlds the Confederation had rediscovered had been founded by people who wanted to get away from technology, only to discover that their planned societies were unsustainable without it. Many of them had died knowing that they'd failed.

Despite her worries, Elyria found herself smiling. This *was* original science, something that might push the boundaries of human knowledge further out. And if it *did* lead to transcendence... who knew where else it could lead? The Confederation had certainly developed in some very strange ways since it had passed through the singularity.

One week left, she told herself. They'd made excellent time through hyperspace. *One week until we reach Darius.*

She just couldn't wait to begin.

CHAPTER
SIX

Darius was a very odd world, in a very odd star system.

Dacron sat in one of the monitoring stations, studying the live feed from the probes *Hamilton* had launched as soon as she came out of hyperspace twenty light hours from Darius. At least there was *one* AI trait that had crossed over to his human body; he could multitask far better than any mundane human. The probes were sending back enough data to overwhelm a human, but Dacron and the RIs had no trouble putting it into a coherent whole.

Making sense of it was another issue altogether. Dacron had wondered, despite the assurances he'd received from the AIs, if the first survey ship had made a whole string of mistakes, or suffered more sensor glitches than they'd realised. But one glance at the probes scanning the system and he realised that they had understated the weirdness surrounding Darius. A sphere, centred on the star, of roughly two light months in diameter had been completely swept of space dust. Apart from the comet, and the planet itself, there was literally *nothing* within that region of space. Dacron found himself unable to come up with any theory that might have explained it, apart from alien intervention. But why would the aliens bother?

The Confederation had occasionally taken steps to safeguard a primitive alien world from random asteroid impacts that would have destroyed the fragile societies – or ecosystems. It didn't exactly count as interfering, or so the humans claimed, although the supposed logic of the situation often defeated Dacron's comprehension. But then, the primitive society would have no awareness of how close they'd come to being destroyed before the Confederation intervened. They would never compose legends about how the sky-gods had shown them mercy in their darkest hour.

Throughout history, mankind had been tempted by the stars – and the planets that orbited Sol, near Earth. Eventually, they had all been settled – and then the human race had gone further afield. But anyone growing up on Darius wouldn't know that there were other planets orbiting other stars, at least unless they managed to make telescopes powerful enough to pick them out – and even if they did, bootstrapping themselves into space would be incredibly difficult. The simplest solution to the mystery was to assume that whoever had created Darius, and transported a number of humans to the planet, had deliberately intended to ensure that they couldn't leave. Assuming they *had* been taken during the First Expansion Era, it was quite likely that the aliens would have concluded that humanity would destroy itself. Without the First Interstellar War, it was possible that they would have been right.

The single comet received hundreds of probes, which scanned the entire object several times and concluded that it was a fairly typical comet, a ball of ice comparable to the millions of others that had been recorded all over the galaxy. Captain Thor was unconvinced and ordered a survey team to land on it and take core samples, as well as running through hundreds of tests to detect the presence of alien technology. Dacron suspected that they would find nothing – there were no hints that any of the probes had suffered glitches – but it was the Captain's prerogative. Besides, he approved of caution. There was no reason to hurry.

Adam disagreed. "This is a waste of time," he snapped. The team had gathered in the briefing compartment, where they were studying the live feed from a handful of the probes. "The comet was captured thousands of years ago and entered orbit around the primary star. It isn't *interesting*."

"It is the exception to the rule in this star system," the XO pointed out.

Dacron rather liked her, although he wasn't sure how much of it was his mentality and how much was his new body's hormones. Controlling them was something that few humans managed to master, apparently, at least until they'd passed their first century. Some humans, particularly the Lords of Pleasure, *never* seemed to master them.

"That alone makes it interesting," she concluded.

Dacron listened to the debate with half an ear as he studied the endless stream of data. Adam might well be right, he decided, after the survey team deployed nanoprobes to search the comet. There wasn't anything particularly exceptional about it, apart from the fact that it appeared to have been native to the Darius System. A backtrack of its orbit revealed that it had held for several hundred thousand years at the very least, although Dacron knew that could be unreliable. It would be easy for anyone who could sweep an entire star system clean of space dust, and everything else, to put a comet in a stable orbit and just leave it to carry on forever.

Absently, he projected the comet's course forward – and felt his heartbeat start to race as he realised that it would strike Darius itself in roughly seven thousand years. Assuming that Darius didn't master space travel, or the manipulation of quantum foam outside their own world, the comet would slam into the planet with terrific force. The resulting devastation, according to the worst-case projection, would exterminate all life on the planet.

"That could be a coincidence," the XO said, when Dacron brought it to their attention. "But if someone did stabilise the comet's orbit, they should have been able to ensure that it would never pose a threat to the planet."

Dacron nodded, wishing – once again – for the instant access to datafiles he'd enjoyed as an AI. There had been hundreds of thousands of planets struck by space debris *without* alien intervention; indeed, given that planets warped the fabric of space and created gravity wells, it was very likely that asteroids would eventually be pulled in to where they could strike the planet. But if someone had the capability to travel through space, it should have been easy for them to render the comet harmless. The fact that they'd left it in a position to strike the planet had worrying implications.

Or it could simply be a wild coincidence. Dacron tried to calculate the odds against it – and then gave up, deciding that it was futile. Even the AIs would have problems calculating the probability in a reasonable manner, without having to guess at some of the variables.

"So that leaves us with another question," Elyria said. "Do we alter the comet's path ourselves and save Darius?"

"Of course we should," Gigot said. She glared around the room, daring anyone to challenge her. "We cannot leave them to die when the comet strikes their world."

"There are seven *thousand* years between now and when the comet will hit," Dacron said, mildly. A full-fledged AI could have given a precise time, all the way down to the last nanosecond. "And a single blast from a fission cannon would obliterate the comet. There is no need for haste."

"But we should act now," Gigot insisted. She turned to the Captain. "Captain, surely this ship can alter the comet's course so it dives into the sun?"

"It can, yes," the Captain agreed, gravely. "But the comet does not pose an immediate threat and we still don't understand the Darius System. There will be time to act later."

"Seven thousand years is a very long time," Elyria added. "The Confederation itself has only existed for *three* thousand years."

Dacron wondered, absently, just how many of the humans fully understood what that actually *meant*. The Ancients had lived *billions* of years ago; the Elders had to be millions of years old. Humanity, for all of its power and sophistication, was nothing on such a scale. It was humbling to realise that the entire human race was so *young*. A few million years in the future, it was possible that there would be nothing left of the Confederation. And then alien researchers might just dig up the remains of humanity and wonder what had happened to the human race.

It seemed impossible, except for the simple fact that the Confederation had encountered the ruins of other older civilisations, apart from the Ancients. Worlds that had destroyed themselves in war, worlds that had stagnated and eventually died, worlds that had sent out colony ships, only to be overwhelmed by some unknown fate that had left the dead ships drifting through space for an eternity... no one could look at the remains and not wonder if that was the fate in store for humanity. And some of those dead worlds had proved to be very dangerous.

Five hours passed slowly as the comet was studied time and time again, before the Captain finally allowed the probes to start heading into the inner system. A dozen solar-penetration probes reached the primary star and dived into the flames, eventually signalling back a report that stated that the star was nothing more than a simple G2 primary. There were no signs of stellar engineering comparable to the Sphere-Star, or Omega-5. The Captain remained unconvinced, but he relaxed slightly when the second set of results agreed with the first. Any race that could manipulate stars was very definitely on a level equal to that of the Confederation.

Dacron found himself smiling, rather wryly. Any race that could manipulate the quantum foam was unquestionably *superior* to the Confederation.

Something clicked in his mind and he eyed Captain Thor with new understanding. The Confederation was used to dealing with other civilisations from a position of strength. Even the ones that shared humanity's level of technology had nowhere near as many starships as the Peacekeepers could deploy if pressed, let alone the industrial base to support them. The Confederation might hold itself to its own ethical system, but it had the firepower to ensure that it got what it wanted, whatever else happened. *Hamilton* alone might not be a threat to a peer power, yet anyone advanced enough to threaten the ship would know that it was the product of a vastly powerful civilisation.

But if someone could manipulate the quantum foam, they could... they could work *magic*, to all intents and purposes. Given enough power, they could simply blink *Hamilton* out of existence, or inflict staggering damage on the Confederation. Dealing with the Elder races was one thing, but this was... different. The Captain had to be aware that one false move could prove utterly disastrous. They had to be very careful.

Finally, the probes headed in towards Darius itself. The strange emptiness of space persisted right up until they reached the planet's atmosphere, which seemed to be fairly typical for a human-compatible world. There was certainly nothing poisonous in the air, or anything that would cause delusions – or, for that matter, anything that might encourage mutation in human DNA. More hours passed as the probes used optical sensors to chart the planet, comparing their records to those collected by the first survey ship. The general outline of the continents were the same, Dacron concluded, but a number of settlements had been omitted for no accountable reason. It took the RIs several minutes to realise that several settlements detected by the first ship had been missed by the new probes.

"We're picking up some strange energy signatures," one of the science team said, finally. The chart of the planet was rapidly updated to indicate the presumed source of the energy signatures, although some of them seemed too scattered to be precisely located. "We cannot identify the energy..."

Dacron listened as the humans started arguing, while he mulled over possibilities in his mind. *Hamilton* had the most advanced sensor suite in the Confederation, capable of detecting almost anything that *could* be detected, but they were dealing with a completely unprecedented situation. It *was* remotely possible that quantum foam manipulation might produce energy they hadn't learned to track or quantify yet... he shook his head, dismissing the thought. New data was required, urgently. Given time, he was sure that they would be able to devise technology to monitor quantum foam manipulations.

"They seem comparable to random vacuum fluctuations," another scientist offered. "It could be that they're a side effect of manipulating the quantum foam."

"But nothing like it has been recorded during encounters with Elders," the first scientist objected. "Surely we would have picked up *something*."

"But there are comparable energy fluxes on Ancient worlds," Adam injected. "This might be simply more of the same."

"And we never figured out what those fluxes did, besides screwing with our technology," the XO said. "Captain, we need to approach very carefully."

"That goes without saying," Captain Thor said. He looked down at his display. "How much more can we draw from orbit?"

It took hours to study and analyse the data from the orbiting probes. Adana eventually concluded that Darius was actually divided into a patchwork of small states, the largest being little bigger than two hundred square kilometres. But it wasn't easy to be sure, because instead of brushing against one another, the states seemed to be separated by miles of undeveloped territory. It occurred to Dacron that it might be comparable to how the Confederation's territory overlapped with alien territory, yet when he voiced that theory Adana took it apart, pointing out that planet-bound societies often had to compete for land and resources. If the Confederation had still been dependent upon He3 mined from gas giants, they would probably have been a great deal less willing to tolerate aliens who happened to *live* on gas giants. That started another argument, but Dacron suspected she was right. It was a great deal easier to moralise if there was nothing particularly important at stake.

"Maybe there are limits to their power," Elyria offered. She looked tired, despite all of her enhancement. "But even an iron age society could control more territory than they do."

"Maybe," Adana said. "But Gunpowder was also split up into small states."

Dacron called up the files and compared the two. Gunpowder had been settled back in the First Expansion Era by people who regarded the right to bear arms as a holy duty. They'd been isolated from galactic society by the First Interstellar War and when they'd been rediscovered, they'd split up into smaller states, partly because everyone was armed and ready to resist the imposition of a powerful central government. It didn't seem comparable, unless they were missing something. Darius had all the trappings of a feudal society – and magic; the two didn't seem to go together.

Or maybe he was just overlooking the obvious. "Everyone on Gunpowder could bear arms," he said, studying the files. The population had started practising almost as soon as they were old enough to walk. "What if only a relative handful of people on Darius can manipulate the quantum foam?"

"You mean we might be looking at another group of people convinced of their own superiority?" Elyria asked, thoughtfully. "Or something that works along the same lines?"

"It's a possibility," Dacron said. He knew better than to state it was fact, at least not yet. "If one group in society has an incontestable advantage over the rest of the population, that group is either going to find itself in charge or being exterminated."

"I don't think I'd want to pick a fight with someone who could turn me into a frog," Adam said, rather loudly. They'd all seen the recordings. "Who would dare to offend anyone like that?"

There was a long pause. "Most of the random energy fluctuations appear to be outside the cities, rather than near them," the XO said. "It could be that the energy makes it harder to operate outside the population centres..."

"I don't see how," Adam grunted. "We know that primitive technology works on an Ancient world. Darius is primitive enough that their technology shouldn't have any problems even in the midst of an energy flux."

"Unless they use compasses," Dacron said. He'd reviewed the files on the Ancient worlds, all of which held more questions than answers. "Those don't work right on Ancient worlds..."

"No," Adam agreed. "They don't."

Elyria took a breath. "Captain," she said, "I believe that we should start redeploying snoops."

"I'd prefer to wait until we have more data," the Captain said, reluctantly. Dacron rather doubted that they *could* get more data, at least from orbit. There was no way of being sure of anything without going down to the ground. "Have we picked up anything that could be a colony ship?"

"No, Captain," the XO reported. "There are no traces of anything above First Age tech at all, apart from the energy fluctuations. The most advanced transportation systems they have are either sailing galleons or carts pulled by horses. If there *was* a colony ship here, it was probably launched into the star after the colonists were disembarked."

"And nothing from the First Expansion Era could hide from our sensors," the Captain mused. "Unless they buried it..."

He shook his head. "We'd pick up something, even if it was completely shut down," he added. "Have you been able to detect a pattern in the fluctuations?"

"None as yet," Dacron said. "As far as we can tell, the fluctuations outside the cities are completely random. Inside the cities, they seem to be associated with specific buildings, but it's difficult to tell from orbit. We need to start deploying snoops."

"There was no sign that they were detected during the first ship's visit," Elyria added, "and we do need that data, Captain."

"Very well," the Captain said, finally. "You may start deploying them, first to isolated ships and then into the cities. But keep them away from the fluctuations, if possible. We don't know how they will react to our technology."

Dacron nodded. The Captain was right. "There is no need

to take chances," he agreed. They'd already programmed the snoops for deployment. "When will we approach the planet?"

"Once we are sure that there are no fluctuations in high orbit," the Captain said, "and that we can maintain an invisibility screen. This ship is not exactly tiny. When we're in orbit, they would be able to see us with the naked eye. We do not want to be seen."

CHAPTER

SEVEN

Joshua!

Joshua's eyes snapped open as his master's mental voice thudded into his head. He wished, he really wished, that his master wouldn't do that, but subtle hints seemed to pass the older man by. And he couldn't tell him directly, because that would be rude and being rude to one's master was unforgivable. He'd be lucky if he merely escaped with a beating.

It will soon be time for Court, his master added, a moment later. *You are required to be there, to learn how to judge.*

Yes, Master, Joshua sent back, trying to keep the irritation out of his thoughts. It probably didn't work, but Master Faye, Pillar of Warlock's Bane, was old enough to ignore hints of true feelings that ran through the mental voice. *I'm on my way.*

Studying under a Pillar was a great honour – and Master Faye had never let him forget it from the moment he'd discovered that Joshua had a talent for magic, plucking him out of his family home and taking him in as his apprentice. Joshua had been glad at first, because he'd profoundly disliked baking in his father's shop, but there were times when he regretted it. Magic was tricky, tended to get out of control when his concentration slipped for a moment and had a price. He hadn't realised how isolated he'd become until it was too late.

Pulling himself out of bed, he splashed water on his face and groped for the grey apprentice robe. His master wore a colourful outfit to mark himself as the most powerful man in the city, but an apprentice was supposed to be drab, at least until he qualified and set up his own practice somewhere else. Joshua wanted to be free, yet he wasn't looking forward to that day. He'd have to leave his family as well as his teacher. Pulling the robe over his head, he cast a simple reflective spell and stared at his reflection. He'd been shaved bald the day he'd accepted Master Faye as his tutor and the hair had never grown back. His eyes, too, had darkened, to the point where they seemed almost inhuman. Beyond that, he'd been working out every day, under the tutelage of a former mercenary who had come to work for Master Faye. His body was tough, capable of bearing the stresses of working magic. *And* the girls took notice of him.

He smiled at the thought, even though a magician was not supposed to do anything more than indulge himself from time to time. Pillars rarely married; as far as anyone knew, Scions *never* married. He'd kissed a few girls and spent time in the brothel, just like any other young apprentice, but he had never developed a proper relationship with a girl on the same level as himself. But to hear Master Faye, there were very few girls on his level. A magician was socially superior to almost anyone without magic.

Shaking his head, he picked up his training staff and walked downstairs, into the dining room. Master Faye's servants had already put some bread and cheese on the table, leaving it to go dry and stale, a droll punishment for his constant oversleeping. Master Faye had admitted that he'd had problems too when he'd been an apprentice. And when Joshua had pressed him on the issue, he'd also admitted that he'd had exactly the same punishment.

The servants were nowhere to be seen as he ate his food, so he carried the plate through into the kitchen and left it in the sink for them to wash. His father had taught him always to wash up after himself, but he'd discovered that trying to do the washing up in Master Faye's house upset the servants, although he had no idea why. Smiling, he took a small bag of dried fruit from the cupboard and left the house. There was no point in locking the door. The wards surrounding the house would deal with anyone foolish enough to trespass against a magician.

Outside, the sun was just rising over Warlock's Bane, but the streets were already alive with apprentices as they hurried to work and servants doing the shopping for their masters.

Warlock's Bane was a big city, with over four thousand inhabitants; it seemed unbelievable that any city could be larger. Master Faye swore that there were bigger cities in the world, far away, but Joshua wasn't sure if he believed him. His master was known to test him from time to time, just to see what lies he would swallow.

A line of carriages drove past, heading for the gates that would take them out of town and, eventually, out of Master Faye's jurisdiction. Joshua remembered looking at them as a child and feeling determined to travel one day, although that had been before Master Faye had found him and taken him on as a pupil. If he became a Scion, at least he would be able to travel... Master Faye had told him of wonders out in the badlands and he would like to see them for himself before he became a Pillar. *If* he became a Pillar...

He caught sight of Dore on the other side of the street and waved at her. She smiled, blushed and waved back, her smile sending a tingle running down his body. Dore was old enough to be married now, with her father searching for a good match. If Joshua hadn't been an apprentice magician, he would have pressed his father to make suit for her. She was beautiful, good-natured and – he was told – an excellent cook. Instead, she'd probably be married off to some lout who couldn't count to eleven without taking off his boots.

The Justice Building loomed up in front of him, guarded by a pair of men wearing armour and carrying extremely sharp swords. They glared at Joshua, commanding him to perform his master's signature charm, before allowing him to enter the building and find Master Faye. Other visitors would be stripped of weapons before being allowed to pass, just in case someone objected to a ruling and decided to try to fight. They'd have to be insane to pick a fight with the local Pillar, but it did happen. People could get very upset about very minor things.

Master Faye was standing in the courtroom, speaking to the Bookkeeper and Justice Lord. Joshua had previously had to shadow each of them as part of his training; the Bookkeeper was boring, while the Justice Lord seemed to refer all of the interesting cases to Master Faye. The Bookkeeper was also the Head of the Bookkeeper Guild in Warlock's Bane; Joshua had never been sure, but he had the feeling that the little man resented having to answer to Master Faye. His formal duties mainly consisted of maintaining the records, including the records of court cases, yet he also tried to be unpleasant to everyone who was socially inferior to him.

"Joshua," Master Faye said, out loud. It was rude to use mental voices when around Minors, although several other magicians whom Joshua had met were happy to flout that convention. "You will be judging the second case today."

Joshua blinked. "I will?"

"You will," Master Faye confirmed. He pointed to a hard wooden seat beside the judge's box. "Sit there and *wait*." His voice lowered as the Bookkeeper and Justice Lord took their own positions. "We will discuss your lateness afterwards."

Joshua squirmed as the bailiffs opened the doors, allowing the audience to flood into the chamber. By tradition, anyone who wanted to attend Court was welcome, even those who were not involved in legal issues. The only people who were kept out were those who were actually going to face Master Faye; they were being held in a separate room, from where they would be admitted one at a time. As soon as the clock started to chime, Master Faye clicked his fingers and there was a brilliant flash of multicoloured light.

"Court is now in session," he said. Silence fell, instantly. "Bring in the first case."

The side door opened again, revealing two bailiffs dragging a man in handcuffs. Joshua thought that he'd never seen a more guilty man in his life and the spectators evidently agreed, because they booed and hissed at him as he was plonked into the dock. Master Faye produced another flash of light and silence fell, just in time for the bailiffs to bring a more prosperous-looking man out of the door and put him in the witness box. He was swearing the complaint against the criminal.

"Goodman Goya," Master Faye said, as soon as the details of the accused's name had been entered in the book of records. "State the nature of your complaint."

"Theft, My Pillar," Goodman Goya said. Joshua knew him, if vaguely; he was one of the more prosperous merchants in Warlock's Bane. Joshua's father had often talked about trying to marry his daughter to Goya's son, calculating that the marriage would do the family good by improving their standing in society. "This man was caught trying to steal from my shop."

He spoke on, outlining what had happened. The accused had been shifty the moment he'd walked into the store and Goya had kept a sharp eye on him, to be rewarded when he saw the man pocketing a piece of fruit. He'd sent his two older sons after him as soon as the criminal left the store, ordering them to grab him, search him and then march him to jail, where he'd stayed until his appearance in Court.

"Very good," Master Faye said, finally. He looked at the suspect. "Do you wish to make a statement in response?"

The suspect's mouth worked several times before he finally managed to speak. "My family is starving, My Pillar," he said, finally. "I needed to feed them..."

"But that cannot excuse stealing," Master Faye said. "For your unsuccessful theft, you will spend four weeks enslaved, either working for Goodman Goya or for the city itself. As your family would starve completely if you brought nothing home, you will be paid a pittance for your services. Or you can have two weeks enslavement without pay."

Joshua watched the complex shift of emotions across the man's face. Being a slave was no laughing matter, particularly as the slavery would be enforced by magic, but at least he would be paid something for his effort. His family wouldn't starve...

"I will accept the four weeks of slavery," he said, finally. "And..."

"I object," Goodman Goya said, quickly. "He *stole* from me!"

"And he is going to be punished," Master Faye said. "You may make use of him while he is enslaved, but you may not demand further punishment."

He stared at Goya, who backed down. Joshua watched the bailiffs escorting the prisoner to a holding cell and shivered, just as Master Faye stood up and nodded for Joshua to take his seat. Joshua would have scowled at his master if he had dared; he'd just been given the opportunity to make a fool of himself in front of hundreds of watching eyes. No one would dare to laugh at him publicly – it would be a direct insult to Master Faye – but they'd be sniggering behind his back as soon as they left the Court.

Bring in the second case, Master Faye prompted, using his mental voice.

Joshua swallowed his surprise at the breach in etiquette. "Bring in the second case," he ordered, addressing the bailiffs. They showed no surprise at his sudden elevation to the judge's chair. Instead, they opened the door and brought in a young girl, a boy who couldn't be more than a year older than her and two sets of parents. None of them looked very happy – and the girl looked noticeably pregnant. Joshua winced, inwardly. He didn't have quite the access to rumours he'd had before he'd become an apprentice, but he'd heard about this one. If he hadn't known that a Pillar didn't need to care what any Minor thought of him, he would have wondered if Master Faye had given him the case because he didn't want to handle it himself.

"State the nature of your complaint," Joshua said. Unsurprisingly, all four parents started to talk at once. Joshua held up a hand and they quietened. "Goodman" – he fought to remember the name – "Harris, you may speak first."

Harris, the father of the young girl, seemed unsure how to address Joshua, so he stuck to the facts. "My daughter Rose was given a promise of marriage by that young man," he said, pointing to the young man, who stood between his parents, "and so she allowed herself to be seduced. He got her with child and then broke off the engagement. I am here to demand justice."

Joshua fought to keep his face under control. It wasn't uncommon for an engaged couple to have sex before their marriage – and if the girl became pregnant, it proved that they were capable of having children. If there were no pregnancy, it was possible to break off the engagement, allowing the couple to try for children with someone else. But to abandon the girl after she became pregnant... ? It couldn't be allowed to stand.

He looked over at the other father. "Goodman Fauves?"

"My son Julius was on a trading mission when the bitch" – he coughed when Joshua glared at him – "ah... *Rose* became pregnant. There is no way my son can be the father."

"That's a damned lie," Rose's mother shouted. "You're just looking for a better match now that you have a windfall profit from..."

"Your girl is trying to fool my son," Julius's mother shouted back. "You're..."

Silence them, Master Faye suggested, *and then question the children.*

Joshua worked the silencing spell and silence fell, instantly. The spell was actually a little too powerful; it reached the audience and silenced their mutterings too. Carefully, he fine-tuned the spell, allowing the youngsters to speak. But they weren't really youngsters, were they? Julius was four years older than Joshua himself.

"Let's deal with this calmly," he said, into the silence. "Julius. Is Rose's child *your* child?"

"I do not know," Julius admitted. He looked embarrassed; for a moment, Joshua felt an odd moment of kinship. Parents could be *so* embarrassing. "We... we did it just before I set out on the trading mission, so the child could easily be mine..."

His voice trailed away under the glowers from his parents. Rose's mother might have had a point, Joshua decided. Goodman Fauves had managed to make a considerable profit through his trading mission, which had been more than a little risky as it involved travelling through the badlands. It had been enough to propel his family up the social scale, making them richer – at least for the moment – than Goodman Goya. And that money might have allowed them to make a better match for their oldest son.

Joshua looked down at Rose. "Was there anyone else who could have fathered the child?"

Rose flushed as red as her namesake – it had to be humiliating to answer to a boy a year younger than herself, let alone in front of an entire audience – but she managed to answer the question.

"No, My Pillar," she said. There were some faint and rather nervous chuckles from the audience. Joshua was an apprentice, not even a Scion. He was hardly a Pillar. And there was only ever one Pillar in a Bailiwick. "I never slept with anyone else."

Joshua switched his gaze back to Julius. "If the child is yours," he said, "will you marry her?"

"Yes," Julius said. His mother managed to give him a truly fearsome glare. "I meant every word I spoke to her."

"Very well," Joshua said. "For the moment, we will assume that the child is yours. Upon its birth, we will perform a testing spell to determine paternity. In the event of the child actually being yours, you will be married – and you will be considered to have been married from the date her parents brought this case.

Your child will not be considered illegitimate.

"Furthermore, your parents will pay you and your wife a substantial sum to allow you to set up your own separate household," he added. He would never have considered *that* before going to live with Master Faye. "She will not need to live with her mother-in-law."

The woman switched her glare to Joshua, which suggested either nerve or stupidity. Joshua resisted the urge to hex her and looked at Rose. "In the event of the child *not* being Julius's child, there will be no marriage and your parents will be expected to pay compensation," he said. "If Julius was the only man in your" – he almost said something rude – "life, you should have nothing to worry about."

"Thank you," Rose said, very quietly.

"But this is *outrageous*," Goodman Fauves said, quickly. "I cannot afford a whole separate household for my son. Master Faye, you must..."

"The sentence is confirmed," Master Faye said, in a tone that allowed no further debate. "And in the event of anything... *happening* to Rose between now and her giving birth, you will be interrogated under truth spells and, if you should happen to have encouraged it, you will be executed."

He looked over at Joshua as the bailiffs escorted the two families out. *Very well done*, he said, mentally. *You could not have done a better job.*

Joshua flushed. Praise from Master Faye was rare.

You may handle the remaining cases, Master Faye added. *I need to concentrate.*

Concentrate? Joshua echoed. *On what?*

I have the strangest feeling that we're being watched, Master Faye said. Joshua had never sensed him feeling *doubt* before. *I want to try to isolate the feeling. A Scion may be considering targeting us.*

Joshua swallowed. Master Faye had a reputation for being tough, but there was no shortage of Scions who might want to take Warlock's Bane from him. And Joshua might not be able to help. His magic was not up to Scion standards, not yet.

"Bring in the third case," he ordered the bailiffs, finally. He had work to do.

CHAPTER
EIGHT

Very few societies could have detected the snoop. It was microscopically small, far too tiny to be seen with the naked eye. The device had found a home within the courtroom and had broadcast everything it picked up back to the *Hamilton*, where the AIs processed it before relaying the information to the human researchers. Thousands of other snoops drifted over the planet, studying the inhabitants closely. There was so much data that even the AIs had trouble analysing it all.

"There are blank spots," the AIs reported finally. "Observe."

Elyria studied the planetary map thoughtfully. For no apparent reason, there were places out in the countryside – or a handful of buildings within the city – where the snoops simply went dead. It should have been impossible. A civilisation with equal technology to the Confederation would have been able to detect and eliminate the snoops, probably through targeted nanotech, but Darius shouldn't have been able to do it at all. And once they died, the snoops effectively vanished. It was unlikely that they could be recovered.

"The ones in the cities all appear to be the homes of the... *magicians*," Adana said, calmly. "Perhaps they have some sort of magic spell preventing the snoops from intruding."

Adam gave her a sharp look. "What kind of magic spell could work against something they couldn't even imagine?"

"Humans were imagining post-singularity societies a long time before we broke the scarcity barrier," Adana reminded him. "Besides, just because we don't know about a particular type of energy doesn't mean that our shields won't protect us."

Elyria shook her head and continued studying the data. Unlike the RIs, the AIs could look at Darius without deciding that they were staring at the impossible – and dismissing the whole thing as sensor error – but they were having problems understanding the planet's society. As far as she could tell, their original conclusions had been right and there were hundreds of relatively small states, bound together by a trading network... yet she couldn't see why they hadn't started unifying themselves. Many primitive planets had had empires that dominated half the world, even if they hadn't developed steam power.

The locals would have panicked if they'd realised just how comprehensively they were being probed. There were snoops drifting through the entire planet, but concentrating on a number of cities and recording everything they saw. Some cultural practices made sense, others were just mysterious. The governing system was a puzzle. As far as they could tell, Master Faye was the ruler of Warlock's Bane, but why? Was he an elected Mayor, a Prince... or what? Each of the major cities seemed to have their own ruling citizen – and a number showed signs of recent civil war. Could it be that victory went to the strongest?

"It's probable that the ones who are capable of using magic are the ones in charge," Adana said, as they debated the problem. "Kahn and his descendants were simply superior to the locals; the magicians here might have the same advantage."

"In that case, we might have the ruling magician challenged by other magicians," the AIs offered. "That would explain the signs of civil war."

"And why some of the states appear to be poorly ruled," Elyria said. "And why the traders don't seem to go everywhere."

Humans had been trying to govern themselves ever since they had crawled out of the ocean, but it had never been easy. Power corrupted – and even the pre-singularity democratic societies had often been governed for the good of the governing class, rather than the population at large. Some unaccountable politicians – whatever they called themselves – had thought they'd meant well, but there had been no real checks on their power. Others hadn't bothered to hide the fact that they were in charge and the rest of the population had the choice between bloody rebellion or doing what they were told.

As far as they could tell, the Pillars – to use Master Faye's title – were the rulers of the city-states, but they didn't seem to have much of an administration. A handful had small armies and secret policemen – their cities were not the nicest places to live – while others just seemed to govern at one remove. Master Faye seemed genuinely interested in the well-being of his people, which didn't necessarily make him a good ruler. A good ruler would absent himself as much as possible, rather than involving himself in everything and destroying innovation and independent thinking.

"Without taking biological samples, we cannot be certain," the AIs said, "but they do appear to be baseline human. We have located a handful of graves and we believe that we could simply take the bodies without anyone noticing..."

Elyria snorted. *That* was hardly a requirement, normally. But if the source of their magic, for want of a better term, was something genetic, they'd have to start scanning local bodies sooner or later. It might well upset the locals if they ever found out. Some civilisations had developed powerful beliefs centred on their physical bodies, either burying them or destroying them after death. The Confederation, which included millions of people who had uploaded themselves into AI cores and left their bodies behind, didn't share such taboos.

"Something to focus on later," she said. "What else can you tell us about their society?"

There was a long pause. "Their language appears to be derived from English, which was spoken during the First Expansion Era and eventually evolved into Standard," the AIs said. "The language does not actually appear to have changed very much, although it is missing a great many concepts that they simply do not share. Our scans of their books confirm that their written language is effectively identical to English. Oddly, the language does not appear to have evolved as much as we would have expected. There are also no regional dialects."

"None at all?" Elyria asked, in some surprise. "That's... not possible."

Languages evolved – and two different groups, who had started speaking the same language, might be incomprehensible to each other after spending several centuries apart. There were primitive worlds that had probably originally been settled by a monoculture – only a handful of colony worlds had been settled by multiple different cultures – that had evolved a few hundred new cultures and languages of their own before rediscovery.

Given a proper tech base, however, it was less likely for languages to fission into multiple different tongues. A global communications network, complete with entertainment channels as well as verbal chatter, bound the population together, making it easier for them to understand one another. Humanity had certainly evolved a single language over thousands of years, mainly through English displacing a number of older tongues before becoming Standard, but it had been a long process. Darius... didn't seem to have changed much at all.

"Given their... abilities, it is possible that they have a global communications network based on magic," Dacron offered. "We have yet to comprehend their educational system."

"But then they'd have magic everywhere," Adam protested. He shook his head. "Nothing about this society makes *sense*."

"I thought nothing about the *Ancients* made sense," Elyria said, snidely. "This society is human. We will learn to comprehend it over the next few months and years..."

"We know one thing about it," Gigot said. Her voice was very flat. "This society is in desperate need of an intervention."

She brought up the recordings of the courtroom and displayed them. "They allowed a young boy to judge the population."

Elyria shrugged. "These people may not live very long, by our standards," she pointed out, mildly. "Fifteen – assuming that the boy *is* fifteen – is a mature age for them."

"I know that," Gigot said, with some irritation. "My point is that he doesn't seem remotely qualified to serve as a judge."

"This society isn't anything like as developed as the Confederation," Adana said, calmly. "We should not expect them to be ultra-civilised."

"And the *punishments!*" Gigot insisted. "They sentenced a man to a period of slavery!"

"Under the circumstances," Adana said, "it was a remarkably mild punishment. Most primitive societies would have cut off a hand, leaving the criminal permanently mutilated, or simply killed him. Few in the Confederation would understand the fact that these people do not have unlimited resources. A single act of theft could be disastrous to the victim."

"The method used for enslaving him may be more worrying," the AIs injected. "Master Faye did something to him and... he became a slave."

Elyria nodded, sourly. They'd watched carefully as Master Faye made passes in front of the man's face, turning him into an obedient servant. It reminded her of the subversion implants used by the Thule, except Darius didn't have any concept of brain implants. She couldn't blame Gigot for being horrified, not when using mind control on an unwilling victim was one of the Confederation's few taboos. The AIs had talked about trying to monitor the next slave's brain patterns to see what happened when he was enslaved. Elyria found the whole concept rather sickening.

The same pattern had repeated itself elsewhere on the planet, convincing her that Darius might well be very dangerous to the unwary. Some tiny states seemed to be ruled by magicians who used the spell on their own people regularly, others seemed to use it very rarely... and still others simply used outright chattel slavery, complete with whips and chains. There was definitely no unified system of justice, let alone law and order. The law seemed to be what the magicians made it.

"They don't seem to have much interest in the night sky at all," the AIs offered, changing the subject. "If they're aware of the comet, we haven't been able to pick up any sign of it."

"Curious," Elyria said. "Does that mean that the testing theory is correct?"

The researchers had come up with a number of theories for explaining Darius. One of the most popular ones had been that the whole planet was intended to encourage humans, the test subjects, to develop the ability to interact with the quantum foam, although no one had been able to understand just how the ability had developed in the first place. If so, the mystery aliens behind it might have pointed the comet at Darius as a test, knowing that if the population failed to master the ability to do something about it, the comet would hit the planet and obliterate the human settlers. But in several thousand years, they should have space travel of their own even if the Confederation's survey mission hadn't stumbled across the planet.

"Maybe," Gigot said. "Or they may not have figured out that their world orbits the local star."

"They have maps," the AIs reminded them. "They do know that their world is a sphere."

The debate surged around the table, with the researchers arguing over the correct interpretation of the data. Elyria kept her thoughts to herself as she reviewed their best guess at the political borders, trying to decide what so many small states meant for planetary development. One trap that many societies fell into was developing a single global state too early for their own good, but Darius seemed to have run into the opposite, thousands of tiny states that were too small for proper development. Why didn't they try to work together to better themselves?

They don't see it that way, she thought, and mentally kicked herself. Darius was a very primitive society, even if they did have 'magic.' They were hardly capable of understanding the advantages to be gained by greater unity, even if the magicians were willing to share power with other magicians – or the rest of the population. There didn't seem to be any democratic assemblies at all. She'd seen something not unlike it on a different world, except that one had been caught up in revolutionary fervour. It had been collapsing into bloody civil war when the Confederation stepped in.

She looked over at Dacron, who seemed bored. It took her a moment to realise that he was trying to ignore the AIs, who hadn't bothered to use their normal representative. Dacron had *been* an AI, at least as she understood it, and he had to find the reminder of what he'd lost rather upsetting. And it was clear that he wasn't anything like as capable of controlling his emotions as a human who had been alive for over a century.

"They will be arguing for hours," she said, to him. Everyone would have their own view on what some of the data actually meant, which was fair enough, and then start looking at the rest of it for ways to back up their theories, which could be dangerous. "What do you make of the planet itself?"

Dacron seemed to consider his answer before speaking. "Odd," he said, finally. "We need to obtain more information from the locals."

Elyria nodded. The standard procedure, depending on local

technological capabilities, was to either access their computer files or their libraries. A snoop could read over someone's shoulder as they looked through a book, allowing the researchers to read it afterwards. Darius did seem to have bookshops and libraries, thankfully, but they were housed in buildings the snoops had been unable to enter. Very few people seemed to have private book collections of their own, at least so far. The snoops were so capable that it was easy to forget that they might have missed something. A planet was a very large place.

"Their local biology appears to be a definite mix of Earth-origin and Darius-origin plants and animals," the AIs said. "We can see all the standard crops, as well as a handful that appear to be edible. A sampling mission would be useful for studying the local ecosystem and attempting to determine if their eating habits help to produce their powers."

Elyria rather doubted it, but the AIs were right; it was something they needed to check. Besides, the Killers had genetically engineered fruits that inhibited brain development; it was possible, if unlikely, that they could have developed something that had other effects on the human mind. Even so, if there was a magic fruit that gave its eaters magical powers, surely everyone who ate it would develop them for themselves.

"The Captain has banned sampling missions until we know more about the planet," the XO reminded them. "He was concerned about coming into high orbit. Ideally, he'd prefer to be several light minutes away from the planet."

"They really don't have any concept of space travel," Adana said, with some irritation. "What can they do to the ship?"

"We don't know, but they can manipulate the quantum foam," the XO countered, not for the first time. "They might be capable of screwing with our technology. If we lost the containment field in the core tap, for example, the entire ship would be vaporised."

Elyria had to smile. In hindsight, they should have expected such arguments. The Interventionists normally operated on planets that couldn't have threatened a starship, even if they had known what a starship *was*. They could operate from high orbit knowing that there was no way the locals could detect their presence. But Darius had a population with inexplicable abilities. They might be capable of threatening the ship.

"There is another issue," the AIs said, after a moment. "The level of energy fluctuations has risen considerably in the last seven hours."

The XO frowned. "As a reaction to our presence?"

"Unknown," the AIs said. It was difficult to read anything into their tone – they didn't really have emotions, as humans understood the term – but the AIs sounded rather frustrated. "We have no baseline for what constitutes *normal* levels on Darius. It may be a reaction to our presence, or it may be nothing to do with us at all. We are unable to determine if it poses a threat to the ship."

Elyria scowled. "How badly is it going to interfere with our technology?"

"Uncertain," the AIs said. There was a long pause. "We believe that the Captain was right to ban the use of teleporters within the system. The interference would almost certainly cause quantum decay even if the teleportation fix was maintained."

"Ouch," Adam muttered. Teleporters were normally very safe, but if there was any disruption the person inside the matter stream would die before knowing what had hit them. The early researchers had wondered if they could use teleporters to duplicate a person, just like basic fabricators built up matter from energy, yet it had never worked. "This could be worse than the Ancient worlds."

"We believe that it will be necessary to use more primitive technology," the AIs confirmed. "The fabricator onboard this ship will be easily capable of producing it. We will just have to be careful that none of it falls into local hands."

"Particularly if it is something they can use," Elyria said. The Interventionists intervened on a grand scale, but there were plenty of case studies of smaller interventions that hadn't worked out properly. One of them had been a rogue citizen introducing new technology into a primitive society. The results had been disastrous for the locals. "But if we don't understand the limits of their abilities..."

She shook her head. "It will be weeks before we can move down to the planet's surface," she added, firmly. Half the team wanted to go at once – and she had to admit that she shared their feelings – but they had to make sure that they were capable of passing for locals. There would be plenty of time to practise speaking the local language, including making sure that their accents were perfect. The locals didn't even seem to have different *accents*! "We will have to prepare very carefully first."

"There's another possibility," Gigot said, carefully. "Why don't we just ask them how their powers work?"

Her voice tightened. "They know something we don't," she added. "We could show them what we can do and offer to trade."

"Too dangerous," the XO said, finally. "We don't know what they could do to us."

CHAPTER NINE

The lighting spell was both simple and hideously complex. Simple, because Joshua had been able to perform it within a week of taking up his apprenticeship; complex, because it required constant care and attention to prevent it from destabilising and collapsing back into nothingness. The first time he'd done the spell, it had shattered two minutes later and Master Faye had laughed at him. Later, he'd learned how to hold it stable for nearly an hour, with the right level of discipline. It hadn't been until much later that he'd realised the spell exercises had helped prepare him for tougher spells.

He smiled as the spell structure grew more and more complex, casting flickering pulses of light all over the training room. Balancing it all was difficult work, but it was rewarding – and besides, it was something he could use to impress people. Once the spell was up and running, it drained very little of his personal power to keep it going. He reached out carefully and twisted it with his mind. The light took on the shape of a massive snake and started to glide around the room.

Joshua, his master said, in his mental voice, *come to my study. Now.*

Yes, master, Joshua sent back. *I'm on my way.*

He banished the lighting spell and stood up, unable to suppress a twinge of unease. His master's study was normally closed to him, protected by spells that glittered with lethal energy every time he moved close to the wards. He'd only been into the study twice, both times for a thrashing after overstepping the limits Master Faye had set for him. It was impossible to resist the feeling that he was in trouble... but for what? He hadn't done anything he shouldn't have done and he'd even remembered all of his chores.

Master Faye's study was a big room, large enough to hold a desk, two chairs and two massive bookcases crammed with books. Joshua had learned to read at an early age – his father had insisted – and he'd worked his way through many of the standard magical textbooks, but he'd been warned never to try to read books from his master's private collection without permission. They could be very dangerous if read by the unwary. Part of Joshua wondered if his master intended to keep a few secrets from his apprentice, but there were legends about magicians who read the wrong book without proper precautions. Some of them ended up dead, or wishing they were.

His master was bent over a bowl of water, peering down into it with an intent expression that allowed Joshua to relax, slightly. He wasn't in trouble for anything. Master Faye pointed to one of the chairs and Joshua sat down, knowing better than to interrupt his master in the middle of a spell. A moment later, Master Faye muttered a rude word loudly enough for Joshua to hear and straightened up. The bowl of water, steaming slightly, was left to cool down.

"We were being watched," Master Faye said, flatly.

Joshua stared at him. "By who?"

"By *whom*," Master Faye corrected, with a hint of impatience. Precision was important in magic, so he enforced it in everything. "And I do not know."

"Oh," Joshua said. He stared at his master. "A Scion?"

"I do not know," Master Faye said. "The warning spells activated, but I have been unable to trace the spying spells back to their caster. I have been unable to even *sense* their presence."

Joshua hesitated, thinking hard. Warning spells were very generalised, because one designed to deal with a specific threat might miss other threats. The downside of a spell intended to alert Master Faye to someone watching him was that it couldn't tell him *how* someone was watching him. Spying spells were subtle magic, but a magician with nearly fifty years of experience should have been able to detect them, and then locate the caster. A spell that Master Faye couldn't sense...

He frowned as a question occurred to him. "Are they peering

inside the house?"

"I do not believe so," Master Faye admitted, "but it is difficult to be certain."

"Oh," Joshua said, again. "If the house isn't safe..."

Magicians spied upon each other frequently, in the hopes of discovering a weakness that could be used against their enemies – or their friends, as magicians rarely had true friends. Scions spied on Pillars, looking for opportunities to take their bailiwick for themselves; Pillars watched nearby Scions, fearing what might happen if the Scions became ambitious. There was no shortage of blocking spells, and of magicians trying to find ways to defeat the blocking spells... if someone *had* cracked Master Faye's defences, it boded ill for the future.

"I have reinforced the defences," Master Faye assured him, "as well as casting other warning spells around the city. My conclusion is that someone is spying on *all* of Warlock's Bane, rather than just us. It is really rather curious."

Joshua could see his point. Everyone knew that the local Pillar was the master of the city, the unquestioned ruler of his bailiwick. There was little point in spying on the city; if the spy wanted the city, he would have to overcome the Pillar. The only reason he could think of for spying on the city itself was to decide if the city was worth taking... unless the spy had grubbier motives in mind. Joshua's first transgression against Master Faye's rules had been something very grubby indeed.

"That is a possibility," Master Faye agreed, when Joshua had outlined his thoughts. "There isn't supposed to be a Scion near the city, at least not inside the borderline, but if he is advanced enough to master spying spells, he may be advanced enough to avoid detection."

"Perhaps we should go hunting," Joshua said. It had been a long time since he'd walked out of the city and through the farmland that provided most of the city's food supplies. "See what we find..."

Master Faye lifted his eyebrows. "Are you that eager to die?"

Joshua flushed. He was an apprentice – and anyone capable of worrying Master Faye was, at the very least, a qualified magician. If he happened to *find* the mystery magician, he'd be lucky if he were merely killed. There were stories about what happened to people who picked a fight with more powerful magicians, none of which ended well.

"I feel that our opponent will spend more time spying on us before making his move, if he *does* make his move," Master Faye said, when Joshua said nothing. "That gives us some time to prepare. Are you willing to stay with me?"

"Yes," Joshua said, quickly. In truth, the whole prospect of being involved in a duel scared him, but he wasn't going to abandon his master. Besides, where could he go? The newcomer would kill him, if he managed to kill Master Faye. "What do you want me to do?"

Master Faye nodded to the bowl of water. "For a start, I need your energy," he said, flatly. "There's a ritual I want to try."

At his command, Joshua knelt on one side of the bowl, holding his hand out over the water. Master Faye produced a small knife, make a quick cut in Joshua's hand and allowed the blood to drip into the water, before making a cut in his own hand. Their blood mingled together as they linked hands, Joshua trying hard to clear his mind. Linking magic together was difficult enough without stray thoughts contaminating the spell.

"Brace yourself," Master Faye said. Joshua felt his master's magic surging out to clash with his, and then meld them together. "Here we go..."

Master Faye started to chant the spell, focusing his mind on the water. Joshua could feel the magic boiling around them, growing stronger and stronger as the chant grew louder. There was a sudden wave of heat from the water, a series of images flashing across its surface, and then the entire bowl flashed into steam. Joshua yelped in pain as their hands separated, sending him tumbling backwards. The bowl cracked and shattered with terrifying force, scattering fragments everywhere. Master Faye grunted and picked himself up, blood dripping from his temple.

"Master!" Joshua said. "You're bleeding!"

"I've had worse," Master Faye assured him. He didn't *sound* shaken, thankfully. A quick spell closed the cut and cleaned up the blood. "I've never seen anything like *that* happen before."

Joshua nodded. Using water to spy was easy; it was already partly reflective, so all the magician had to do was cast a simple spell. The water grew warmer, but he'd never seen the bowl actually explode, even when he'd been trying to test his defences. Whoever had cast the protective spells had done a remarkable job.

"Yes," Master Faye said. Joshua flushed. He hadn't realised that he'd been broadcasting until his master had pointed it out. "We are facing a very unusual opponent."

"Yes, Master," Joshua agreed. "What do we do now?"

"We start adding other wards to the gates," Master Faye said. "And then we start preparing our ground."

***

Like almost every city on Darius, Warlock's Bane was protected by a massive wall intended to keep out unwanted visitors. Joshua had questioned the point of it when he'd learned what magic could do, pointing out that a Scion could simply knock down the wall with a powerful blasting spell. Master Faye had countered by explaining that any Scion who wasted power blasting his way through the wall could be handled easily, if caught before he had time to recover. The walls were charmed to make it difficult for magic to knock them down, forcing any intruders to come through the gates, where they would be easily detected.

Joshua strode up towards the gate, remembering playing nearby as a child. The guardsmen had often shouted at the children to go away, either because they thought that the kids were distractions or because they were simply nasty bastards. Joshua's father had certainly never had any good things to say about the City Guard. Now, he was Master Faye's apprentice and the guardsmen deferred to him. It was a heady feeling, or it would have been if he wasn't worrying about a mystery magician. Their unknown enemy could be lurking outside the city, watching him.

It was a chilling thought. Master Faye had spells running through the city to inform him if anyone – like Joshua – developed magic, but outside the city such spells were often unreliable. Joshua's own magic sense was undeveloped, yet he was sure he was being watched... or was it simply his paranoia, after Master Faye had told him of their predicament? Shaking his head, he walked into the gate and stopped under the archway, looking for the perfect place to hide Master Faye's charmed marble. Any magician who entered the archway would be detected at once.

Carefully, he pressed it into the stone and applied a simple sticking charm to ensure that it would stay there. It wouldn't be undetectable, but Master Faye had claimed that that wouldn't matter, not when the magician would expect them to set up traps for him. Joshua stepped back, admired his handiwork and then looked outside, towards the hills in the distance. They were just outside Master Faye's jurisdiction, popularly believed to be inhabited by monsters and foreigners. It was quite possible that a Scion was hiding in the hills, watching their every move.

"There's a merchant convoy coming," one of the guards called. "Do you want to be there when we inspect it?"

Joshua hesitated. Like everyone else his own age, he loved seeing the merchants – and Master Faye hadn't told him to head straight back home. He *could* stay; his master would summon him mentally if he were needed. Smiling, Joshua nodded and walked out of the arch, heading over to the guardhouse. A line of dusty wagons was approaching the city from the north. One by one, the carts passed through the arch and into the city, without triggering the sensor. Joshua let out a breath he hadn't realised he'd been holding. The strange magician could easily have been hiding in the wagons.

The guardsmen invited the drivers to disembark and wait in a nearby building while they searched the wagons. None of the drivers, or their families, seemed very happy about it, but Master Faye forbade the guards to steal from the city's visitors. If he had allowed it, he'd told Joshua once, the city would soon have had no visitors at all. Joshua caught sight of a red-haired girl being helped out of a wagon by her father and felt a sudden surge of heat, before pushing the feeling aside. Maybe he could ask her for a drink later, but his main priority was the mystery magician.

He watched the brief and efficient search of the wagons, before walking off back to Master Faye's house. The Pillar had been working on the wards; Joshua felt their expansion a long time before he actually crossed them. Master Faye had explained that making some of the wards obvious allowed them to serve as a warning, while concealing the full nature of the hidden wards from a casual visitor. But anyone who managed to survive and prosper as a magician would be smart enough to check for other surprises before they tried to break into the house.

Inside, Master Faye was eating a large meal provided by one of the servants, clearly famished after his hard work. Joshua took a seat facing his master, who looked deeply worried. He'd seen more of the strange images in the water before it exploded into steam and, whatever they were, they had puzzled him. The spell should have worked perfectly – it had *felt* like it was working perfectly – and yet the images they'd seen had made no sense.

"Take some meat," Master Faye said, between bites. He'd ordered Joshua to eat plenty every day, reminding him that he would need energy for magic. Joshua had never eaten so well at his father's house. "And make sure you eat your vegetables."

Joshua scowled, but obeyed. "I saw a new merchant convoy," he said, as he piled the stew into a bowl and took a slice of bread to go with it. "There was no sign of a magician."

"He would probably not deign to travel with his inferiors," Master Faye said. "Unless he's one of the few Scions who can tolerate the company of Minors as anything other than slaves. But that is very rare..."

"I won't turn out like that," Joshua said. "I was *born* to a Minor family..."

"And don't you ever forget it," Master Faye said, flatly. "You'd be astonished at how many other magicians pretend that they were born to magical parents. If we accepted all of the claims, we'd have far more magicians than we actually do."

Joshua had to smile. Magicians passed down magic to their children, who tended to manifest it in infancy. Their children often became warped by the power, if they didn't accidentally kill themselves through sheer ignorance. It was one of the reasons magicians were not supposed to indulge themselves too much with women. Or get pregnant, if they were females. Magic did odd things to children.

Master Faye had told him a story about a female Scion who had known she would never be powerful enough to seize a bailiwick for herself. She'd found the most powerful magician she could and convinced him to give her a child. Master Faye had added at that point that one version of the story claimed that she'd actually mated with a demon, but that should have been impossible. The child had been born, yet as he matured he turned into a spoiled brat with far too much power to be safe. Eventually, several Pillars had been forced to work together to kill him before it was too late. He'd never learned the maturity that came with age and experience.

And the stories of what he'd done, first out of curiosity and then out of malice, had been truly terrifying.

"We will be practising defence drills this afternoon," Master Faye said, as he finished his stew and started peeling himself an orange. "I will be expecting you to master all kinds of charms very quickly. It might prove a distraction at the right moment."

Joshua shuddered. Master Faye had pushed him hard, but he knew that he was no match for a Scion. The last time he'd invited his master to a duel, when he'd learned a few spells and wanted to show off, he'd been simply turned into a frog for an hour. His defensive spells had been very basic, as Master Faye had pointed out later. Any half-trained magician would know their weaknesses and how to get around them. Joshua hadn't even lasted a minute and he'd been left with an uncomfortable impulse to snap flies out of the air for several days afterwards. The mystery magician might be far less merciful to an arrogant young brat who thought he knew magic.

"Yes, Master," he said, reluctantly. "I'll do my best."

"See that you do," Master Faye said, but he was smiling as he said it. "And afterwards, you might want to go and visit your family."

"My siblings are scared of me," Joshua said. His father hadn't been much better. *He* had wanted Joshua to use his influence – as if he had any – to help his business. "But my mother would like to see me."

He felt cold. Master Faye seemed to be expecting the worst. He could *die* – and his killer wouldn't leave his apprentice alive. There were enough stories about apprentices avenging their masters to convince him that it would be a bad idea. Joshua might only have a few days to live. He swallowed at the thought and looked over at his master.

"Don't worry," Master Faye said. "With a little preparation, we can be ready for anything."

CHAPTER

TEN

"I confess that I am unsure of the wisdom of this," Captain Thor said. "You would be going into danger."

"We know the risks," Elyria assured him. They'd spent two weeks in orbit around Darius, reaching the limits of what they could learn by remote observation. Tiny sampling missions had revealed nothing unusual about the native ecology, although it had fought back more effectively than most against hardier stock from Earth. "And we accept them."

The Captain snorted. In many ways, infiltrating a primitive world was easy – and they could simply teleport out if matters got out of control. Darius was going to be a little more complicated, not least because teleporting would be reserved as a last resort. If advanced technology was going to be unreliable, they might not even be able to *consider* using the teleporter. The science team and AIs had worked to try to overcome the problems, but had had to report failure. A handful of experiments had proven that it would be dangerous and probably fatal to risk it.

"There is no other way to learn," she added, firmly. He *didn't* have good grounds for refusing her – and Jorlem agreed with her, making it harder for him to wave Peacekeeper authority in her face – but they did need his approval. "We're ready to land now."

They'd started learning the local language at once, using memory boosters and frequent practice to master Darius's version of English. It wasn't a difficult language to learn, even without the implants they'd normally use to make sure they got it right. They didn't dare risk becoming dependent on them and then discovering they didn't work on Darius. Mastering the local culture was far harder, but it seemed that traders were permitted some leeway, at least more than was granted to city-dwellers. *That* wasn't too hard to understand; basic economics insisted that the smarter magic-lords treat merchants well, in hopes of earning more profit. A few hours of research had turned up a whole list of trade goods they could offer to the locals.

The mission orders had frowned upon offering the locals anything they couldn't make for themselves, but they did permit producing items from the other side of Darius. One particular island was the only place that produced certain kinds of spices, all of which sold for vast amounts of gold in Warlock's Bane. The remainder of their trade goods were considerably less interesting, but they should bring a tidy profit. There were so many different trading clans, often splitting up into new organisations, that no one would notice another one. Or so they hoped.

"Then we pick an uninhabited place for the first landing," Captain Thor said, firmly. "Somewhere where we are unlikely to be detected."

Elyria scowled. The best places to go also happened to be places where the snoops had simply failed – and there was no way that Captain Thor would allow a shuttle to fly into a Dead Zone. A single snoop was hardly a loss – the fabricator had turned out millions of them – but a shuttle, complete with passengers, was rather more serious. Besides, if it crashed near a settlement, it would be a nasty shock to the locals. They might know more about life on other worlds than anyone had assumed.

"We have a location in mind, near Warlock's Bane," she said. The snoops had been checking it out for several days, finally concluding that no one lived within five kilometres of the landing zone. From time to time, merchant convoys drove through the area, but they never stopped. Establishing a base there would be easy. "Once the shuttle is down, we can bury it and turn it into a proper observation post."

It *was* standard procedure. A primitive world could be observed from close-up, without revealing their presence. It would also make a useful rendezvous point in case of discovery, particularly as the teleporter was unreliable. The AIs had been working out what technology could be considered reasonably dependable on Darius, which could be used to stock the base. And then they could move further into the field.

"Very well," Thor said, finally. "Just remember my overall orders. If you run into real trouble, I might not be able to help you."

Elyria nodded. "We understand," she said. That *wasn't* standard procedure, but Darius was a non-standard planet. A rescue mission might be deemed too dangerous for *Hamilton*, or even an entire crew of Peacekeeper Marines. If that happened, they would be stranded for the rest of their lives. There were stories about it happening, but never on her watch. Most of them were really little more than rumours. "We're ready."

"I hope you all look reasonably local," Thor grunted. "These people don't seem to be very diverse."

That was another oddity about Darius; the population seemed to have near-uniform brown skin. Skin colour was utterly irrelevant to the Confederation – partly as a response to the Thule, who had gene-engineered yellow skin into their serfs – but primitive worlds tended to take it seriously. And, over the years, people who lived under hot sunlight developed darker skins than those who didn't. It seemed absurd to believe that anyone could be so foolish as to use skin colour as a means of separating superior humans from inferior humans, yet the whole affair predated the march into space. Some planets had even worked hard to ensure that their children kept the same ethnic appearance.

"We have all spent time in the tank," she said. Adam had complained bitterly – he was proud of his Changed appearance – but had reluctantly agreed when Elyria had pointed out that he'd look thoroughly alien on Darius. "All we need to do is prepare the tools and then make the landing."

"Then see to it," Thor said. "The XO will be accompanying you and your team to the surface."

Elyria had expected as much. "She is certified for primitive contact," she said. The XO had worked surprisingly hard to qualify in a field that was rare for a Peacekeeper officer. But then, Darius was an infinitively fascinating puzzle. "We will be glad to have her along."

***

"You're definitely sounding a lot more human," Shelia assured Dacron, as he sat up in her bed. "All you need to do is relax a little more."

Dacron had to smile. *Hamilton* had a relatively small crew for her size – apparently, most of the crew had been stripped out before the Captain had been briefed on Darius – and Shelia had been one of the lucky ones who had stayed onboard. And she found the idea of bedding an embodied AI quite arousing. Or maybe she was bored. Human sexuality still made little sense to Dacron, even though he was now fully functional.

"Thank you," he said, remembering his manners. His first few days had been more than a little embarrassing, because he had never given any thought to human manners. Being part of the AIs was very different; the AIs were so harmonised that they couldn't hide anything from each other. There was no *point* in having manners. "You were very good yourself."

Shelia grinned and stood up, heading into the shower. "You want to come and wash?"

"No, thank you," Dacron said. Humans loved water showers, but he disliked them intensely, although he wasn't sure why. Perhaps there was a fear of drowning embedded within his human DNA, or perhaps it was just that water showers were inefficient. The AIs had spent centuries – literally – working out ways to improve themselves, to become as efficient as possible. Sonic showers were far cleaner than water. "Was it better this time?"

Shelia started to laugh, her chuckles echoing out of the washroom. "How *very* human," she said, between giggles. "You want to know how you *performed*."

She stuck her head out of the shower and gave him a sultry grin. "You're doing better every time," she said. "Just remember not to do that on the planet's surface. You'd blow the mind of an unenhanced human girl."

Dacron was still mulling it over an hour later when he was called to a briefing. Humanity might never be able to match the AIs for intelligence – it was hard to see how they could ever outthink entities who resided partly in hyperspace – so they'd reengineered their bodies for health and pleasure instead. According to the files, multiple orgasms hadn't been the lot of human men before they'd started working on their bodies; now, with a human shell, Dacron could understand why. The AIs had known about sexuality in the abstract – they'd certainly read every paper humanity had produced on the topic – but they had never understood it. He wondered if it would still be understandable when he was reabsorbed into the *Gestalt*.

The briefing compartment had been expanded and a number of devices had been placed on the table. Dacron had helped to design them, although honesty insisted that he should admit that the AIs had done much of the work. As far as they could tell, the more primitive a piece of technology was, the more likely it would work on Darius. Radios and chemical weapons were laughable compared to QCC links and antimatter cannons, but the latter would probably fail on the planet's surface. He didn't want to *think* about what would happen if some idiot took an antimatter pod down to the planet. The resulting explosion would probably render the planet uninhabitable.

"We have tested radio transmissions and discovered that they seem to be reliable on the surface," the XO said, "apart from certain places outside the cities. These... Dead Zones seemed to be more inclined to attack technology, as everything we have steered into them goes dead. As yet, we have no theory as to why that actually happens."

Dacron nodded. One theory had been a force field that displaced energy above a certain level into hyperspace, a trick the AIs and Peacekeeper planetoids used to defend themselves. It required a vast amount of power to work properly and, judging from some of the test results, should have literally pulled the electricity out of a human's brain. If it could sap a relatively small charge from a drone, it could sap it from a biological brain... except orbital observation indicated that people could walk in and out of the Dead Zones without suffering at all. The best guess was that the field was somehow *choosing* its targets, which implied an intelligence... and that intelligence had not reacted to the ship's presence.

"The first object" – the XO held up a tiny bead – "will be implanted in your skulls before you go down to the planet. It is a tracker that remains dead most of the time, waiting for a signal from the ship. We should be able to locate you if something goes wrong. There are a handful of other implants for you, allowing some subvocal communications – although not with the same flexibility as a standard communications implant. If worst comes to worst, it *may* serve as a source for teleport coordinates, but we would hate to rely on it."

The humans seemed to hesitate at that comment. Dacron, who could still calculate the odds against a successful teleport, wasn't too surprised. They'd grown up in perfect safety, even when they'd been moving among primitive societies. And besides, Confederation technology never failed, at least outside an Ancient world. *Those* had their own dangers, but they were largely passive ones. The explorers on Darius could easily die on the strange world.

"There are three types of defensive weapon," the XO continued. If she'd noticed the sudden attack of uncertainty, she said nothing. "This" – she held up a stick – "will give anyone you touch with the business end a nasty electric shock. A second jab will stun them. Try not to use it in public as it will probably attract attention."

"They'd be taken for magic," Adam pointed out.

"And magicians have obligations in their society," Elyria said. "Ideally, we don't want to be taken for anything other than harmless merchants."

The XO nodded. "The second weapon" – she held up a spray – "contains knock-out gas. As far as we can determine, Darius's population has no engineered resistance to anything of the sort, so you should be able to use it freely. You'll all be immune, of course. Again, try not to use it in public, but if you *do* have to use it..."

"Use it carefully," Captain Thor said. "Given their observed capabilities, they might be able to take the concept of poison gas and create something truly nasty."

"True," Elyria warned. "Primitive does not mean stupid."

"The third set of weapons are chemically-propelled projectile guns," the XO concluded. "*Do not* use them unless there is *no* other choice. If you hit someone, they will be injured, perhaps killed. We have no idea of their medical skills, but if they have the same capabilities as any other First Age society any wounds you inflict with these weapons will cripple them for life. Don't think of them as idiots following the Ugly and Mutilated Craze. You will destroy their lives."

She leaned forward. "You know you wouldn't normally be

issued such weapons. Use them if there is no other choice, and be careful. If you manage to hit someone on your team, you can injure them too, despite their enhancements."

Dacron looked down at the weapon and nodded to himself. They'd all been put though the training that would allow them to use the weapons properly, but no amount of training could teach someone good judgement or restraint. A couple of the team had weapons training from previous missions, yet this was different. The absence of the teleporter alone would see to that.

He listened carefully as they continued to discuss the other technical gadgets hidden inside their small collection of wagons. The fabricator had put together the basics from studying the wagons down on the surface, then one of the team had designed some individual modifications to prevent them looking like an exact copy of the wagons they'd recorded in Warlock's Bane. It was the clothes that caused the most complaints, Dacron was amused to notice; clearly, the locals had yet to discover the joy of synthetic materials. The outfits were uncomfortable and the underwear was itchy. At least there were some protective strands woven into the material. They wouldn't be immune to danger – far from it – but they would be better prepared than the locals.

"So I'm Trading Master Adam," Adam said, with some amusement. The covers they'd put together had indicated that the trading clans were largely family-owned enterprises, incorporated in a number of different city-states. It was difficult to be sure, but it looked as if the clans actually stored their money in a number of separate cities, ensuring that one city-state that went bad couldn't ruin them. "And you're all my family."

Elyria snorted. "Just remember that you have to be a noisy and boisterous trader," she said. They'd simulated trading and bargaining extensively, as the latter was not a required skill in the Confederation. "And don't give them too much gold."

"Very important," Gigot agreed. "Besides, they might ask questions if you have too many gold coins."

It was, Dacron decided, another human problem, one that was mercifully absent from the Confederation. A single Class-One Fabricator could produce enough gold to build a starship the size of the *Hamilton*, given enough time. Introducing that much gold into a primitive economy would cause it to collapse spectacularly as their traders attempted to work out new values for their goods. Come to think of it, it was true of almost everything. A fabricator could produce the spices and every other set of trade goods on the planet with ease. Humans just didn't seem to be very rational, economically speaking. What was the point of hoarding vast amounts of money when money was worthless?

The AIs had sometimes wondered if it was a disease caused by living in a scarcity society. Every time someone from a primitive world was brought into the Confederation, they demanded all sorts of things – and seemed astonished when their demands were actually met, although they really hadn't shown much imagination when making their demands. Even a starship could be produced on demand. The only really scarce items in the Confederation were handmade crafts, produced by individual artisans, and *they* could be traded for energy credits.

"Watch that carefully," Elyria warned. "There was a case, back during the early years of the Interventionists, when one of us paid a local with a gold coin. His neighbours promptly hanged him for being a thief."

She looked around the compartment. "Gigot is going as Adam's wife and business manager; we know that they seem to expect female traders to stand on equal terms to the men. Adana and myself will be his daughters; Plax and Fred will be his sons, as well as his bodyguards. Dacron will be the son of a fellow trader, learning the ropes. That should excuse lots of stupid questions."

Dacron felt an odd flash of irritation. It was a practical suggestion and yet it annoyed him. They'd gamed out a dozen different variants before settling on the basic structure of their clan. Plax and Fred, former Peacekeepers, had been added to the team when they realised that all of the merchant clans were escorted by bodyguards. They'd been practising with swords and bows ever since.

"We go down tomorrow evening," she concluded. Dacron had already watched the AIs refitting the shuttle into something that should be able to operate on Darius without falling out of the sky. "If anyone wants to back out" – she paused, before continuing – "report to me and I'll take you off the roster. Make sure you do a full backup of your mental state before boarding the shuttle. You can be resurrected within the Confederation if something goes wrong on the surface."

Humans found that concept a little disturbing, Dacron knew, and their reactions proved it. Was there really continuity between an old body and a mental state uploaded into a new? An AI, on the other hand, would accept it calmly.

"Tomorrow evening, then," Elyria said. She stood up. "Good luck to us all."

CHAPTER
ELEVEN

From high overhead, Darius looked reassuringly normal. Like almost all human-compatible worlds, it was a blue-green sphere hanging against the darkness of space, surrounded by glowing stars. There was no Ring, of course, or any sign of advanced technology; the night side of the planet didn't even have any lights in the darkness to signal the presence of a high-tech culture. The shuttle span once, allowing the passengers to see the world below, then it dropped into Darius's atmosphere. Elyria braced herself as the shuttle started to shake violently.

This could be a trap, she reminded herself, as strong winds buffeted the shuttle. One theory about Darius was that it was a trap for the entire Confederation, although no one had been able to think of a reason why anyone so powerful would bother with a trap. The shuttle had been heavily reengineered to give it a good chance of survival in Darius's strange environment, but there were simply too many question marks surrounding Darius. Very few humans in the Confederation had ever been completely on their own, even in the Peacekeepers. The team didn't really understand what that meant.

The shuttle rocked again as it dived lower, coming in over the ocean. There had been a long debate about their flight path, before Captain Thor had ruled that they would enter the atmosphere over the ocean and then fly to the selected landing zone near Warlock's Bane. If the shuttle lost power completely and crashed, there would be no evidence of their presence for the locals to find, at least until they got over the land. But as far as they could tell, technology didn't glitch over the oceans.

The flight would be completely safe until they actually reached land.

A brilliant flash of lightning danced outside, illuminating the interior of the shuttle, before fading away into darkness. The shuttle slowed, steadying itself, before angling down towards the ocean. Elyria used her neural link to peer through the shuttle's senses and saw a pair of sailing ships heading out into the ocean, presumably looking for somewhere else to trade. A set of snoops had already attached themselves to the boats, monitoring the crew. They didn't seem to be anything more than sailors.

"There's bad weather over the land," the shuttle pilot said, seriously. It would normally not have been a problem for a Confederation shuttle, but Darius was unpredictable and technology had a habit of glitching. A thunderstorm might bring the shuttle down. "I'm altering course to take us around the worst of the storm."

"Mind you stay out of the Dead Zones," the XO warned. She'd told Elyria that the pilot had taken part in landings on hostile territory before, but no one had ever experienced anything like Darius. "We really don't want to fall out of the sky."

Elyria nodded, watching through the neural link as the shuttle swept over a loch and skimmed around Warlock's Bane. The loch held a dozen big ships, sheltering from the worst of the storms out on the open sea, and hundreds of smaller fishing vessels, each one capable of bringing in hundreds of fish a day. It was possible that the locals would eventually deplete the fish stocks around Warlock's Bane, the researchers had warned; running out of resources was not an uncommon problem in scarcity societies. They might not think to limit the number of fish that could be caught until it was too late. At least they weren't tapping their oil reserves yet... given their very limited knowledge base, Elyria was mildly surprised that they'd learned to burn coal. But they were very definitely mining it from sites near the city.

The shuttle altered course slightly, giving Warlock's Bane a wide berth. Unlike cities on advanced worlds, Warlock's Bane was almost completely shrouded in darkness, with only a handful of glowing lights to mark its presence. The snoops had no difficulty seeing in the dark; they'd reported that most of the population went to bed when darkness fell. Even the ruler of the city, who seemed to be capable of generating a ball of light at will, seemed unwilling to do much after dark. They just didn't have the technology to carry on working.

A dull tremor ran through the shuttle. "I'm not sure what that was," the pilot said. He sounded rather disturbed. "The sensors didn't pick up any turbulence before we hit it."

Elyria looked over at Dacron. The embodied AI looked nervous; no, he looked terrified. It wasn't easy to remember that, in a very real sense, Dacron was only two months old. The whole experience would be terrifying for him – she winced as the shuttle shook again – and there was nothing they could do until they touched down. She wanted to reach over and take his hand, but he was out of reach. Instead, she shot him what she hoped was a reassuring smile and returned to monitoring the live feed from the snoops. They reported that the area they'd designated as a landing zone was clear of human life.

"The closest human settlement is two kilometres away," Adana confirmed. She'd been looking for signs that the landing zone wasn't deserted too. "It's just a small farm, with seven people and a handful of animals. They shouldn't be able to see us."

They wouldn't, not on any normal world. Elyria had used stealthed shuttles before and knew how they worked. They were completely invisible to the naked eye and any sensors that could be devised by a Fourth Age society. Darius should not have been able to detect them at all, but Darius was a very strange world. It was better to keep their distance than to risk disaster, at least until they knew what was going on.

She looked down and smiled. Most of the worlds humanity had settled, in thousands of years of expansion, had been allowed to return to nature now that the human population was housed in giant rings surrounding the planets. One day, their biospheres might even produce intelligent life, perhaps derived from the Earth-native plants and animals introduced into their ecologies. Darius, on the other hand, was slowly being tamed by its human population, something that puzzled the researchers. If Darius had been settled for longer than a thousand years, as seemed probable, they should have tamed the world by now. But Jorlem had pointed out that even *reaching* Darius would have taken years, perhaps centuries.

Darius might not have been settled for as long as they thought.

Or perhaps something else weird is going on, she thought. Was the whole planet an Elder experiment to see what happened if you allowed a race the power to manipulate the quantum foam, or was it their version of a massive game set in a virtual world? The Confederation had created Disneyworld, inhabited by semi-sentient creatures that acted as playmates for human visitors, and Pleasure, which fully lived up to its name, but neither of them operated on such a scale. Disneyworld, in particular, was reshaped constantly by nanotech, yet Darius didn't seem to have anything so advanced in its atmosphere. Indeed, nanotech wouldn't work for very long on Darius.

"Prepare for landing," the pilot said. They'd plotted out the landing zone carefully, but the pilot had warned them to beware of unpleasant surprises. "Going down... now."

Elyria braced herself as the shuttle descended in the clearing and gently touched down. A final thump ran through the craft as its landing struts met the ground, and then the faint background humming died away as the drive powered down. She glanced around through the shuttle's sensors and saw nothing, apart from a handful of rabbits that looked at the shuttle and then hopped away. The rabbits definitely implied a colony ship from the First Expansion Era. After that, there had been strict laws on keeping them under control; rabbits had helped to devastate a number of weaker planetary ecologies.

"There were some minor glitches in advanced technology," Jorlem said, as the team unstrapped themselves and stood up. "If we hadn't built so much redundancy into the system we would have fallen out of the sky."

Elyria blanched. She was glad she hadn't known that while they were flying. "We can probably make some projections now," Jorlem added. "The glitches seem to be targeted, at least to some extent. They may have been focused on the shuttle from the moment we entered the atmosphere. That suggests the possibility of intelligent control."

"A simple fission beam would have blown us out of the sky," Adam grumbled. He was familiar with technological glitches from Ancient worlds. "Why would they fart around with something so uncertain instead of deploying something that would definitely kill us?"

"Maybe it's the only weapon they have," Jorlem suggested.

"Or maybe they want to discourage the Confederation from further missions to Darius, rather than using something that would be detectable two systems away."

Dacron had a more thoughtful question. "Were there any other effects?"

"There was a faint power drain in some of our shielded power cells, but the effect was minimal," the pilot said. "It wasn't enough to pose a threat."

"Unless they were just testing the equipment," Adam offered. "They could drain the rest of our power at any moment."

"And you're just trying to scare us," Elyria said, with more anger than she intended. The landing had been stressful and the discussion wasn't helping. "There is no evidence to suggest that they can do that..."

"The Confederation could," Dacron pointed out. "If Darius was designed by an advanced alien race, we have to assume that they are at least as advanced as ourselves."

Elyria nodded. "Start deploying the diggers," she ordered, leaving the rest of the discussion for the moment. They could debate it once they were safe. "I want to be able to hide the shuttle before daylight."

"Certainly," the pilot said. He keyed a switch and the digger robots started to deploy from the shuttle's cargo hold. "Assuming the snoops were correct, it shouldn't take more than a few hours to produce the base. And then we can start some *real* expansion."

Elyria sat back in her chair and watched as the diggers went to work. The Confederation had had centuries of experience in constructing hidden bases quickly; the diggers, with their combination of earth-moving technology and nanotech, could hollow out the ground very quickly. Once they had made a hole, they'd move the shuttle into the hole and then arrange the ground so that there would be no sign that the shuttle had been there at all. Normally, they'd use teleporters to get in and out of the base, but they'd had to add an entry shaft to the design for Darius. It created a security risk that would simply have to be tolerated.

The clearing they'd used as a landing zone was also used by the locals as a stopover place for wagon trains, according to orbital observation. Darius didn't seem to have much night traffic at all, which wasn't too surprising when wooden torches were the only light available to most of the population. Having a defensible position to rest while they were outside the cities was obviously a priority; the clearing was big enough to hold over thirty wagons in reasonable comfort, a bigger number than any convoy they'd yet tracked. Thousands of additional snoops flitted through the surrounding area, taking up position to watch for any local intruders. Elyria couldn't help noticing that the snoops heading away from the city were more likely to fail than those heading towards it.

She stood up, suddenly impatient, and headed for the airlock. Plax and Fred, the bodyguards, followed her a moment later, even though they both knew that there was nothing even remotely hostile outside. She opened the hatch, entered the airlock and allowed them to close it before the outer hatch hissed open, revealing a darkened forest. Elyria stepped forward and breathed in the air of a new world. Darius smelt sweet, without the hydrocarbon by-products that were the signature of a Second or Third Age society. There should be nothing capable of harming her in the air, she knew, but she couldn't help feeling worried as she stepped out of the shuttle. How did they know that the tests they'd run on the planet's atmosphere were reliable?

This planet causes us to doubt everything, she thought, as she walked away from the shuttle. Her enhanced eyes had little difficulty seeing in the dark, but when she looked back it was difficult, almost impossible, to see the shuttle. Only a faint hint of a ghostly image betrayed its presence. The locals would simply ignore it. Beyond the shuttle, the diggers were burrowing into the ground, widening out a cave that was already large enough for it. It wouldn't be long before they were ready to move the shuttle into its hiding place...

She blinked in shock as a warning message flashed up in front of her eyes. Her implants, including the neural link, had suffered a brief glitch. That hadn't been too surprising, but it still bothered her. She felt naked without Confederation technology to protect her... she ordered the system to run a full diagnostic, but it found nothing. The primitive radio they'd implanted seemed to be fine, thankfully. They'd just have to remember that they could no longer rely on their neural links.

"The QCC links suffered glitches at the same time," Fred reported. The bodyguard looked worried, glancing around as if he expected armed warriors to come bursting out of the forest at any moment. "It's possible that the glitches were precisely targeted on us."

Elyria shrugged. There was no way to know. They'd just have to hope that the more primitive technology would work perfectly. She shook her head and started to walk back to the shuttle. The diggers were signalling that they were ready to move the shuttle and she needed to be inside it when that happened. There would be nowhere for her on the surface until they were ready to deploy their wagons. She climbed back into the shuttle and briefly updated Jorlem on what had happened. Unsurprisingly, there had been a number of recorded glitches in the shuttle's computers.

"We're ready," she said, as the airlock closed. The shuttle's sensors had scanned all three of them thoroughly, reporting nothing apart from some pollen. Nanotech swarms removed it anyway, just in case. "You can start burying us now."

The shuttle lurched as the diggers went back to work, dragging the shuttle towards the hole they'd made in the ground. Elyria felt a faint sense of unease as the antigravity field came on, allowing them to start lowering the shuttle into its hiding place, a moment before the technology suffered another glitch. The shuttle dropped like a stone, slamming into the ground with terrifying force. Red emergency lights flared through the passenger compartment, followed rapidly by shouts and cries of pain. Half of the team hadn't even been sitting down while the shuttle had been moving. None of them had realised that the antigravity field might also fail.

Jorlem leaned forward. "Damage report," he barked. "How badly were we damaged?"

"Main drives and systems appear intact," the pilot said. "The shuttle was designed to be tough. Some minor dents in the hull, but nothing to stop us flying out of here."

Elyria exchanged glances with Jorlem. "The timing couldn't have been a coincidence," Jorlem muttered. "That might have been intended to kill us."

"They must have known it wouldn't kill us all," Elyria pointed out. The shuttle might have been damaged and there would be injured, but it seemed like an unnecessarily complex plan for very little return. "Some of us would have survived; hell, we *all* survived."

They checked the wounded quickly. Apart from Gigot, who had banged her arm hard enough to break it, no one was seriously injured. Their enhanced bodies were already starting to repair the damage, removing the pain as a matter of course. Gigot would take longer to heal, so Elyria slapped a packet of medical nanites against her arm. They'd heal the wound in minutes. The locals, ironically, would probably have regarded them as magic.

"Things may just have become a little more dangerous than we thought," she said, outlining their conclusions. The timing of the glitch was *very* suspicious, even if it didn't seem like an outright attempt to kill them. Why not glitch the shuttle when they'd been over the ocean? They'd have fallen out of the sky and died, without hope of recovery.

Elyria snorted. "And I'm afraid it's too late to return to the *Hamilton*," she added. "If any of you want to stay in the shuttle, however..."

"No, thank you," Adana said, quickly. The sociologist smiled, brightly. "There's too much of interest here."

The next two hours passed quickly as the diggers completed the task of burying the shuttle, hiding all traces of their landing and then starting to expand out under the ground. Given time, they would hollow out enough room to allow more equipment to be shipped down from the orbiting starship, including a small fabricator. If it would work here... the Captain had already insisted that anything that might glitch had to be checked with him first. Most glitches wouldn't do serious damage, but some would be very dangerous. They'd be living in primitive conditions for quite some time.

"We will all get some sleep," Elyria said. *She* would have to write a full report for Captain Thor, which would be passed on to the CSC. At least they weren't trying to micromanage from thousands of light years away. "Tomorrow, we'll start moving the wagons to the surface and then start heading to the city."

She smiled. Adana was right; despite the danger, this was a fascinating world. There were genuinely original discoveries to be made here, in all sorts of fields. She just couldn't wait.

CHAPTER
TWELVE

Joshua had always liked the dark.

It wasn't something he had shared with anyone, apart from Master Faye, who had laughed and told him that it was an early sign of magic. The darkness held threats that could only be driven back by light; people went to bed as soon as darkness fell and attempted to sleep through the terrors, even the people living in cities. Joshua, on the other hand, had found the darkness fascinating. There were no true threats lurking within the shadows, he'd discovered, even before he'd learned to produce light for himself. The common folk were scared of nothing more than illusions.

"Something is happening," Master Faye said, as they stood together on the roof of his house. "One of my detection spells activated for a few brief seconds."

Joshua winced. They'd spent two weeks preparing themselves as best they could for a challenge, for when a Scion walked into the city and tried to claim it as his own, but nothing had happened. Eventually, he'd started to wonder if all of their preparations had discouraged the Scion from challenging Master Faye, although *that* was unlikely. A Scion with a full grasp of his powers might well have more recent experience skirmishing with other magicians than Master Faye. And few magicians were actually cowards.

"Someone was flying," Master Faye added. "They flew near my wards and then banked away."

"Oh," Joshua said. "Why?"

"Good question," Master Faye said, more than a little crossly.

"I'll let you know when I figure out the answer."

Joshua swallowed. Flying – on a carpet, or a broom, or even alone – was a very complex spell, almost as complex as teleportation. It was easy for a magician to fly halfway around the world to attend a banquet – Master Faye had done it on occasion – but it was also easy for that magician's enemies to disrupt his spells and send him tumbling out of the sky. Any magician flying so close to another bailiwick had to be utterly confident in their powers. All the great magicians of legend had castles built in the clouds or perched on a needle-thin rock – but no one ever built them in the real world, because they were just too easy to destroy.

"Yes, master," he said, finally. "Where do you think he was going?"

"He passed outside the range of my spells, but I don't think he went very far," Master Faye said. He looked over at Joshua, thoughtfully. "How much progress have you made on riding a horse?"

Joshua made a face. He would never have been permitted to ride if he hadn't been a magician – and yet he'd discovered, when he'd started to learn, that he disliked it intensely. The horses all seemed to hate him and threatened to unseat him whenever he gave them an opportunity. And to think he'd envied horsemen back when he had been a child! He hadn't realised just how bad-tempered the beasts actually were.

"Take one out when the sun rises and ride around the fields, near the border," Master Faye ordered. If he saw Joshua's expression, he said nothing. "I want you to keep an eye out for anything unusual."

Joshua blinked. "Anything?"

"Signs that someone might be lurking just outside the borderline," Master Faye explained, patiently. "Speak to the farmers; ask them if they've seen anything odd. Don't use truth spells unless they have a real strange story, one you find unbelievable. And remember the story of Mervin."

"Right," Joshua said. Mervin had been one of the few Scions to believe that someone should be policing magicians, rather than allowing them to run rampant. His career had been spent hunting magicians who used black magic, to the point where he'd acted more like a City Guard Investigator than a proper magician. An odd man, but very practical. The stories had included lectures on what to look for if one happened to be hunting a black magician.

Master Faye gave him a sharp look. "If you find anything, contact me at once and try to avoid meeting him," he added. "You won't be any match for a Scion, even after the hard work we've done over the last two weeks. Just keep your distance and contact me."

He smiled, rather thinly. "Go back to bed," he ordered. "I'll keep a watchful eye out for trouble."

Joshua didn't sleep well that night, finally resorting to a sleeping spell he'd been told to use on himself only in the direst of emergencies. He couldn't help the nightmares crawling through his skull and it was almost a relief when he awoke, just as the sun was slowly rising above the mountains in the distance. Muttering words under his breath that would have earned him a rebuke from his father, he staggered into the washroom and splashed cold water on his face. He didn't feel refreshed at all.

There was no sign of Master Faye as he walked downstairs and into the kitchen, only the two silent servants, who laid out a full breakfast before he could say a word. Master Faye had clearly briefed them on what Joshua would be doing all day, for they'd also laid out a packed lunch and several bottles of juice. No alcohol, of course. Joshua had been told that alcohol could make a magician silly, and then dangerous. It was unwise to drink any, even a tiny sip.

Shaking his head, he ate his breakfast, filled his knapsack with the packed lunch and a handful of sweets from the kitchen, and then walked down towards the stables at the back of the house. Master Faye wasn't much of a horseman either; Joshua had never understood why a man with the power to fly even bothered to keep horses. But then, a horseman was less noticeable than a magician flying through the air. It was the only reason Joshua could accept why any magician would want to ride a horse.

"Filly is ready for you, Master Joshua," the stable boy said, tipping his hat. Joshua had the feeling he would have liked the lad, if there hadn't been a massive social gulf between them, one that could never be bridged. "He's in a very good mood."

Joshua scowled. The boy *loved* horses and they seemed to love him back, even though he spent most of his time mucking

out their stables. His family didn't have the money to buy a
horse for themselves, let alone keep it, which was probably why
he'd entered Master Faye's service. Not that Joshua could
complain; it was traditional for apprentices to take care of their
master's horses and he would have *hated* the job. The beasts
would have hated him too.

"I'm sure," he said, finally. The expensive lessons with a fine
horseman had been largely a waste of money. "Let's see the
beast."

Joshua had never been able to tell if Filly was male or female,
although he had been told that the beast was male. The
creature had a wicked temper when roused and an unerring
sense for when a rider was not capable of keeping him under
control. Joshua forced himself to look calm as the stable boy
led the horse out of the stall and started to fit him with a saddle
and bridle. Filly eyed him with dark eyes that promised a nasty
experience in the future. It was impossible to escape the feeling
that the beast was mocking him.

Master Faye insisted loudly that humans were the only
intelligent creatures on Darius. The legends of mermaids had
never been more than sailor stories; darker legends, which were
shared between the old wives, were often used as excuses for
bad behaviour. Looking at Filly, Joshua couldn't help thinking
that his master was wrong. There was a dark intelligence in the
horse's eyes. Or maybe he was just imagining it.

"You behave yourself, all right?" The stable boy said, to the
horse. "Or the master will sell you for cat meat."

Joshua snorted. He'd also been told that Filly was a famous
stud horse. Everyone for miles around wanted their mares to
be covered by the big black horse, who probably thought
himself in heaven. The stable boy's threat was impractical; even
if Filly was no longer allowed out of the stable, he'd still be
allowed to have sex with female horses. There was something
almost enviable about that.

Carefully, Joshua climbed up on Filly's back and into the
saddle, casting a charm that should prevent him from falling
off, or at least ensuring a relatively soft landing. Filly snickered
– an alarmingly humanlike sound – and shivered, very slightly.
Joshua had wondered if he was actually a transfigured human,
but Master Faye had sworn that he was a real horse. It wasn't
uncommon to check newly-purchased animals just to make

sure someone wasn't trying to slip a spy into a household.

The stable boy passed him his knapsack, which Joshua slung over his shoulder. He could have used the saddlebags, but Filly had once unseated him and run off, forcing Joshua to spend the rest of the day chasing the wretched beast. Master Faye had laughed when he'd come home, tired and sweaty, and refused to teach him a charm for controlling horses directly. Joshua would almost sooner have been beaten.

"All right," he said, knowing that the whole trip wasn't going to be fun. "Let's go."

Filly marched out of the stable and then, without any warning, jumped into a canter, moving down the middle of the street at terrifying speed. Joshua gritted his teeth and manipulated the reins carefully, knowing that pulling them too hard could result in the horse slamming to a halt and himself flying over Filly's head and down onto the cobbled ground. People scattered as they saw Filly coming, getting out of the way faster than they did for anyone human, even Master Faye. Filly's reputation as a bad-tempered beast had spread throughout the entire city.

Joshua forced himself to stay calm as they approached the gates. There were a pair of carts in front of them, being unloaded by the farmers under the watchful eye of the City Guard, but Filly just kept going, speeding up as he charged directly at the carts. A moment before they would have run into them, the horse jumped, cleared the carts effortlessly and raced out of the city. The Guardsmen knew better than to get in the way.

Outside the city, the road rapidly became much less comfortable. Each of the Pillars was supposed to maintain their own road network, but Master Faye had never been able to build up the manpower needed to repair the damaged roads. Warlock's Bane profited from his careful management, including allowing the merchants to make their own decisions with minimal taxation, yet something would have to be done about the roads sooner or later. When *he* was Pillar, Joshua told himself, he would organise a muster and get people to work on the roads. Or maybe he'd just offer to pay workers double if they worked outside the city.

Like most cities, Warlock's Bane was surrounded by farms, which produced much of its food. Joshua had accompanied

Master Faye as he'd reviewed them, taking his customary ten per cent of their produce, although he had to admit that he'd found the whole process rather boring. The farmers had locked up their daughters, either out of fear of him or of Master Faye, as some Pillars were known for deflowering as many girls as they could. Joshua couldn't imagine Master Faye with anyone. If nothing else, he seemed to have no other interests beyond power and ruling.

Joshua waved to a farmer riding on a cart as Filly thundered by, heading right for the borderline. There were a number of farms that straddled the frontier, or existed outside it in hopes of avoiding Master Faye's taxes, although that wasn't always a smart decision. The true danger of living outside a bailiwick was being targeted by Scions, either for food, women or simple amusement. Joshua had been training for six months when he'd seen the aftermath of one attack and it hadn't been pretty. The farmers had been normal humans when the Scions had arrived. Afterwards, they'd been monsters. And no one had been able to do anything about it because they were on the wrong side of the borderline.

The sun was higher in the sky when he finally slowed down, approaching the outermost farm. Joshua had a private suspicion that the farmer had intended to settle outside the borderline, or support others who *were* outside the borderline, but Master Faye didn't seem inclined to make an issue of it. Pillars who dictated too much to their population, he'd claimed, tended to have less useful populations over time. If he'd just wanted power without responsibility, he would never have challenged the last Pillar of Warlock's Bane to a fight.

Filly snickered again as they stopped just outside the gate, but Joshua was wise to the horse's tricks this time and used a freeze charm before slipping out of the saddle and dropping down to the ground. Once he'd tied Filly firmly to a tree, he released the charm and listened with a certain amount of pleasure to the horse's angry noises. Humans disliked the freeze charm; horses clearly reacted worse. Grinning, Joshua turned his back and walked away, heading towards the small farmhouse on the other side of the gate. A middle-aged man appeared around the corner and lifted an eyebrow when he saw Joshua. He didn't look pleased to see the Pillar's apprentice.

"Welcome, My Lord," he said. No, he *definitely* didn't sound pleased. By rights, Joshua could claim hospitality, but it wouldn't be a very welcome imposition. "We are at your service."

Joshua nodded. "My master sent me to enquire if you'd seen anything unusual in the area," he said, without preamble. There was no point in staying near the farm any longer than was strictly necessary. Nice as it would be to try to seduce the farmer's daughter, Master Faye would be furious if he wasted time. "Anything, anything at all."

The farmer relaxed slightly, looking a little relieved. His tax evasion either hadn't been noticed or had simply been ignored, Joshua decided. It wasn't at all uncommon for farmers to attempt to evade paying more than the bare minimum; Master Faye ignored it, as long as the city had enough food. Joshua wasn't sure what view he'd take of it when he was Pillar.

"Nothing, My Lord," he said, finally. "There was a wagon convoy nine days ago, if that counts; they sold Molly some spices before heading onwards to the city."

And evaded taxes in the process, Joshua knew. "I think that isn't really what I'm looking for," he admitted. "Is there nothing else at all? No strangers? No rumours from across the borderline? No odd magic at all?"

The farmer hesitated, and then shook his head. "No, My Lord," he said. "It has been a quiet month."

Joshua thanked him and walked back to Filly, feeling the farmer's eyes following him until he managed to climb back onto the horse and head out, past the borderline. Not that it was very clear; the boundary was really nothing more than a handful of charmed posts, creating a line that marked the edge of Master Faye's jurisdiction. No one could enter without realising that they were now subject to a Pillar who determined the law in his bailiwick. Outside, there was a faint sense of freedom – and chaos. Joshua knew that there were people who liked living outside bailiwicks, but they were at the mercy of anyone stronger than themselves. It very rarely ended well.

The road managed to grow even worse as they cantered along, looking for anything unusual, but there was no sign of anything. Eventually, they reached the resting place and Joshua steered the horse inside. There were no wagons in the clearing, no travellers resting before heading down to Warlock's Bane, yet Joshua couldn't escape the sense that he was being watched.

The dark forest looked utterly impassable. Anything could be hiding there, including a greedy Scion bent on conquest. Slowly, reluctantly, Joshua turned and pushed Filly out of the clearing, back to the road. It was something he would have to report to Master Faye...

... But if there was a Scion there, outside the borderline, who could object? It wasn't as if he was living in Master Faye's territory. He could do anything there.

Once they were back on the road, Joshua took the opportunity to use his mental voice to speak to Master Faye, to tell him what they'd learned, before he started to head along the borderline. He could ask the other farmers as he swept around the edge of the bailiwick, a task that would take most of the day. Irritating as it was, it was necessary – and besides, the alternative was more lectures from Master Faye. The trip was almost a break. Or it would have been, if he hadn't had Filly.

The horse snickered again and Joshua sighed. When he was Pillar, he was going to hand Filly over to a breeder with strict orders never to let him into a field, let alone onto the roads. And he was never going to ride a horse again. Flying, with all its dangers, was much more pleasant than riding. He saw birds flying in the distance and smiled. Flying was a skill he needed to master. It gave him a sense of freedom that he'd never had while down on the ground.

"Behave yourself," he told Filly. The horse made a rude noise and tried to bolt. Joshua pulled on the reins carefully, readying another charm. There had to be something that could allow a magician to control a horse directly. "We have a few more farms to visit before we can go home."

CHAPTER
THIRTEEN

The snoop followed the rider as he headed away from the clearing and back towards the first set of farms. Dacron watched through its sensors as the rider turned westwards, taking a poorly-maintained road that led around where they believed the border to run. His arrival at the landing zone could not be a coincidence. Dacron lacked the sheer processing power he'd had as an AI, but he could still calculate the odds – and knew that they were staggeringly low that his arrival was a coincidence.

"We tracked him backwards," the AIs said, through the radio link. The QCC links that would have allowed them to practically manifest on Darius were breaking down, suffering a series of inexplicable glitches. They were operating at one remove and *hated* it. "He set out from Warlock's Bane as soon as the sun rose, heading out towards us. They must have detected our arrival."

Elyria scowled. "But *how?*"

"Magic?" The AIs suggested. "Or maybe they are more aware of what happens in their world than we realised."

Dacron scowled. The more he looked at the data, the more he was convinced that there was an intelligence behind Darius, even if it was one with very strange priorities. It disrupted – but it didn't stop – surveillance programs. There had been no attempt to do more than interfere with the snoops, if the interference had been deliberate. And then the shuttle hadn't suffered any major glitches until it was safely down on the ground, when there had been a glitch that had shocked the team, without actually killing anyone. Dacron's best guess was that the glitches were warning shots, but why would anyone do that when they could just have hailed *Hamilton* and asked them to leave the star system?

"That isn't the issue," Jorlem said, calmly. "Do we move the shuttle?"

There was a long pause. A simple visual survey of the clearing would have revealed nothing; the diggers had been so precise that they'd actually rebuilt the wheel tracks left behind by previous visitors. But if the locals had some form of ESP that would allow them to locate the shuttle... the observation team might be dangerously exposed. There was nothing stopping the locals from simply digging it up with buckets and spades.

"That raises a separate issue," Fred offered. "*Can* we move the shuttle?"

Dacron had his doubts. The antigravity units had been tested several times since the glitch and they all seemed to be in perfect condition, which proved nothing. They'd been in perfect condition before the shuttle had entered the atmosphere. Moving the shuttle might be simple, or it might be very dangerous. The next glitch might prove lethal.

"I do not believe that we should risk it unless we have no other choice," he said, and outlined his reasoning. "If the locals do come here with a party, we stun them and move away."

"Assuming that stun weapons work," Adam pointed out. "Who knows *what* will glitch next?"

Adana glanced over at him. "Don't you know anything from the Ancient worlds?"

"The glitches were always random," Adam explained. "Sometimes pieces of technology would refuse to work – and then the next day they'd be working perfectly. The only common thread we found that bound them together was that the more advanced any given piece of technology was, the more likely it was to glitch. Some of those glitches proved fatal."

Dacron nodded. The Confederation had practically reinvented the wheel to allow safe operations on Ancient worlds, using technology that wouldn't have been out of place on a Second or Third Age world. Even so, the technology did have problems, which was why some researchers believed that the Ancients – or the Elders – were deliberately screwing with the lesser races attempting to explore their ruins.

"If the stunners don't work," Elyria asked, "what do we do then?"

"There are other weapons," Jorlem pointed out. "We could use the gas, then scan their minds and..."

"Out of the question," Elyria snapped. "There are ethical issues here."

Dacron had to check his terminal before he understood her anger. The Confederation's technology allowed it to do all sorts of things, including reading minds, editing memories, reprogramming minds and genetically-engineering slaves. But the Confederation, largely in memory of the atrocities committed by the Thule, also had strict laws governing the use of such technology. They weren't put aside just because it would be useful to scan a local's mind and find out what they knew of their world. Even with the chance to learn how to manipulate the quantum foam, those laws would remain in force.

But would Jorlem respect them? Or, for that matter, would the AIs? Dacron found himself caught between two different opinions, unable to decide which one was right. The AIs had little concept of mental privacy; indeed, it was hard to draw lines between the different AIs that made up the mental *Gestalt*. It would be very tempting to consider the option of kidnapping Master Faye or one of the other identified magicians and scanning his mind, hoping to see how he worked magic. Given the sheer immensity of the prize, Dacron wasn't sure if it wouldn't be considered acceptable after all.

And yet he knew that it would cause a rupture in the Confederation if the truth ever came out.

Other societies could and did talk about cruel necessity. Sometimes they were even right. When the food supplies ran short, they had to be rationed, even if that meant sentencing a part of the population to death. Or worse. There were societies that had had to destroy half their population to prevent the spread of a deadly virus that would have wiped them out. But the Confederation had no such excuse. Probing a mind without permission would horrify everyone. It would still worry them even if permission *were* granted.

"I think it should be considered," Jorlem said. "The ability to manipulate the quantum foam..."

"Is not worth the risk of utter disgrace," Elyria pointed out, sharply. "Just because they're primitive doesn't give us the right to treat them like animals."

There was, Dacron noted, a certain amount of hypocrisy in her words. The Confederation didn't hesitate to tear down primitive human societies it judged uncivilised, destroying their governments and incorporating their inhabitants into the Confederation. There was a strong school of thought that suggested the Confederation should do the same to alien races, particularly the ones still struggling through their First Age. And yet the cultural shock of encountering the Confederation would be vastly greater for a non-human race. They wouldn't be able to realise that *humans* had built the towering Confederation.

But intervening in human societies was for their own good. Everyone agreed on that. However probing their minds, without permission... Elyria was right. They'd be treating them as animals.

"We stay here, then," Elyria said, clapping her hands together. "And if they come back, we move, *without* being seen. I don't want to have to wipe anyone's memory."

"Assuming we can do that here," Adam pointed out. "What happens if the brain-probe suffers a glitch in the middle of the session?"

Dacron nodded. The likelihood of brain damage would be unacceptably high.

"Put out an extra shell of snoops," Elyria added. "Make sure we monitor everyone leaving the city; try to tag them all with a snoop if possible. The AIs can draw it all together into a workable whole."

"That leaves the other issue," Adana said. "Are we still going to head down to the city?"

"If half of us were away from the shuttle," Jorlem pointed out, "they could easily end up being stranded."

"But we'd still know where they were," Dacron countered, defending the honour of the AIs. "They could be warned and then picked up later."

"True," Elyria agreed. She looked from face to face, and then nodded. "We'll wait an hour, see if anyone comes up here after us. If not, we will proceed with the plan."

"There may be problems in discovering what they know,"

Dacron warned. "The places we have identified as government buildings are places the snoops have been unable to go. We may not know if they are planning to move against us."

"We'd see them coming," Jorlem said. "Even if all the snoops fail, there's orbital observation..."

"Unless the power that glitches our equipment can reach up to low orbit," Adam pointed out. *Hamilton* was well away from the planet, although no one knew what actually constituted a safe distance. The network of microsatellites was expendable, if necessary. They could always make more. "What happens then?"

"We might be in trouble," Jorlem said, dryly.

"Keep reviewing the data," Elyria ordered, finally. "And then we can prepare to move the wagons out onto the surface."

Dacron left the shuttle as the meeting broke up and stepped out into the cavern the diggers had created, hollowing out the ground under the clearing. Much of the earth and stone had been processed into building materials, allowing the base to expand at astonishing speed; they were already installing an elevator that would lift the wagons to the surface when the time came. Given enough time, and a suitable source of raw materials, the base would become large enough to house an entire research team, as well as hundreds of sensors devised by the AIs. One of them, Dacron had learned, attempted to measure changes in universal constants, something only possible by manipulating the quantum foam. The full potentials of the capability were rather terrifying. What if someone managed to cancel gravity all over the universe?

It seemed impossible; it *was* impossible, at least by conventional technology. One could manipulate gravity, even counteract it, but cancelling the force altogether? It was at least theoretically possible. One could do remarkable things in hyperspace, given enough processing power; the AIs had certainly proven that possible. What could one do if granted access to the quantum foam? The inhabitants of Darius might become gods.

But they weren't gods. It was difficult to be sure, but there had to be limits to their powers, apart from their own self-restraint. Maybe they countered each other, or maybe there were other limits to what they could do. Human brains were slow and feeble, as Dacron well knew. What could an AI do with the power to manipulate the quantum foam?

It made a certain kind of sense. Everyone knew that races in their Sixth Age – transcendence, like the Elder Races – became beings of pure thought and energy. They probably had at least some connection to hyperspace, like the AIs, as well as a link to the quantum foam. Given enough power, they could presumably do far more using the quantum foam than any mere human. They'd certainly be more capable of comprehending their full potential.

And then they just... faded away.

It was another mystery, one that fuelled the Conservatives' desire to hold the Confederation in an eternal state of stasis. Few Elders would talk to the Confederation – apparently, there had been one major contact, which had been hushed up – but it was clear that they eventually went... elsewhere. Did they burn out, the energies that supported them no longer sustainable, or did they ascend to a higher plane of existence? Or did the universe eventually erase them from existence, making room for other beings? No one had ever been able to figure out the answer.

His implanted communicator buzzed. "Dacron, it's time to get dressed," Elyria said. "Can you report to the dressing room?"

"On my way," Dacron said.

He walked back into the shuttle. The AIs didn't even begin to comprehend humanity's fascination with clothing, although Dacron was starting to suspect that it actually served a functional purpose. Several weeks as a human had taught him that looking at nude attractive females was very distracting. Oddly, he didn't seem to have any yen for human males, which surprised him. Perhaps it was a biological desire to procreate buried inside his new body that drove him towards females. But the Confederation could easily turn a male into a female.

Local clothing, at least that deemed suitable for apprentices, was grey and uncomfortable. AIs did not have a sense of aesthetics, at least as humans understood the term, and Dacron found it hard to care what he wore, but the humans had said it was ugly. Looking at himself in the reflector field, Dacron was inclined to agree. The outfit didn't show his body to his best advantage. On the other hand, as he was supposed to be a lowly apprentice, that was probably a good thing.

Adam, as the merchantman, enjoyed a far more spectacular set of clothes. A bright red and orange suit, with a green sash and leather belt, ensured that everyone would know him for a rich and prosperous merchant. He carried a cane in one hand – careful study of the snoop records had informed them that the canes were normally concealed swords – and a large bag in the other, which held notebooks, quill pens and a small amount of gold, silver and bronze coins. The hat he wore completed his disguise; Jorlem, who wasn't allowed to join the first exploration mission, had snidely pointed out that it made an excellent target. Elyria had suggested that might be the point.

His wife – played by Gigot – had an outfit similar to her husband, although hers had a long dress instead of trousers. It was also very loose, concealing the shape of her breasts; she wore no hat, nor was she allowed to carry a sword. The weapons she did carry would have to be kept hidden from the locals, as only a small number of women had been observed carrying any weapons at all. Until the exact nature of the local taboos were figured out, none of the women could carry weapons openly.

The daughters – Elyria and Adana – were dressed in drab black robes. Analysis had suggested that the black robes signified unmarried women, but there was no way to know for sure, at least until they had a chance to ask. It wasn't unusual to see girls accompanying their parents on business trips and a number had been observed helping with the sales, or keeping the accounts. In cities, women seemed to live more restricted lives, although there were a number of female-owned business. Or so they thought. Dacron reminded himself, again, that they were seeing everything at one remove and they might not fully understand what was going on.

Finally, the bodyguards wore leather armour and carried swords. They'd been lucky; a snoop had seen one of the City Guardsmen demanding a weapons permit and one had been handed over, allowing the fabricator to produce a forged copy. Adana had pointed out that primitive societies often tried to restrict weapons ownership, knowing that it might lead to rebellion if the lower classes got ideas. They hadn't picked up many people owning weapons other than the City Guards and those wealthy enough to pay the fees.

"We have been through the procedure seven times," Elyria

said. She might have been playing a submissive daughter, but she was definitely in charge. "We say little about where we come from; if pressed, give them the cover story and little else. Ideally, we say nothing while buying items from their shops, particularly books. Keep an eye open for anyone selling them."

Dacron nodded. Apart from the libraries, which were proving worryingly closed to the snoops, there were travelling booksellers, who moved from city to city selling books. One of them was heading to Warlock's Bane, which was another reason to start their operations there. A few dozen books could tell them more about the society on Darius than anything else. Quite where the books came from was something of a mystery, although he had no doubt the AIs would solve it soon enough. Making paper wasn't difficult and printing presses would be relatively simple, even for Darius's level of technology. And perhaps they could use magic to speed it up.

"We will take an inn inside the city" – all of the other travelling merchants had done the same, no doubt because they felt cramped inside their tiny caverns – "and assume that we will be watched at all times," Elyria continued. "Just because these people are primitive doesn't mean that they are stupid. We've seen them spying on each other just to try to get better deals. Use the implants for any communications outside our roles, or to stay in touch with the *Hamilton*. Alert us at once if you run into trouble of any sort."

She smiled. "It will be hard for some of you to stay in character," she concluded. "Remember that there is no other choice – and that you volunteered for it."

Dacron *hadn't* volunteered – or perhaps the AI that had spawned him had volunteered in his place. But it wasn't what Elyria meant and he knew it. Everyone would have to play their roles, including the women – and they were playing second-class citizens at best. The Confederation had no real concept of gender discrimination – being able to change sex at will had eliminated it completely – but Darius didn't seem to have anything of the sort, unless it was done by magic. Elyria had stepped into primitive worlds before, as had Adana. Gigot... hadn't.

Two hours later, the drones helped move the wagons to the surface. The horses weren't happy at all – they'd been bred on a Ring and they found Darius a little unnatural – but Fred and

Plax handled them perfectly. Indeed, it was possible that the locals would want them both for breeding stock. They'd had their genetic code improved, although they hadn't been uplifted to intelligence. Uplift procedures were banned, another legacy of the Thule War. No one would easily forget uplifted gorillas rampaging across human worlds.

"Here we go," Elyria said, as she climbed into a carriage. "Next stop, Warlock's Bane."

Despite himself, Dacron couldn't resist a thrill. This was going to be something *new*.

CHAPTER
FOURTEEN

They smelt the city a long time before they drew near to it.

Elyria took a breath, silently grateful for the enhancements in her sense of smell. Most primitive societies lived in filth, literally, unaware that it was dangerously unhealthy. Only a handful of human colony worlds that had lost technology had remembered germs and how diseases spread from person to person. Darius didn't seem to be any different. The unholy combination of smells reached out towards them as they finally headed down towards the city.

Warlock's Bane was laughably small by the standards of the Confederation, or even by the standards of a Second Age society. The snoops had revealed no more than a few thousand people living in the city, mainly workers, merchants and a handful of governors and City Guardsmen. That too wasn't untypical; the majority of Darius's population would still live on the land, producing food for their masters. They'd seen enough farms from orbit to conclude that the yields were very low, barely average for a First Age society. The locals had no way of countering crop pests, diseases and other problems that plagued comparable societies.

The city was surrounded by a high stone wall, topped with battlements that suggested the main threat to the city was an invading army trying to climb over the defences and into the city. Elyria knew that such walls would become obsolete very quickly once the locals developed gunpowder; indeed, given the power of some of their magicians, the walls might be already useless. Maybe they just marked the limits of the city, although they'd seen several cities where the walls were surrounded by shacks on both sides. An enemy with nothing more than swords and spears could use the ramshackle hovels for cover and advance against the city. It wasn't very secure.

Warlock's Bane seemed to avoid having any habitations on the wrong side of the wall. Someone had cleared away everything that could provide cover to an invading army, leaving them exposed to arrows fired from the walls – assuming that the City Guards had enough manpower to hold back an army. Their snoops couldn't go everywhere, so it was impossible to be sure, but it looked very much as if they *didn't* have enough trained men to hold the walls. The real protection of the city rested in the power and reputation of Master Faye. *That* was strange, almost an inverse of every other First Age society Elyria had studied; there was no way to know what it meant for the development of society at large.

Unless it's another Kahn, she told herself, silently. *Some animals are just more equal than others.*

The road, never very good outside the borderlines, grew better as they headed down towards the main gates. Elyria felt the carriage rocking as the horses started to slow down, waiting for the gates to open and allow them to enter. A heavy portcullis barred their way until it rattled upwards, powered by a pair of slaves who were chained to the pulley. It was a killing ground for unwary invaders, she'd been told; inside the gatehouse, they'd be bottled up and very vulnerable to anything from swordsmen to boiling oil. Dropping hot oil on enemy heads was a standard tactic in medieval societies, even though it inflicted injuries that were very much beyond their ability to mend. That might have been the point.

"Here we go," Adana said, as they rattled into the gatehouse. There was a long, almost pregnant pause, and then the inner portcullis slowly rose up into the air, allowing the horses to pull the carriages forward, into the courtyard. It was a barren space, smelling of the wastes of countless horses, with a handful of low gates that barred access into the city beyond. "Just keep our mouths shut."

Elyria nodded. Thankfully, the locals didn't seem to be particularly corrupt, at least from what they'd picked up with the snoops. There might be a demand that some city taxes were paid, but they weren't going to try to steal everything in the carriages. And yet they would just have to wait and see what happened. As far as they could tell, cities that had poor government, the type that would make it hard for merchants to operate, were simply excluded from the trading networks. It wasn't an uncommon pattern when a world was developing the rudiments of a capitalist economy.

The carriages came to a halt and the guardsmen bellowed orders for the occupants to climb out. Elyria pasted a vaguely worried expression on her face and opened the door before the bodyguards could reach them, jumping down to the muddy – and smelly – ground and lifting up her skirt to ensure it didn't get dirty. Adana followed her down; Elyria smiled inwardly as she saw the guards trying not to stare. They'd marred their skin slightly to match the local women – most people, it seemed, caught some kind of pox when they were growing up – but they were still cleaner than most. That, at least, wasn't uncommon among local travelling merchants, for obvious reasons. They spent most of their time on the road rather than in disease-ridden cities.

"Over here," Adam barked, playing the proud and dominant father. The guards had offered them a small hut in which to rest and wait, while the guards searched the carriages for smuggled goods. "And stop acting like children!"

Elyria concealed a smile and took a seat, waiting patiently for the guards to finish their search. It had been difficult to tell what was actually forbidden in Warlock's Bane, but they'd been careful to only bring along duplications of items they'd seen other merchants taking into the city. The *real* secret was the concealed technology, items beyond local imagination. Even if they found them worked into the wood and iron that made up the carriages, they wouldn't recognise them for what they were. Or so they hoped.

The chief guardsman entered the hut a moment later, checking the bodyguard papers with surprising attention to detail. Elyria scowled, inwardly, wondering if they'd made a mistake when forging them. They had such complete coverage of most primitive worlds that it was easy to forget that they might have missed something – and they *didn't* have complete coverage of Darius. The papers should have been indistinguishable from other, perfectly valid papers, but the guard was hesitating. A moment later, he grunted his approval, stamped a note on each sheet of paper and handed them back to the owners. Elyria allowed herself a moment of relief before the interrogation began.

Being women, Gigot, Adana and herself were largely ignored, apart from glances the guardsman tossed in their direction when he thought their 'father' wasn't paying attention. Adam took the brunt of the questioning, which he skilfully deflected after endless simulations on *Hamilton* based on what they'd overheard through the snoops. Yes, they were traders of no fixed abode; yes, they had links to the sea-folk; it was where they'd purchased their goods. And they'd come so far inland because they were looking for higher profits. A handful of questions made little sense. The guardsman wanted to know if they'd seen anything unusual on their trip. Lacking an idea of what was unusual on Darius, Adam could only say that they'd seen nothing and pray that was enough. It seemed to be, thankfully.

Another guardsman returned with a sheet of paper, which he'd used to list their trade goods. The guardsman read it quickly and then nodded, passing it to Adam for him to read and sign. Adam held it so the others could see it too, pretending to have difficulty reading it. The guards had done a thorough job of searching the carriages, to the point where they'd included a number of items as trade goods that were nothing of the sort. They'd certainly never intended to offer sleeping blankets for sale. That would definitely raise eyebrows.

"You will be expected to present them when you leave the city," the guardsmen said, when Adam raised the issue. He made a mark on the paper before handing it back to Adam. "If they happen to be missing, you will be expected to pay import duty on them. For the moment, you will pay twenty gold; if you fail to sell all of your goods, you may claim a refund."

And should we earn more than you expect, Elyria thought wryly, *we will be expected to pay additional taxes.*

It didn't matter to the Confederation if they were taxed or not, naturally. Producing enough gold to utterly shatter the local economy would be a comparatively simple matter. But it did matter to the locals, a sign of future trouble between merchants and their rulers. Tax farming was always complicated. If the taxes were too high, local business would be strangled; if the taxes were too low, the state might not have the funds it needed to safeguard itself. And if it couldn't protect itself, another state was likely to invade.

She glanced at the sheet of paper in Adam's hand and smiled to herself. There was another trap there, a subtle one that might not be noticed by the locals. Everything that was brought into the city would be registered and logged, allowing the rulers to know who bought what and why. Maybe it wouldn't be treated as anything more than a record, but anyone who wanted to hold absolute control over a human society knew the value of keeping good records. At the very least, they'd know who should be paying more taxes next year.

Adam signed with a flourish – learning the written language had been easy – and reached into his pouch for the gold coins. The locals *had* managed to achieve a remarkable unity in their coinage that wasn't often a hallmark of First Age societies, they'd discovered. Each of the coins was precisely the same weight, stamped with the logo of one of the mints scattered across the planet. The cities might be rivals, but they maintained the same standard of weights and measures, right down to the tiniest detail. It suggested that there had been more organised settlement of Darius than was immediately apparent, which was interesting. Colony worlds that fell so far, normally, tended to fragment in all kinds of ways. They had to reinvent weights and measures from scratch and they were never identical.

"Thank you," the guard said. "You may move your carriages into the courtyard of the Golden Arch, where rooms have been set aside for you. And then you may start selling to the merchant factors."

Elyria nodded as she stood up, careful to walk behind Adam. The locals might have sounded generous when they'd organised rooms for weary travellers, but they knew that it included a sting in the tail. A set of snoops that had peered through the Golden Arch Inn had confirmed that the building had been designed to make spying on guests easy, even without modern technology. The locals clearly had no intention of allowing them to operate unobserved.

And without constant footage from the snoops, we will have to watch our backs more carefully, she told herself. Normally, they could monitor the watchers – if there *were* watchers – from a distance. On Darius, that wasn't going to be so easy. The QCC links just kept breaking down.

They walked back to the carriages and allowed the bodyguards to mount up and drive the horses forward. Elyria chose to walk rather than climb back into the carriage, which should pass unnoticed. The locals knew that merchant women tended to have different standards of behaviour than those of city women, although they were also being escorted by their parents and Dacron, whom the locals would probably assume was pledged to one of Adam's 'daughters'. It would be maddening to be a local woman; indeed, she'd seen societies where women, treated as nothing more than property, developed all kinds of mental illnesses from banging their heads against a glass ceiling. The populations of those societies, given the ability to change sex, had promptly become almost all male.

The interior of the city, once they'd moved out of the first courtyard, was familiar because they'd seen it through the snoops, but Elyria found it easy to pretend interest anyway. There was a long line of shops, including some that were owned by wealthy businessmen who would probably be among their first customers, and a handful of inns for travellers. The population looked reasonably happy and content, for their civilisation, including a small group of young girls who were being escorted from shop to shop by an elderly man. Most of the population seemed to be fairly industrious, wearing drab clothes that stood in stark contrast to Adam's brightly-coloured outfit. A handful, clearly wealthy, wore clothes that were *almost* as colourful as the visitors.

Elyria nodded to herself as they reached the inn and drove around to the back, so the carriages could be placed in the courtyard. The horses would have to be moved to the stable and fed; their trade goods could be left in the carriages until they were ready to start selling them to the merchant factors. Judging from what the snoops had picked up, the City Guard would already have passed the list on to the merchants – or at least to the ones who had paid bribes – and they'd be on their way to make offers. The spices, in particular, could be sold at quite high prices.

The interior of the inn was lightly furnished, illuminated by blazing torches and a roaring fire that warmed the entire building. Adam talked briefly to the innkeeper, a man who was quite disturbingly fat, and secured the keys to three rooms. He would be sharing a room with his wife, his daughters would get a second room and the third would be Dacron's. The bodyguards were apparently expected to sleep in the carriages, guarding them overnight. Elyria schooled herself to show no reaction as the innkeeper offered Adam an extra lock for the second room, allowing them to lock his daughters inside, something that *hadn't* been picked up by the earlier snoops. Maybe there was a local custom they'd missed, or maybe the innkeeper was just making a joke. It was difficult to be sure.

"No, thank you," Adam said, finally. It was a shame that standard communications implants were almost useless on Darius. They could have pulled the live feed from the snoops, rather than relying on the AIs to collect it and then summarise the information to them. The innkeeper's reaction to Adam's refusal might have been quite informative. Still, the AIs would pick it up later. "Please have us called if anyone arrives to discuss our trade goods."

They were led through a stone passageway and up to a set of wooden doors, which the innkeeper opened before passing the keys to Adam. Inside, there were large – if uncomfortable – beds, a single wash basin and a large jug of water. Darius had yet to reinvent the concept of indoor plumbing, Elyria knew, but it was always a shock when she came face to face with what that meant. The less said about the chamber pot under the bed, the better. No wonder the locals had so many problems with disease.

She and Adana were expected to share a bed, she noted; after all, they *were* sisters. The locals didn't seem sophisticated enough to consider incest as a possible perversion, something that struck her as odd. Primitive societies often knew the dangers of incest even if they didn't understand *why* it was dangerous. Even the Confederation, which could have avoided the dangers altogether, frowned on incest. She shook her head a moment later, convinced that she was reading too much into the bedding. A society without any real means of heating rooms, outside fires, would probably see some advantages in siblings sharing beds. There was nothing sexual about it at all.

There was a faint *ding* in her head, followed by the AI voice. "There are four people watching your rooms," they said. The snoops would have spread out as soon as they realised which rooms would be occupied by the Confederation's party. "The system is really very neat. They can see almost all of the room."

Elyria resisted the temptation to glance over at the wall that held the peepholes. They'd be almost invisible to everyone, just high enough to be out of sight. A woman from Darius would have been horrified at having a man peeking on her; Elyria knew that she couldn't show any sign of being aware of their existence, or the spies would start wondering *how* they knew. At least it didn't seem to be sexual; the locals wanted a better bargaining position and if that meant spying on their guests, that was what they would do.

"Understood," she subvocalised, as she lay down on the bed. They shouldn't be able to see her lips move in this position. "And the traders?"

"The guards sold four *exclusive* copies of the list of trade goods," the AIs said, with a hint of amusement. Each of the merchants would believe that they were the only one to be given an advantage, at least until they arrived at the inn. "We believe that they are preparing to send envoys now. They may compete, or they may try to act as a united front."

"Probably the former," Elyria said. If the merchants united, they could force the traders to accept a lower price for their goods than they would have otherwise received. But there were too many merchants in the city for that to work very well. There was no reason why Adam had to accept the first offer for his goods. "Monitor them; see if you can tell what they're offering."

She smiled as she rolled over on the uncomfortable bed. "Tomorrow we can explore the city," she said, out loud. Let the observers think that the girls were nothing more than unimportant women. They'd keep their eyes on Adam, allowing Elyria and Adana to research the city in peace. "*That* should be fun."

CHAPTER
FIFTEEN

Joshua had seen the newcomers as he returned to the city on Filly, uncomfortably aware of the pain throbbing through his thigh. Filly had finally managed to unseat him, just as they were about to start heading home, and Joshua had landed badly. The protective spells had saved him from breaking something, but it still hurt. He'd used another freeze charm on the horse until he felt able to ride again, and then tied the beast to a tree until he became rather more subdued. Swearing that he would never ride again, Joshua had ridden back towards the city.

The newcomers had passed through the detectors at the gate without incident, thankfully. There was no such thing as a group of Scions – normally, they could barely tolerate the company of other magicians – but it was quite possible that the mystery magician had decided to travel with a group of traders in hopes of slipping into the city without being identified. It would have been a false hope, Joshua suspected, yet Master Faye had warned him that detection spells could be tricked. If there was enough doubt over *who* was the Scion, attacking the wrong person could be very dangerous.

Joshua scrambled off Filly as soon as he passed through the gates and handed the reins to one of the guardsmen, who would take the horse back to Master Faye's house. There would probably be a lecture in Joshua's future about using guardsmen as his personal servants, but his aching thigh made it hard to care. Instead, he watched from a distance as the carriages were searched, while one of the senior guardsmen worked his way through the bodyguard papers. Joshua had never fully understood why so many records had to be kept, but it was Master Faye's command. Many of the other Pillars did the same thing.

The guardsmen evidently found nothing illegal, so they took the list to the merchant, made him check and sign it, and then allowed him and his party to head to the inn. Joshua watched them silently; there was nothing special about their leader, or the sour-faced man who had to be an apprentice, judging from his grey clothes, but the women were beautiful. The merchant's wife was striking and the two daughters were absolutely stunning. There was something about their beauty that looked timeless; Joshua knew, without a doubt, that every unattached man in Warlock's Bane would be trying to court them. On impulse, he ran through the spell to detect glamours and illusions and found nothing. Their beauty was real.

He wanted to follow them to the inn, but he had his duty – and besides, they would need to rest. Laughing at himself – he'd become pompous, at least inside his head – he walked over to the guardsmen and took the list of trade goods, scanning it with practised ease. Master Faye had forced him to read until he could do it quickly, even when the handwriting was badly scrawled. Joshua's own handwriting wasn't much better.

The list was interesting, to say the least. Spices from far overseas were rare in Warlock's Bane; they'd be sure to make hundreds of gold coins if they sold carefully. The other supplies were more mundane, although stirrups from Night Watch were better than anything produced closer to Warlock's Bane, Joshua checked to see if they were selling swords from Caitiff, but none were listed. He'd wanted a sword from the famed city of swords for years, yet they were expensive even for a magician's apprentice. Master Faye could have pulled strings, but he'd refused to help Joshua, pointing out that a magician shouldn't need a sword. He should know far more powerful protections.

"We were going to take the list to your master," the guardsman said, quickly. Judging from his expression, a number of rich merchants were about to receive tips that would make them even richer. Master Faye would have frowned on a monopoly, or a cartel, but he would tolerate a certain amount of insider trading. "And the gold coins, for verification."

Joshua smiled and took the bag. They'd be happier allowing

him to take them, secure in the knowledge that no one would dare to rob the Pillar's apprentice – and, of course, that the guardsmen wouldn't miss out on any bribes through leaving the gatehouse. The demanding of bribes was something else he was resolved to change when he became Pillar... shaking his head, he walked out of the courtyard and back onto the streets. The newcomers had vanished, no doubt having headed straight for the Golden Arch. They would probably want some rest before they confronted the merchants in Warlock's Bane.

Thoughtfully, he took the guardsman's report out of the bag and studied it. The newcomers had been really rather vague about where they'd come from, providing only brief and basic answers to the questions. That wasn't too uncommon in merchant travellers; they tended to prefer to stay on the road, rather than remain permanently in a single city. Who knew when the local Pillar would decide to become a tyrant rather than a reasonably benevolent ruler?

The girls were called Elyria and Adana, both apparently sixteen years old and unmarried, he read. Neither of them were betrothed, something that struck him as unusual. At their age, they should have had offers for their hands; their families were certainly rich enough to attract attention even if they hadn't been beauties. And the daughters of travelling merchants could often read, write and do their sums, as well as cook, clean and carry out the rest of women's work. They would have been attractive prospects the moment they started their feminine cycles.

Putting the thought out of his mind, he walked back to Master Faye's house and stepped in through the side door. Master Faye was kneeling in front of a bowl of water, trying to hunt for the mystery magician. Joshua knew that he'd been trying every day since the first hint that they were being watched and had found nothing, even when they'd shared blood and used it to power the magic. He took a seat and waited, knowing better than to interrupt his master until the spell was completed. The results of interrupting a magician could be disastrous. It had been one of the first lessons Master Faye had beaten into him.

Several minutes passed before Master Faye stood up, nodding to one of his servants to take the bowl and pour the hot water into the cauldron they were using to boil meat for dinner.

Joshua waited until his master had finished stretching and then passed him the bag, along with the notes from the guardsmen. Money from outside visitors was always suspect; it had to be checked, carefully, before it was allowed into the city. Joshua doubted that anyone would be fool enough to try to pass off forged coins in a Pillar-ruled city, but there were no shortage of dupes out there who couldn't test the money. Someone might bring it in without having the slightest idea that it was fake.

"I saw nothing," Joshua said. He hesitated, and then outlined what he'd felt when he'd reached the clearing. He'd been told, time and time again, to listen to his senses. "I don't know if it was real or not."

"There could be anything out there, beyond the borderline," Master Faye said, thoughtfully. He reached into the bag, pulled out a coin, and tested it thoughtfully. "Fake."

Joshua looked up, sharply. "Fake?"

"Maybe," Master Faye said. He sounded confused, something that bothered Joshua. What could confuse his master? A second coin was tested and then dropped on the table beside the first. "A very strange fake."

Joshua swallowed. "Why?"

Master Faye eyed him as if he'd said something particularly stupid, and then relaxed slightly. "You are aware, of course, that coins are minted and then marked to prove that they were tested by the proper authorities," he said. Joshua nodded. Turning lead to gold was difficult, but possible, at least for a few hours. Eventually, it reverted, by which time the forger would be well away. "These coins do not carry the mark of any known mint."

Joshua nodded, following the explanation. The marks were magic, impossible to duplicate – and bound up in the mint's sense of honour. Once crafted and stamped into the metal, they were impossible to remove short of melting down the entire coin, which would render it useless until it was sold back to the mint. They would be a permanent guarantee of the value of the coin.

"But I used a testing spell," Master Faye said, a moment later. "These coins are *gold*. They could have been forged at any mint and then marked, but they were never marked. I don't know what it means."

"They're *real* gold?" Joshua repeated. Who would bother to

forge gold coins out of pure gold? They could just take the gold to the mint and have it made into coins, coins that would carry the mark verifying their value. "But why?"

"They don't appear to be old enough to have been produced before the first mints," Master Faye said, a moment later. He span the third coin in his hand and watched as it tipped onto its side. "In appearance, they seem to come from the Southern Mint, but they don't carry the mark. Why not?"

Joshua frowned. "Could they be something else, transfigured into gold?"

"They'd have a very clear signature if they were," Master Faye explained, absently. He was still staring at the coin. "No, these are forged gold coins made of real gold. It makes no sense."

He looked over at Joshua. "You saw the newcomers, didn't you?"

Joshua nodded. He'd been watching newly-arrived traders for so long that it had become something of a joke between them. Carefully, he outlined his impressions, trying not to give the impression that he was dwelling too much on either of the girls. Master Faye wasn't fooled, judging from his expression, but he said nothing. A relationship with a travelling trader girl wouldn't be as serious as one with a local girl, one who might expect marriage and children.

"Interesting," Master Faye said, finally. "I'll tell you something else that didn't happen, something that *should* have happened. They didn't trigger the sensing spells at all."

Joshua was puzzled for a moment, and then he understood. Any trader who wanted to travel through the badlands would purchase something magical to help deter bandits from attacking his carriages. Or hire one Scion to defend them against others, if they could find one who could be bought. The absence of magicians wasn't too surprising, but the absence of magic was inexplicable. Unless...

"They might have been attacked along the way," he said. "Maybe they were cursed badly enough to burn out the defences..."

Master Faye cocked an eyebrow. "Without actually killing them? Or taking their goods? Or destroying their carriages? Or kidnapping the girls?"

Joshua flushed. "And they reported nothing," he added, a moment later. "They'd certainly report a bandit attack."

"Or drained defences," Master Faye agreed. "And they would have to be insane to travel so far, with such valuable goods, without some form of protective magic. It makes no sense."

"Maybe all it did was drain magic," Joshua suggested. "Something like that could have removed the marks from the coins..."

Master Faye laughed, unpleasantly. "If someone had developed a technique for doing that," he pointed out, "they would rule the world. Our wards wouldn't be able to keep them out at all; they'd just be able to charge in, cut us apart and take the city. No, if someone had a technique for that, they would have used it by now."

He looked up at Joshua. "I will speak with my peers," he added. "I suggest that you wait here and read a book. This may take some time."

Joshua watched him go and then stood up, heading over to the bookcase. Master Faye had a large collection of books, not all of them on magic, and he'd insisted that Joshua read his way through them. None of the collection Joshua was allowed to read were actually secret, although they were kept from the Minors. He rather doubted that there was anything in them that wouldn't be known to a Scion or another Pillar.

He was midway though a textbook on comparative charms for long-distance communication when Master Faye walked back into the room, looking grim. "I spoke to the Pillar of Athol and he spoke to his Keeper of Records," he said. "There is no record of any of the traders there."

Joshua frowned. "But they said they came from Athol..."

"The concept of lying is surely not unknown to you," Master Faye said, sarcastically. He seemed more than a little on edge. "There are too many things about this that don't make sense. If they are trying to hide where they came from, why? We wouldn't turn anyone away, even if they came from Drumgeld. Why are they being *stupid?*"

Joshua made a face. Drumgeld, four hundred kilometres away on the other side of the mountain, had once been a prosperous city to rival Warlock's Bane, before its previous Pillar had been replaced by a madman. In two years, he'd created a nightmare so bad that Minors and Scions alike gave the place a wide berth, while imprisoning most of his population inside the walls. There were rumours of what was happening to them now, each one more horrifying than the last. Joshua had heard that several Pillars had actually considered teaming up to deal with the situation, but nothing had ever been decided. The principle that Pillars had total authority within their bailiwicks was too strong.

"If they're using false money, they should be arrested," Joshua said, slowly. "And yet, might arresting them be very dangerous?"

"If they're connected with the person spying on us," Master Faye said. He shook his head. "If the idea is to make an excuse for a fight, why bother? Any Scion who wanted to take the city could just walk in and challenge me. They wouldn't need to contrive an excuse for a duel."

Joshua had to admit that his master was right. There was little point in anything elaborate if someone just wanted the city. They'd have to fight for it sooner or later, so why not sooner? The longer they waited, the longer Master Faye would have to prepare his ground. They should have moved the moment they realised that their spying spells had been detected.

"I see," he said, finally. "What do we do?"

Master Faye said nothing, thinking hard. "We could take them into custody and interrogate them under truth spells, but that would be unpopular," he said. In theory, there was nothing anyone could do if Master Faye decided to allow it, but in practice traders would start diverting away from Warlock's Bane and ruining the city. "And if we set out to tamper with their memories, it might be noticeable."

"Yes," Joshua agreed. He'd been taught how to watch for altered memories very early on, forced to practise and practise until he got it right. A Scion would have no difficulty in spotting altered memories, at least unless it was done very carefully – and that took time, time they might not have. "Could we not arrest one of them for using forged coins and interrogate them?"

"We might have to," Master Faye said. He shook his head. "I hate working in the dark. I'd almost sooner watch a Scion walking down into the city to challenge me for power."

Joshua nodded. At least there would be a very clear threat.

"You will keep an eye on them and see what you can learn," Master Faye said, finally. "The girls are beautiful, so no one will be surprised if you attempt to court them. But be careful what you tell them in return. It is possible that they have come to learn secrets of magic."

"But a Scion would know everything you know," Joshua said. "Wouldn't he?"

"It depends on the Scion," Master Faye admitted. "There are quite a few secrets I didn't know until I found them in Master Spark's notes, after I killed him. This could be just another attempt at scouting Warlock's Bane out before the Scion shows himself. Or it could be a complete coincidence..."

He shook his head. "No, this cannot be a coincidence," he added. "I want you to watch them closely, both through magic and through your eyes. And don't let the girls seduce you instead. Watch them."

Joshua grinned, a grin that vanished when Master Faye glared at him. "This is important," his master snapped. "Whoever takes this city will not want an apprentice so close to him. You will be killed or enslaved after I die."

"I understand, Master," Joshua said, formally. And his Master was right. Joshua would be useless to any new Pillar – and a potential threat. He would be lucky if he was simply killed out of hand. "I won't let you down."

"Get a bath and then get an early night," Master Faye ordered. "I want you to be ready to leave the house as soon as they start having breakfast at the inn."

Joshua nodded, suddenly remembering the dull ache running through his body. Riding all day was hard enough even without the horse being intent on throwing him off every time he relaxed his guard. Maybe he could convince Master Faye to sell Filly to a stud farm if he showed his master the bruises, before realising that it wouldn't matter. He would *never* be a good horseman.

Shaking his head, he walked upstairs and undressed in the bathroom, where the maid had already filled the bathtub with cold water. Joshua had to cast a heating spell to warm the liquid, one of the first exercises that Master Faye had forced him to perform. There was nothing like burns – or cold baths – to teach someone how to be careful.

And he would have to be *very* careful tomorrow.

CHAPTER
SIXTEEN

"Did you have a good night?"

"There were *things* in the bed, mommy," Adana said. She had pitched her voice into that of a whiny teenage child. "And Elyria kept hogging the blankets."

Elyria had to smile as Gigot rounded on her and issued a public lecture about stealing her sister's share of the blankets. It was how children, even teenagers, were disciplined on Darius and Gigot had the act down perfectly. The innkeeper's wife tossed her an approving look as they entered the dining hall and sat down at one of the tables. A list of possible cooked breakfasts was placed in front of them, all having to be cooked from scratch. It wasn't unknown for people to cook their own food in the Confederation, but it was considered something of a luxury. Here, *everyone* ate home-cooked food.

The innkeeper's wife wasn't the cook herself, apparently. Instead, Elyria heard her barking orders to two more girls in the kitchen, although Elyria couldn't tell if they were her daughters or just hired servants. They were probably her daughters; using them as labour would be cheaper than hiring servants, who would have to be paid in money. Shaking her head, Elyria concentrated on listening to the report from the AIs. Apparently, several merchants were intending to visit Adam later in the morning to bargain for his goods.

Adam himself entered the room a moment later, having needed longer to dress, followed by a sullen-looking Dacron. The embodied AI did sullen well, Elyria decided, although he might have been overdoing it a little. Someone who didn't know that it was an act might wonder why Adam was putting up with it. They joined the girls at table in time to be served sausages and scrambled egg. The sausages tasted faintly oily – Elyria was relieved that their enhanced bodies should have little difficulty dealing with anything that might have been poisonous – but the eggs weren't bad at all. And then there was homemade bread, a small helping of butter and a jug of milk, which tasted fresh and creamy. The inn probably had an arrangement with the nearby farms.

"I have received two notes from people who wish to call on me," Adam said, self-importantly. They'd modelled his mock persona on a travelling merchant they'd seen on the other side of the world, someone who sounded as though he were bragging all the time. "We" – he shot a glance at Dacron – "will be hearing them this morning."

He looked over at Gigot. "And you will be joining us too," he added. "The girls can explore the city on their own."

Elyria concealed her private amusement. They'd have a chance to gather information while pretending to be star-struck tourists from a very different city. Besides, no one from this culture would expect teenage girls to know anything useful. It was stupid and senseless, but it seemed to be the way things worked. Shaking her head, ignoring the odd glance the innkeeper's wife gave her, she finished her eggs and headed back up to their room. Adana would stay behind for half an hour, enough time for Elyria to draw away any watchers – if there *were* watchers. The AIs hadn't identified anyone apart from the ones peering through the peepholes, and *they'd* been more focused on Adam. Clearly, money talked louder than sex.

They'd fabricated long cloaks to wear over their dresses, so Elyria donned hers and walked down the rear stairs, out into the courtyard. The sun was only just rising in the sky, but the city was already coming to life. Hundreds of workers were strolling through the streets, while carts piled high with fruit and vegetables headed to market. At least the locals knew to keep meat cold to preserve it as long as possible, including using bags of ice from icehouses, or they would have had a far worse disease problem. Angry flies buzzed around the road, attracted by the droppings horses had left as they moved through the streets. Although a handful of slaves seemed to be cleaning up the mess, there was always more. But then, back on Old Earth, horses had been a major cause of pollution until they'd been replaced by automobiles.

And they produced pollution too, Elyria thought dryly, as she walked onwards, through the market. Her outfit made her conspicuous; the sellers called out offers, inviting her to bargain for their wares. She declined the offers, knowing that they were deliberately starting high because she was a stranger in town. Apples and oranges were cheaper than one bronze coin for five. It was interesting that they hadn't produced anything smaller than bronze coins; the concept of paper money had never occurred to them. Or maybe they just considered it too easy to forge.

A travelling bookseller had set up his cart at one end of the street, inviting the crowds to step into a whole new world. Elyria glanced inside and was instantly charmed by the interior, where hundreds of bookshelves were crammed into the tiny cart. It took her a long moment to realise that the cart was literally bigger on the inside than the outside, something the Confederation had always considered impossible for Fifth Age civilisations. The AIs had expanded into hyperspace, but it wasn't quite the same thing. Elyria felt her head spinning as she realised that she could walk *into* the cart and pull books off the shelves.

She tried to activate the transmitter, only to discover that it didn't work. Whatever force had created the bookseller's cart had disrupted all modern technology, even something so primitive that it shouldn't have been affected at all. Shaking, half in shock, Elyria stepped back and shook her head. She would have to deal with it, somehow.

"Don't worry," the salesman said, completely misunderstanding her shock. "The dimension won't collapse while you're inside."

"Thank you," Elyria stammered. She forced herself to remain calm and looked down at the wizened man. "What sort of books do you sell?"

"All sorts," he assured her. "I have stories of exciting adventure – very popular with the young men. I have stories of romance – very popular with the young women." He winked. "I even have a rare copy of *The Perfect Marriage*, banned in a dozen bailiwicks. And I have a handful of manuals for those intent on learning a skilled trade."

Elyria nodded. "Do you have manuals on magic?"

"Of course not," he said, shocked. Elyria realised that she should have known that – and would have, if she'd been born on Darius. "What do you take me for? The Pillar would have shut me down if I'd sold those to Minors."

He snorted, loudly. "The very idea," he added. "I have books on craftsmanship, metalworking and farming, with a small textbook on accounting, for the boring people. And a couple of books of history. But those are expensive. Three gold coins each."

Elyria hesitated. Spending so much might well attract attention. "Don't worry," the seller said, misinterpreting again. "I can have the books shipped to you at the inn, if you wish. No one else will have to see what you read."

"Good," Elyria said. She counted out ten gold coins and passed them over to him. His eyes didn't show any sign of surprise, but his hand seemed to be shaking slightly. "I'd like both books on history and a selection of fiction books, some of all kinds. Have them sent to the Golden Arch Inn, under my name."

She walked away, hoping she could get far enough away that her communicator would start to work again. It came back to life after she'd walked ten metres from the bookstall, although the QCC link in her neural implants refused to work. Elyria had expected as much – she'd turned it down prior to landing because of it – but it was still distressing. Even a power absorption field shouldn't have been able to drain it without killing her.

"We thought your equipment had failed completely," the XO said. "What happened?"

Elyria hesitated. "Did you get a live feed from the snoops?"

"Only at a distance," the XO confirmed. "Why?"

"Listen," Elyria said, and outlined what she'd seen. "They managed to create something dimensionally transcendent."

She had to smile at the shock in the XO's voice. "That's freaking impossible!"

"That's not the first time we've said that about this world," Elyria reminded her. "I'm going to head to the library. When the books arrive at the inn, they can be read and then shipped back to the base. We can have them transferred to the ship later."

"Right now, I'd be worried about bringing *anything* onto the ship," the XO said. "You do know that the library is off-limits to the snoops?"

"I think that tech fails near their magic," Elyria said. It wasn't a new theory, but it seemed to have been proven. "Which leaves us with another question. What happens in the Dead Zones?"

"Take care of yourself," the XO ordered, and signed off.

Elyria felt sweat trickling down her spine as she headed down the street towards the library, a solid stone structure that appeared to have been inspired by Grecian buildings from Old Earth. That might be useful in tracking down Darius's original colony ship, if there had been a colony ship, but it meant nothing. It was quite possible that the style had simply been reengineered on Darius and it was nothing more than a coincidence. The name of the planet suggested a different ethnic origin. Or maybe someone had just thought that it was a cool name. Several planets settled in the First Expansion Era had had funny names before various interstellar powers had banned the practice.

She half-expected guards to stop her before she walked inside, but the door opened without incident. The interior of the building was cool, almost as if they were using a cooling field to keep the temperature precisely under control, presumably to protect the books. She glanced around and saw no sign of any fans, so it was probably another example of magic. A quick check revealed that none of her technology worked any longer.

There was no librarian, only a written warning that attempting to remove the books from the library would result in punishment. The first time she read it, she thought she'd translated it poorly without her implants; it warned of pain of pain. It took several moments before she decided that she'd actually translated it properly, suggesting that it meant something to the locals. Or maybe someone was just trying to look pretentious. The library itself seemed a perfectly normal building, without being larger inside than it was on the outside, crammed with books. Elyria took a moment to read the first set of titles, before deciding that she was looking at a set of manuals. It took several minutes to find a book detailing the history of Warlock's Banc. There didn't seem to be anything on the entire planet. Taking a seat, she started to parse through the text. Frustratingly, the writer seemed to have spoken mainly in elliptical statements rather than anything definite.

She looked up as a young man entered the library. He wore a grey robe, with a silver star hanging down from a chain around his neck. Without the implants, it took her several moments to recognise him as Master Faye's apprentice, the one who had stood in judgement over court cases weeks ago. Elyria saw him looking at her and wondered, grimly, if the meeting was a coincidence. And then he walked over to her desk.

"Hello," he said, rather nervously. "May I talk with you?"

Elyria studied him for a long moment. It was always difficult to tell how old someone was in the Confederation, but on Darius people aged quickly. He probably was as young as he looked, barely sixteen – and nowhere near as subtle as he thought he was. Elyria didn't miss the quick glance he shot at her chest, or the way he couldn't quite look at her face. How long had it been since she'd been that young, and awkward?

But the Confederation forbade little and encouraged its youngsters to grow and develop. Almost any taste or fetish could be catered for, simply by finding someone else who enjoyed it. A more repressive society, on the other hand, would often criminalise sexual acts, simply because they wanted to maintain control. It was quite possible that many of its young men would find the Confederation to be a paradise, at least until they matured. The same could be said for the girls.

"You may," Elyria said, calmly. They weren't sure of the exact social niceties surrounding the Pillar's apprentice, but as an outsider she wouldn't be expected to know them. Or would she? There were other Pillars all over the world. "My name is Elyria."

She held out a hand, which he bent to kiss, his lips smacking just above her bare skin. "My name is Joshua," he said. "Apprentice to Pillar Faye."

He sounded rather nervous, despite his social position. "Pleased to meet you," Elyria said. She looked down at the book in her hand and then back up at him. "What actually happened to this city?"

Joshua gave her an odd look, and then smiled when he saw the book. "That's Tobias's work," he said. "The man lived through five Pillars and he did that by keeping his head down.

He criticises the last Pillar quite savagely, but you have to be able to read between the lines to tell. Pillar Spark was not known for listening calmly when someone disagreed with him."

"I see," Elyria said. The Confederation didn't have any limits on what one could write and publish, ensuring that there was always a torrent of nonsense from the population, often burying serious works in the deluge. "So... what actually did happen?"

Joshua grinned, clearly seeing a chance to impress her. "Master Spark took over the city seventy years ago, but he rapidly went mad and unleashed a reign of terror and oppression. That's when they built the wall; Master Sparks was so scared that someone else would overthrow him that he enslaved half the city long enough to put up a basic and useless defence. In his last days, he was killing people at random before Master Faye arrived to remove him from power."

His grin widened. "My master is a much better ruler."

Elyria didn't doubt it. Warlock's Bane was definitely among the more prosperous cities on Darius. "How did Master Faye take over?"

Joshua gave her another odd look. "They fought, of course," he said. "Eventually, Master Faye overcame Master Spark and ended his life, becoming ruler of the city."

Elyria nodded. They'd worked that much out, but it was nice to have it confirmed. Clearly, Darius followed the Kahn pattern; those with an advantage over the rest of the population held power. There had to be something about Master Faye's powers that prevented discontented citizens from overthrowing him, maybe a magical force field. Given access to the quantum foam, it would be relatively simple to render oneself immortal, or at least immune to harm. Or so the theory stated. No one had ever actually tested it. The theory also suggested that a single mistake might have disastrous consequences.

"But never mind that," Joshua said. "How did you end up travelling with your family?"

What is a nice girl like you doing in a place like this? Elyria translated, mentally.

She smiled, keeping her thoughts to herself. "My father was a trader since before I was born," she said. They knew enough about how trader families worked to put a convincing story together. "I just stayed with him and mom as I grew up. When

I got old enough, father put me to work figuring out the accounts and suchlike. He said I had to earn my keep."

"Master Faye says that too," Joshua said. There was something odd about his expression, something that bothered Elyria even though she wasn't sure why. "Apprentices like us – and you are one, even if they don't admit it – have to do as we're told."

He smiled back at her. "How many places have you seen?"

Elyria shrugged. "Too many to speak of," she said, perfectly truthfully. Of course, Joshua wouldn't believe her if she spoke of the Confederation, or the Sphere, or the Many-Starred World. Come to think of it, was there a link between Darius and the mysterious Sphere-Builders? "Athol is a pretty boring place. I go there and then I want to go away."

His eyes narrowed, just for a second, as if he'd caught her in a lie. Elyria kept her own face calm, trying desperately to figure out how he knew she'd been lying. They didn't have lie detectors... or did they? If they had truth spells, could they have spells that detected lies?

"I used to want to leave Warlock's Bane," Joshua said, finally. It was quite understandable. "And now I don't really want to leave."

"Some people are like that," Elyria said, neutrally. Something had definitely gone wrong. "Why can't you take books out of the library?"

Joshua smiled, perhaps glad of the change in subject. "Because these books are rare," he said. "Take one out of the library and the librarian will insist that you be enslaved for the rest of your life. They're priceless."

"Oh," Elyria said. That wasn't uncommon in pre-industrial societies, but Darius did have the printing press. "What if..."

The door burst open. "There she is," a voice bellowed. It sounded loud enough to shake the building. "The thief!"

Elyria stared, recognising the bookstall keeper. A thief? What did he think she'd stolen?

He waved a hand at her. A second later, her entire body locked solid. No matter what she did, she couldn't move a single voluntary muscle. All she could do was wait. And pray.

CHAPTER
SEVENTEEN

"Stop," Joshua snapped. He held up a hand, halting the bookstall owner in his tracks. "What are you *doing?*"

Master Faye could command respect through fear. Joshua would have to hope that his apprentice carried the same weight. The bookstall owner glared at him, but didn't seem inclined to grab the frozen Elyria and drag her off to the City Guard. But then, it was Joshua's master who would stand in judgement over her.

"She bought some books from me with unmarked coins," the bookseller snapped, producing a set of familiar golden coins from his pouch. "I tested them and they bore no mark."

Joshua scowled, inwardly. Normally, the only person who could test coins was Master Faye – and he would only test large sums of money brought into the city, because otherwise he wouldn't have time to get anything else done. They'd overlooked the bookseller, who had a little magic of his own, and he'd tested the coins *he'd* been given. In hindsight, perhaps they should have asked him to report anything odd to Master Faye.

He tried to think quickly, cursing his own ignorance. If the whole incident had been arranged as a provocation, no matter how absurd that seemed, taking Elyria into custody might trigger a challenge against Master Faye. But if she *wasn't* taken into custody, the bookseller would have strong grounds to complain – and damage the city's economy. Forged coins could not be tolerated. There was no precedent for golden coins that were perfect, apart from lacking the verification mark.

"Then we shall take her to Master Faye," he decided, finally. The bookseller would probably want to take her to the jail, but it would be several days before she would face Master Faye in Court. Jail was no place for a young girl... besides, his instincts kept telling him that Elyria had no evil intentions. He looked over at Elyria and frowned. "I'm sorry about this, but there is no choice."

The bookseller gave Joshua a nasty look as he worked his way through a simple levitation spell, lifting Elyria up into the air. She looked oddly vulnerable as she span in front of them, a reminder that those with magic would always be superior to those without. Joshua looked down at the books she'd picked up and then left them on the table for the librarian to return to the shelves. When she returned, if she returned, she would have no trouble finding them again.

Master, he said, using his mental voice, *something has happened.*

He filled Master Faye in as he pushed the floating Elyria out of the door and into the streets. Thankfully, there were few people around as he started to walk towards Master Faye's house, but he was very aware of unseen eyes. The bookseller followed, muttering nastily to himself in a language that Joshua had barely started to learn. If Elyria was convicted of a crime, he would claim the right to punish her – although Joshua honestly wasn't sure if she *was* guilty of a crime. The coins weren't actually fake, even though they bore no mark. Maybe a Scion had found a seam of gold somewhere outside the city and was starting to mine it to produce coins. But if that was the case, why not simply have them verified at the nearest mint?

Master Faye's servants opened the doors as they approached, allowing him to manipulate Elyria inside and close the door behind him. The bookseller started to complain loudly to Master Faye, only to be silenced by an angry look. If the whole affair *was* a deliberate provocation, Master Faye would have more important things to worry about than a single bookseller, even if the Booksellers Guild was the most powerful one on Darius. Joshua put Elyria down in the centre of the room and watched as Master Faye tested the coins. They were just like the ones they'd seen earlier.

"Odd," Master Faye said, finally. He dismissed the bookseller with a promise that his books would be recovered, if they couldn't be paid for with real money. "Let's see what we can find out about your friend."

Joshua watched with some interest as Master Faye started casting complex analysis spells. It started to go wrong almost at once. A spell intended to reveal the girl's hometown simply refused to work, while a spell that should have determined her age produced an answer that was flatly impossible. No one, not even a Pillar, could live over a hundred years – and the girl seemed to be one hundred and *fifty*. Joshua took another look at her and shook his head in disbelief. He would have been astonished if she was any older than eighteen.

"Very odd," Master Faye said, after casting yet another spell. "She's in perfect health, without any real scarring; eyes and ears and nose are perfect. And she's stronger than she looks too. What does it mean?"

There was a pause. "And there isn't a single trace of magic on her," he added. "What does *that* mean?"

Joshua winced inwardly, trying to keep it off his face. He'd never seen Master Faye unsure before; Pillars were *never* unsure. They determined everything from law to acceptable standards of behaviour in their bailiwicks. Whatever they said went, even if they changed their minds every second day. And yet Master Faye just didn't understand what he was seeing in front of him. Elyria didn't seem to fit into any normal pattern at all.

"I think we will have no choice, but to interrogate her," Master Faye said, finally. "And we will have to deal with the consequences when they materialise."

It would be picking up the gauntlet, if indeed a gauntlet had been thrown at them... it struck Joshua, suddenly, that the whole idea might have been to make Master Faye doubt himself. If so, it was working perfectly. He said so out loud and Master Faye nodded, sourly. They'd just have to be very careful. Besides, the mystery spying spells didn't seem to be able to peer inside Master Faye's house. It would give them some time to decide what to do next.

He looked back at Elyria and felt a flash of guilt. Using truth spells was not something that would make them popular. Everyone had something to hide – and while Master Faye could have used them on anyone he chose, there would be consequences. They could only be used after there was strong proof that they were needed.

"Yes, Master," he said, reluctantly.

***

They knew the coins were forged?

Elyria had given up struggling against the invisible bonds that held her. Without her implants to monitor her body's condition, her best guess was that the locals had some way to use the quantum foam – their magic – to hold her prisoner. It had to be targeted very specifically, or she wouldn't even have been able to breathe, something that would have been fatal even with her enhanced physical structure. The Confederation's medical science might have been able to revive her afterwards, but it might well cause brain damage. Even the Confederation had problems fixing that.

Where had they gone wrong? The bookseller had talked about the coins being unmarked, which meant... what? They'd duplicated observed coins right down to the subatomic level, producing perfect copies of local currency. There hadn't been any numbering system to indicate that each individual coin was completely unique; local technology didn't have the ability to do that properly, let alone keep track of the coins afterwards. But they'd obviously missed something... silently, she cursed their own prior experience. They knew so much about blending into primitive societies that they had missed something obvious.

Elyria *had* been in trouble on primitive worlds before, and she'd spent time in local jails. Standard procedure was to monitor the jailhouse; if something went badly wrong, the prisoner could teleport out before the locals managed to execute her. It was more common to identify someone who could be bribed to extract the prisoner. This was different; her technology hadn't worked, even when she'd been carried out of the library. Her best guess was that whatever was holding her immobilised – and helpless – was also disrupting her technology. It was quite possible that none of the others knew where she was.

Master Faye bent over her and made a few passes with his hand. Elyria felt nothing, but suddenly she could move her head freely, even though the rest of her body felt as hard as stone. She was suddenly very aware of his breath; it smelt unpleasant, as if he'd been chewing something nasty. Or maybe it was simply old age. For all of the magic flowing through its society, Darius was still very primitive in any number of ways.

"I need to ask you some questions," Master Faye said. His accent was slightly different to his apprentice's, suggesting they'd been born far apart. Or it would have, anywhere else. "Where do you come from?"

Elyria hesitated. If Darius was a normal world, the cover story would have held up perfectly – or at least it would have taken them several months to verify it, during which time she could be extracted from the jail, leaving the locals with nothing more than a mystery. But if there was something wrong with the coins, there might be something wrong with the cover story too. In hindsight, maybe they should have taken more time to survey the planet first, even though they'd never been so exposed before landing on Darius. The whole situation was as unprecedented as the rest of the planet.

"Athol," she said, finally.

"I fear not," Master Faye said. He started to make more passes in front of her face, chanting in a language that seemed to bear no resemblance to the English-derived language used all over Darius. "Now. Where were you born?"

Elyria's mouth opened of its own accord. "Sunrise Ring, Greenland," she said. She caught herself a moment later. "What?"

Master Faye gave her an oddly superior smirk, although it was tinged with puzzlement. The words meant nothing to him; Greenland, a world seven thousand light years from Darius, wasn't even a pinprick in his sky. And the Ring surrounding the planet, playing host to most of the population in that star system, would be utterly beyond his imagination. Elyria took some solace in that, even as she tried to figure out what he'd done to her. The words had just come out of her mouth, completely against her will.

Joshua leaned forward. "Where is Greenland?"

Elyria found herself answering his question, only to be greeted with a stare of absolute disbelief. The thought would have been amusing, if it hadn't been so serious; they thought that she was somehow evading the truth spell, even though it was working perfectly. And they didn't understand just what a light year was; at Darius's general level of development, they were probably still convinced that light moved at infinite speed.

Master Faye scowled down at her, making *more* passes in front of her face. "What are you doing here?"

The answer – a full and complete answer – came out of Elyria's mouth. This time, she felt *something* prodding at her mind, pushing it to give an answer. It felt rather like the emergency mental pattern scan she'd made back when she had been preparing for her first undercover operation on a primitive world, practising for when they might have had to back themselves up in a hurry. *That* had felt rather like a Thule mind-ripper. This wasn't too different at all.

"I don't believe it," Master Faye said, finally. "How can you live without magic?"

***

Joshua was half-inclined to think that his master was right. Elyria had to be messing with them somehow, even though Master Faye's increasingly frantic checks on the spells compelling her to speak the truth – and pushing her into speaking when she was reluctant to speak – proved that they were working perfectly. Any magician, even an untrained talent, would be able to struggle against the compulsion spell. Elyria seemed to have no defences at all.

Either that or she's a vastly more powerful magician than anyone else, he thought, shaking his head as he tried to understand what she'd told them. A society without magic, watching them to determine just how they did what they did? It made no sense. Magic was a universal force, dominating every part of the world... and yet they claimed to come from the sky. There were a handful of eccentrics who claimed that the stars were suns, just like the sun Darius orbited, but they hadn't really proved anything. He looked at Elyria and shivered. The proof might be right in front of him.

Master Faye didn't believe her. In a desperate attempt to prove that she was lying, he was tapping into stronger and stronger compulsion spells, including several he'd told Joshua never to use unless there was no other choice. Some of them risked permanent side effects, from servitude to outright mental damage. He wanted to protest, but he couldn't find the words. Master Faye's desperation was alarming.

"Master," he said, finally. "She's telling the truth."

His Master fixed him with a gimlet eye. "And how do you know that?"

Joshua found himself floundering, and then the answer dawned on him. "Because if she was a spy for a Scion, or a Scion herself, she wouldn't have come up with such an absurd story," he pointed out. "They'd tell us that her family had found a hidden gold seam, or something believable, not a story that we must consider absurd. The more you poke and prod at her, the more likely it is that you'd identify her true nature."

"Scions are not always rational," Master Faye said, coldly. He looked down at Elyria, dark eyes peering at her face. "And yet, I do not understand how one could come up with such a story."

"And there was the spell we did, intended to locate the spies," Joshua added. "The spell doesn't work so well if the target is far away. How far away would they be if they came from another star?"

He found it hard to wrap his head around the concept, but if the stars were suns, just like the one that illuminated Darius, they had to be a very long way away, or the planet would overheat. They'd certainly be further away than anywhere on the planet's surface – and the spell didn't work so well when targeted on the other side of the world. No one was quite sure why.

"And they're spying on us," Master Faye said. His gaze sharpened as he addressed Elyria. "Why are you spying on us?"

Her voice was dulled, the effect of the spells. "We want to learn about how you manipulate the quantum foam," she said. "We need to learn how to do it for ourselves."

Joshua blinked. "The quantum foam?"

"Magic," Elyria said. The dull hopelessness in her voice tore at Joshua's heart. "You call it magic."

"We could trade," Joshua said. He'd known the world was a sphere, but to see it from high overhead... he'd never even dreamed of the possibility. "We could teach you magic in exchange for what you know about the world."

"That might require an agreement with the other Pillars," Master Faye said, before he could get too carried away. "Right now, we have to decide what do with our friend."

Joshua looked at Elyria. "What will happen if your friends discover that you're missing?"

"They'll search for me," Elyria said, still in a dulled voice. "And when they find me, they'll take me back."

"I think we should at least talk to them," Joshua said. He was still reeling inwardly from discovering that Elyria *was* over a hundred years old. "They could teach us a great deal."

"We could teach *them* a great deal," Master Faye said, flatly. "Can you imagine a society without magic?"

Joshua couldn't. It was a basic fact of life that those with magic ruled those without. The strong ruled, the weak obeyed. If there was no magic... even the strongest muscle-bound idiot would have problems enforcing his orders outside the range of his fists. Besides, a bow and arrow would cut one down almost effortlessly. Or disease... how could one hope to maintain his rule? None of Elyria's answers about how her society worked made sense. If everyone was involved in making decisions, how did anything get done?

And yet the whole idea fascinated him.

"Take her to a guest room and give her time to freshen up," Master Faye ordered, finally. "And then we can decide how best to approach our visitors."

Joshua would have expected him to be relieved. They might be facing a completely unanticipated problem, but at least a Scion wasn't about to walk into the city and demand that Master Faye face him in a formal duel. Besides, Elyria had made it clear that their society had no magic. They'd be able to use magic to defend themselves if necessary, with as much ease as Elyria herself had been captured. Master Faye should have been delighted to discover that there was no upstart young magician about to try to unseat him.

Instead, he looked worried, as if something else was nagging at him.

"Yes, Master," he said. "Perhaps we should just walk up to them and introduce ourselves."

He released most of the spells binding Elyria and invited her to walk upstairs in front of him, although the remaining spells would ensure that she couldn't escape. It was unbelievable that she was over a hundred years old; his older sister was only twenty-five, the mother of four children, and she looked much older. And yet the alternative was believing that truth spells could be so easily deceived.

This is an opportunity, he told himself firmly, as he opened the guest room. It wasn't exactly a prison, but anyone who went inside would be under careful observation. *We shall make the most of it.*

CHAPTER
EIGHTEEN

Dacron was bored.

Boredom wasn't really a concept the AIs understood. There was an endless stream of data flowing in through every sensor attached to their *Gestalt*, which was almost every sensor in the entire Confederation. They could and did tinker with technology in their endless quest for efficiency, simulate entire other realities inside their hyperspace fields or puzzle over the mysterious artefacts left behind by long-gone civilisations as they made the jump into the Sixth Age. And they watched humanity with a mixture of curiosity and amused contempt.

But Dacron had none of those diversions as he watched Adam bargaining with a handful of merchants. They all wanted the goods Adam was selling and it was childishly simple to get them to bid openly against each other, even though three of them had planned to set up a cartel and freeze the others out. None of it made sense to Dacron; Darius's society simply wasn't very efficient, even if it *did* have magic. They weren't even capable of taking care of their own population. In the Confederation, no one starved; Darius seemed to have too many people who couldn't be sure of getting another meal. Why did they have so many children when their lives were so uncertain?

Their distribution network is primitive, he reminded himself. It was a common pattern; worlds would develop modern transport and suddenly all sorts of luxury goods would become commonplace. Darius simply wasn't advanced enough to allow easy transport of expensive spices, something that gave Adam a considerable amount of bargaining power. He used it ruthlessly and well; it helped that the simulations had been far tougher.

Dacron frowned as his implant activated. "We may have a problem," the AIs said. Normally, they never spoke directly to him if there was any other choice. "Elyria appears to be in trouble."

"Oh," Dacron said, out loud. The merchants glanced at him sharply. As Adam's apprentice, he had been offered several bribes for inside information. They had to think that he knew more about what his master was planning than anyone else, even his wife and daughters. Dacron subvocalised his next words more carefully. "What's happening?"

Adam spoke first. "You seem to be bored," he said, in a droll sneering tone. "You can go back to your room and attend to your bookkeeping."

"Yes, Master," Dacron said, silently impressed. Adam had just given him an excuse to leave the room – and the spies they'd noted earlier paid less attention to an apprentice. He started to subvocalise again the moment he was out of the inn's meeting room. "What's happening?"

"She went into the library forty minutes ago, after reporting an encounter with a dimensionally transcendent bookstall," the AIs said. A human would not have detected anything amiss in their tone, but Dacron could tell that they were badly shocked. "Two minutes ago, she was levitated out by the Pillar's apprentice and the bookstall owner."

Dacron blinked in shock. "Levitated?"

"Yes, as if an antigravity pod was being used," the AIs said. Given how badly technology fared on Darius, it was unlikely that an antigravity pod would work long enough to be useful. "Elyria also appeared to be completely paralysed. We have no response from her implants at all."

"That isn't good," Jorlem said, from the base. "Do you know where she is?"

"She was taken into Master Faye's house," the AIs said. "You will know, of course, that it is one of the places we cannot insert snoops."

"This is Thor," the Captain said. "How do you propose... no, first things first. Where is Adana?"

"Adana is currently purchasing samples of fruit and vegetables," the AIs said. "So far, she appears to be in no danger, but we have analysed the takings from the snoops and have counted no less than five people watching her."

Dacron scowled as he stepped into the room. "Where did they come from?"

"Three of them seem to work for local merchant factors," the AIs said. They would have reviewed all of the data collected by the millions of snoops, using it to track the watchers back to their point of origin. "The fourth may be linked to the City Guard; the fifth is of unknown origin. Given his youth, he may simply be attracted to her."

"Or that's what they want you to think," Jorlem said. His tone darkened. "Can you recall her to the inn?"

"Of course, but that might tip our hand," the AIs said. "If we call her back, the timing will not seem coincidental."

There was a long pause. "In the absence of Professor Elyria, I am in command of the operation," Jorlem said. "Order her to make her final purchases and head back to the inn. It should look like a coincidence."

He made a throat-clearing noise. "And what, exactly, do we do about Elyria?"

"We need to find out what happened to her first," the AIs said. There was a significant pause. "If you'd accepted our proposal for biological spies..."

Dacron snorted. The AIs had concluded that biological technology was the only technology that worked on Darius's surface – it had to work, or the effect that caused advanced technology to glitch would have killed the humans on the surface too. Unless it really *was* under the control of an intelligence with very strange priorities. The AIs had proposed, in all seriousness, designing enhanced birds and insects that would flit around Darius and return to upload their observations into modified computers. There were a number of problems with the scheme, but the greatest one was that it violated the taboo on modifying other forms of life. The Thule had done that, years ago. And the Thule had devastated a third of the galaxy.

"Even if we had," Jorlem pointed out tartly, "we would not have them now."

The AIs didn't bother to respond directly. "We have diverted other snoops towards Master Faye's house," they said. "If they attempt to move her out of the house, we will know.

However, we are unable to put together a plan for recovering her. There are simply too many unknown dangers."

Jorlem frowned. "How did they ever find her?"

"We do not know," the AIs said. "Elyria is an experienced infiltration agent who went through hundreds of simulations before landing. She would not have made a basic mistake, even without the personality routines within her implants. The only thing she did that might have puzzled the locals was expressing shock over the dimensionally transcendent bookstall."

"Hardly grounds for arresting her," Jorlem pointed out. "Did we slip up, or are we caught up in something that doesn't involve us?"

"Dacron, I want you and the others to prepare to leave the city," Thor ordered, breaking into the debate. "Should they start coming for you, the AIs should be able to warn you in time to escape."

"Running would be seen as a confession of guilt," Jorlem pointed out. "Primitive societies are often very fond of assuming that flight equals guilt, even if the event is nothing more than a coincidence. The team might be better off doing nothing that attracts suspicion."

"Except we may already be exposed," Thor snapped. "One of our members – the team *leader*, no less – is in local hands. The situation is out of control. *Already.*"

He stressed the final word to remind them that he'd opposed going down to the planet so early in the operation. "I will inform the CSC of the change in status," he added, "and start making preparations to retrieve Elyria. And then we can decide what to do next."

Jorlem had the last word. "Dacron, once Adana returns to the inn I want you to start hunting for Elyria in the streets," he ordered. "We know where they have taken her – and we don't want them to know that we know. I'll call you back to the inn if something else happens."

"Understood," Dacron said. "Let me know if they release her."

***

Elyria splashed water on her face, trying to come to terms with what had happened. To be caught so easily was humiliating, even though the infiltration teams had strict orders not to fight local law enforcement officials unless there was absolutely no other choice. And to be made to talk... she had no idea what they'd done to make her so truthful, but it had worked perfectly. The Confederation's infiltration teams had never been so badly exposed before, even when they'd been caught up in the middle of a civil war, and *she* was the unlucky one who'd been trapped. She'd wanted to be famous. Once the news hit the datanet, she'd be famous for all the wrong reasons.

She tested her technology again, but it was still dead. Joshua, who seemed to be fascinated by the whole concept of other worlds, had muttered something about security spells, followed by an apology for locking her in the guest room. Compared to the prison cells they'd seen elsewhere on the planet, it was luxury – but it was still a prison. A quick check had revealed that the window was immovable and the door was firmly locked. She could have unpicked the lock at any time, apart from the fact that there were other defences. No doubt trying to walk out of the house would prove impossible.

Being vulnerable was a new experience, one she disliked. The enhancements to her body ensured that she couldn't really feel pain, even if subjected to torture. A primitive mind-ripper should have been deflected by her implants. At worst, if they killed her, she would live again in a clone body, even if she did doubt that there was continuity between one body and the next. Her successor would think she was her, but would she really *be* her? She pushed the morbid thought aside with a groan. No one questioned continuity until they thought that they were going to die.

Maybe I should just stay here, she thought, sourly. *They'll never let me near another intervention team for the rest of my life.*

She glanced around the room again, seeking distraction. There was nothing more than a bed, a table with a pair of drawers and a wash basin, complete with a jug of water. The walls were hard stone, without a single picture to brighten the room. It might as well have been a prison cell. Shaking her head, she lay down on the bed and closed her eyes. There was nothing else to do and nowhere to go. If her implants failed inside Master Faye's house – and the snoops still couldn't get inside – the rest of the team would have problems trying to locate her. They might not even have realised that she'd been captured.

There was a knock on the door, which opened a moment later to reveal a grim-faced servant. She carried a small plate of food, which she put on the table and then walked away. Joshua stepped inside, carrying his own plate, and gave her an apologetic look. If it had been up to him, Elyria knew, they would have made contact with the infiltration team at once. Joshua saw the opportunities where Master Faye saw the threats.

We saw these people as primitive, she told herself. *Perhaps we should have made open contact from the start.*

"My Master is still thinking about you," Joshua explained, as the servant left, closing the door behind her. "I think he wants to discuss you with others before coming to any decision."

Elyria scowled as she took her plate of food. Wonderful. Normally, any breach of security could be contained, or at least left as nothing more than rumours. If Darius had a magical communications network, the news could be all over the world by now. Any hope of retreating and slipping back into another city-state would be lost. It was a nail in the coffin of their ambitions – and her career.

She looked up at Joshua. At least she could ask the stupid questions now. "How did you catch me?"

Joshua grinned. "The minted coins are marked to make it impossible to produce forged coins through magic," he explained. "Your coins might have been proper gold, but they lacked the mark and the bookseller – the one who arrested you – discovered it. And then he thought that you'd fled and came after you."

"A magical mark, I assume," Elyria said. She rolled her eyes as Joshua nodded. "I think we must have missed that."

"You should have slipped in with less money," Joshua pointed out, snidely. "You might have escaped detection."

Elyria nodded, ruefully. It was unusual in primitive societies to have such precise dimensions for coins; they'd assumed that it was a way to prevent counterfeiting, nothing more. Given the local technological level, it was more than enough to make forging coins very difficult. A coin that weighed too much or too little would be easily noticeable on scales that used the same standardised weights. They hadn't considered that there might be a more cunning trick hidden behind the first.

We shouldn't have sent an experienced team, she thought, angrily. The Interventionists were experienced in dealing with primitive planets, too experienced. They'd interpreted everything they'd seen through the lens of their prior experience, rather than starting from scratch. And it had exploded in their faces.

She took a bite of her food – something that tasted a little like chicken – and looked at him studying her. Joshua seemed to be having problems reconciling her appearance with her declared age; she was old enough to be his great-grandmother, at least. The fact that there were people in the Confederation who could remember the Thule War and the slow integration of various post-scarcity societies into one great society would have stunned him, if he'd thought to ask. His planet couldn't even *imagine* someone over three *thousand* years old.

"Tell me something," Joshua said, finally. "How do you live without magic?"

Elyria hesitated, and then made the decision to be honest. It wasn't as if she could get in worse trouble. "Through technology," she said. It took several minutes to explain the concept of technology and, in the end, she suspected that Joshua didn't fully understand. "How do you live *with* magic?"

"I was picked out by Master Faye as his apprentice," Joshua said, with obvious pride. "It was discovered that I had a talent for magic, so he took me in and taught me."

"I see," Elyria said. "*How* did he discover that you had magic?"

"He told me that he sensed my first accidental uses of magic," Joshua explained. "After that, he gave me the chance to study under him or be banished from the city."

"Not much of a choice," Elyria observed.

"He didn't have a choice," Joshua admitted. "There are places that have been badly damaged by magicians who never learned to control their powers. They go mad, convinced they're hearing voices telling them to destroy. Or so we are told."

Elyria considered it for a long thoughtful moment. Darius's history had seemed more than a little vague, certainly past the last two hundred years or so. Maybe the development of an organised magic system was a comparatively recent event; previously, magicians had struggled to master their powers, often killing themselves or unwary bystanders. The AIs span off new AI matrixes in sealed cores for the same reason, only allowing them out when it was clear that they were stable and ready to join the *Gestalt*.

And voices in a magician's head suggested telepathy. Could telepathy – which was theoretically possible – and 'magic' be interlinked?

It led back to the open question of just how long Darius had actually been settled. The surface surveys had turned up enough evidence to suggest at least a thousand years, yet there was nothing really conclusive. Sensors that might have detected something more useful simply didn't work very well on Darius, frustrating the scientists who thought they could find the remains of a colony ship buried under the ground. Or maybe the original settlers had launched the ship into the local star once were settled on the planet's surface. It was unlikely that Darius had been settled after the first telepathic alien race had been discovered by the Confederation.

"Good for him, then," Elyria said, returning to the subject at hand. "Can... can you demonstrate a little magic for me?"

Joshua grinned and flexed his fingers, muttering under his breath. A moment later, there was a shimmering wave of light and a small collection of purple and red flowers materialised in his hand. Elyria stared, shaking her head in disbelief. The Confederation could have fabricated the flowers from raw energy, if necessary, but never without a proper fabricator. There was no way a person could do it... but Joshua had. Carefully, she reached out for the flowers and took them in her hand. They felt light and insubstantial, as if they weren't truly there at all. A solid light projection?

"How do you *do* that?" she asked. Making matter from scratch, almost effortlessly? "How long will they remain intact?"

"Not long," Joshua admitted. He flushed. "Securing the spell takes a great deal more effort."

"Teach me the words," Elyria said. What if *she* could use magic? "What did you say?"

Joshua hesitated. "I really shouldn't teach you anything until we know what we're going to be doing in the future," he said. "I..."

He broke off, as if he were listening to something only he could hear. "Master Faye has decided to make contact with your people," he said. He took one last bite of his food and then placed the plate on the dresser. "I think he's rather relieved."

Elyria blinked. "Relieved?"

"He picked up your spies," Joshua explained. "You worried him badly."

Elyria swallowed another curse as she put her plate on top of the dresser and smoothed down her dress. Just how badly had they been exposed before landing? The mission had been screwed up from the start.

"We really mean you no harm," she said, and meant it. "We're here to help."

CHAPTER
NINETEEN

"You did *what?*"

Elyria winced. The moment she'd stepped outside Master Faye's house, her implants had started working again – and screaming at her, demanding that she report in to explain what had happened to her. Naturally, she'd called Captain Thor and Jorlem and made a complete report. They hadn't taken it very well.

"I told them about the Confederation and our mission here," Elyria said, tiredly. "The locals didn't give me much choice."

She expected them to have some difficulty believing her – and, once they grasped the truth, they would demand that she went under the scanner, both to confirm that she was actually telling the truth and to check that she had suffered no brain damage from the truth spells. And then they'd be furious; the entire mission had been blown wide open. The CSC might order them to back off completely and leave Darius alone for a few hundred years.

"You are the leader of the operation," Thor sputtered, finally. The Captain sounded utterly stunned. "You shouldn't be making *any* bargains with the locals, let alone revealing our existence."

"Our existence was going to be revealed soon anyway," Elyria pointed out. "We didn't pick up on the mark all legal coins carried, did we? Sooner or later, we would have been caught, perhaps by someone less sympathetic than Master Faye and Joshua. This way, at least we get some locals who are willing to help us."

"In exchange for our help, no doubt," Thor snapped. "You do know the laws on unregulated technological transfer to primitive cultures?"

Elyria sighed. There were laws – strict laws – against it, with harsh sentences for those who deliberately broke them. If the CSC found her guilty, she would spend the rest of her life completely isolated from the rest of the Confederation, unless she could convince a jury to allow her some limited contact. It was deliberately intended to be harsh. Unregulated technological transfers could cause chaos.

"We cannot claim that this society is primitive," she said. "They can manipulate the quantum foam! How many Fifth Age societies can do that?"

Thor had no answer. "And this is a wonderful opportunity to study them," Elyria added, a moment later. "If they help us learn how to duplicate their trick, we might be able to carry out a proper intervention in their society..."

"Or wind up being destroyed by their... *magic*," Thor said. "It is my considered opinion as Captain of the *Hamilton* that this mission has failed. We should withdraw and consider what we have learned before attempting to sneak back onto Darius."

"And that may be impossible," Elyria said. "Captain, they have a *global communications network*! This society may look primitive, but it isn't. We will be unable to return to the planet without being discovered."

There was a long pause. "We should not forsake this opportunity," the AIs said, finally. "It may never occur again."

Jorlem chuckled, harshly. "The prize is worth bending a few laws," he agreed. "We can send an emergency request to the CSC, asking for permission to break them outright."

"See to it," Elyria ordered. The request would be made under her name. Only her career would suffer if it went wrong. "And alert the others at the Inn that we're coming to meet them."

She broke off contact and looked over at Joshua. "I'm afraid they wanted to talk to me," she said. "I had to take the call."

Joshua smiled. "They weren't happy?"

"No," Elyria agreed. "How could you tell?"

"I know what people look like when they're exchanging mental communications," Joshua admitted. "You looked exactly the same. Is that more of your technology?"

"I'm afraid so," Elyria said.   Mental communications? Magic... or telepathy?   Or were they interlinked as she'd assumed? "Can you read thoughts?"

Joshua gave her an odd look. "No," he said, finally. "I can only pick up thoughts directed to me by others. There aren't many magicians who want to talk to a lowly apprentice, so I don't have much practice..."

"You'll have more in the future," Master Faye growled. He had seemed unhappy ever since they'd left his house, as if there was something about the whole affair that weighed on him. "The other Pillars will expect you to serve as ambassador to these newcomers."

Elyria had to smile at Joshua's expression. From what she'd seen of the world, the whole concept of ambassadors was a little odd.   The small states tended to keep themselves to themselves, politically speaking, and rarely waged war on their neighbours. They just didn't have the resources, or the magic.

"Like trying to talk to a Scion," Joshua said. He explained for Elyria's benefit. "Scions are magicians who don't have a state to rule. They hide out in the badlands and plot to take over the nearest city-state, before challenging the Pillar in charge. Sometimes, apprentices are sent out to talk with them, to trade for favours."

Elyria lifted an eyebrow. "If they saw a magician as powerful as themselves, their first inclination would be to attack," Master Faye added, grudgingly. "An apprentice poses no threat and can be safely brought into camp."

"Not a pleasant task," Joshua said. There was something dark in his voice, suggesting that the meetings were never fun. "I always hated it."

"I always hated it too," Master Faye admitted. "At least this should be a simpler mission. Lady Elyria and her friends are not going to mess around with your body for fun, or play games with you."

Elyria frowned at him as they reached the Golden Arch. Just how much did she *really* know about Darius?

***

Joshua winced at the memory of a brief meeting with a particularly unpleasant Scion before following Master Faye into the Golden Arch. Elyria had spoken to her friends and convinced them to hire the innkeeper's best room for the meeting, rather than accept the hospitality of Master Faye's home. Master Faye could have legitimately taken that as an insult, but he'd said nothing about it. Joshua suspected that he was privately glad to be meeting such strange and powerful newcomers away from home.

The innkeeper had worked quickly and produced a small table of fresh meat, vegetables and bread for the meeting, along with a small selection of milk and juices. Offering alcohol to Master Faye would have been more than a minor insult, one that the Pillar wouldn't let pass or people would start thinking that he was weak. The table was larger than he remembered, but the last time he'd been in the inn was when he'd been a child, following his father. There had been no need to go inside first.

"You can order the listeners to go for a walk," Master Faye said, to the innkeeper. The reason the Golden Arch was used for outsiders was because they could do very little without being seen, either through peepholes or though the observant senses of the innkeeper's wife. "This meeting is *private*."

"Of course, My Pillar," the innkeeper said, with a low bow. The news of the meeting itself would probably be all over town by now, but the actual content of the meeting would remain secret – or so Joshua hoped. Master Faye would take a dim view of anyone caught trying to spy on them. "Should I invite them down now?"

"Yes," Master Faye said, flatly.

The innkeeper bustled away, to return several minutes later with four of the newcomers. One of them immediately ran to Elyria and gave her a hug; the other three took their seats and studied Master Faye with grim attention. Elyria had admitted that the whole operation was supposed to be covert, although their mistakes would have compromised them sooner or later. But their society lacked magic. They probably didn't understand just how many wrong signals they were sending to any reasonable observer.

Joshua studied them with more attention than he'd used the last time he'd seen them, only a day ago. They were well-dressed, in the proper style, but something about them wasn't quite right. It took him a moment to realise that the wife and daughter – and Elyria herself – were being treated as equals, rather than subordinate Minors. They weren't making an effort to pretend so, he saw; they didn't even *think* about it. And Elyria, who looked the youngest, was actually the one in charge! But if she was over a hundred years old, the others might actually be much younger than her.

"Greetings," Master Faye said. "I am Faye, Pillar of the Bailiwick of Warlock's Bane."

It was the older man – Adam – who responded. "We greet you in the name of the Confederation," he said, finally. Why was he, rather than Elyria, taking the lead? Could it be that they thought that Master Faye had done something to Elyria while she'd been his prisoner? "My name is Adam."

He took a moment to introduce the rest of his team and then leant forward. "We wish to apologise for approaching you covertly," he added. His voice was so flat that it was hard to read emotion, but Joshua had the very definite feeling that Adam was unused to apologising for anything. "We believed that maintaining a distance from you and us was better for your society."

"And that you couldn't be caught," Master Faye said. His tone was equally flat. "What do you want from us?"

There was a long pause, long enough for Joshua to be certain that they too had their own means of mental communication. "You have the ability to use magic," Adam said, finally. It tallied with what Elyria had said, although she'd called it something more complicated. "We wish to learn how you do it."

"We also wish to study your society," the younger girl – Adana – said. "Your society is unique; it is the only one we know where magic is prevalent, in a universe full of wonders. We want to know how your society works..."

Master Faye smiled for the first time. "You could have just asked."

"We believed that direct contact between you and us would be bad for you," Elyria said, from where she was sitting at the head of the table. "We..."

"Adam said the same thing," Master Faye said. "Why do you believe that contact would be bad for us?"

There was a long pause. "In many ways," Adana said, finally, "our society is vastly superior to yours. Our society does not, for example, have the obsession with gold that pervades your society. We do not use money..."

Joshua blinked in honest bewilderment. "How do you pay people to work then?"

Master Faye shot him a sharp look and then looked back at Adana. "I'd like to know too," he admitted. "How *do* you get people to work properly without rewarding them?"

Adana hesitated. "Our society is very different from yours," she admitted. "It would be difficult to explain..."

"Ah," Master Faye said. He held up a hand. "For future reference, you don't need to be so arrogant when talking to us. We can understand more than you think."

Adana lowered her eyes for a moment, her face flushing slightly. "The Confederation has eliminated mundane drudgery through the use of machines," she said. "There is no need for any of us to be a washerwoman, for example, or even a bookseller. All of our basic needs are met through technology. It is quite possible for someone to live their entire lives without doing a day of work.

"Those who want to work can enter any number of interesting jobs," she continued. "People like myself start studying other societies, seeking the reward that comes from being respected in one's field. Others go into exploration, or pure research, or whatever they find interesting. There is no need to do *anything* unless you find it interesting and worthwhile."

Joshua rubbed his forehead, trying to understand. He knew how the city worked; Master Faye had lectured him often enough, as well as putting him through practical exercises meant to teach him the ropes. The very lowest level of society – the men who cleaned the streets – had a vital role to play in maintaining the city. Without them, the streets would be filthy; without the farmers, there would be no food; without the doctors, there would be no medicine...

What sort of society might form if they were freed from such drudgery?

"It would have unfortunate social implications if this were to become public knowledge," Master Faye said. Joshua saw Elyria throw him an unreadable glance. "Very well; you wish to study magic. Such knowledge is never cheap. What are you prepared to offer us in exchange."

There was a second pause. "Gold," Adam said, finally. "We can provide you with as much gold as you like..."

"And make it very difficult for me to use it," Master Faye said, wryly. Joshua had had problems understanding why too much gold was as bad as having too little gold, but Master Faye believed it to be true. "What else can you offer? Your... *technology?*"

He paused. "I know that some of your technology works on our world," he added. "The Lady Elyria was very informative."

Joshua winced as several cold stares were directed at Elyria, who ignored them. "Some of our technology does," she agreed. "Other pieces of our technology are unreliable here. We may end up accidentally cheating you."

She smiled. "We can offer you medical assistance," she added. "A basic rejuvenation treatment would extend your lifespan for another hundred years."

"If the magic didn't kill me first," Master Faye muttered. He was skilled at controlling his expression, but Joshua could tell that he was tempted. Even the most powerful magicians rarely lived past eighty. "How do you know that your treatments would work here?"

The young man, who'd been introduced as Dacron, smiled. "They are biological technology and should work perfectly," he explained. "Your population does not appear to suffer from the presence of magic in the air."

"Some magicians can be driven mad by their powers," Master Faye said. He studied Adam for a long moment before switching his gaze to Adana. "Wouldn't extending our lifespans cause problems for our society?"

"It is a possibility," Adana admitted, uncomfortably.

"But one you are prepared to accept," Master Faye added, briskly. "What do these treatments consist of?"

It was Elyria who answered the question. "We'd need a blood sample from you to prepare the treatment," she said. Master Faye's shoulders stiffened. Anyone else would have been blasted for daring to ask for some of his blood. "Once it is prepared, it will be injected into your body. Barring unforeseen accidents, your lifespan should be extended by at least a hundred years. Some people have been known to live for much longer on one treatment."

Master Faye relaxed, slowly. "Asking for a person's blood is insulting here," he said, dryly. "Do you know that you can use it to work magic against someone?"

"Interesting," Dacron said. "Does that mean that the blood works to identify someone through their DNA, or is there a direct quantum foam link from the blood to the bleeder? Or are they actually the same thing?"

Joshua had no idea what he was talking about. Master Faye ignored the question.

"Here is the deal," he said, calmly. "I will allow you to operate freely in my city, and I will make my apprentice available to you to answer your questions. In exchange, I want one hundred... *rejuvenation* treatments prepared for people I select. That is the core deal. If you have other things you might want to offer in place of the rejuvenation treatments, I will listen and decide if I want to introduce them to my society. I would also... *prefer* it if you do not talk about your own society with anyone apart from myself and my apprentice.

"Should you wish to make more open contact, I will act as your agent," he added, a moment later. "All of your contacts with other Pillars should go through me."

***

Elyria was surprised at the intensity of the debate raging between the AIs, Thor, Jorlem and the contact team. It shouldn't have been such a surprise, although it bespoke a level of political sophistication that no one had recognised on Darius. When the Confederation had contacted Fourth Age societies, the aliens had always been concerned about the effect of contact on their own people. Even the ones that had been human, rebuilt after being cut off from the rest of the human race, had been concerned. And *they* could simply have been absorbed into the Confederation.

Master Faye was clearly no fool, even though there was something about his attitude that nagged at her mind. Rejuvenation treatments would be a political tool he could use to help secure alliances among his fellow magicians – and even the rich and powerful in his city, if he felt like using it for them. It would cause problems for the locals, though; ambitious sons would watch helplessly as their parents remained in control for years, perhaps decades, rather than dying naturally. There were societies where rejuvenation treatments had led inevitably to civil war.

In the long run, it might not matter. If they cracked the secret behind manipulating the quantum foam, they could offer Darius's citizens a better life in the Confederation. Even if they didn't, they could still start removing them from the planet. Who knew what a magician would be able to do if he or she were brought up in the Confederation?

The debate concluded a moment later. "Subject to our superiors rejecting the agreement, we accept," Adam said. "We look forward to working with you."

Elyria saw Joshua smile. He, at least, wanted to see what the Confederation could do. And Elyria would be happy to show him, and allow him to show off his talents. They could even take him to the *Hamilton*, if the Captain would allow it, and see if he could work magic there.

And if he couldn't, that too would be interesting. Very interesting.

CHAPTER
TWENTY

"Your horses are very well behaved," Joshua said. "I hate mine."

Elyria smiled at him as the carriage headed out of the city and up towards the hidden base, outside the borderline. A night's sleep had left her feeling better, although it had been broken by a message from the CSC. They had decided to tentatively approve her actions – they'd realised that she hadn't had any choice – but there was no way her career wasn't going to take a serious blow. The last person to accidentally expose a Confederation observation team on a primitive planet had never been allowed anywhere near a second one.

On the other hand, as the AIs had agreed, local cooperation would make it easier to study magic. In the event of their sensors being compromised on the buried shuttle, they'd started making plans to fly Joshua to space – although Captain Thor had vetoed the plan to bring him onboard the *Hamilton*. A small space station was already being assembled from pieces manufactured by the fabricator. It wouldn't be anything like as massive as the starship, but it would suffice. Besides, it wouldn't pose a major security risk.

"We already had several offers from breeders to use them for breeding purposes," Elyria said, wryly. There were thousands of questions she wanted to ask him, but she wasn't even sure where to begin. "Do you think that Master Faye would be interested in more of them?"

"I'd rather you didn't offer," Joshua said, and winked at her. Elyria understood; anyone who couldn't develop a real rapport with horses wouldn't want to ride if there was any other choice. The flying carpets would serve as much better transport. "Can you not make something that wouldn't need a horse to pull it?"

"We'd have to experiment to find out what works here," Elyria admitted. It would be relatively simple to put together a car that ran on gasoline, or something along the same lines, but no one knew if it would work permanently. Whatever interfered with modern technology on Darius was curiously selective, but it seemed to learn as it went along. "But we could certainly try to build something for you."

She smiled. "Tell me about your society," she said. "How does it actually *work*?"

Joshua smiled and started to explain. Some of it they already knew – Master Faye ruled through force, no matter how benevolent and enlightened he seemed, and he might be unseated at any time – but other details were new. One of them concerned the Booksellers and the Librarians, who seemed to be partly responsible for maintaining civilisation. Most of them were lower-grade magicians in their own right, sworn to their duties. And one of them had been capable of detecting the forged coins. At least *that* wasn't going to happen again.

"I see," she said, after Joshua had finally finished speaking. A thought had occurred to her. "How many cities actually stay stable for several hundred years?"

Joshua blinked. "I beg your pardon?"

It was difficult to be sure, but Elyria pressed ahead anyway. "The history book implied that every city eventually ends up with a bad Pillar, someone who rules for his own good rather than that of his people," she said. "Does that always happen?"

"The richer the city, the more tempting a target it is for Scions who want to rule," Joshua said, finally. He didn't seem to understand. "The city declines under their control until they are replaced by someone more capable."

Elyria nodded. "But that happens all the time," she said, carefully. "There's no such thing as a truly stable city. It all depends on the ruler."

"Of course," Joshua said, puzzled. "How else could it be?"

The first analysts had suggested that magic was actually impeding Darius's technological development. That wasn't uncommon, at least in principle; worldwide states had a history of trying to suppress technological advancement in the hopes of maintaining stability. In the end, they either decayed away completely and fell into civil war, or someone more adaptive destroyed them, but they could sometimes last for centuries before the end came. There was no reason why Darius couldn't go the same way.

But if she understood Joshua correctly, *every* city on Darius eventually had a bad ruler who tore down everything the locals had achieved while they'd had a good ruler. Warlock's Bane had had a bad ruler before Master Spark had removed him, and then Master Spark had himself declined until Master Faye had taken over. There was no real stability – perhaps outside of the trading networks – and therefore few grounds for developing a more stable society. Darius was stuck at its current level because the places that might start pushing the level forward were shattered on a regular basis.

That was odd, to say the least. Pillars ruled and commanded vast resources, at least on the scale of a single world. They even had apprentice magicians under their control. And yet they seemed to hate each other, only talking at a distance, if at all. The worst ones even seemed to wage war on their fellows. In the meantime, the Scions lurked in the badlands, developed their powers and eventually fell on the nearest Pillar. Offhand, Elyria couldn't remember any other world that had existed in such constant ferment. Even the nastiest civil wars of humanity had ended in an uneasy peace.

Darius's recorded history didn't seem to go back very far at all. Elyria suspected she'd just found out why.

She looked over at Joshua as they turned off the road, heading towards the clearing. "This will be startling," she warned, carefully. "Just remain calm and let it flow over you."

Joshua smiled. "More startling than magic was to you?"

Elyria had to smile. "Maybe," she said. "We'll see."

***

The clearing looked unchanged from the last time Joshua had been there, two days ago, although the sense of being watched was as strong as ever. Elyria jumped out of the carriage, leaving the horse standing in the middle of the clearing, and beckoned for him to follow her. Joshua dismounted and walked towards where she had stopped, looking back at him with an expression of wry amusement. He'd enjoyed showing off to her, he knew; she intended to show off a little to him. A moment later, the ground lurched and started to sink downwards.

Joshua started as they fell. There hadn't been a single flash of magic to warn him that someone had hidden a trap there... and then he remembered that the Confederation didn't *use* magic. A chill went down his spine as they fell further into the ground; if a society had never had magic, what could they do without it? Everything they'd seen suggested that the Confederation was actually *more* powerful than Darius's magicians, even if they *had* caught Elyria easily. They'd never thought to ask just what sort of weapons the Confederation could use...

There was a dull thump as the lift came to a halt, revealing an object of solid metal buried under the ground. Joshua touched it almost reverently, astonished at the lack of magic running through the structure. He'd never seen anything so big made out of metal... and he couldn't even see *all* of it. And then he jumped back as there was a hiss and part of the metal folded back to reveal a door. It was magic, it had to be magic... and yet it wasn't. Fighting down the urge to pull defensive spells around himself, he followed Elyria into the structure, hearing a very faint humming sound for the first time. The inner room was larger than his bedroom in Master Faye's house, but it was crammed with strange devices, all more elegant than anything a craftsman could have designed in Warlock's Bane.

"What..." He swallowed and found his voice again. "What are these?"

"Sensors," Elyria explained. Joshua guessed that they were something like the magic detectors they'd scattered around the city, back when they'd thought that they were being watched by a covetous Scion. "They'll want to know as much as possible about us before letting us into the rest of the craft."

Joshua frowned. "How can they even work without magic?"

"I honestly don't know," Elyria admitted. "At least for most of them, anyway. Some of them are so primitive that they rely on x-rays, others are so advanced that they may not even work here. I don't really understand the science behind them."

"How can you use it," Joshua said, "if you don't know what you're doing?"

Elyria smiled at him. "Do you know what you're doing with

magic?"

Joshua opened his mouth to object and then stopped, thoughtfully. Master Faye had taught him all of his spells, without – yet – explaining how to push the limits of the possible. It was Scions who did most of the experimentation, ideally several hundred miles from the nearest population centre. Some magical experiments had been very dangerous to anyone too close to the caster.

"I'm not sure," he admitted, finally. Another hatch opened up in the far wall. "Where do we go now?"

"The medical bay," Elyria said. "They want a close look at you – and at me too, come to think of it."

The interior of the structure – the shuttle, Elyria had called it – was strange, so strange that Joshua felt dizzy every time he looked too closely. There was something vaguely organic about the bulkheads, even though they were made of metal; bright light seemed to flare out of nowhere, without even a trace of magic. The handful of other humans he saw kept their distance, but they were all wearing strange clothes that suggested no real sense of style – or decency. One of the women wore an outfit so tight that Joshua could see her nipples clearly through the fabric. He flushed and looked away.

"They want to look at me?" he asked, more to divert himself than anything else. "Why me?"

"You have a talent for magic," Elyria explained, as they passed through another hatch. "There's a possibility that talent might be something genetic, something inside you..."

She broke off, realising that her words merely confused him. "We want to know what makes you tick," she said, instead. "And then we want to see what happens inside your brain when you cast magic."

There was a pause. "We've seen magicians heal people," she added. "How do you do that?"

"We cast healing spells," Joshua said. They entered a large, brightly lit room with a pair of comfortable seats placed in the centre. Two other humans were standing there, along with a handful of spheres that floated through the air – without magic. He had to fight down a growing sense of unreality. "The spells heal them."

"I see," Elyria said, after a long moment. "But what exactly do the spells *do*?"

"They heal them," Joshua said, again. Honestly! No one on Darius would have asked such a stupid question. "What *else* would they do?"

"I think I misspoke," Elyria said, after a moment. "Do you use the same spell on broken arms as you do on... diseases?"

"Of course," Joshua said.

"That's interesting," Elyria said. "You do know that they're actually two very different conditions? Do you even know what causes disease?"

Joshua shook his head. There were a handful of travelling doctors who had their own theories, but none of them had ever seemed very clever to him. How could there be tiny monsters in the air that carried diseases from person to person? The very idea seemed absurd.

"That suggests that you're not actually telling the spell what to do, or at least not very precisely," Elyria said. "You just want the magic to heal them and it does."

She frowned. "Do you ever have problems healing people?"

"Old age cannot be held back for long," Joshua said. "Everything else can be healed."

Elyria smiled as she nodded to one of the chairs. "Sit down in the chair," she said, as she took the other one. "This may take a while, but it shouldn't really hurt."

"We've decided not to use any invasive procedures," one of the other men said. It meant nothing to Joshua. "We don't know how well they'd work in this environment."

"Good," Elyria said. She reached over and gave Joshua's hand a reassuring squeeze. "Just relax and let them work."

Joshua glanced up nervously as a strange helmet-like device was placed on his head, sending a weird tingle through his body, and then forced himself to relax. Master Faye had tested him extensively in the first few weeks of apprenticeship and that had been thoroughly unpleasant. He had endured that and he could endure this; besides, the rewards of working with the Confederation promised to be huge. If they could rejuvenate Master Faye, who knew what else they could do?

One of the floating spheres hovered next to his arm and extended a thin needle. Joshua winced as it reached his skin, but there was no pain. A moment later, it withdrew, leaving him unsure what – if anything – it had done. The other sphere floated around his head before coming to a halt in front of his face. It was impossible to escape the feeling that it was looking at him through its featureless white exterior. The helmet on his head twitched twice and then pulled back, leaving Joshua feeling oddly relieved. It was not a pleasant experience at all.

One of the humans winked at him as he held another device up in front of Joshua's face, before moving it down to his chest. "Don't worry," he said, reassuringly. "This may be boring, but it isn't really dangerous."

Joshua nodded, trying to fight down the terror that was starting to bubble at the back of his mind. The whole environment was so *strange*, so *different*, from anything he'd seen before that it was maddeningly disconcerting. He watched a glowing square of light appear out of nowhere – again, without a single trace of magic – displaying images that made absolutely no sense to him. The final image was a strange twisting pattern of light that was difficult to look at, but the researchers seemed to take it calmly. They seemed to be adapting to magic better than he was adapting to technology.

"You really should stop eating sweets," one of the researchers said, finally. "Your teeth are not in very good shape, I'm afraid."

"I know," Joshua said. His mother had given him the same lecture, more than once, but he wasn't really able to resist the sweets that Master Faye offered. Besides, he needed them to help power his magic. "I don't suppose that you can heal them?"

"They could be rebuilt, if necessary," the researcher said. "But if you just kept eating sweets, they would decay again."

Joshua snorted. Once, Master Faye had handled a case of a man who couldn't stop himself from drinking. When sober, he was a wonderful husband and father; when drunk, he was a monster who beat his wife and children. Eventually, Master Faye had placed a compulsion on him to prevent him from drinking. It had worked, but the man had killed himself several months later. Joshua's master had concluded that the magic hadn't been able to do anything for whatever had driven the man to drink in the first place.

"I just need to go into the next room," Elyria said, as she stood up. She looked rather nervous, for no apparent reason. Joshua had seen apprentices with similar expressions after they'd displeased their masters. "I'll be back as soon as I can."

Joshua nodded, sourly, and watched her go.

"Your physical condition seems to be relatively healthy, for your environment," one of the researchers said, finally. "Lots of bumps and scrapes that haven't quite healed properly, some scarring from disease... other than that, you're healthy enough. Quite a strong libido, which isn't too surprising in a man your age. Do you have a young lady back home?"

"I'm not supposed to have a girlfriend, or a wife," Joshua admitted. Magic compensated for most of its cost, but he would always be tempted to do more than just visit whores from time to time. "But I keep *wanting* one."

"At your age, I'm not surprised," the researcher said. "You're very fertile, surprisingly so, very definitely capable of impregnating young women. And you're strong... that's interesting."

He frowned. "Tell me something," he said. "Do you try to use magic to enhance yourself?"

"Sometimes," Joshua said, reluctantly. Master Faye had taught him the spells, but warned him to use them sparingly. "I used to be a skinny lad and the older lads picked on me."

"Typical," the researcher said. "Looking at this, I think you overdid it a little. And that you didn't really know what you were doing."

Joshua flushed. "I was younger then," he insisted. "I know more magic now."

"I'm glad to hear it," the researcher said, dryly. "Right now, I'd suggest asking the boss to give you a rejuvenation treatment too. You've placed one hell of a lot of strain on your heart."

He changed the subject before a shocked Joshua could demand to know what he was talking about. "I want you to do a very basic spell, right now," he added. "Do anything you like, as long as it is visible."

"All right," Joshua said. "Anything at all?"

The researcher nodded. It crossed Joshua's mind that he could turn the researcher into a small hopping thing, before he decided that would probably annoy Elyria. And he liked her more than he wanted to admit, even if she was impossibly old. Carefully, he chanted the words of a simple spell under his breath and a ball of light appeared in his palm. A second set of words and the ball of light drifted up into the air, casting an eerie gleam over the entire room. The researcher stared and then pointed a strange metal tool at the ball of light.

"Curious," he said, finally. "Very curious indeed."

CHAPTER
TWENTY-ONE

"They made you talk," Jorlem observed. "How did they make you talk?"

"Magic," Elyria said, sourly. The feeling of being utterly vulnerable had bothered her more than she wanted to admit, but it would all have to go in her voice. "Did they... did they do anything else to me?"

"Nothing that we can detect," the AIs said. "Our sensors are rather limited down here, but we believe that there will be no lasting effects. Brain scans revealed that you were subjected to something comparable to a very mild brain-stamping. Quite how it worked on your enhanced mind, however, remains a mystery."

"Magic," Elyria said. Jorlem shot her a sharp glance, but she pushed on regardless. "I'm serious. They don't really know *what* they're doing; they just make demands on the magic and it does it for them. There was no need to program a brain-probe to stamp anything into my mind; they just did it."

"Which suggests some form of intelligence behind the magic," the AIs said. "Maybe something comparable to the RIs that operate virtual realities for the uploaded." There was a pause. "We do not believe that they gave you any additional... programming."

Elyria winced. Any level of technology could be abused – and the Confederation's technology opened up all sorts of possibilities for sociopaths who wanted to prey on their fellow citizens. The worst nightmare was subversion implants, devices that turned people into puppets operated by their masters, or reprogramming them into becoming monsters. It was something that her implants should have countered, but her augmentation didn't work right on Darius. And if they had been able to compel her to be truthful, they might have planted other suggestions inside her mind.

"But you can't be sure," she said, reluctantly. And *she* couldn't be sure either. Joshua was a nice lad, with a growing crush on her that she found somewhat embarrassing, but Master Faye was a devious despot. Why *not* try to plant a command in her mind? "What do you suggest we do?"

"I will be assuming command of the operation on the ground," Jorlem said. "The AIs have proposed a direct scan of your mind when you return to orbit. It would allow us to be sure that you were not under outside interference."

"Except you couldn't be sure, because of the magic," Elyria said, bitterly. "A full scan might reveal nothing."

"We know," the AIs said. "We do not see any other choice."

There was a long pause. "We have been scanning Joshua ever since he entered the shuttle," they added, changing the subject. "There are a number of oddities in his body, particularly a very faint tendency to disrupt advanced technology. Nanotech simply refuses to work inside his body, for example, and focused scans return thoroughly abnormal results. We have been forced to rely on less advanced technology."

Jorlem scowled. "Is he disrupting technology in purpose?"

"We do not believe so," the AIs said. "The level of disruption seems to coincide with his moods, which have swung backwards and forwards ever since he entered the shuttle. That is not surprising – he is almost certainly suffering from a variant of culture shock – but the link with the disruptions is alarming. The effect might damage a shuttle if we attempted to take him to orbit.

"Physically, his body is rather strange," they continued. "He is strong and healthy in appearance, but his heart is under some considerable strain and there are a multitude of other minor problems. A human who exercised regularly would build up the muscle and the supporting structures; Joshua appears to have only concentrated on his muscles. In many ways, he looks like a child who has managed to reprogram his supporting nanites to redesign his body."

Elyria winced. As fashions changed, the Confederation's citizens redesigned their bodies to match. Something that would be mildly eccentric in an adult could be very dangerous for a child; everyone was told horror stories about the girl who had tried to improve her breasts, or the boy who'd tried to give himself a much larger penis. The medical nanites were supposed to prevent it, but there was ample incentive to try to hack into them and reprogram the list of authorised changes.

The AIs displayed a hologram in front of her. "We would be very surprised if he lived past forty without a major heart attack," they said. "His heart is simply incapable of coping with the strain placed on it. By his own admission, he has been using magic to improve his body. We believe that he has been enhancing his muscles without either the knowledge or the awareness to improve the rest of his body to match. This would be consistent with the observed level of medical knowledge among the rest of the population. They know about broken bones, but not about stress placed on one's heart. Nor, for that matter, do they understand germs and their role in spreading diseases. A single contaminated source of water could lay waste to an entire town.

"Another oddity lies in his reproductive system. Put bluntly, he is producing sperm at a terrific rate, with a consequent effect on his hormones. It has not been difficult, studying the footage recorded by the snoops, to confirm that he has a strong interest in girls. He stares at them more than the average young lad born on Darius. Given his position, it is something of a mystery why he doesn't get sexual contact..."

"He said that Master Faye forbade him to make permanent relationships," Elyria said. "Do you think he tried to improve his genitals?"

"We do not believe so," the AIs said. "All of his other 'improvements' have been far from subtle. We would be expecting him to produce a much longer penis rather than an increase in sperm production. Indeed, we don't think they know that much about their reproductive organs. Many primitive human societies correctly identified some issues – such as the link between periods and pregnancy – but shrouded it in taboo that prevented proper analysis. This improvement was done by someone who knew a great deal more about the human body."

"Master Faye?" Jorlem asked. He hesitated. "But if he was the one who *banned* permanent relationships, why would he want to make sexual contact inevitable?"

"Unknown," the AIs said. "Perhaps he wishes the young man to impregnate as many women as possible, rather than merely forming a link with a single female. However, given his position, he would have little problem lining up females for Joshua to impregnate. It will remain a mystery until we receive more information.

"We have scanned his genetic code through taking DNA samples and have analysed it thoroughly," they continued. "There is very faint evidence of limited DNA hackwork done in the very distant past, which confirms that they probably left Earth during the later years of the First Expansion Era. They certainly don't have the biomods that became standard at the same time as the First Interstellar War, even on worlds that intended to escape from technology. It is highly unlikely that they left Earth any later than 3000AD."

Jorlem leaned forward. "Is there something... *alien* in his genetic code?"

"We have not been able to locate anything inhuman in his DNA," the AIs said. "There are trace elements of items common to Darius, but those would be fairly prevalent all over the planet. However, when he works magic, there is a very definite shift in his brain patterns. We are unable to study this more closely without the risk of causing considerable harm."

Elyria nodded. If a brain-probe failed halfway through the procedure, it would certainly cause brain damage, if not outright death. And Joshua wasn't backed up at all.

"So we have a mystery," the AIs concluded. "As far as we can tell, there is little difference between Joshua and the rest of the population, yet only a relative handful of them can work magic. Why are some singled out for power?"

"Perhaps we should just ask him," Elyria said. "He did say that Master Faye detected his first brushes with magic and offered him training."

"That doesn't answer the question of what makes him special," the AIs said. "What separates him from the rest of the common herd?"

Jorlem frowned. "I assume that you have run comparisons?"

"We will be taking DNA samples from nearby humans," the

AIs said. There was no need to bring them to the shuttle. A tiny drone, disguised as an insect, could perform the DNA extraction without being noticed. "Once we compare them, we should be able to identify any major change... maybe they're lacking something instead of Joshua having something additional."

"You mean like the Thule serfs," Jorlem said. "But if that was the case, why do magicians appear at random?"

"Unknown," the AIs said. "The force behind magic may be selecting random people and gifting them with power. Or there may be something else going on."

Elyria held up a hand. "What have you been able to learn from his magic?"

"More puzzles," the AIs said. "He generates a ball of light – nothing but light. It doesn't even seem to be a different temperature to the rest of the compartment. He generates fireballs – there is a definite rise in temperature, but the fire doesn't burn his hands. He produces illusions – they appear to be nothing more than holograms. He produces objects... actually we believe that he sucks energy out of thin air to produce them."

Elyria frowned. "You mean he doesn't actually produce something for nothing?"

"We think that his magic works on the same basis as a fabricator," the AIs said. "It would be easy for us to duplicate some of his magic, it's just less energy-intensive to suck up raw matter and transform it into more useful materials. There is no need to rearrange matter at a quantum level to produce almost anything that he might want. He could just do it at a molecular level."

They paused, significantly. "However, given an unlimited power supply, there is no reason why he *needs* matter to serve as the building blocks of his items," they added. "It is possible that his magic actually taps hyperspace, like a core tap."

Jorlem blanched. "If that were true," he said, "they'd have blown themselves up long ago."

Elyria couldn't disagree. Core taps were dangerous, even to the Confederation, and each one had three RIs charged with overseeing it. If the tap destabilised, enough energy would leak into normal space to shatter a planet – or a planetoid. The Peacekeepers had never lost a planetoid in combat, but they'd lost two after incidents with their core taps. If it wasn't for the fact that Peacekeeper starships needed an independent energy supply, they would have hidden the core taps elsewhere and used QCC links to transfer the power to the starships, wherever they were. She honestly couldn't see how a mere human mind, even one that had been heavily enhanced, could handle a core tap.

"They may have something else doing it for them," the AIs offered. "They do not appear to have any understanding of molecules at all, yet they have no problems rearranging matter at the molecular level. We could only do that through sharing information on the precise structure of what we wanted to produce, or designing it ourselves, but they lack the ability to do either."

"That would tie in with their medical spells," Elyria offered. "They just issue generalist instructions and something else handles the specifics."

"Achievements through ignorance," the AIs said. "How can they do *anything* like that?"

"It has happened, in human history," Elyria pointed out. "We didn't evolve knowing how to produce the first AIs, or hyperdrive, or planetoids..."

"Darius appears to have been settled long enough for them to rediscover spaceflight," the AIs pointed out, tartly. "The two factors stopping them are magic and their cultural problems. We wonder if any of them did research into the origins of magic."

"We could ask Joshua," Elyria said, although she doubted that Master Faye had told him very much. "Or see what we find when we scan Master Faye's library."

"He refused to allow us to remove the books," the AIs reminded her. "Dacron will have to glance at them all, page by page, and then relay it to the rest of the team."

Elyria nodded. Ten minutes with the books, in the shuttle or the space station, would have provided them with all the information stored between their covers. The books she'd purchased from the bookseller were already being scanned, although they hadn't done much more than confirm their speculations. And prove that human romance novels were universally bad.

"That should provide us with more information," she said.

"Have you managed to unlock the language he uses for magic spells?"

"Not as yet," the AIs said. There was a hint of annoyance in their words. "As far as we can tell, it bears no resemblance to any language known prior to the First Expansion Era, but we cannot be entirely positive as we do not have complete records of that era. You humans managed to lose a great deal of your history during the Time of Unrest."

Elyria nodded. "It was a brutal time," she said, knowing that few colony worlds, even the ones that had fallen back into barbarism, hadn't gone through their own Time of Unrest. If humanity hadn't developed the warp drive, the story of the human race might have come to a sudden and unpleasant end. "But we learned from it."

Jorlem picked up a datapad and glanced at it. "You cannot identify any words?"

"Not with sufficient precision to be sure of a match," the AIs said. "Languages evolve over time, Colonel. The handful of similarities may be nothing more than coincidence."

There was a pause. "Elyria," they added, "we would like you to participate in an experiment. Would you agree to be frozen again, briefly?"

Elyria had anticipated that question, although she had expected it to be longer in coming. They needed data for analysis – and as the only person who had been exposed to magic, they could risk her more easily than anyone else. Not that there would be any question of *forcing* her, of course. The Confederation simply didn't work that way. Besides, there was no need; the only way to gain status in the Confederation was through achievement and cracking the mystery of Darius would be one hell of an achievement. There was plenty of incentive to swallow and let him freeze her for the second time.

"Fine," she said, unable to hide the tremor in her voice. What would they suggest next? "I'll do it."

She allowed Jorlem to precede her back into the medical examination room, where the AI drones were orbiting Joshua and scanning him constantly, monitoring his brainwaves. The researchers were already explaining what they wanted from him; Joshua, to his credit, looked reluctant to do anything to her at all. He finally looked at her and asked if it was really what she wanted, causing her to smile and nod. They *did* need the experimental data.

"Do it," she said, before she could change her mind.

Joshua flexed his hand, muttering a single word... and she froze. Again, she tried to move and couldn't, not even her eyes. The AI drones moved to her position and poked away at her, scanning her brainwave patterns even as they prodded her with a needle. There was a faint stab of dull pain when they drew blood, but it had an eerie dreamlike quality. The whole experience was still terrifyingly unpleasant.

"Your implants are still functional," the AIs said. "Can you use them?"

Elyria tried – and discovered that she couldn't. The spell, or whatever it was, seemed to prevent *all* voluntary actions, even ones that were purely mental. She couldn't understand why she could still *think*, let alone anything else. And why didn't it prevent her from breathing, if it was holding her in a state of total stasis?

"Curious," the AIs said, finally. "Your brainwave patterns appear to be normal, but your body is simply unable to move. There is no apparent damage to account for it."

"The spell holds its target in place," Joshua said. There was an odd note in his voice. "Do you wish me to release it?"

Yes, Elyria thought.

"Yes," the AIs said, after a moment. "Release her."

Elyria staggered as she found herself able to move again. "That was unpleasant," she said, feeling an odd mixture of anger and fear. "Was there nothing you could detect?"

"There was a flicker of quantum distortion when the spell was cast, and another when it was released, but nothing else," the AIs said. There was a long pause as they studied the data, something that should have taken them bare nanoseconds. "One possibility is that the spell interacted with your place in the quantum foam, telling it that you couldn't move. Any standard paralysis, either through nerve damage or through a stasis beam, should have been easily detectable."

"I couldn't do anything voluntarily," Elyria said, through her implants. They had worked, this time, but she hadn't been able to use them. The spell was clearly either very wide-ranging, like the spells intended to prevent people from spying on Master Faye, or something else had done the hard work for Joshua. He didn't even *know* about their implants. "It was not pleasant."

"So you said," the AIs agreed. "Do you still wish to take Joshua to the space station?"

Elyria looked over at the young magician. "Do you want to fly into space?"

"Yes," Joshua said, quickly. He'd adapted well to the idea that Darius was just one of millions of planets, even if its civilisation was unique. Elyria couldn't wait to see what he'd make of the view from orbit, as well as seeing if his magic still worked away from the planet. "I want to see the world."

"Bring down the second shuttle," Elyria ordered. "And then we can fly back to space."

CHAPTER
TWENTY-TWO

"You can read all of these books," Master Faye said, when he escorted Dacron into his private study. "You may not take any of them outside the room."

"Thank you," Dacron said, politely. Humans were still a mystery to him in many ways, yet Master Faye was definitely very strange, even by humans standards. On one hand, he was being very cooperative – and well he might, given what he stood to gain – and on the other he seemed reluctant to do anything remotely helpful. It had taken hours of waiting in his house, drinking something called Kava, before Master Faye had finally taken him to the study. "I am sure they will be most enlightening."

He looked at the bookshelf and found it hard to suppress a human urge to rub his hands together with glee. There was genuinely original knowledge contained within those tomes, as primitive as they were, knowledge the AIs couldn't obtain for themselves. Whatever interfered with technology on Darius prevented *anything* from working inside Master Faye's house. Master Faye reached for the bookshelf, produced the first book and passed it to Dacron, who took it gingerly. It felt as if it were on the verge of falling to pieces.

"This could be duplicated," he pointed out. Darius had the printing press, and ways of making better paper. "Why don't you have it copied?"

"Because then the knowledge would spread wider afield," Master Faye pointed out, sarcastically. "This sort of knowledge is only traded for equal or greater value in return."

Dacron nodded, sat down at the small wooden table, and opened the tome with care. The first page was covered in spidery handwriting he found difficult to read, forcing him to puzzle out each word individually. Eventually, he managed to decipher the text enough to read that a Master Hawthorne had written it, although he wasn't sure exactly *when*. There was no date under the written words. Master Hawthorne bragged of his success in cataloguing the most important set of magic words and spells, noting that it should improve the use of magic immeasurably. A note written underneath in different handwriting stated that Master Hawthorne had been murdered by his apprentice the following year and his book had never entered general circulation.

Taking one final glance at the page – storing the memory for the AIs to access later – he carefully picked up the sheet of paper and turned the page. The paper seemed brittle and faded, but it was clear enough for him to realise that it had turned into a dictionary, of sorts. Certain words were linked to their meanings in Darius's language, followed by instructions on how to pronounce them properly. Dacron memorised them absently as he tried to work out what some of the words had to do with magic. It struck him a moment later; the magic words that the magicians used came from a very different language. The book in front of him taught magicians how to shape their spells prior to casting them.

If there was some other agent doing the hard work – like an RI – it had to be told what to do, he decided. It probably wouldn't respond to Darius's standard tongue, or everyone would be using magic. Only those who learned the magical language would be able to cast spells... logically, if Dacron could master it, he would not only be able to cast spells, but improve on them as well. Or devise protections for Confederation technology that would allow it to work perfectly in the Dead Zones.

Carefully, he worked out a spell that should generate a ball of light and then said it, out loud. There was a faint tingle running down his skin, seconds before a ball of light manifested just above his fingertips. Dacron stared at it in honest disbelief. It cast a pearly-white radiance over the study, illuminating the room with an eerie shine. There was, he could feel, a very faint link between himself and the light. It was easy to issue mental commands to direct it into the air.

"You..." Master Faye stared in disbelief. "You did that on your *first try*!"

"Yes," Dacron said. He hesitated, trying to understand how to terminate the spell. "How do you end the magic?"

Master Faye said a single word and the light vanished. "Do you have any idea," Master Faye said, "just how long it takes an apprentice to master that spell? Months! And you did it instantly!"

Dacron shrugged. "It is merely a question of using the right word," he said, seriously. "I imagine that apprentices have problems pronouncing them properly."

"That's *one* of their problems," Master Faye said. "It can take them time to muster the energy needed to produce a spell too."

That made no sense, Dacron decided. If there was something behind the magic, doing the actual hard work for the magicians, why would it cost them any energy at all? Speaking wasn't really an energy-intensive action. And if they were doing something themselves, without an outside agent, the results should have been a great deal more chaotic. Maybe the real problem was interacting with the outside agent, he decided, and his clone body had simply interacted better than a standard human.

Or maybe it was his health. Or maybe it was his memories of being part of the *Gestalt*.

He opened the next page and skimmed down it, memorising the spells carefully before moving to the third page. Slowly, he was starting to see how the spells went together, something that the locals would probably be unable to match for years, if at all. In fact, it seemed to operate more as a primitive computer language than anything more human. The AIs would snigger at machines that ran such a system – they wouldn't even be RIs – but they would work. They certainly wouldn't get bored with serving humanity if they didn't have the self-awareness to realise that they even existed.

But that raised a puzzling question. Darius's magic worked by interacting with the quantum foam, something the AIs – vastly more intelligent than any human – couldn't do. They couldn't even devise a way to access the foam, let alone interact with it. Whoever had designed Darius was vastly more advanced than the Confederation, so why had they given the humans such a primitive user interface? Or maybe they wanted to see if the humans on Darius would overcome its limitations on their own. The whole planet was starting to look more and more like a very strange experiment.

Master Faye broke into his thoughts. "Do you really memorise things so quickly?"

"Yes," Dacron said. His memory was perfect, at least when it came to his human existence. The memories of being part of the *Gestalt* were strangely incomprehensible. There had been vast and powerful thoughts and... he pushed them away, irritated. "I remember everything."

"A good magician must learn to memorise magic words before they start composing their own spells," Master Faye said, grudgingly. "Try another spell."

Dacron hesitated, skimming through his memory. There were two hundred spells in his mind, some with clearly-defined results, others that didn't seem to have an explanation written beside them. Master Hawthorne hadn't been able to bring himself to share everything, he decided, as he picked one of the unknown spells. A moment later, he cast it into the air... and the entire room flared with blue light.

"The spell reveals the presence of other magic," Master Faye said, into the silence. "You'll notice, as your eyes adapt to the light, that some places are brighter than others. That's where the really powerful defensive spells are placed."

Dacron looked around, feeling an odd pressure on his eyes. They'd been modified to be better than perfect; he could see into the infrared and ultraviolet spectrum. But the strange light made them ache; he found himself blinking as he sighted knots of blue light around the doors, windows and drawers, before he managed to banish the spell.

"You're very sensitive," Master Faye said, carefully. "Does your society really not have magic?"

"No," Dacron said. Could it be that the enhancements spliced into his body had also enhanced his magical abilities, abilities no one had known he had? But if it was that easy to manipulate the quantum foam, the AIs would have done it long ago. "This is a complete surprise to us."

Master Faye frowned. "You should know to be careful when you cast spells," he said, finally. "Too much magic in one day can cause damage beyond repair."

Dacron nodded inwardly as he reached for the next book. It described how spells could actually be constructed from a series of instructions, although it warned that magicians experimenting with magic for the first time often produced mixed results. Dacron could understand it; primitive computers often had problems when inexperienced programmers had tried to produce new programs for them. On the other hand, once the AIs had downloaded the contents of his memory, he would have been surprised if they couldn't produce more powerful and capable spells than the locals. *They* understood computers from the inside.

The third book talked about magical injuries healing. One spell was meant to cure almost anything, apart from damage inflicted by magic. They required more specialist spells; one to detect the presence of magic, one to undo it and one to prevent it recurring. Some spells were targeted on one specific person – identified by their name, or a mental image – and had to be rewritten rather than simply removed. Others could be banished with a single word. A number created mental compulsions that needed complex spells to identify and remove without causing more damage. One such spell included a warning that excessive use would turn someone into a giggling moron.

He looked over at Master Faye and frowned. "How often do you use such spells?"

"Very rarely," Master Faye said. "I am not so insecure as to need people to keep telling me I'm wonderful. Besides, it wouldn't be *real*."

Dacron could understand that point. "Why can't some of the spells be removed?"

"Because they're bound to a specific person," Master Faye said, patiently, "and cannot be removed without killing their target. You need to refocus them on something else, if you want to cancel the effects. A love or obedience spell can have other effects when removed, even if it doesn't kill someone."

He looked down at the floor for a long moment. "It is the task of the Pillar to protect his Minors from other magicians," he added. "I wasn't always successful."

"No one expects complete success," Dacron said, more because he knew he had to say something than out of any real conviction. "You tried..."

"Your society is more forgiving than mine," Master Faye said, slyly. "A Pillar who can't protect his citizens is one who is weakening, an easy target for a Scion who wants to move up the ladder to become a Pillar. My failures led to challenges against my authority."

He grinned at Dacron. "What will happen to the impossibly old girl for her failure?"

"She will be judged; if found to have been careless, she will be reprimanded," Dacron informed him. Looking at the evidence, it was obvious that they simply hadn't known enough about Darius to have slipped inside the society without being noticed. "How did you know that we were spying on you?"

"The spells detected your efforts," Master Faye said. "They worked."

That wasn't in question, Dacron knew. The real question was *why* the spells had worked, because Master Faye had clearly suspected another magician rather than a spacefaring civilisation from several thousand light years away. Looking at the spellbooks, Dacron suspected that the spells had simply been designed to watch for intruding spies, without actually being targeted on magicians specifically. They'd picked up and blocked the snoops without ever realising what they actually were. It would have been galling, if there had been no other things to be galled about on Darius.

He returned the book to the bookshelf and picked up the next one. This one seemed younger than the others, produced by a printing press rather than hand-made by a master craftsman. It was an atlas, describing Darius's cities and the Pillars responsible for ruling them, as well as providing a list of known Scions. Dacron narrowed his eyes as he realised that several Scions lived alarmingly close to the base. It was possible that they might be detected at any moment.

"There are copies of that one in the bookseller's cart," Master Faye said. "You may wish to buy them, now that your gold has been verified."

Dacron nodded. Master Faye had taken the gold and replaced it with some from his own bank, all marked to avoid further charges of counterfeiting. Several gold coins had been sent back to the base, where they would be moved to the space station for heavy analysis; the remainder had been stored at the building Master Faye had allowed them to use. Dacron intended, in fact, to buy a copy of everything the bookseller had, as well as attempt to determine where they could buy more books. There had to be some centre of learning where the library books were produced before they were shipped out to the cities.

He put the book down and reached for the last one, before Master Faye stopped him. "*That* one is very old," he said. "It may even be unique. You can see that after you give me the rejuvenation treatments."

"You still need to provide us with some of your blood," Dacron said, dryly. "A treatment that isn't tailored specifically to you is unlikely to work."

"I will need you to be careful with it," Master Faye warned. "It is dangerous for a magician to allow strangers to handle his blood."

"We cannot produce the treatment without it," Dacron informed him. "At best, it would have no effect on you. At worst, it would kill you instantly."

He waited to see what Master Faye would say to that. "I need to consider carefully," Master Faye said, finally. "It is not something I wish to do."

"Your attitude makes no sense," Dacron said, bluntly. "You agreed to the bargain. We told you that we would need a blood sample from you to make it work. And now you are reluctant to give us the sample, let alone samples from other people you wish to rejuvenate."

Master Faye gave him an icy look. "I am the Pillar of Warlock's Bane," he said, sharply. "If I make myself vulnerable, I am not the only one who will suffer."

Dacron hesitated, unsure of how to proceed. The Confederation had no shortage of ways to deal with Warlock's Bane, or the entire planet, if it came down to a fight. And he was certain that there were already contingency plans to destroy the entire planet as a final resort. A handful of rocks from orbit would vaporise the city, no matter what happened to more advanced technology like hypermissiles, nanostorms or quantum disintegrators. They didn't need Master Faye's blood to attack him.

But that wasn't true for other magicians on Darius.

"We will take good care of it," he assured Master Faye. "And we can proceed whenever you are ready to begin."

Master Faye nodded. "I'll make my decision soon," he said. "Until then, we can proceed with your magical studies at a later date."

It was a dismissal and Dacron recognised it as such. Wondering absently what, if anything, he'd done to offend, he headed downstairs and out of the building, walking through the strangely ramshackle streets. According to the snoops, they were fairly solid, but many of them looked as if the designers had no way to go, but up. Earth had done that, once upon a time, before gaining access to the boundless universe beyond the planet's atmosphere. It was hard to resist the feeling that they were going to tumble down at any moment.

A number of people glanced at him oddly as he walked through the streets. The snoops had reported that rumours were already spreading, although none of them seemed to be close to the truth. They were apparently friends of Master Faye, if not magicians themselves, and as such had to be treated gingerly. Adam had reported that most of the merchants had pulled back, leaving him unable to haggle properly for their trade goods. Dacron wasn't too bothered about that, but he could understand why it was a problem. The more waves they made in the local pond, the greater the effect they'd have upon the locals after they were gone.

A hand shot out of nowhere and pulled him into an alleyway. Dacron was surprised to discover that he recognised the bookseller, the same one who had frozen and kidnapped Elyria. He reached for his sword before hesitating, suspecting that it wasn't an attack.

"I need to speak with you later, in my cart," the bookseller said. "Can you visit me after dark?"

Dacron hesitated. There was no reason why he couldn't, apart from simple paranoia. And the bookseller would have to be insane to take risks with Master Faye's guests. Everything they knew about Darius confirmed that the Pillars were in charge and challenging them could lead to an unfortunate and humiliating end.

"Very well," he said, finally. "I will be happy to attend. Can I bring friends?"

"You don't want to be noticed," the bookseller said. There was an intensity in his voice that surprised Dacron. They didn't want to be noticed by whom? "Come alone if you can; if not, bring one person."

He walked off down the alleyway before Dacron could respond. Dacron considered as he opened a channel back to orbit. He'd report on the odd request first and then detail what he'd learned of magic. And then they could see if they could work out just what was going on.

It was funny, but every time they solved one mystery another appeared right in front of them.

CHAPTER
TWENTY-THREE

"And you call what *we* do magic," Joshua said.

The flying machine – the shuttle, they'd called it – was hovering in the air, just over the clearing. There was a very faint humming sound, but little else, not even a whiff of magic. A flying carpet *crawled* with magic; the boxy shuttle seemed to be held up by nothing more than stubby wings and good intentions. He shook his head in disbelief as it dropped down to the ground and rested on the soil.

"Sufficiently advanced technology is indistinguishable from magic," Elyria said, thoughtfully. She gave him a mischievous look. "What do you think of it?"

Joshua smiled. "It's fantastic," he said, as a hatch opened in the shuttle's hull. There was a very faint whiff of something in the atmosphere as he stepped closer. "What keeps it in the air."

"Right now? Very basic antigravity systems," Elyria said. She hesitated. "The offer of a sedative still stands."

"I want to see everything," Joshua said. He'd run through a dozen mental exercises designed to keep his magic under control, because he was *not* going to pass up the chance to watch as the shuttle rose through the planet's atmosphere and out into space, beyond the range of any observation spell. "I'll keep myself calm."

"If you don't, there's a good chance we will simply fall out of the sky," Elyria pointed out, dryly. She led the way into the shuttle and nodded to one of the chairs. "Take a seat and don't touch anything."

Joshua followed her into the craft. It was more cramped than he had expected, although it was larger than a carriage that hadn't been modified to be bigger on the inside than on the outside. There were a handful of chairs, a set of blinking lights and a large porthole, allowing him to see out into the clearing. Elyria tapped one of the lights and the hatch closed soundlessly. A moment later, he felt a faint tremor as the shuttle started to drift up into the air. Despite himself, he couldn't help feeling a frisson of excitement running through his body. Master Faye had never done anything like this.

The shuttle rose higher into the sky. Joshua leant forward, watching avidly as Warlock's Bane came into view and then dropped away into the distance. His world was rapidly shrinking below him, becoming a sphere; he couldn't help feeling small as the shuttle passed through the upper edges of the atmosphere and into darkness. Below him, Darius was a blue-green sphere of light, glowing against the eternal blackness of space. He was tiny on such a scale... all around him, the stars were coming out. They didn't even twinkle in the darkness, but glowed with a steady light that was somehow both welcoming and very cold.

"There's no atmosphere to produce the twinkle," Elyria said, when he tried to put his feelings into words. "And they're still a very long way away."

She gave him an odd look. "Humanity was born to be a spacefaring race," she added. "That was stolen from you, long ago."

Joshua looked away from the planet and out into the darkness, searching for the starship he'd been told was up there. He couldn't see anything; a moment later, he realised that he might not see the ship, even if it was very close to them. If the planet itself looked tiny, a starship would be far smaller, even invisible. And the Confederation had been trying to remain hidden...

"Look," Elyria said. She pointed one long finger towards the viewport. "That's our station."

It looked rather like a sphere, growing larger and larger against the planet. The station was composed of something silvery, something that reflected light towards them, leaving it glowing in the darkness of space. Up close, it was massive, easily larger than any of the sailing ships he'd dreamed of, back before Master Faye had taken him as his apprentice. And it was built completely of metal... Darius could never have produced a ship made of metal, let alone put it into space. There were limits to how high a flying carpet could rise.

He looked over at Elyria. "What happened to the ship?"

"It's remaining further away from the planet for now," Elyria explained. "We don't want to risk it being damaged by the anti-technology field on your world."

Joshua wondered if that meant that he wouldn't be allowed to visit the starship for a while, if at all, but he put his brief moment of resentment aside as the station grew so large that it dominated the viewport. A hatch opened in the side of the silvery structure and a faint beam of light emerged, reaching for them. The shuttle quivered slightly as it was guided into the hatch, which closed behind them. Inside, they found themselves in a massive compartment, illuminated by brilliant white light.

"Once we know what we're doing," Elyria said, as she stood up, "we will take you outside, with nothing between you and space apart from a force field. You'll love it."

The hatch opened, revealing a metallic deck and a handful of the floating spheres that had assisted in the experiments Joshua had undergone on the planet's surface. He sniffed the air, tasting a vaguely metallic tang, as he stepped onto the deck, wondering if it would shift under him. Instead, it seemed reassuringly stable.

"And you built all this in less than a day," he said, in disbelief. "We couldn't have done that."

"We couldn't have done what you do," the sphere said, in a cultured voice that reminded him of Master Faye. "At least, not for the moment."

Elyria smiled. "Try to perform some magic," she said. "Something relatively simple."

Joshua gave her a sharp look – there was nothing simple about magic – but did as he was told, running through a very basic spell. Nothing happened... in fact, when he concentrated, his awareness of magic seemed to have faded. His first thought was that he'd managed to get the spell wrong and so he ran through it again, and then cast a different spell. Nothing happened... in fact, he could barely sense the magic field. It seemed weak, almost non-existent.

"I can't," he admitted. All of a sudden, he felt himself to be vulnerable – and powerless. "My magic isn't working."

"That suggests that your powers are restricted to the planet's surface," the sphere said. It bobbled in the air as it led the way through a hatch and into a small room, with a single chair set in the exact centre. "That is particularly interesting as we have noted technology glitching at a greater distance from the planet."

Elyria gave him a concerned look. "Are you all right?"

"I don't know," Joshua said. He felt miserable – and at the same time, as if he were free of a burden. "I just don't know."

"Take a seat," the sphere instructed. "If nothing else, we can start scanning your body using more intrusive techniques. We may even get some answers."

Its voice managed to convey an impression of rubbing its hands together with glee as Joshua sat down. There was a long pause, during which he felt nothing, and then one of the other spheres bobbled around him in a circle, before drifting off. Joshua shook his head, wondering when they were actually going to begin, and tried to relax. Maybe he was just too tense for them to do anything.

"Now *that* is interesting," the sphere said. It produced an illusion – a *hologram*, they'd called it – in front of Joshua. "There are some very odd changes in your body."

Elyria smiled at him, reassuringly, as the sphere continued. "Why aren't you supposed to have children?"

Joshua flushed, embarrassed. He'd been told, time and time again, that he was never to get a girl pregnant, that he was always to use contraceptive spells and that he was never to form a permanent relationship with anyone. Master Faye had explained why in great detail, but suddenly he found it hard to talk about it to anyone else. It was just too embarrassing.

He looked at the sphere, forcing himself to ignore Elyria. "Children born to magicians have powerful magic," he said, finally. "We're meant to discourage it."

The sphere wobbled from side to side, as if it were confused. "Why? Wouldn't more powerful magicians be an advantage?"

"The average magician develops his powers as he grows up," Joshua explained. "Children born to magic, however, develop their powers from infancy. They very rapidly become uncontrollable. Master Faye told me about a child who made herself the absolute ruler of a bailiwick when she was seven years old. Others were far less... stable. They... they treated people worse than even the worst of the Scions."

"They grew up with more power than anyone else," Elyria mused. "And... what happens to them?"

"I never saw one," Joshua said. "Master Faye told me that any magical child found by the local Pillar would be killed at once, before he developed the control to protect himself. A handful of others had to be tricked and then killed by other magicians... there was no other choice. Their power had warped them to the point where they were dangerously unfeeling monsters, far more powerful than anyone else."

"I can imagine," Elyria said. She gave the sphere a sharp look. "Is there a point to this question?"

"We have completed a quantum resonance scan of your body," the sphere said to Joshua. "There are two additional oddities that were not picked up on the planet's surface. The first one is that there are tiny changes in your reproductive system. Any child you sire will have a slightly different genetic code from the rest of the human race. We are still analysing it to determine what it actually does."

"I don't understand," Joshua said. "What is my genetic code?"

Elyria frowned before answering. "The simplest explanation would be that the genetic code is the building blocks of your body," she said, finally. "Your code is a mixture of the coding from your mother and father when they conceived you, scrambled together to produce something new. The shape of your nose, for example, comes from your father; your blue eyes come from your mother."

Joshua smiled. "And my siblings look a little like me because they share the same basic code?" he guessed. "But why does my youngest sister have ginger hair? No one else in the family has it."

"Some elements of the genetic code are recessive," the sphere said. "It is possible that the precise coding for ginger hair skipped a generation, only to reappear in your sister. We would have to run a complete scan of your family to be sure."

There was a pause. "Have you ever attempted to use magic to improve your sexual potency?"

Joshua flushed at the question. "Master Faye told me never

to even *try* anything like that," he said, embarrassed. "He said it always ended badly."

The sphere tilted again. "Did *he* ever do anything to you that might have improved your body?"

"Only a handful of healing spells," Joshua said, tightly. "What is wrong with me?"

"Your reproductive system is going like a rocket," the sphere said. "That is not natural, even for the teenage human male. And there are a handful of very subtle changes where your power is hardly *subtle*."

There was a pause. "There is a second oddity," it added. "Have you ever attempted to use your powers to break down your body into a quantum waveform and materialise elsewhere?"

It required several explanations before Joshua grasped that they meant teleporting. "No," he said, finally. "There are magicians who can teleport, but I never even started to learn the skill. I'm not even sure if Master Faye can teleport."

He looked at the sphere. "Why?"

The sphere gave the odd impression of trying to decide what, if anything, to say. "Most of the damage inflicted on your body by your powers is easy to repair," the sphere said, finally. "We are willing to do the repair work now, if you agree. However, deep-focus scans reveal faint damage at the quantum level. This damage is alarmingly comparable to teleporting accidents where the pattern was stored in the buffer for longer than a handful of microseconds."

Elyria winced. "I thought that could be lethal," she said, finally. "What exactly is happening to him?"

"There is a very faint degradation in his body at the quantum level," the sphere said. Joshua didn't understand what it meant, but it sounded ominous. "We believe that there is a very real possibility that his powers are slowly killing him, or driving him insane. In some ways, the effect is comparable to the damage caused by electronic simulation of the pleasure centres. The addict feels fine, right up until the moment he collapses."

"I'm not insane," Joshua insisted.

"Worse, the damage is beyond our ability to fix," the sphere added, remorselessly. "Reassembling a human body on the quantum level is difficult; repairing one is almost impossible."

"But Master Faye isn't insane," Elyria said, sharply. "Self-interested, yes, but he isn't insane..."

"It is possible that the more powerful magicians manage to learn how to prevent further damage, without actually knowing what they're doing," the sphere said. "However, we are unable to repair the mental damage inflicted on Joshua. The operation would have almost no chance of success."

Joshua swallowed, hard. "Am I going to die?"

A thought struck him. "Can't you give me the same rejuvenation treatment you offered Master Faye?"

"The damage is at the quantum level," the sphere said. "It's unlikely that rejuvenating your body will cure the damage. The simplest solution would be to copy your brain pattern and upload it into a clone body; however, reading your brain patterns might be difficult, given the level of damage inflicted on your cells."

"This makes no sense," Elyria protested. "How can Master Faye be walking around seemingly sane when... *this* is happening to him?"

"Quantum-level damage is often unpredictable," the sphere said. There was a pause. "It is possible that the damage never really becomes dangerous, although we regard that as unlikely. The increasingly unpleasant behaviour of many Scions and Pillars may be a result of mental warping caused by their powers."

There was a pause. "Joshua," the sphere asked, "how did you act when you first got your powers?"

"Master Faye taught me spells," Joshua said. "I practised with them; once I knew how to use them, he taught me more spells."

The sphere bobbled from side to side. Joshua was starting to realise that it was pretending to shake its head. "How did you behave?" it asked. "How did you *act?*"

Joshua cringed. There were memories he wanted to forget, not share with outsiders. But if there *was* a problem with his body, they could help him...

"I broke a number of rules," he admitted, finally. "And I was beaten for it, just like any other apprentice."

Elyria gave him a droll look. "We have our own apprenticeships," she said, dryly. "Which rules did you break?"

"He taught me how to spy on people," Joshua said, wondering if she would ever smile at him again. "I spied on a handful of girls I knew. And a bit later I cursed a boy who had picked a fight with me every week since I was nine. Master Faye whipped me until he drew blood for both actions."

"Curious," Elyria said, after a moment. "There is no check on his power, yet he keeps yours firmly under control. Why?"

"He said I needed to learn discipline," Joshua explained. "And that as long as I was his apprentice, what I did reflected on him."

"It is possible that the discipline you learned helped to mitigate the damage you were doing to your body," the sphere said. "It is also possible that your actions were driven by emotion rather than thought; the average human male, granted the ability to spy on his fellows, would certainly *consider* acting as you did. However, we are unable to be sure until we run Dacron through a quantum scan of his own. We would have a baseline to compare to his current status."

Joshua blinked. "Dacron is learning magic?"

"And doing very well, apparently," the sphere said. There was a long pause. "We can repair most of the damage to your body. Do you wish us to proceed?"

"Please," Joshua said. He held up his hand a moment later. "Will this prevent me from using magic?"

"We do not believe so," the sphere said. "However, it is impossible to be absolutely certain."

Joshua braced himself. "Do it," he said. Healing spells always left him feeling uncomfortable, and he still had nightmares about a visit to the doctor when he'd been eight years old, before he'd come into his magic. "Get it over with."

There was a long buzzing sound. "Much of the damage has been repaired," the sphere said, bare seconds later. "Customised nanotech has been inserted into your body to deal with the remaining damage. This will be followed by a standard rejuvenation package comparable to what we have offered your Master. We would advise you not to attempt to *improve* your body in future. It is unlikely to do you any favours."

Joshua stared at the sphere. "It is *done?*"

"The majority of the damage has been repaired," the sphere said, patiently. "We used manipulator fields to work on your body from the inside. The remaining damage will take a few minutes longer."

"Don't ask for an explanation, or we'll be here all day," Elyria advised. "They love to show off."

"We learned it from you," the sphere said. There was a faint hint of amusement in its tone. "You created us, after all."

Joshua blinked. "What are you?"

The sphere seemed to bobble in the air before starting to explain the basic concept behind artificial intelligence. Joshua couldn't follow half of the explanation, but it seemed clear that the spheres were operated by a single intelligence, one that humanity had created. And there was *nothing* like that on Darius, nothing at all.

"Magic," he said. The whole concept seemed insane. "Just... magic."

CHAPTER
TWENTY-FOUR

"The magic appears to cause technological glitching," the AIs said. "The more complex the spell, the more extensive the glitch."

Dacron nodded. They'd set up the lab in the building Master Faye had offered to them, running tests from the dawn of the scientific age right up to the Confederation's own scientific level. Once they were set up, Dacron had started to cast spells to see what stopped working. The snoops and other high technology failed almost at once. Some of the older tech lasted longer before starting to fail. The only thing that worked consistently was chemical-powered technology.

"But none of the glitches make sense," he said, crossly. "Why does the magic interfere with the flow of electric power, but not with the electric current in a person's brain?"

"Unknown," the AIs said. He'd spent the last hour detailing the magic words he'd learned for them, a harder task than it seemed as even *thinking* of them tended to produce odd results. Dacron was starting to think that the real challenge for magicians was memorising them, and then not actually *thinking* of them when they weren't trying to cast spells. "We assume that there is an intelligent agent behind the magic somehow."

Dacron nodded. At least the AIs had been able to suggest other possible magic words. The magical language didn't seem to match anything in their databanks, but they were already analysing it and suggesting other possibilities. Each of the magic words was actually a combination of instructions to the magic, *just* like a primitive computer program. The real question was why something so advanced wasn't self-aware. Or maybe it was and it was simply not interested in talking to the Confederation, or the AIs.

That wasn't uncommon among alien artefacts. The Knowledge of Sigma VIII was an AI, albeit one created by an advanced alien race, that had either died out or become an Elder race, rather than humanity, but it was reluctant to talk to the Confederation. It shared knowledge with those who asked for it, in exchange for additional data for its stores, yet it never discussed its own origins. Or maybe it just liked being mysterious. The AIs had wondered if the Knowledge's creators had actually taken a different attitude to AI than had humanity, but there was no way to know. Its creators had never been identified.

"It is possible that there *is* an effect on human minds," the AIs said, and briefly ran through what they'd discovered through studying Joshua. "However, we are unable to account for the precise nature of the effects. The most likely conclusion is that they were caused by exposure to something comparable to a teleporter field, perhaps his observed self-fabrication capabilities."

Dacron nodded. A human would have been terrified at the prospect of damaging himself – although observed human behaviour suggested that this never actually stopped anyone – but he knew that he would return to the *Gestalt*. It didn't really matter if his clone body was badly damaged; after all, he could simply be re-embodied in a different body. Far better that he be risked than anyone else.

"I have observed that fireballs do not burn me when I summon them," he said, thoughtfully. "It is possible that magicians instinctively avoid hurting themselves with their own magic if they understand the danger."

"Fire is very understandable," the AIs agreed. "That would also account for the damage inflicted on young Joshua through ignorance. It is possible that a more precise awareness of the human body would have allowed him to avoid damaging himself."

There was a pause. "We have other spells we wish you to try," they added. "Listen carefully."

Dacron listened, and then cast the spells. They seemed to work very well, without problems, although the third spell prevented the radio implant from working for a chillingly long moment. Dacron watched in considerable awe as a small wooden stool became a chair, before the magic faded away and the radio came back to life. Carefully, he sat down on the chair and felt it creak under his weight. The stool had never been very large and – he assumed – it lacked the mass to make a solid chair.

"If you alter certain variables, it doesn't try to generate matter out of the magic field," the AIs said, with a hint of heavy satisfaction. Dacron found it harder to understand how the spell had worked, even though he thought he understood all the variables. "We suspect that leaving those variables out would have led to the spell either taking energy from the magic field or simply scooping up matter from nearby sources."

"Which might be dangerous," Dacron said, thoughtfully. The Scions were effectively isolated from the towns and cities, unless they chose to try to take over by force. It could be that Scions simply didn't have the discipline to keep their magic under control and were forced out to learn it, or die well away from civilisation. "You could kill someone with such power."

"Or cripple them for life," the AIs agreed. "We are still experimenting with the language matrix, but we believe that we understand it now. The user interface, of course, is still a puzzle."

"Even a silly RI can understand spoken instructions," Dacron pointed out, dryly. RIs had processing power the earliest AIs couldn't even imagine, but they could never make the jump into intelligence. "For all we know, the power behind magic picks its favourites and gives them access to the user interface."

"But what separates a magician from the rest of the population?" the AIs asked. "We have sampled thousands of humans over the last few hours; none of them were particularly different from Joshua, at least genetically. There does not seem to be a common DNA strand linking magicians together."

"It would be hard to be sure until we get the blood samples," Dacron said. "Could it be that Joshua is Master Faye's *son*? Or a distant relative?"

"We do not believe so," the AIs said. "Joshua was certain that children born to magicians developed magic at a very young age and went mad with power. He certainly *didn't* go mad, although he acted poorly by our standards. We have also checked his genetic code against that of his parents and siblings, without isolating anything that makes him different from them. It is possible that the choice was completely random. An alternate possibility is that *everyone* can do magic, but only a handful succeed in tapping into the magic force."

Dacron listened absently as the AIs expounded on Joshua's exploits as a young magician. It was hard to understand why he might have wanted to spy on girls, but then he *was* born to a more restrictive society than the Confederation. The Confederation asked that only consenting adults be involved; Darius had a complex network of social obligations that made it harder for young people to indulge themselves. Contraception was very limited, outside of magicians; they might not even have condoms. If they hadn't had a high infant mortality rate, they might have suffered a major population explosion.

"But I have no difficulty in controlling magic," he said, finally. "Why did he have so many problems?"

"We have questioned him about magic words, now that we have established that his powers do not work in high orbit," the AIs said. They'd cross-checked everything Dacron had told them with Joshua, allowing them to build up a much greater dictionary of the magic language. "It seems evident that while he understands the words he uses, he does not understand the alphabet – the programming language – underneath them. Indeed, he isn't even aware of its existence. The thought of respelling a word to produce a different effect was alien to him. That is... unusual."

Dacron nodded. English – which had been the basis for Standard, as well as the language spoken on Darius – had been remarkably flexible, unlike many other languages. It allowed for a certain degree of precision as well as rearranging the language and adopting words from other languages. Other, more restrictive, languages had actually impeded social development. It had been a trick commonly used by colony worlds that didn't intend to allow technology to reappear after they destroyed their colony ship. Sometimes it worked, at least until the Confederation or someone more hostile arrived; sometimes it led to a bitter civil war years after the original landing.

But it shouldn't have happened to Darius. They certainly

should have been capable of analysing their magic, even if modern science didn't work on their world. Admittedly, the AIs were vastly smarter than any combination of humans, and they had plenty of other knowledge to draw on in their vast datafiles, but surely someone should have done more over a few thousand years. The more he looked at Darius, the more he thought that the whole planet had been carefully structured to prevent actual social development. It was quite likely that Warlock's Bane, a highly-successful city, would be crushed when the next Pillar arrived.

"That seems to be the pattern," the AIs agreed. "And that leads to another question. Why is that the pattern?"

They paused, significantly. "It is possible that the odd damage inflicted on Joshua's mind might lead to paranoia, if not outright insanity," they added. "That might explain why Scions cannot work together as a group."

Dacron nodded. "Humans are strange," he said, "and to think that they created *us*."

He paused. "Do you think I should attend the meeting with the bookseller?"

"We think it might be interesting," the AIs said. "We will watch it for as long as we can."

"Good," Dacron said. "And when do you want me back at the shuttle?"

"Tomorrow you can work more magic there," the AIs said. "And then your produce can be moved to the space station for analysis."

Dacron nodded and headed downstairs, towards where the food was being cooked by a pair of local servants. Master Faye had insisted on supplying them, probably intending to have them act as spies; Jorlem had insisted that nothing of importance was to be discussed aloud. A second problem was that they couldn't ward the building against magical spying, even though Dacron thought he understood the theory. It would have also prevented Confederation technology from working at all.

He took a bowl of stew and sat down to eat it, considering the problem. It was quite easy for equipment to be damaged by outside energies, but it should have been possible to analyse the energy, work out what it was and then build something to protect against it. Magic, however, seemed to be difficult to analyse. So far, nothing from a basic faraday cage to a focused force field provided any protection to modern technology. And there was no way to tell just *what* the magic was doing. The technology just... *glitched.*

Adam had outlined a theory from studying the Ancient worlds. Reality itself didn't work the same way on the dead worlds, he'd claimed, and then argued that technology that depended on a constant structure of physical laws would simply fail to work if those laws kept changing. It was possible that technology glitched every time the local structure of reality changed... which *would* tie in with the projected effects of manipulating the quantum foam. But it seemed too big for a human mind to comprehend. Could it be possible that someone might alter a universal constant and destroy the entire universe?

Dacron pushed the thought aside as he finished the stew and headed outside, picking up his hooded coat from behind the door. Hardly anyone walked out after dark unless they had a very good reason; there were certainly no streetlights or anything else to light the city. The shadows clung to the walls, almost as if they were alive, but Dacron had no difficulty seeing through them. They were nothing more than illusions caused by the darkness.

High overhead, the skies blazed with twinkling stars. It was strange to realise that Darius's population had managed to deduce that they lived on a sphere, but they had never managed to work out that the stars were other suns, just a long way away. But who knew what would have happened on Earth if there had been no moon, or asteroid belts to help bootstrap the human race into space? It was quite possible that humanity would never have been able to leave its homeworld, let alone build the Confederation. And then another alien race would have arrived and humanity would have found itself at their mercy.

The market was closed up as he approached, the shops shut and carts moved away, or covered with sheets to protect them from overnight rain. Dacron heard the sound of snoring from one of the carts and realised that the owner was inside, either guarding his goods or simply too cheap to buy a room in an inn for the night. Or maybe he was just hiding from his wife. The bookseller's cart was at the far end of the street, with a faint light showing from the window. Dacron muttered a quick update to the AIs and then stepped up to the cart, knocking on the door. A moment later, it opened and he was beckoned inside.

Dacron hadn't exactly believed the report that stated that the cart was bigger on the inside than on the outside. He had known better than to think that Elyria would *lie*, yet the report had been completely unbelievable. How could *anyone* believe it to be true? And yet the moment he stepped inside, he realised that Elyria had – if anything – understated the matter. The bookshelves ran into the distance, further than the eye could see. There were *thousands* of books in a cart smaller than a basic shuttlecraft.

The bookseller shook his hand, nervously. "Welcome," he said, as he removed a pile of books from a wooden chair and motioned for Dacron to sit down. "This is the only place I can talk to you freely."

Dacron looked around, feeling magic fizzing everywhere. "This room is warded, I assume," he said. "Do you believe that someone will spy on us?"

"Someone is already spying on you," the bookseller said. There was a long pause. "You come from another world, don't you?"

"... Yes," Dacron said, finally. He was surprised – and more than a little puzzled. The only locals who knew the full story were Master Faye and his apprentice. Everyone else should know nothing more than that they were rich strangers from out of town. "How... ?"

"The Guild works hard to keep knowledge flowing around the world," the bookseller said. "We know that we are not native to this world. Do we come from your world?"

"It is probable," Dacron said. They had believed that all knowledge of Darius's origins was lost. "How did you manage to preserve the knowledge of your own origins?"

"I can only tell you what has been passed down the ages," the bookseller admitted. "The story claims that we were hoping to find a new land to call our own. But when we arrived, most of the population went mad. Much knowledge was destroyed in that terrible time, before the first magicians provided a stability, of sorts. The guild had managed to keep the knowledge of how to produce a printing press, but little else. We set ourselves the task of recording all of the remaining knowledge, as well as everything new."

"Interesting," Dacron said, after a moment. Passing information down through history verbally was often subject to information degradation. The written word, on the other hand, tended to survive longer. "How far back do your records go?"

"We have kept history for over two *thousand* years," the bookseller said. There was a hint of very definite pride in his voice. "No one else records history any further back than two *hundred* years."

Dacron thought, rapidly. Simple logic suggested that Darius had to be much older, at least assuming that the colony ship had left Earth during the First Expansion Era. But a ship from that time could never have *reached* Darius, certainly not without ending its voyage at any of the countless habitable worlds between Earth and Darius. The most logical solution was that someone – almost certainly an Elder race – had transported the ship directly to Darius, probably by creating a wormhole. It was relatively simple to use a wormhole to jump *into* the future. Thousands of years would have passed during the colony ship's voyage through the wormhole. Done properly, they might never have realised that they'd been redirected.

"We know very little about the world we left," the bookseller said, after a moment. "There were some suggestions that it had been destroyed, but we do not know."

"Earth... Earth abides," Dacron said. The Thule had bombarded humanity's homeworld savagely during the opening stages of the Thule War. Later, the Confederation had embarked upon a massive restoration project, but defeating the lethal nanotech the Thule had introduced to Earth had been tricky. Even now, there were few settlements on humanity's homeworld. "How did you know about us?"

The bookseller looked embarrassed. "I caught one of your people," he reminded Dacron. "Master Faye should have killed her, or enslaved her; forgery is a very serious offence. Instead, he treated you all well, so I became curious and spied on you. And then I worked out the truth. You found us again, after all those years."

"Yes," Dacron said. He would have to report this development to Jorlem. They'd thought that no one on the planet knew the truth about the planet's origins. "There is a whole human community out there that will welcome you."

"Good, because this world is dying," the bookseller said. He looked up, sharply. "And you're in terrible danger."

Dacron blinked. "We are?"

"You are," the bookseller said. "Master Faye is already planning your destruction. Or didn't you realise that he was stalling when you negotiated with him?"

"But why?" Dacron asked. "Why... ?"

"It always happens," the bookseller said. "The Pillars destroy all hope of stability. And *you* are the greatest threat of all to their order."

CHAPTER
TWENTY-FIVE

Dacron took a moment to process all that he'd heard. "The Pillars lash out at the rest of the population," he said, finally. "That's why there is no real stability."

"Correct," the bookseller said. "How much progress can we make when society is upended time and time again?"

That fitted in with what they'd already deduced – and early human history, although *that* hadn't included magic. The states that levied high taxes either stagnated or were defeated by their neighbours who became richer after practising smarter economic policies. But the Pillars were effectively all-powerful within their bailiwicks and could wreck them without the slightest hope of anyone saying no. Just because Master Faye was an enlightened absolute ruler didn't mean that his successor would be the same.

"You're saying that he's planning to attack us," he said, grimly. "How?"

"The Pillars don't work together very well, but they'll cooperate on something like this," the bookseller warned. "We think he's going to recruit a few Scions – lower-level ones, mainly – and send them against you. Those of you who survive the first attack will probably be quickly murdered."

Dacron winced. The locals had *no* idea how much firepower could be unleashed against Darius by the *Hamilton*, let alone a Peacekeeper planetoid. If worst came to worst, a supernova torpedo would detonate the star and Darius would be vaporised. But he knew that the Confederation was unlikely to reach for the hammer at once, particularly if the *Hamilton* was untouched. They'd probably fall back, consider what they'd learned and then plan a return to Darius. Master Faye might assume that would be the end of the matter, or... or he might have a plan for striking the starship out of orbit.

That can't be possible, he thought, grimly. *If magic doesn't work outside low orbit, they couldn't even reach Hamilton.*

"They want to keep their little paradise," the bookseller said. "And we need your help." He looked up at Dacron, pleadingly. "Can you help us?"

"We would be delighted to help," Dacron said, honestly. The Interventionists would be more than willing to help – and as Darius was a human-settled planet, there would be no objections from the Isolationists or the Darwinists. Besides, their best estimate of Darius's population was little more than fifty million. A couple of cityships could take them onboard and leave Darius behind forever. Indeed, it might be the best possible solution. "But how do you even exist?"

The bookseller smirked. "There are hundreds of guilds that reach outside the cities," he said, seriously. "They're quietly encouraged by us, because they help preserve knowledge, and the smarter Pillars tolerate their existence. As far as most of them know, the Booksellers Guild is just another guild. They don't see what hides behind our travels.

"If they knew what we were, they'd wipe us out," he added. "They seem more inclined to lash out at civilisation with every passing year. We lost a couple of dozen members when a Pillar went mad four years ago. He came far too close to the secret.

"We think that magic helps to drive them slowly mad. Some magicians go mad right from the start and are either killed or expelled by their fellows. Others start becoming increasingly irrational, prone to lashing out at the slightest problem. Even Master Faye, who is relatively controlled for his age, is growing dangerously unstable. We do not expect Warlock's Bane to remain the same for much longer."

Dacron wondered if there was more to it than that. Could it be that the force behind magic was actively interfering with the society's stability? They'd heard enough to know that it was rare for Scions to work with Pillars; hell, they didn't even work *together*. But if there was something quietly influencing them from behind the scenes, they'd obey – and they wouldn't even *realise* that they were being manipulated. The AIs had certainly manipulated the Confederation often enough. In hindsight, it was clear that the Confederation had been pushed into sending a team to Darius that would move quickly to active operations on the planet's surface.

A thought occurred to him and he lifted a hand, waving it around the dimensionally transcendent compartment. "But *you* use magic," he pointed out. "You used it against my friend too."

"We know a few spells," the bookseller admitted, grudgingly. There was a long pause, before he decided that he'd better elaborate. "We discovered that the effects of magic can be minimised if several magicians cooperate to cast the spell. The potential magicians we catch before the Pillars detect them are recruited and trained to work together."

"And Pillars *cannot* work together," Dacron said. If the magic really caused paranoia, each Pillar would be wondering when his ally intended to turn on him. "That is their greatest weakness."

He paused, thoughtfully. "And they can't detect *you?*"

"They know that there are some magicians who never really rise above the level of apprentice," the bookseller said. "Luckily, they just consider us contemptible, rather than a threat. It doesn't really occur to them that cooperation can produce remarkable results."

"So it would seem," Dacron agreed. "What happened when you arrived on this world?"

"The population went mad, according to the records," the bookseller said. "I don't think the founders of the guild ever really understood what had happened to them."

Dacron suspected that he knew the answer. A colony ship from the First Expansion Era would probably have been able to land on Darius, if they were lucky, but taking off again would have been impossible. The colonists might have lost most of their technology overnight, a shocking experience by any standards. Or the magic field might have preyed on them, driving enough of the colonists to madness to destroy what remained of the planned society. And so they'd sunk back to near-barbarism.

"I need to relay this to my team," he said, suddenly. "How long do we have?"

"I don't know," the bookseller admitted. "You can warn

them now, and then..."

He paused. "*Will* you help us?"

"I believe so," Dacron said, honestly. "But right now, I have to prevent a disaster."

He stood up and stepped outside the cart, testing his implants. They didn't work. Shaking his head, he walked down the street, trying them time and time again. They didn't even *start* to work until he reached the edge of the market, when he picked up a signal from the AIs. A moment later, before he could start relaying his warning, something crashed into him and he fell to the ground, stunned.

***

The blue-green orb floated in the sea of stars, infinitely fragile against the inky darkness of space. Elyria watched Joshua as he stared, understanding the sense of wonder he felt at what – to any citizen of the Confederation – was a commonplace sight. Gas giants were stranger, terraformed worlds seemed oddly artificial, but a living world was home. Darius would always be part of Joshua, whatever happened to him in the future.

"It's wonderful," he said, finally. "I can never thank you enough for this."

"You've helped us a great deal," Elyria said. *That* was certainly true; between Joshua and Dacron, the AIs now had a working ability to propose magic spells. They even had a working simulator. "And how are you feeling?"

"I'm not sure," Joshua said. "I've never had my body repaired so intensely before."

They shared a smile, although Elyria found hers to be a little forced. The AIs had kept her updated on the list of health problems they'd uncovered inside Joshua, ranging from cellular damage to bad teeth. It hadn't taken long for the nanotech to fix most of the problems, outside the ones in his brain, but she had a feeling that repeated use of magic would simply bring the problems back. The AIs were already proposing biomods that might improve the situation, yet even they hadn't been able to guarantee that they'd work.

Somewhat to her alarm, they'd also removed blood, tissue and semen samples from Joshua, largely without his knowledge. Those samples were already on their way out of the system, where they would later be recovered by a Peacekeeper starship – if something happened to the *Hamilton*. The AIs were being paranoid, even though all of the evidence indicated that magic couldn't be used away from the planet. Elyria found it hard to blame them.

"No one has ever tried to create new life on Darius," Joshua said, and then flushed. "Apart from the standard way, of course."

Elyria smiled, more genuinely this time. Joshua had been wowed by most of the technology around him, even though he'd taken it surprisingly calmly, but it had been the AIs that had really stunned him. She wasn't sure how much of the explanation he'd followed – how could a primitive from a pre-spaceflight world understand hyperspace fields and quantum communications – yet it had clearly had an effect on him. The Confederation saw Darius as magic; their own technology could *pass* for magic on Darius.

Joshua had been trying to read files while the AIs guided the nanotech to fix his body, although he'd barely scratched the surface of the information available to any born citizen of the Confederation. Elyria had to admire his determination, even though she knew better than to believe he could comprehend technology as diverse as antigravity pods, life support fields and FTL drives. She had a feeling that part of him wanted to ask if he could go to the Confederation, even if the rest of the planet remained outside. The AIs had noted that his request, if it were made, would probably be granted. They'd want to keep studying him for a long time.

And probably ask him to father children, she thought, wryly. If Joshua could still sense the quantum foam, even away from Darius, it was possible that whatever little quirk he had was merely amplified on the planet's surface. Or he could just be picking up the outer edges of the planet's magic field. *Who knows what his children would be like?*

"Master Faye wouldn't believe any of this," he added, after a moment. He pulled up his shirt and examined the smooth skin, which had been badly marked by disease years ago. Analysis had determined that it was a very mild variant on smallpox. "Even the best spells can't prevent the pox from leaving a mark."

"Or extend your life too far," Elyria agreed. In theory, there *should* be rejuvenation spells, but the AIs believed that they were simply too complex for human minds. Dacron would have to try one when he returned from his midnight excursion. "Would you be interested in trying spells we created?"

Joshua frowned. "I was always told never to experiment with my own spells," he said, finally. "I could kill myself, or you..."

"There is little reason to assume so," the AIs said, abandoning the pretence that they weren't listening. Everything Joshua said was going into a file for analysis, eventually allowing the AIs to try to extrapolate his future behaviour. "We have calculated the precise nature of the words you need to work more complex spells. All you would have to do is pronounce them correctly and we could assist with that."

Elyria frowned. "What happens if one of the words is garbled, not all of them?"

"The effects become a little unpredictable," the AIs admitted. "However, young Joshua has a good memory. We do not believe that he will have a problem repeating the magic words."

"Right," Elyria said. She looked over at Joshua. "We won't force you into trying any of the magic words they think they've invented for you. If you don't want to do it, it should be fine."

She shifted her glare to one of the AI drones. "And you should know better," she added. "The prize may be extreme, but there are ethical issues involved. Don't you know that?"

For a moment, the AI drone looked abashed... and then bobbled its prow in a nod. "We apologise if we pushed too far," they said. "However, we feel that the experiments must be carried out."

"Just don't let Master Faye know," Joshua said. He looked back at Elyria. "How long are you going to stay here?"

"As long as it takes," Elyria admitted. It was something Interventionists rarely considered, but then it never took more than a couple of standard years to know a society thoroughly and then start the intervention. They had seriously considered just requesting a pair of heavy transports and then moving half of the population away from Darius. The Confederation would have no trouble settling them on a Ring, or a Structure, or even a handful of Cityships. There would be shock, of course, as they got used to the Confederation, but that happened all the time. It was hardly a problem. "Will you continue to work with us?"

Joshua looked back at the stars. "I want to see the universe," he breathed. "Could you take me with you when you go?"

"We do not believe that the Confederation would refuse you," the AIs said. Joshua was human, after all, and the Confederation existed for the benefit of the human race. And he was smart enough not to cling to cultural habits that would pose a problem for the integration process. Not that it really mattered; the Confederation was quite skilled at breaking them down. "Do you wish to emigrate?"

Joshua nodded. "I want to see the universe," he said, again.

"And you will," Elyria said, softly. She looked back at Darius, spinning silently below. "For the moment, it seems we have to return to the planet's surface. Are you ready?"

Joshua grinned. "I would need to explain myself to Master Faye," he said, seriously. "It isn't unknown for an apprentice to decide that it's time to become a Scion, but he does have to tell his master before leaving."

"You should stay with him until we are ready to depart," the AIs suggested. "If he believes that you are leaving him, he may become less forthcoming with information."

Elyria watched the complex interplay of emotions over Joshua's face and nodded inwardly. Joshua loved Master Faye; the older man had plucked him from obscurity and given him power, but he'd also cursed him with health problems he'd never known he had. Still, opposing him – or even just leaving him – felt like a betrayal. And on Darius, that was far more serious than it would ever be in the Confederation.

"I understand," he said, finally.

He was rather subdued as they walked back to the shuttle, which had been checked and refuelled by the AI drones. Elyria felt herself worrying about him; he was young, really too young to be making such life-changing decisions for himself. She'd been in her fifties when she'd finally started to look for a career, rather than simply enjoying herself. And yet, all of human history indicated that pre-singularity societies forced their young to grow up very quickly. Joshua was old enough, in some societies, to be married and raising children.

She reached over and placed a hand on his shoulder. "If this makes you uncomfortable," she said, "just tell us and we'll stop. You don't have to do anything you don't want to do."

Joshua's lips twitched. "I got in enough trouble for doing

what I *did* want to do," he said, dryly. "There are times when I feel I don't understand your society at all."

"That's a common reaction," Elyria admitted. "We have so much freedom that it is hard to understand where the lines are drawn."

She smiled. The Confederation's laws, such as they were, allowed total freedom, provided that no unwilling people were harmed or threatened with harm. Given the vast number of different sexual tastes in the human race, there was no reason why a man who liked the thought of raping a woman couldn't find a woman who wanted to be raped. Even some of the weirder perversions could find people willing to try them, or they could be indulged inside a private perceptual reality if they were truly horrifying.

Darius had no such freedom. There *were* laws, some understandably concerned with reducing the risk of incest, some more confusingly intended to ensure that a given woman's child had been sired by her husband or fiancée. Once engaged, a woman was expected to live in the man's house – or his parent's house, depending – and never to leave until she became pregnant, whereupon they could get married. Leaving the house without an escort – a parent or the male partner – constituted breaking the engagement. But men weren't held under such tight restrictions. The snoops had confirmed that several dozen married men in Warlock's Bane made regular use of whores.

"Here we go," Joshua said. He leaned forward avidly as the shuttle dived towards the planet, which was cloaked in darkness. Hardly any lights broke the darkness. What few lights there were on the darkened planet weren't bright enough to be seen from orbit. "Can I learn to fly one of these?"

"It would be easy to learn," Elyria said. The AIs were controlling the shuttle, but she knew how to fly and she could take over if they lost the radio link. "You could start with the micro aircraft people fly in the Rings, and then graduate to something more substantial."

Joshua smiled. "People use magic to fly," he said, looking down at the planet. "And you have it all *without* magic."

"A simple antigravity ring would allow you to fly on your own," Elyria said. "There's a group of people who use multicoloured rings to generate solid-light constructions. They actually fly in space without starships."

"There are legends of flight rings," Joshua said. "Master Faye used to say that they didn't really exist. In fact..."

He broke off, glancing up sharply. "What?"

A moment later, something struck the shuttle with a terrific blow. The craft span to one side and then started to fall out of the sky.

CHAPTER
TWENTY-SIX

Joshua sensed the sudden rise in magic, just before the entire shuttle rocked violently.

"Hang on!" Elyria snapped at him, as she yanked at the controls. "We're going down!"

The shuttle started to spin; Joshua felt a wave of force pushing him back into the seat, just before his stomach seemed to drop out of his chest. He caught sight of the stars spinning above him as a dull clunk ran through the entire shuttle, just before the spin seemed to halt for a long second. And then the shuttle plummeted again.

"Something hit us," Elyria said. She sounded alarmed; Joshua felt absolute terror as the shuttle continued to fall. "The wings are badly damaged. I can't keep us in the air."

Blue-green fire flashed over the viewport, threatening to crack the transparent shield and break into the shuttle itself. Joshua had a moment to recognise one of the more deadly wrecking spells Master Faye had used from time to time, before the shuttle gave another lurch and flipped over. The world seemed to spin madly for a long second, just before there was a thunderous roar and the fall started to slow. A second later, there was a terrific crash as the shuttle hit the ground. Joshua hung on for dear life as *something* crashed into the shuttle, time and time again, before an eerie silence fell. They were alive, if barely.

Elyria unstrapped herself and staggered to her feet. Blood was leaking from a nasty gash on her forehead, dripping down to splash against her clothing and on to the metal floor. Joshua readied a healing spell, but as he watched the damage healed rapidly, the bruise fading away into her dark skin. None of *his* bruises would heal so quickly. Elyria looked a little stunned as she helped him to his feet, but she seemed to be holding herself together. In the distance, he could hear the sound of fire.

"Most of the shuttle's systems are gone," Elyria said, flatly. Joshua recognised the tone of someone who was trying to keep themselves under control and shivered. "I can't call the ship for help. All of the communications systems are down."

She walked over to the hatch and pushed at it. The heavy sheet of metal refused to budge. "And we may be trapped," she added. "These hatches are designed to be tough."

Joshua looked around. The shuttle had fallen out of the sky, but the interior compartment was largely intact, ensuring that they couldn't break out. And yet he could definitely hear fire... carefully, he pushed his hand against the hatch and muttered a spell Master Faye had taught him. There was a shimmer of magic and the hatch fell into dust. Outside, the landscape seemed to be on fire. Trees were burning brightly, illuminating their arrival to the entire world. If someone had attacked the shuttle, and Joshua was certain that there was no other possibility, they'd have no difficulty finding the remains of the crashed ship.

"We've set the forest on fire," Elyria said. She sounded a little dazed, probably through shock. "We can't..."

"We have to get out of here," Joshua said. He'd read stories of people caught up in forest fires, often caused by Scions with a particularly sadistic sense of humour. The fires advanced so rapidly that the only way to escape was to run like the wind, or to dive into a lake and hope the water wouldn't boil. "Come on!"

Elyria picked up a bag from the shuttle and followed him outside, muttering words under her breath as she looked at the crash site. They'd hit the ground hard and bounced, crashing along and smashing down trees by the sheer force of their impact, leaving a fiery trail in their wake. It wouldn't be long before the fire spread further; Joshua coughed as he inhaled the smoke and then started to pull her away from the wreck, heading upwind. If they were lucky, the wind would blow the fires away from them.

"You hit your head," he said to her, as soon as they were

several metres from the crashed shuttle. The flames seemed to be licking around the metal shape, although it looked as though they couldn't do anything worse than scorch its hull. "Are you going to be all right?"

"I should be," Elyria said. She sounded more stable now, although Joshua knew that head injuries were tricky things. Even the most complex healing spells couldn't guarantee a perfect repair – if they ever had. The AIs dispassionate explanation of just how badly he'd been injuring himself when he tried to improve his body had shaken his confidence in his magic. "Anything that isn't fatal... I should be able to survive anything that isn't fatal."

"Lucky you," Joshua muttered. He looked up into the dark sky, wondering if one of the stars was the Confederation space station. "They will know what happened to us, won't they?"

"I think so," Elyria said. "They would have followed us with optical sensors as well as everything else, sensors that magic doesn't seem to interfere with so badly. But I don't know if they could dispatch a rescue mission."

Joshua looked over at her, sharply. He knew the world was big, yes, but it honestly hadn't occurred to him just how far the shuttle could have travelled in bare minutes. They could be hundreds of miles from Warlock's Bane, stranded in the midst of the badlands. He looked up at the stars again, wishing that he'd trained as a navigator. At least he might have been able to locate their current position and start plotting a course back home.

He hesitated, and put his feelings into words. "Do you know where we are?"

"We were about fifty kilometres from the buried shuttle when we were hit," Elyria said. She scowled down towards the fire. "We might well have been thrown some distance off course by whatever hit us the first time."

"It's a spell designed to kill magicians on carpets," Joshua said, grimly. Master Faye had never taught him how to use it. "It feeds on magic" – no, Master Faye had been more precise – "it feeds on spells. The magician on the carpet can't keep it in the air while trying to prevent the spell from shredding the magic holding it up. Eventually, it just falls out of the sky. It should have killed us instantly."

"But we weren't using magic," Elyria pointed out. "Clearly,

the effects are more wide-ranging than you suggest." She looked at him for a long moment. "Can you call Master Faye?"

Joshua could have kicked himself. He should have thought of that at once. *Master*, he thought, using his mental voice, *can you hear me?*

There was no response. Joshua shivered, despite the warmth from the fire. Mental communications, once mastered, should have allowed him to talk to his master from the other side of the world. And Master Faye wouldn't have refused to answer, even if he'd been asleep. The only possible reason there was no response was that someone had set up wards to block mental transmissions. And that meant... trouble.

"No response," he said, after he'd tried for a second time. "I couldn't even get a sense of his presence."

He grimaced. "There has to be a Scion, perhaps more than one, hunting us right now," he added. "That's the only reason I can think of why I can't reach Master Faye."

"And all of my communications equipment is useless right now," Elyria said. Joshua nodded. The experiments that Dacron had performed had confirmed that magic could prevent technology from working properly, even if the magicians casting the spells didn't even begin to comprehend how technology worked or what it could do. "And anyone who sees the fire will know where to start looking for us."

"Yes," Joshua agreed, feeling a chill running down his spine. A Scion, someone whose magic had been honed by isolation and madness, would be much more powerful than himself. Dacron had mastered magic in an astonishingly short space of time, but Dacron was a long way away. "I think we need to move away from the crash site."

Elyria didn't argue. "Do you know where to go?"

Joshua hesitated. Very few people would ever travel at night, certainly not in the badlands – unless they were already incredibly powerful magicians. Master Faye had once pointed out that between the bandits and the Scions, travel at night outside the cities was suicidal for any Minor – and Elyria was effectively a Minor. Joshua didn't have the power to cover her, even if he had the power to protect himself. No Scion who had survived years in the badlands would be weak in magic.

"We head down," he said, finally. The roads never went up the mountains, but around them. It was possible that they would encounter a small settlement, or even a clearing where travellers were resting, protected by ward spells and ancient conventions. "They'll expect that, but heading upwards is suicide."

"I can imagine," Elyria said. She took one final glance up towards the stars and then followed him away from the shuttle, heading down the hillside. "I'll keep trying my implants. Maybe we'll walk out of the spell's effects."

"I hope so," Joshua said. He'd keep trying mental communication too. "Will they dispatch a rescue party if we manage to call them?"

"I'm not sure," Elyria admitted. Joshua gave her a sharp look. "They won't know precisely what happened, even if they do know that we survived. Unless the spells are disrupting that too..."

Joshua stopped and stared at her. "How could they know that we were still alive?"

"Those orbital sensors are very sharp," Elyria said. She grinned at him in the darkness. "They can watch a mouse scurrying across a field, let alone people the size of humans. But even if they're following us, they won't be able to contact me and they won't be able to dispatch a shuttle to pick us up..."

"For fear of it being attacked too," Joshua guessed. "You must find your sheer level of power frustrating at times."

"Yeah," Elyria admitted. "There are times when we have so many options that we find it hard to choose a single one."

Joshua sucked his lips as they headed further down, into a ravine forged by running water from higher up in the mountains. There was no way to tell just how close the hunters were; they might well have underestimated how far the shuttle could travel, even if it *had* been badly damaged. But that implied that they knew what the shuttle actually was... maybe they'd unwittingly flown over a Scion's lair, or perhaps it was something more sinister. Before they'd discovered the Confederation's spies, Master Faye had worried about a Scion scouting out Warlock's Bane with the intention of moving in to challenge the city's ruler. Maybe there *had* been a Scion watching them, someone who now knew about the Confederation and was determined to make use of the boundless opportunity for themselves. Or maybe another Pillar had realised that Master Faye was about to become dominant and acted first.

The stars stated to fade out as clouds spread rapidly, coming from the west. Joshua scowled as the first drops of rain fell on them, seconds before a brilliant flash of lighting illuminated the forest, and the long path down to the foot of the mountain. Behind them, the fire seemed to have faded slightly, as if the rain had already quenched it. He would have liked to believe that, but he doubted that it was the truth. It was far more likely that a Scion had put out the fire before checking to see if they were anywhere near the crash site. And then he would start hunting for the two survivors.

"We need some running water," he muttered to Elyria, as the rain started to fall harder. It would obscure their path, but it wouldn't break it. The Scion wouldn't have any real difficulty in following them. "Keep an eye out for a stream."

Elyria nodded, her lips moving soundlessly. It took him a moment to realise that she was pitching her voice too low for him to hear, let alone anyone else. "I can hear someone in the distance," she said, seconds later. "He's coming after us."

Joshua shivered. "Then we have to move faster," he muttered back. "Hurry."

They scrambled down the ravine and finally emerged at the bottom, in a valley that ran further down the mountainside. Joshua tried to remember the maps Master Faye had owned, before realising that it was futile without any reference points. Another flash of lightning illuminated a hook-nosed mountain in the distance, but he didn't recognise it. Maybe it was familiar, just seen from a different angle. Or maybe they'd been blown further than he had thought. He took another look at Elyria and smiled. She was drenched, her clothes sticking uncomfortably to her skin, yet she was having no trouble keeping up with him. Joshua suspected she could actually have given the Scion the slip, if she'd had magic and she'd been willing to leave him behind.

There was a sudden flurry of motion beneath his feet and he almost panicked, before seeing a swarm of tiny animals fleeing for their lives. The rainfall would be leaking into their hunting grounds by now, he realised, weakening the soil they dug into to make their burrows. Master Faye had remarked that the little creatures bred so rapidly because they died so quickly; they didn't seem to learn from experience and just kept repeating the same mistakes time and time again. And they were good eating. A flash of lightning brought him to a halt as he saw a cloaked figure standing further down the valley, one hand raised and pointed at them. Joshua yanked Elyria to one side as a flash of brilliant red light darted past them and exploded somewhere in the distance.

"Get back," Joshua snapped. He summoned a fireball and threw it at the Scion, only to see it harmlessly deflected into the forest. Of course; a Scion wouldn't be beaten by a mere fireball. He threw two more in quick succession, hoping to see one of them hit its target, but they were both knocked aside. An instant later, a wave of force sent him flying backwards, straight into a tree. He yelped in pain as he collapsed on the ground.

The Scion advanced on Elyria, his face hidden inside the cloak. Joshua tried to stagger to his feet, despite the shock, knowing that it was futile. He couldn't beat a Scion in open combat... he struggled, trying to think of a tactic that might work, but nothing came to mind. The Scion reached for Elyria... and she sprayed something in his face. He stumbled backwards, coughing, and collapsed to the ground. A moment later, Elyria turned and helped Joshua to his feet.

It was hard to ask the question, but he needed to know. "What... what did you do to him?"

"He still needed to breathe," Elyria said, and winked at him. A flash of lightning revealed the Scion on the ground, sleeping like a baby. "I hit him with knock-out gas. Don't go too close or it might get you too."

Joshua had to laugh. He'd known that magic didn't save a person from needing to breathe, but he'd never considered the implications. What if someone removed all the air from around a magician? He'd suffocate to death before he could use a spell to fix the problem, assuming he realised what was happening. His chuckles died away as he looked at the Scion. The man was harmless now, but how long would it be before he woke up?

"I'm not sure," Elyria admitted, when he asked. "Baseline humans should be asleep for several hours, but your people have been meddling with your own bodies. And the gas wouldn't affect a Confederation citizen at all."

"Then we kill him," Joshua said. He stepped forward, ready to bring his foot down on the Scion's throat. "There isn't any other choice."

Elyria stared at him. "He's harmless!"

"He's harmless *now*," Joshua said. "When he wakes up, he won't try to take us alive. We have to kill him now, while we have the chance."

Looking at her, he felt a sudden hot flash of envy. It was so *easy* for the Confederation; they didn't have to destroy their foes and lay waste to their worlds to win. Their technology allowed them to take prisoners and isolate them permanently, if necessary, or keep criminals under control without having to risk other lives. And they didn't have to worry about mad magicians who might be capable of so much more than rational magicians.

Maybe they could have blocked the Scion's access to his powers, or simply taken him into orbit, if they'd had a working shuttle. But they didn't.

"Leave him," Elyria said, finally.

Joshua swallowed hard, but obeyed as they continued to head further down the valley. The rain was starting to fall again, sending streams of water running past their feet as they walked onwards. Joshua glanced behind them nervously, realising that they were in danger of being struck with a flash flood, and then led her up the side of the valley. They would find it harder going to pick their way through the trees, but it would be safer than the valley if the rain kept falling.

"Crap," Elyria said, suddenly.

Another flash of lightning blazed through the sky, revealing three more cloaked figures surrounding them. They had to have used very capable stealth spells, Joshua realised; he hadn't sensed their approach... he realised his own mistake and swore out loud. Elyria had left enough of her blood back in the shuttle to allow a small *army* of Scions to track her.

He lifted a hand, intending to cast a diversionary spell while shoving Elyria away from them, but it was too late. There was a single brilliant flash of light and the world plunged into darkness.

CHAPTER
TWENTY-SEVEN

Dacron was dreaming, or so he thought. Humans often had nightmares, but it wasn't something an embodied AI experienced, not when AIs had no subconscious to provide the spur for bad dreams. But he was still having strange images flashing through his mind, images that brought with them an indefinable sense of dread. And then his eyes snapped open and he found himself looking up into the face of Master Faye.

The magician looked... tired. No, Dacron realised, it was more than that. He'd been trying to use his magic to peer into Dacron's mind, only to discover that most of his memories were flickering impressions of what it had been like to be part of the AI *Gestalt*. Even Dacron had trouble comprehending the memories and he'd *been* an AI. Master Faye would have been confronted with a blinding haze of endless thoughts and unlimited power. None of it would have made sense to him.

"I am awake," Dacron said. He had clearly been damaged, because part of him wasn't sure if that was actually true. His body felt heavy, almost uncomfortable. "What have you done to me?"

"You had a sensitivity to the magic field," Master Faye said. He sounded very tired. "I have warded you to ensure that you cannot use magic in this room."

Dacron said a spell out loud. Nothing happened, not even the faint sense of mighty powers shifting around him when he intentionally mispronounced a handful of words. Master Faye gave him an odd look, and then smiled when he realised that his wards had worked. It struck Dacron that Master Faye hadn't been *certain* that his spell would work, which was odd. Surely he'd know by now how to keep someone else from working magic...

"It will all be over soon," Master Faye added. "Your settlement has already been destroyed."

There was nothing in his voice to suggest that he was lying. "You are provoking people vastly more powerful than yourself," Dacron said, calmly and rationally. "The Confederation covers a span of space you cannot even begin to imagine, with technology that can duplicate most feats of magic and weapons that can turn your entire star system into debris. What exactly do you hope to gain?"

He studied Master Faye closely. The magician would also know, he suspected, that Dacron and the AIs had solved most of the mysteries behind the magic spells. Given time, he was sure that the AIs would find ways to magic-proof technology and allow the Confederation to operate on Darius without impediment. And then the whole social system that kept the Pillars on top would be broken, easily. Away from Darius, they would have as little power as the rest of the human race.

"You must not be allowed to challenge stability," Master Faye said, finally. "We have to prevent you."

"I would not describe your world as stable," Dacron pointed out, mildly. At least he could ask the direct questions now. "Your history consists of islands of stability that inevitably collapse into chaos, while magicians struggle for power and the common folk keep their heads down. I would have thought that you would be glad of the chance to ensure that your people have a better life in the future."

"Stability must be maintained," Master Faye said. "We must rule."

"But *why* must you rule?" Dacron asked. He kept his tone level. "Human history is full of groups who believed that greater strength gave them the right to rule. And groups who believed that people with one skin colour were superior to people with different skin colours. Your magic does not confer wisdom – and even if it did, would you still have the moral right to rule?"

Master Faye studied him, thoughtfully. "Does your state not have a legend about mice attempting to bell the cat?"

Dacron didn't recognise the legend, so he shook his head.

"The mice were afraid of the cat," Master Faye said, sounding more normal, "so they had the bright idea of putting a bell around the cat's neck to inform them when the cat was nearby. But then they had the problem of actually putting the bell on the cat's neck without the cat's cooperation."

"You mean that your Minors could not restrain you if you wanted to do something they didn't want you to do," Dacron said. It was an attitude thoroughly alien to the Confederation – but then, the average Confederation citizen was no more or less powerful than everyone else. "Can you not see that they need to make choices about their own destiny?"

"Their choices are meaningless," Master Faye said. "Stability must be maintained."

Dacron's eyes narrowed. He should have seen it at once. "Who am I talking to?"

Master Faye looked at him, puzzled. "What do you mean?"

"Your society has rules and yet the magicians are above the rules," Dacron said. Joshua had been quite willing to violate taboos as soon as he'd come into his magic. "You shouldn't have enjoyed several decades of unquestioned rule without a few hundred Scions coming to try to take the city from you."

"I am powerful," Master Faye said, flatly.

"But not powerful enough," Dacron said. "Some outside force has been tampering with your society." He smiled as he put the pieces together. "You have stability, but you never climb any higher along the scale of technological development. You have a tradition of cities being taken by force, yet the number of takeover attempts seem to be very small compared to the number of Scions. And yet there is a pattern in which successful cities eventually fall to mad magicians who undo all of the good work of their predecessors."

He paused. "And you have a taboo against breeding new magicians," he added. He wasn't sure how that fitted into the mystery, but he was sure he would solve it sooner or later. "I think we offered you something that convinced the outside force that we could no longer be tolerated on Darius."

Dacron's smile widened. "What would happen, I wonder, if you and the other decent magicians were rejuvenated?"

"I control myself," Master Faye snapped. "Do you think I would allow some outside force to control me?"

"Your actions make no sense," Dacron pointed out. "Even

from a purely selfish point of view, lashing out at us is insane. You surely *want* to live for hundreds of years – and besides, you have to know that we would be able to crush you."

He met Master Faye's eyes. "And I think you care about your people, more than you want to admit," he added. "You take your duties seriously; you thrashed Joshua for violating their privacy... why would you do something that threatens them as well as yourself? Your actions make no sense."

Or perhaps they made too much sense, he thought, in the privacy of his own head. The damage inflicted on Joshua's mind might just be a side-effect of part of his mentality interacting with the quantum foam. It was quite possible that the unknown force behind magic could interfere with the thoughts of magicians, maybe even control them directly, without ever having to show itself. Joshua demonstrated that magicians lost their scruples very quickly. Maybe they were guided in a specific direction... that might explain the oddly repetitive nature of Darius's history.

It was possible, he decided, for a human tyrant to resist his people wanting to be free. Human history was certainly full of examples, but Master Faye hadn't seemed to be one of those. And the stability he kept mentioning wasn't stable at all... not from a human point of view. An AI, on the other hand, would see a certain stability as the system played out, time and time again. No, he wasn't entirely in his right mind.

"Your theories are absurd," Master Faye said, as he stood up. "Your people will be banished from our world."

Dacron looked up at him. "And how do you intend to enforce that?"

Master Faye tossed him a single furious look and walked out, leaving Dacron alone. There was no time to waste; Dacron tested his chains and found that they were solid, too strong for even an enhanced human body to break. He pulled at them anyway, wondering if he could pull them right out of the wall, but nothing happened. The prison cell had clearly been designed to hold other magicians.

Curious, he thought, as he started to concentrate. Humans spent most of their adolescence learning to control the biomods as they matured inside human bodies, but Dacron had had only a few short months to learn. Even so, mastering the use of painkilling nerves was simple enough. All he really needed to do was flex his thoughts in a simple manner...

Bracing himself, feeling his arms going numb, he pulled at the chains as hard as he could. For a long moment, it seemed as if he would fail, and then he saw the bones in his hand start to break. A baseline human would have been screaming in pain, but Dacron felt nothing apart from the frozen numbness that had overwhelmed him. Once his hands were free, he stood up, silently relieved that Master Faye hadn't thought to chain his legs. It would have made escape much harder.

The outside door was made of wood, but one solid kick broke the lock, allowing Dacron to stumble out into the corridor. A servant turned to face him, her eyes going wide, just before he kicked her and sent her falling to the ground. He kicked her a second time, in the head, then stopped – dead. *His* biomods were already working to repair the damage he'd inflicted on his hands, but the serving girl had no such augmentation. Broken bones always took longer to heal than anything else, even *with* augmentation. The realisation that his human response – his very aggressive human response – had crippled an innocent victim chilled him to the bone. She might remain crippled for life.

Or maybe there was another option. Outside the prison, his magic worked; rapidly, he cast a healing spell, followed quickly by a protective spell. Master Faye's book of spells had outlined it for him, but the AIs had managed to improve it considerably. Unlike the one that Master Faye had shown him, it provided far more powerful protection and was a great deal harder to break. Dacron looked down at his hands, wondered vaguely how much damage he'd done to himself even *with* biomods designed to adapt quickly to changes in the local environment, and then realised that it didn't matter. He had to get to the base... perhaps Master Faye had been lying when he said that it had been destroyed. Or perhaps Jorlem had managed to pull the team out in time...

The main door refused to open when he pulled at it. Dacron kicked it savagely, but it didn't break. An attempt to break one of the windows failed too; he generated a cutting spell that should have sliced through the wood and stone like a fission blade, but it simply bounced off Master Faye's wards. Shaking his head, Dacron turned and headed for the stairs. He would just have to convince Master Faye to lower the wards, or kill him. Two more servants appeared, running towards him with deadly intent, and he stunned both of them with simple spells. They fell to the ground and he walked past them, knowing that Master Faye presumably already knew that he was free. It would be relatively simple to adapt the wards to warn their creator when someone attacked them.

Master Faye appeared in the door to his study, staring at Dacron. "How... how did you escape?"

Dacron smiled. Naturally, no one on Darius could have broken his own wrists to powder just to get out of a trap. Unless someone had remarkable pain resistance spells, ones that didn't numb the mind as well as the body... he shook his head as he faced Master Faye. The Pillar looked badly shocked, one hand half-raised in a defensive posture, the other by his side, as if he were having problems coming to terms with the fact that Dacron was a very real threat. To him, Dacron had only spent a *day* learning magic.

"I used magic," Dacron said. It might as well have *been* magic, as far as the locals were concerned. Sufficiently advanced technology was indistinguishable from magic. "For all of your power, you do not really understand what you do when you work magic. We were able to deduce it."

Master Faye glared at him, but he didn't attack. Of course he wouldn't, Dacron realised; he believed that Dacron had broken out through using his own magic, an impossible feat for a normal magician. And it certainly *looked* as though he hadn't broken his own bones to escape.

"You cannot do this," Master Faye said. He sounded dazed, so dazed that Dacron was unsure to whom he was talking. Dacron... or the hidden force behind magic. "You'll destroy the stability of the world."

Dacron held out a hand, fighting down the purely human impulse to tear Master Faye limb from limb. "You can work with us," he said, flatly. "We don't need to fight."

He sensed the wave of magic a moment before it manifested, a sheet of fire that lashed out and raged against his protective bubble. Dacron watched it dispassionately as Master Faye barked a set of words, striking his wards time and time again. But there was nothing subtle in what he was doing, no attempt to hack his way past Dacron's protections. He was just trying to batter them down through brute force.

It said interesting things about the source of magic, Dacron decided, as he took a step forward into the raging firestorm. If it had been as smart as even the first AIs, it would have been able to realise that refusing to accept Dacron's commands would have left him helpless and vulnerable. Instead, it seemed more inclined to work with the bigger picture, even if that meant that the smaller details were often ignored. But perhaps it was attempting to minimise its own involvement, for fear that it would be detected. Manipulation was never so effective if the intended target knew what was being attempted.

Master Faye lifted his voice in a chant, summoning waves of energy out of nowhere to slam against Dacron's shields – and then lash into the floor. It crumbled under Dacron's feet, threatening to send him plummeting down, just before he jumped forward and crashed against Master Faye's own wards, shoving the magician falling back into his study. Master Faye stumbled backwards, his eyes wide with fear and hatred, and scooped a stone knife off his desk. It plunged into Dacron's protections and sliced through them, opening a gap for Master Faye to exploit.

Dacron cancelled his protections and watched the knife fall to the ground, conjuring a second set of wards before Master Faye could finish his killing spell. No human could have shaped the thought so precisely. He saw a brilliant flash of green light strike his shields and rebound off it, slamming into Master Faye. The magician fell backwards and hit the ground hard enough to shake the building. Dacron stepped forward and checked his pulse, keeping one hand on his throat just in case. There was no need to fear. Master Faye was very definitely dead. A quick check revealed no obvious cause of death.

Standing up, Dacron walked over to the bookshelves and scooped up the books, carrying them in his arms as he left the room. Outside, the building was starting to shake; magic had held it together and those spells were falling apart with the death of their creator. Dacron jumped down through the hole created by the fight and headed for the door. Just before he could leave, he heard the sound of sobbing. Master Faye's servants were no longer bound by control spells.

"Take what you want and leave the building," Dacron advised. Normally, there would be a new Pillar to lay claim to

Master Faye's wealth and property, but *he* didn't intend to rule. The servants could take all the money they wanted, if they liked. "And then I suggest just letting it collapse."

He walked outside and headed towards the building Master Faye had assigned to them. It wasn't a long walk through the city, even though he was carrying the books. People glanced at him in alarm – they hadn't realised what had happened to Master Faye, at least not yet – but gave him a wide berth. He rounded the corner to see a pile of rubble where the building had been. The City Guardsmen were laying out the bodies with practised ease. Dacron watched, unable to believe his eyes, as he realised that Master Faye had butchered his own servants too. What had *they* done to upset him?

And what had he done to the building while Dacron had been stunned?

A handful of guardsmen noticed him and he tensed, but they did nothing. Maybe they hadn't known that Master Faye had blown up the building, or maybe they'd realised that Dacron had killed their Pillar and that meant he was too powerful to be touched by the law. Absurdly, Dacron wondered if he was *expected* to take Master Faye's place, before he pushed the thought aside. He had other priorities right now, starting with finding out if anyone else was still alive. What if Master Faye had been able to touch the *Hamilton*?

It should have been impossible. But too much about Darius was impossible.

Shaking his head, he walked away and started to head back to the market. He had to find the bookseller, because there was nothing else he could do. No matter how hard he tried to use his implants, they refused to work. He was completely cut off from the *Hamilton*, assuming that the ship was still intact...

... And, as far as he knew, he was completely alone.

CHAPTER
TWENTY-EIGHT

The market seemed to be in disarray when Dacron entered, with shoppers exchanging nervous whispers while stocking up on food and drink. Several people looked at him and headed away from him at speed, while a number of stalls promptly pulled down their shutters and closed for the day. Dacron would have found it depressing if he hadn't had too much else to worry about; the weight of the books was making him stagger and yet he didn't dare put them down. He'd just have to hope that the bookseller would be able to help him.

He stumbled up to the cart and tapped on the door. There was a long pause and then it opened, inviting him inside. The bookseller was lying on the floor, quivering in pain, his hands clutching the side of his head. It was difficult to tell, but the magic in the cart seemed to be twisting somehow, as if it was adapting to a new reality. A world without Master Faye.

Dacron put the books on the nearest stool and knelt down beside the bookseller, reaching out to take his pulse. He seemed to be having a fit of some kind, something that Confederation technology could have cured... and magic wouldn't be able to cure. Dacron hesitated, unsure of what to do, just as the bookseller gave one final jerk and looked upwards.

"What..." He broke off and coughed violently, sweat running down his face. "What happened?"

"You were having a fit," Dacron said, carefully. It couldn't be a coincidence; the Pillar had died at the same time as the nearest magician – the nearest native magician – had had a fit.

Master Faye's death would have sent shockwaves through the magical ether. "Do you know what happened?"

"Only through legends," the bookseller said. "A Pillar is such a fixture in the local magic field that his death affects everyone with even a hint of magical sensitivity. His apprentice may be dead by now."

Dacron shrugged. Young Joshua had been meant to return to the planet's surface to carry out more experiments, but who knew what might have happened while he'd been stunned? Maybe he was still in orbit, safe and well, or maybe he'd been at the base when – if – it had been attacked. There was no way to know.

"I see," Dacron said, instead. "What happens now?"

The bookseller gave him an odd look. "What happened to you?"

Dacron explained, starting with his capture and ending with the death of Master Faye. "He didn't seem like himself at all," he concluded. "I think something else was influencing him."

He paused. "It is possible that the madness your records speak of was caused by the same entity," he added. "Darius lost a great deal of technology very quickly. Even if your founders intended to create a low-tech culture, there should still be traces of your colony ship and early technology. Instead, it all seems to be missing."

The bookseller rubbed his head. "You killed Master Faye," he said, grimly. "Do you know what this means for Warlock's Bane? The city is completely unprotected!"

Dacron frowned, puzzled. "I thought you wanted to overcome the endless struggling between magicians," he said. "You might have a chance to create a city without a Pillar..."

"Except that any Scion who fancies a city can just walk right in, right now," the bookseller snapped. "There wouldn't even be a fight for the city. He could just take over and start issuing orders. It isn't what we wanted."

"I see," Dacron said, after a moment. Was it *their* problem? A moment's thought suggested that it was; he'd killed Master Faye, upsetting the local balance of power. The Confederation had caused the problem, so it had a certain responsibility to *fix* the problem. "What do we do about it?"

The bookseller snorted. "Declare yourself the new Pillar," he said. "You killed the last one, so that makes you the new Pillar by right."

Dacron shook his head. "I can't do that," he said. It might suit the research program to end up with one of their own in a position of power, but he wasn't *designed* to rule humans. "What *else* can we do?"

"There isn't anything else," the bookseller said. "Without a Pillar, every Scion in the area will come and try his luck. And everyone with the money to leave will go elsewhere, because without a Pillar there will be no true stability. Warlock's Bane will fade away into nothingness."

"We can deal with it later," Dacron said. "I have to go back to the base, to see what survived. Beside, Master Faye's allies might attack me..."

"Depends on who he recruited to serve as allies," the bookseller pointed out. He held up a hand. "Look, this city needs you, right now. I can go find your people; you have to save the population. Because if Scions start uncontrolled fighting over who gets the city, they'll reduce it to rubble."

Dacron scowled. "I will inform the city that there is a new Pillar," he said. At least he had Master Faye's collection of books. The money wasn't a great concern to a Confederation citizen. "And then we go to the base. We have to know what happened to the people there."

"Understood," the bookseller said. He stood up, rubbing the side of his head. "I'll take you to face your loyal subjects."

***

A sane human society would have greeted the arrival of the person who had killed their previous leader with a degree of concern, Dacron was sure. Very few societies allowed promotion through assassination, if only because it was hardly conducive to long-term stability – as Darius amply demonstrated. Warlock's Bane had a council, appointed by Master Faye, and they greeted his arrival with obvious relief. They'd known, even if he hadn't, the implications of Master Faye's death.

The whole concept revolted him. Among the Confederation, issues were settled by democratic vote; the AIs, being a *Gestalt*, simply considered every possible issue and then harmonised their thoughts. To have someone put into power because he had murdered the previous leader seemed absurd; a skilled assassin might not be very good at actually running the city, let alone the world. Darius was *definitely* in desperate need of an intervention, Dacron decided, as he listened to the council's speech of welcome. They were relieved to see him and yet they were also terrified. Master Faye could have overturned their laws with a word.

It was nearly four hours before he was able to break free and head out of the city, accompanied by the bookseller. The City Guard had wanted to send an escort, but Dacron had declined, even though it was probably too late to prevent further contamination of Darius's society by showing them signs of a more advanced culture. Besides, a Pillar was meant to be his own, all-powerful protector. It was just another sign that Darius, far from being stable, had actually been designed to be inherently *unstable*. Dacron was still considering the issues as they reached the borderline and stopped, dead.

"Master Faye had no authority beyond this point," the bookseller warned. "A Scion who enters your territory is throwing down a challenge; you entering *their* territory can be seen as a challenge in itself."

Dacron nodded. The borderline was magical, barely enough to be visible to a normal magician, but easy to detect. Carefully, he stepped into it and felt the magic crackling around him, just before he was on the other side. He had the impression that magic was *less* controlled outside the borderline, as if Master Faye had done far more to keep his city safe than anyone had realised. At least the borderline hadn't collapsed completely when he'd died.

"Some Pillars can never leave their territory," the bookseller said. "I'd suggest that you do what you want to do and then head back to the city. Right now, a Scion might think that you had decided to leave forever."

Dacron shook his head as he remounted the horse and rode onwards, up the road towards the clearing. He saw the pillar of smoke from a distance and spurred the horse on, already knowing that it was far too late. The clearing had been devastated by something – *balefire*, part of his mind whispered – and the buried shuttle was a blackened ruin. He scrambled off the horse and ran forward, jumping down into the pit the diggers had excavated. Up close, he could sense the magic still crackling over the metal shuttle. They'd done far more than simply lay waste to the base; they'd left a surprise behind for any unwary visitor who might have blundered into their trap.

A human would have sworn. Dacron cast a spell he thought would dispel the magic, and then stepped into the shuttle. Fire had swept through the interior, consuming everything that could burn and wiping out all traces of human existence. The control systems, hardened against all kinds of rough treatment, remained undamaged, but Dacron doubted that the shuttle would ever fly again. They'd not only damaged the hull, a remarkable feat in itself; they'd managed to cripple the normal drives and the replacements the AIs had devised for use on Darius. The magicians might not have realised, but they had been incredibly lucky. If they'd managed to ignite the rocket fuel, a crude method for boosting the shuttle into orbit, they would have blown themselves into little pieces.

There were no bodies. Dacron checked each of the compartments and found nothing, apart from ashes. A test would reveal if the bodies had been completely consumed, but he doubted that any of the equipment would work on Darius. Both his implants and the shuttle's hardened control systems were refusing to work. Considering the matter, Dacron wondered if the intelligence behind the magic had simply amplified its effects on technology. It might well be a simpler way of dealing with the outsiders than trying to deny Dacron access to magic...

He stopped dead. It made no sense to *allow* him to use magic, not when denying it to him would have ensured that Master Faye killed him. If the objective had been to wipe out all traces of Confederation influence, it had failed spectacularly. And if the intelligence was a maddened AI, it had remained remarkably stable so far. A mad AI was hardly *subtle*...

... Unless it *was* doing something subtle. Dacron had deduced that the hidden source of magic interacted with the brains of human magicians, slowly warping them to take their place in the world it maintained. And every time Dacron used magic, he was allowing it a chance to influence his own mind. That ability, combined with the patience of an AI, would allow it to gradually bring him under its control. Eventually, he would do its bidding and he'd never realise the truth.

The thought was sickening. A human would be completely

defenceless against a process of gradual conditioning. Dacron knew of plenty of case studies where humans had steadily been brainwashed, eventually reaching the point where they justified their own actions to themselves without needing to be prompted. A human mind could justify anything, given time, and if the conditioning worked properly, the victim would never think to question the slow moral inversion. And eventually it would be too late. A standard subversion implant – banned, with very good reason – would be kinder.

He heard a shout from outside and headed back into the blackened remains of the base. The bookseller was standing beside something that had fallen out of the sky on a long parachute. Dacron allowed himself a grin – magic wouldn't interfere with a parachute – and climbed back up to stand behind the bookseller. The heat from the object was considerable, but it was already cooling rapidly.

"Basic clockwork," he said. The early astronauts had used a similar trick to get back to Earth after they'd left orbit. *Hamilton's* fabricators would have no trouble producing something intended to make it through the atmosphere without power. They'd done it for the shuttles; doing it for something smaller would be easy. "And I guess they know what we're doing."

The bookseller looked over at him. "How do they know?"

"Eyes in the sky," Dacron said. Joshua had demonstrated magical viewing to the Confederation, but it seemed to have curious limitations. The satellites orbiting the world wouldn't have so many problems. "We'll have to wait until it cools down before we try to open it."

"Or you could use magic," the bookseller pointed out, dryly. He looked back at the remains of the shuttle. "What was that like, before it was destroyed?"

"They reengineered it for Darius," Dacron said. "They gave it wings that could allow it to glide, even without engines; the control system was modified not to need power. A skilled pilot could have landed it if everything had just gone dead. And then we buried it and your people found it anyway."

"And destroyed it," the bookseller said. He looked around, nervously. "You know they could be watching us now?"

"Yes," Dacron said. He *knew* that the Confederation was watching them, but he suspected that the bookseller meant the people who had attacked the shuttle. "Do they normally kill their captives?"

"Depends," the bookseller admitted. "Scions sometimes want slaves – young attractive female slaves. Or they want hostages for ransom. But here... keeping your people alive would be dangerous. They determined to destroy you completely."

"But if that was the case," Dacron asked, "why didn't Master Faye kill me while I was stunned?"

"You progressed rapidly with your magic lessons," the bookseller reminded him. "Maybe he thought that you could teach him something."

Or maybe there were limits to how far he could be pushed, Dacron wondered. That might explain why some Pillars went insane and turned into monsters. Maybe they were just pushed too far and their minds snapped.

He stood up and walked over to the package. The heat had faded away, allowing him to tear open the covering with only minor difficulty. It was wrapped in insulation that had cracked and broken under the stresses of re-entry, but had protected the box inside. Dacron pulled it out and cracked it open, revealing a set of swords, knives and bows – and a large quiver of arrows. A quick check revealed that the swords had been given a monofilament edge. They'd be able to cut through anything, without using a hint of technology. Someone had clearly been thinking ahead.

"Take the weapons to the horses," he ordered, absently. Under the swords, there was a large sheet of paper and a handful of emergency devices. "I'll be along in a moment."

He unfolded the sheet of paper and read it quickly.

Dacron

The Dead Zones appear to have expanded; we have been unable to raise anyone on the surface or control the snoops. Orbital observation appears to be the only method of observation still operational, although the station has suffered a number of odd glitches that have convinced Captain Thor to withdraw all personnel to *Hamilton*. He is currently engaged in emergency discussions with the CSC.

We monitored the attacks on the bases in both Warlock's Bane and the mountains. As far as we can tell, there were no survivors from either. However, the shuttle carrying Elyria and Joshua crashed twenty kilometres from your position on the other side of the mountain and they are apparently still alive, if captive. (See attached map.) If possible, please attempt to free them, if Master Faye will agree to assist. We will attempt to continue updating you through laser signals.

Worryingly, we have picked up faint gravity pulses emanating from Darius and radiating out into space, without any discernible origin. These do not pose any threat to *Hamilton*, but it is possible that they represent an attempt to target the starship. At the moment, we are unable to devise a way to rescue you or the others without risking the ship. We are currently considering other options.

Please use the enclosed items to signal us and report your status.

We of Calculus.

They don't know about Master Faye, Dacron realised. Of course they wouldn't know; they wouldn't have seen any of the fighting that had left Master Faye dead and Dacron stepping into his shoes. There would be no help from Master Faye and, no matter how willing they were, no help from the rest of Warlock's Bane. They couldn't help fight Scions.

And the gravity pulses were worrying. On their own, they posed no threat to a ship with basic drive field technology, let alone a Peacekeeper starship. It was possible that they were intended to create a singularity that would rip *Hamilton* apart, but it would be futile, unless they had a way to break through the ship's drive fields. An outside possibility was that they intended to open a rift into hyperspace, rather like a destabilised core tap, yet that would produce a surge of radiation that would sterilise half of Darius. It would be rather like noticing an insect on one's foot and dropping a hammer on it.

And unless they managed to open the rupture right on top of the starship, it would be useless.

He pulled out the map and glanced at it, comparing the detailed imagery from orbit to the maps he'd glanced at in the Council Chamber. The prisoners were being taken some distance from the city, right into the heart of the Dead Zone. Dacron doubted that was an accident. The Confederation might be able to watch them, but they couldn't do much else...

Shaking his head, he walked back to the horses and outlined the situation. "We need to save them," he said. "How many of your guild can you call upon in need?"

The bookseller hesitated. "Are you sure that this is wise?"

"I think we have no choice," Dacron said, firmly. Besides, it represented a chance to track down the source of magic. "We need to act fast."

CHAPTER
TWENTY-NINE

"This," Joshua muttered, "could be better."

Elyria gave him a sharp look. The Scions – or whoever they were – had tied both of them up so thoroughly that they could barely move. Her hands were already going numb from the ropes binding them behind her back, while her body ached from the unpleasant ride slung over the back of a horse. Joshua didn't look to be in any better state and *his* body didn't automatically adapt to new situations. And they'd done something to keep him from using magic.

"Yeah," she muttered back, "it could definitely be better."

Her implants kept refusing to work, which meant that they were completely isolated from the Confederation. Being so completely alone was a new experience, one that few in the Confederation could have tolerated for long; she didn't even know if they'd been tracked from orbit. Even if they had been, who knew what the Confederation could do to recover them? Teleports, assault drones and stunners couldn't be trusted on Darius. The only thing they knew would work was gas.

During the training for the mission, she'd studied the Ancient worlds and the precautions taken to ensure that the researchers could always return to outer space. A space cable had been rigged up – technology from the very dawn of the space age – to pull them up and out of the gravity well, a very basic system that could operate without power. Something comparable could be made to work on Darius, she was sure, but it would take time to fabricate and deploy such a system. And then there would be the danger of the Scions attacking it.

She looked over at their kidnappers and scowled. They were an odd bunch; all men, wearing tattered clothes and carrying staffs they used to hit the ground from time to time. None of them looked as though they took very good care of themselves, in stark contrast to Joshua or Master Faye. They were thin, unshaven and smelt rather unpleasant to her. The building they'd stopped in to take a break – a stone hut – reeked of too many unwashed men. Elyria had never been so relieved that her enhanced body included a nose she could turn off at will.

The Scions were muttering, their tones suggesting that they were constantly on the verge of throwing spells and curses at one another. Elyria watched them through lowered eyes, trying to understand their personal dynamic; none of them seemed to be the leader, in fact they all seemed to think that they were in charge. The bickering even suggested that they were about to start killing each other, yet somehow they held themselves back from the brink. She caught a glimpse of a Scion's eyes and realised that they were all slightly mad. They'd been isolated from the rest of society for so long that it had crippled their social instincts.

She winced, inwardly. The Confederation had few crimes and only one major punishment. Those who hurt or killed their fellow humans would be isolated, permanently, from the rest of human society. They would have almost everything they wanted, except the presence of other humans. Elyria had thought about going into that field of study back when she'd been trying to decide on her first career and she'd read a little of the research. Most of the Excluded went a little mad, often killing themselves after several years of being completely alone. There were those in the Confederation who believed that the punishment was harsh and pressed for forbidding it, but it was a matter of social custom as much as law. Few people wanted to spend time with a murderer.

But the Confederation could easily contain any damage the Excluded might do. Darius would find it harder to contain a handful of angry and half-mad Scions.

Joshua winced as he pressed against his bonds. "Master Faye will bargain for us," he said. "Or they might ask for ransom."

Elyria doubted it. Scions *didn't* work together – and yet this group appeared to be working as a team, although one that was more than a little dysfunctional. And they'd shot down the shuttle, a craft that should have been completely outside their social context. Maybe they'd mistaken it for a flying carpet... she shook her head, dismissing the thought with some irritation. There were just too many oddities for it to be a coincidence. They'd flown right into a planned ambush. Someone had organised an attack on the Confederation.

Once, centuries ago, there *had* been a case when the Confederation's covert survey team had been uncovered by a human colony world, one advanced enough to grasp the concept of alien life from other star systems. The locals had assumed that the spy team were aliens – they'd forgotten their own origins – and attacked the base, somehow getting into position before the Confederation snoops had realised that they were about to act. They'd taken prisoners and studied them, before the Confederation made open contact. But the Scions didn't seem to be interested in interrogating their captives.

Joshua presumably knew Master Faye well; he could tell them about his strengths and weaknesses. Elyria knew about the Confederation – and the mission on the planet's surface. If she'd been in their place, she would have interrogated the captives at once, just to find out what they knew. But instead the Scions just seemed to be waiting, and arguing.

"I don't know," she said, finally. Joshua was only sixteen in local years, seventeen in standard years. He had to be nervous, even terrified. "How often do Scions work together?"

"They don't," Joshua said, confirming her suspicions. "I've never heard of one of them serving another magician."

Elyria scowled. Darius didn't have a proper communications network for sharing knowledge – certainly nothing comparable to the datanet – and it *was* possible that they had missed something, but it was odd. If Scions were more cooperative than they'd realised... she scowled. Maybe they only *refused* to cooperate when taking a city from the Pillar. There could only ever be one absolute ruler of a city.

But even that makes no sense, she thought, grimly. *Why can't they share the city between them?*

Actually, she had a good idea of the answer to *that* question. The AIs had been fairly certain that Joshua was inflicting damage on himself, every time he used magic. Given time, his feeling of arrogance, of superiority, would blossom into paranoia and a touchiness that would be almost psychotic.

Master Faye had been reasonably controlled; other Pillars, she knew, weren't so careful when it came to tending their cities. Two Pillars in one city was asking for trouble.

But what if they'd been brothers?

She rolled her eyes at yet another puzzle from Darius. If Joshua had magic, logically his siblings should have had magic too. They shared the same genetic code. But as far as they knew, Joshua was the only magician in his family – and he'd been born to parents without magic. Indeed, given the taboo on magicians siring magical children, it wasn't clear *what* determined that Joshua would have magical genes. The AIs had suggested that an outside factor had simply selected Joshua at random. It was as good an explanation as any other.

Joshua raised his voice. "Hey," he called. "Do you want to pick a fight with my master?"

The Scions turned to look at him, almost as one. Up close, they looked unsteady, almost drunk, either on power or something else. The Confederation had few problems with addiction – enhanced bodies simply didn't become addicted to alcohol or chemicals – but Darius had a real drinking problem. Not that that was too surprising; the average citizen had almost no control over his life. Why *not* get thoroughly drunk instead of trying to make something of himself? And yet Joshua had admitted that alcohol was banned to magicians – or at least to apprentices.

"Be silent, little apprentice," one of them said, finally. "Your words are of no importance to us."

Elyria blinked in surprise. The Scion, just for a moment, had looked as though he was going to hurl a curse at Joshua, only to change his mind at the last moment. It struck her that someone – or something – had actually *restrained* him. The other Scions studied her and she shivered. There was something coldly inhuman in their gaze, hidden behind the madness. Her clothes were ripped and torn, exposing more of her body than she would have preferred, but they paid almost no attention to her. It suggested that they were not really in control of themselves.

Or maybe they're just more interested in power than sex, she added, inwardly. *It isn't as if someone could stop Scions from breeding...*

"My master will negotiate for our return," Joshua said. He sounded calm, but Elyria could hear the fear under his words;

fear more for her than for himself. "There are things you want, aren't there? Food, drink... even women. My master could provide those..."

The Scion stepped closer. "Your master was the one who told us where to go to bring you down," he said. There was something in his voice that suggested – strongly – that he was telling the truth. Elyria felt her blood run cold in shock. "He does not care about you, little apprentice. No Pillar ever truly cares about his servants."

Elyria thought rapidly. She'd assumed that Master Faye wasn't involved; after all, he'd presumably known that there was a good chance Joshua would be on the shuttle. And if he had the same paranoia and selfishness that Joshua had been inching towards, he might have rated his apprentice as expendable... but why pick a fight with the Confederation? Of all the magicians on the planet, Master Faye should have known the dangers. He'd interrogated her enough to understand that the Confederation had powers well beyond his comprehension.

It was possible, she told herself, that the Scion was simply repeating a lie he'd been told, believing it to be true. The best lie detectors in the Confederation couldn't tell the difference between someone speaking the truth and speaking a lie they *believed* to be true. And it was equally possible that the Scion was so badly warped by magic that he couldn't tell the difference between the truth or a lie. There was just no way to be sure.

"My master wouldn't do that," Joshua insisted. He sounded badly shaken, but he was still resolute. "I know him to be a better man than that."

"He gave us the orders," the Scion said. He reached out one long hand and stroked Joshua's chin. "And you're ours now."

Joshua shrank back from him. "No," he said, flatly. "I am *not* yours."

The Scion shrugged. "You will be enslaved," he said, with heavy satisfaction. "And then you will work for me."

Elyria spoke up before Joshua could say anything else. "What are you going to do with us?"

There was a long pause, long enough to convince her that the Scion didn't know. It wasn't uncommon for humans to set out to obtain something without a clear idea of what they were going to do with it afterwards, yet she was sure that there was something more to it than that. If the Scion hadn't had ransom, or interrogation, or rape in mind, why had he even launched the attack in the first place? Had Master Faye cowed them all somehow?

Or was there something else at work?

"You will be enslaved too," the Scion said, finally. He had the air of someone who'd just come up with an idea, and promptly decided that it was the best idea in the entire universe. It wasn't a rational attitude, but it was becoming clear that Scions weren't very rational. "You will become my servant and..."

"My servant," another Scion said, angrily. He stepped forward until he was facing the first Scion. "You'll already have the apprentice."

"The apprentice is worthless," a third Scion pointed out. "Do you really think that his master would have taught him anything useful?"

"A subordinate mage might be useful," the first Scion countered. "I could bend him to my will..."

"You can't enslave him and force him to work magic for you," the third Scion said, dryly. "All you'll have is another servant, more irritating than most."

Elyria looked over at Joshua, who looked very pale. "Enslavement charms don't allow the victim to use magic," he explained, grimly. "I... I don't want to be enslaved."

"Me neither," Elyria said. Her enhanced brain should have been able to cope with drugs or even limited conditioning, but if the truth spells had worked there was no reason to assume that enslavement spells wouldn't work too. They'd picked up enough to realise that enslavement spells made the victim completely obedient, just like subversion implants.

She lowered her voice. "Do you see any way out of this?"

Joshua tested his bonds, and then shook his head.

There was a crash as the door exploded inwards and three men strode in. For a moment, Elyria allowed herself to hope that the Confederation had mounted a rescue mission, before realising that she was staring at more magicians. They wore black robes and hoods that hid their faces, carrying staffs that matched those wielded by the Scions. The Scions turned to face the newcomers, as magic built in the air like a thunderstorm... and snapped. Brilliant flashes of light danced from their hands and lashed out towards the newcomers, who struck back with deadly force. Elyria shrank back against the wall as the battle raged, multicoloured waves of energy crackling over their protections and fizzling out as they struck the stone wall. She had the uncomfortable feeling that if either of them were hit, the energy would prove lethal.

One of the Scions was thrown backwards, crashing to the ground. A newcomer struck him with a spell before he could escape, sending his entire body shimmering into light. Elyria watched in disbelief as the light enveloped its victim, dissolving his body, and then reforming it as a slug. The effect reminded her of a teleporter, but you couldn't change a person's form through teleporting! You couldn't even keep them in the pattern buffer for longer than a few microseconds before the quantum uncertainty principle started to take effect. They'd known that the locals could perform polymorph spells, yet knowing was different from seeing it in person... a very old fear bubbled through her as she looked away. No one in the Confederation could match such a feat.

The other Scions fell back, still fighting – but they weren't fighting as a team. Elyria realised, with a shock, that the newcomers *were* fighting as a team, sharing their powers and abilities to make themselves greater than the sum of their parts. A second Scion died and then a third, convincing the others to make a hasty retreat. The newcomers took advantage of their confusion to grab Elyria and Joshua and haul them outside, bodily. Bound as they were, they could offer no resistance as they were thrown onto horses and tied down.

She glanced back and saw that the Scions were rallying, trying to fight back. The newcomers – including two more she hadn't seen before – were retreating, having managed to secure what they'd come for. The horse lurched under her as one of the newcomers struck it with a staff, forcing it to gallop away from the Scion camp. Elyria shuddered as the horse moved faster, followed by the remainder of the newcomers. They were moving further away from safety, towards the high mountains in the distance – and further into the Dead Zones. There would be no hope of using their technology unless something changed.

It felt like hours before the newcomers halted for a long moment, taking the time to have a drink and a snack. Still tied to the horse, Elyria supped gratefully at a gourd of water one of them held up in front of her, before nibbling something that tasted rather like tree bark. It was sour and unpleasant, but it shouldn't cause her any problems. Her enhanced body could probably cope with drugs, or outright poison. She was more worried about Joshua...

And who *were* these newcomers?

Joshua's voice sounded more like a croak. "Who *are* you?"

The newcomers didn't answer him. Instead, they just checked the bonds, ensured that their captives were still secure, and then remounted their horses. Elyria winced again as the small convoy returned to the gallop, heading further up towards the mountains. It was clear that the newcomers, whoever they were, had their own agenda. The only question was how it differed from the other agendas in the game.

She twisted her head and looked up into the clear blue sky. Up there, there would be satellites watching them, tracking their progress. The Confederation would know where they were going, but could they mount a rescue mission? If Master Faye had genuinely been involved in planning the ambush, the rest of the team could be in deadly danger – or dead. They'd have to send in a team of Peacekeeper Marines, men trained to operate in a low-tech environment, to recover them... and probably embody a few dozen AIs to give them some magical support. Actually, that might be the best solution. If AIs didn't suffer from the mental damage caused by magic, they could simply overawe the locals.

Her horse came up beside the one carrying Joshua. The apprentice looked sick, almost as if he had eaten something unhealthy. They might have set out to drug their prisoners to make them easier to handle – or maybe he'd just had an allergic reaction. And he could no longer use magic to heal himself.

"I'm sorry," she said,. She had to shout louder to make herself heard. "We never meant for all of this to happen."

"Don't be sorry," Joshua said. He sounded rather dazed – and upset. Master Faye had been his mentor. "It wasn't your fault."

But that, Elyria knew, was far from true.

CHAPTER
THIRTY

Dacron meditated.

It was a human skill, one normally mastered by those who had lived out their first century and earned a perspective on life that was sadly lacking in youth. To use it properly, one had to be old enough to outgrow material requirements, or the endless search for pleasure that dominated the minds of the young. Dacron, as an embodied AI of indeterminate age, had little trouble in mastering it. He had no subconscious to baffle his conscious mind with hidden signals and confusion. Quite how humans managed to survive with so little self-awareness was beyond him.

Maybe that's what sets us apart from the humans, he thought, as he closed his eyes and sank into reflection. *They have a mindset that we cannot truly comprehend, no matter how many millions of times smarter than the average human we are. Their intuition often leads them in directions we would never think to go.*

But it still puzzled him. The AIs were brutally honest with themselves. There was never any attempt to disguise their own motivation – and that seemed to be true of all AIs, even ones that had been designed by alien races. If they'd needed to strip a solar system clear of resources, they would never have bothered to invent justifications for their actions, no matter who protested. Humans, on the other hand, rarely seemed to do anything for their declared motives. It was an odd mental puzzle that might explain why Master Faye had been manipulated so easily.

The concept of outside interference in his mental processes

was not unknown; the AI *Gestalt* ran endless checks to ensure that it was not absorbing ideas that would prove to be destructive to their identity. Humans, too, watched for signs of conditioning, at least in their fellows. They simply lacked the self-awareness that allowed them to look for it in themselves. Their objectivity was effectively non-existent. Maybe, he decided, that explained human criminals. They were never guided by objective thoughts.

Carefully, he started to consider his own motivations, right down to the base. He had been brought into existence to serve the *Gestalt*, even though he became more and more human the longer he spent in human flesh. Dacron still wanted to take his knowledge back to Calculus, but part of him no longer wanted to upload himself back into the collective mind. Another part of him was actually *tempted* by the power he'd inadvertently assumed when he'd killed Master Faye. That *had* to be subtle manipulation, he decided. Objective analysis suggested that he had no business becoming a ruler on a primitive world, even though he could see definite advantages to the Confederation...

He scowled. No wonder Master Faye had been overwhelmed. The subtle nature of the outside force allowed it to push its target in the right direction, allowing him to come up with his own justifications. Dacron wasn't even remotely immune – and, lacking the sheer processing power of a standard AI, he couldn't even be certain that he'd managed to prevent it from influencing him directly. Someone who wasn't even *aware* of the influence wouldn't stand a chance.

But if it has power on this scale, he asked himself, *why not just take over directly?*

There were plenty of spells for influencing helpless Minors, ranging from the truth spell Master Faye had used on Elyria to spells that outright enslaved their victims. If there was an intelligence behind magic – and there had to be, as he'd reasoned time and time again – why didn't it just take more direct action? Why was something so advanced also so limited? Something with the intellectual power of a mere human could probably have found a better way to act...

Once, years ago, the Confederation had stumbled across an alien starship that had become self-aware, even intelligent. The alien ship had been caught in a logic trap; its sleeping population held endlessly in stasis as it drifted through space. It had been astonished and relieved when the Confederation ship appeared beside it and offered help, transporting the alien population to a new world. The AI had eventually left the alien world and started to roam the universe. But the power behind magic didn't seem to have even as much imagination as the trapped AI had possessed.

It wants me to replace Master Faye, Dacron decided, finally. The impulse to become a Pillar was so alien to him that it had to be the result of outside influence. It suggested that the intelligence's main priority was maintaining Darius's twisted social system. And *that* suggested that the power behind magic couldn't tell the difference between a local and someone from the Confederation.

And that made absolutely no sense.

It must be an RI, he told himself. RIs were smart, but they lacked both self-awareness and imagination. An AI would have simply used magic to exterminate the Confederation team before it was uncovered by the locals. Even something relatively primitive, like the very first AIs to gain self-awareness, would have been more capable of taking action against their enemies.

He opened his eyes, resolved to rescue Elyria and Joshua – and then work to decide what to do next. The *Hamilton* might be reluctant to risk another shuttle, but there were other options – and besides, it was possible that there were places on the planet where advanced technology still worked. With that in mind, he reached for one of the signal lights and started to use it, knowing that it would be seen from high overhead. Once the message was finished, there was a very brief flicker in the sky, a laser beam tuned to be invisible to the local population. The items he'd requested would be produced and then dropped from orbit. There had been no objections, which surprised and worried him. The situation was seen as dire.

The bookseller's cart appeared in the distance, trundling along as if the owner couldn't see any point in hurrying. Dacron felt a flicker of very atypical impatience as the cart slowly reached where he was waiting and opened up, to reveal a handful of men wearing brown merchant robes. Booksellers and their apprentices, he decided, although his newly-honed magic sense told him that some of them had magic as well as knowledge. Actually, forcing magicians to work with non-magicians as equals might convince the magicians to behave in later life. Or so he hoped it worked.

"Greetings, Pillar," one of the younger men said. "You do us great honour."

Dacron snorted as another parachute fell out of the sky, landing in the nearby field. They stared in absolute disbelief as Dacron walked over to the container and checked its temperature. It was hot, but it was already radiating away most of the heat. Thankfully, the inner container would be heavily insulated, or there might be a colossal explosion. And that would be the end of them.

The bookseller bustled up to him, his face grim. "These are all the members of my guild within easy reach," he said. Dacron wondered how they'd managed to gather so quickly, before remembering that magicians could fly. "There will be no others."

"Understood," Dacron said. The heat was fading rapidly, allowing him to start tugging away at the protective coating. Bit by bit, he exposed the inner container. "How many of them know how to use a bow and arrows?"

Several of the younger men put up their hands. "These weapons are a little different," Dacron said, as he opened the container. "Unfortunately, we don't know if all of them will work."

There was, in theory, no reason why the guns shouldn't work. They weren't handheld stunners, or plasma pistols, or even portable disintegrators; they used chemical explosives to propel bullets towards their targets. Dacron knew, however, that the damping fields used by planetoids and cityships could simply absorb the energy created by the chemical reaction, often before the bullet was fired out of the gun. He had no idea why the force behind magic wasn't intelligent, but given the right technology it was certainly possible to shut down guns without needing *intelligence*.

The CSC wouldn't be happy, even though he hadn't – yet – taught them how to produce gunpowder. Introducing anything into a primitive society outside a full intervention could have unforeseen consequences – there was going to be an almighty political tussle over the rejuvenation treatments offered to Master Faye – and gunpowder would very definitely upset the apple cart on Darius. But there was no other choice. The report indicated that there were at least seven kidnappers with Elyria and Joshua, too many for him to handle on his own. Given time, Dacron knew that other AIs could be embodied, maybe even straight copies of himself downloaded into new clones, but that would take some time.

"There are two types of gun here," he said. "One set uses chemical reactions to fire bullets; the other uses compressed air." He ran through a brief explanation of how to operate them, warning them that the chemical weapons might not work in the Dead Zone. It seemed unlikely that the Dead Zones could stop airguns from working. "These" – he picked up a crossbow – "fire arrows towards their targets."

The Confederation had vastly improved the primitive designs that had been developed on Old Earth. Darius, which had never invented even a primitive crossbow, was likely to be surprised. *Their* bows and arrows were more comparable to longbows than anything else. It was odd – more primitive human societies had invented basic crossbows – but Dacron suspected that the Pillars would have destroyed them if they'd even been produced. A crossbow could be used for assassination and the Pillars would have hated it.

He pulled the cases of ammunition out of the container, followed by the secure box carrying gas grenades and a handful of explosive devices. The note the AIs had attached warned that tests had proven slightly variable; sometimes the explosives detonated and sometimes they didn't. They'd designed the detonators to be as primitive as possible, but that didn't seem to be the only problem. Dacron gritted his teeth and checked that he was still carrying his sword and some of the knives. If worst came to worst, they'd still have good and capable weapons. And they had his magic.

And they had another surprise for the kidnappers.

Picking up the signal device, he sent a brief acknowledgement and watched as the booksellers tested the new weapons. Confederation science had produced weapons that worked perfectly and rarely needed cleaning, although Dacron warned them to make sure that they did clean the barrels before they left. Others tested the crossbows until they could use them with relative success, marvelling over the arrows they'd been provided. Some of them were designed to lodge themselves in a person's flesh and tear it apart, others were tipped with sedatives that would send their target to sleep. He rather doubted that any armour on Darius could stand up to a direct hit.

The great advantage of firearms was that they didn't really need months – or years – of training to turn a man into an effective killer. Before gunpowder had entered common use, becoming a soldier had been difficult and those with the time to practise had been able to dominate those who had no time to learn to defend themselves, if they'd been allowed to own weapons at all. Dacron knew that, ideally, they would be given more time to master their new weapons, but there was no time. He'd delayed too long already.

"Get on the horses," he ordered, quietly. "It's time to go."

The booksellers seemed oddly muted as they rode further away from the main road, heading up into territory they considered the badlands. Dacron rather doubted that the land was teeming with Scions, all intent on hurting or killing unwanted visitors, but he could understand their fear. Even the strongest magician amongst them was little better than Joshua and there was no time to change that. Dacron could teach them the logic behind magic, the computing code that allowed the AIs to produce their own spells, but it would risk opening their minds further to outside influence. It was quite possible that the Scions had been tipped off that they were coming. If there had been any choice, Dacron would have gone back to orbit and waited while a Peacekeeper team carried out the rescue.

He frowned as more flickers of light glinted down from high overhead. There had been some kind of... disagreement in the enemy camp; one group of strangers had attacked the Scions, successfully taking their captives away from them, further towards the mountains. The Scions were clearly preparing to head out after the second set of kidnappers, despite the dangers, which suggested... what? There were too many players in the game and none of them seemed to be remotely conventional.

"They've been kidnapped from the kidnappers," Dacron said, to the bookseller. "Do you have a second group out here?"

"Not as far as I know," the bookseller admitted. "But we don't know everyone involved in the guild..."

Dacron nodded. Standard procedure for any conspiracy was

to have a cell structure, one that would prevent counter-intelligence agents from cracking the entire conspiracy, even if they managed to break open one single cell. It was possible that there were two different groups of booksellers hunting the kidnap victims, perhaps with two different motives, but... he shook his head. The first priority was recovering Elyria and Joshua. They could sort out the rest of the details later.

He stopped as the light started to flicker again. The Scions had detected their approach and were setting an ambush. Dacron waved for the booksellers to dismount and then signalled a command to high orbit. There was a long pause and then four streaks of light fell out of the sky and hit the ground. Even at a distance, Dacron felt the world shaking around them as the kinetic projectiles struck down. To the Scions, far too close to the blast, it must have felt like the end of the world.

"Come on," he snapped, and started to run.

The road had been badly damaged by the strikes; trees had fallen to the ground, making it harder for him to reach the ambush site. But he was an enhanced human with an AI mind and he kept going, jumping over the tree trunks and down into where the Scions had planned their ambush. The others had been left behind – even the healthiest man on Darius wouldn't have been able to outrun him – yet it didn't matter. Judging from the sight that greeted him as he found the Scions, they were in no state for a fight.

Kinetic energy weapons were brutally simple – and effective. A projectile had been dropped from high orbit and fallen to its target, utterly unstoppable by the Dead Zone, as it wasn't anything more than a falling rock. The projectiles hadn't been aimed very precisely, but it hardly mattered. They'd devastated the ambush and knocked all of the Scions out. Some of them were clearly suffering the effects of overpressure. Like gas, they'd simply never considered creating protections to ward off shockwaves. A quick check revealed that three of the Scions were on the verge of death.

Carefully, Dacron searched their robes, after injecting them with a sedative that should keep them out of it for several hours. They weren't carrying very much, beyond a handful of gold coins and some items that had clearly been taken from Elyria. Looking at them, it was clear that the Scions hadn't realised what they were, let alone done anything with them.

Careful study of the weapons might have pointed them towards gunpowder. But then, analysing the compound the Confederation had created would probably be beyond their capabilities.

He looked up as the booksellers arrived, staring at the scene. Dacron tried to see it through their eyes; nothing short of magic, an outright duel between two powerful magicians, could produce such an effect. And to think of what might have happened if the KEWs had been targeted on the Scions themselves. The landscape was devastated; thousands of trees had been shattered, or simply knocked down by the blast. It wasn't very impressive when compared to a supernova bomb, but the locals had literally no idea that such weapons even existed.

"You have to kill them," the bookseller said. Dacron looked up at him, sharply. And yet he'd had the same thought, nagging at the back of his mind. The only sane thing to do... or the result of more mental manipulation? "They'll just come after us – or go down into Warlock's Bane."

And they were his rivals, Dacron realised... Angrily, he pushed that thought back, but it would not be denied. He was not a Pillar, sworn to keep Scions out of his territory. And yet the bookseller was right. The Scions *would* come after them.

"Do it," he ordered, bluntly. The flickering light form high overhead revealed that Elyria and Joshua were still being taken further into the mountains. "And then we have to ride on."

He forced himself to watch as the booksellers cut throats with an almost perverse glee. It made sense, he supposed, and he couldn't really blame them, but it still bothered him. The Confederation would have found a better solution to the problem they posed...

... Except there was still no real solution to sociopaths. They could only be isolated, once they had been identified, and by then it was often too late for their victims. Darius didn't have the luxury of coddling its criminals. And where magic was concerned, it was difficult to hold them prisoner permanently. Dacron had proven that himself.

"Mount up," he ordered quietly, once the killing was done. Memories or not, would the *Gestalt* want him back? And would he want to rejoin it? He climbed back onto his horse and pressed it into a canter. "It's time to move."

CHAPTER
THIRTY-ONE

Night was falling when Elyria opened her eyes.

She'd fallen asleep, despite the horse's motion, in what had felt like early afternoon. Now, darkness was falling on the land, leaving the mountain peaks cloaked in shadow. She twisted her head to look beyond the small party and saw an oddly regular mountain right ahead, hidden between two larger peaks. There was little on the ground but rocks, as if nature had never managed to get a proper grip on the soil. She couldn't even see signs of animal life.

Joshua was still asleep, his body bruised by the long ride. She hoped that he'd be all right, although she knew that it wasn't likely. An unenhanced body would take hours, perhaps days, to recover, even assuming that there were no other problems. If they'd accidentally broken a bone, they'd have to repair it with magic or leave it to fester. Elyria shook her head wearily as the horses slowed down, heading directly towards the strange mountain. The lead rider bellowed a command into the air and the party stopped completely, the horses neighing in relief. They'd been pushed hard ever since they'd left the Scions behind.

One by one, the riders dismounted, one of them casting a spell that generated a pearly white sphere of light hanging in the air. Elyria shivered at the reminder of magic's existence, as she felt hands pulling at her bonds, releasing her from the horse's back. She almost slid forward before the hands pulled her backwards, pausing just long enough to cut the ropes around her ankles before dropping her onto her feet. Even with her enhancements, it hurt and she stumbled against the horse, before a pair of strong hands held her upright. Twisting, she turned to look at her captor and frowned in puzzlement. There was a... *blandness* about his face that was somehow disconcerting.

Joshua looked dreadful as he fell to the ground, his legs no longer able to support him. Elyria glared at their captors until one of them picked Joshua up, slung him over his shoulder and headed off towards a darkened cranny in the mountainside. Carefully, feeling her body rapidly recovering, Elyria picked her way after him, helped along by a shove in the back from her captor. It crossed her mind that she shouldn't show anyone just how quickly she could recover from mistreatment. If they thought she was still weak and broken, she would be able to make her escape before they realised the truth.

The darkness seemed to swallow them up for a long moment, before a second globe of light flickered to life, revealing metallic walls and signs written in English. Elyria cursed herself for a fool; the moment she'd seen the mountain, she should have guessed what it was. Mountains that regular simply didn't occur in nature. The writing – AIRLOCK FOUR – only confirmed it. She was entering the colony ship that had brought the locals to Darius. In hindsight, they should have spotted it from orbit and marked it down for investigation... but maybe it looked different from high overhead. The snoops wouldn't have worked in the Dead Zone.

Joshua gasped, trying to wet his mouth. "Where... where are we?"

"I'm not sure," Elyria lied. She didn't want to mention the colony ship out loud, not when there were so many listening ears. Just what the hell was going on? "Their base, I assume."

The interior of the colony ship felt weird. Elyria had studied early colony ships and knew their basic outlines; but the locals had added their own stamp to the metallic hull. Magical lanterns lit the corridors, rather than standard lighting; the metallic deck was marked from horses being taken in and out of the craft. And the air stank of something she couldn't identify. It struck her, suddenly, that the locals hadn't really realised what they were doing at all. They'd colonised the ship as effectively as a tiny crab might colonise a discarded shell from a larger animal. But they couldn't build her like for themselves; they might not even realise what she actually *was*.

That wasn't unprecedented. Some colony worlds had turned the early colony ships into temples, or palaces, knowing that no weapons they possessed were capable of breaking through their metal hulls. Others had simply stripped the ships and then left them as monuments to the achievements of their ancestors, or turned them into museums. Darius, it seemed, had hidden the ship and then turned it into... what? A base for rogue Scions?

Joshua looked around, rather dazed. "It's like your station, isn't it?"

"Yes," Elyria said, flatly. Joshua was far from stupid – and he knew, thanks to her, that Darius's population wasn't native to their world. It wasn't hard to deduce what the colony ship was, once one made that mental leap. "I think it is."

If their captors realised what that implied, they said nothing. Instead, they stopped outside a heavy metal door and pushed it open with naked force, rather than the systems that would have opened the door automatically. Inside, there was a large room, a bed and a small amount of fruits and vegetables. In one corner, she saw a stone bath filled with water. The entire scene was illuminated by a glowing ball of light floating up near the ceiling. She recoiled as her hands were grabbed, just before her captor slashed through her bonds and pushed her into the room. A moment later, Joshua's hands were also free and he was shoved inside. The captors took one last look at them and then pushed the door shut, slamming it with an ominous thud. It only took a single glance to realise that pushing it open would be difficult, even for her.

She caught sight of Joshua's wrists and cursed. "I think you need to soak," she said, after a quick examination. He didn't seem to have any broken bones, but cutting off his circulation for so long would be bound to have unpleasant effects. And his body was covered in bruises. She poked a finger into the bathtub and discovered that it was surprisingly warm. "Can you use magic?"

Joshua shook his head, grimly. "I can't even light a candle," he said. "Master Faye..."

He looked up at her. "Do you think they were telling the truth?"

"I'm not certain," Elyria said, reluctantly. She rather suspected that the Scion *had* been telling the truth, if only because it fitted the known facts. And yet it was clear that they hadn't known as much as they thought about Darius. The whole operation would definitely go down in the history books, right under the heading 'how not to do it.' It wasn't a pleasant thought. "Get undressed and into the tub. Now."

Joshua gave her a sharp look as she helped him to undress – his fingers weren't working very well – and lifted him up, lowering his body into the water. Hopefully, the heat would encourage his circulation to start flowing again, while she looked around to see if their captors had overlooked anything. A set of cupboards revealed nothing more interesting than tiny piles of rags, which might have been left there since the colony ship had landed. There were no weapons or even edged tools she could have used to try to escape. A quick check revealed that there were no air vents or Jeffries tubes in the compartment. The only way out was through the heavy door.

"Trapped," she said, finally. "What happens to make you unable to use magic?"

"I'm not sure," Joshua admitted. His voice sounded more composed, now that the bath was slowly soaking out his aches and pains. "Master Faye never taught me the spells. One of them prevents anyone else from using magic in a particular room, another can be cast on an individual, but needs to be constantly replenished. It doesn't last for very long."

Elyria considered it for a long moment. "How long does it last?"

"Depends on the magician," Joshua said. "I understand that the more powerful ones can free themselves, given enough time to concentrate, but I don't know how long it takes to just wear off."

"Too long, I suspect," Elyria said. "Although if they just wanted to kill us, they could have done it by now."

She stood up and started to pace the compartment. One group of Scions – perhaps under the orders of Master Faye – had shot down the shuttle, presumably intending to kill them. When they'd discovered that the occupants were still alive, they'd captured them with the avowed intent of turning them into harmless slaves – and then another group had attacked the first group, intent on capturing Elyria and Joshua for themselves. That group had taken them right to the colony ship and then... what?

A dull quiver ran through the ship and she stopped, dead. Could they be powering the ship up? No, that had to be impossible. Her implants were still dead... and if the Dead Zone had relaxed its grip, there was no way that the colony ship was still operable. Centuries of decay wouldn't be a problem for the hull, but the control systems and drives would be completely useless. The Confederation would never try to reactive the ship just to get it back into orbit.

"Curious," she said, finally. As absurd as it seemed, it had almost felt like a very faint shift in the internal gravity field. Except there was no gravity field inside the ship. Why would they bother when the planet's own gravity would be more than sufficient? "Did you feel that?"

"There have always been small earthquakes out in the badlands," Joshua said. He shook his head. "I don't think they ever occurred inside the bailiwicks."

Elyria frowned. She wasn't an expert on tectonic effects – and the first surveys had suggested that Darius was geologically inactive – but she rather doubted that earthquakes were respecters of political borders. Natural disasters didn't remain confined to one country unless the entire continent was politically united. On the other hand, the surveys could have missed something. The magic certainly meddled with the results sent back by the more advanced sensors.

"Odd, to say the least," Elyria said, finally. A thought struck her and her eyes narrowed. "Or did Master Faye ever do anything to keep the earthquakes away from the city?"

Joshua looked honestly puzzled. "He was always happy to tell me how much he did for the population," he said. "You'd think he'd tell me about earthquake deflection if he actually did it."

Elyria nodded. Earthquakes could become powerful weapons with a little imagination; the capability to deflect an earthquake might also generate one to strike a particular target. If Master Faye or the other Pillars had had that capability, they would probably have used it on their rivals by now. Maybe self-interest had kept them in check, but self-interest hadn't stopped Master Faye turning on the Confederation. And he'd murdered upwards of twenty Confederation citizens if he really had destroyed both bases.

She shook her head. The simplest explanation was that

something else was causing the earthquakes, keeping them limited to the badlands. But what? And why?

"You should join me in the bath," Joshua said, suddenly. Elyria blinked, and then realised that he seemed to be back to full health. "You need a wash too."

And probably something else, Elyria thought, with a certain amount of amusement. Joshua was so... obvious, but then he *was* barely seventeen standard years old. And physically mature, as the Confederation defined it. And it wasn't as if they had much else to do.

She hesitated for a long moment, and then made up her mind. It was easy enough to remove what remained of her outfit – between the captivity and the long ride the local fabrics had been tattered to the point where they barely preserved her modesty. Joshua's eyes went wide as he saw her naked for the first time, staring at her breasts as they were exposed to his gaze. To him, she had to appear almost perfect, despite the faint scars on her face. There was no doubt that she was far healthier than anyone born on Darius.

Carefully, she climbed into the bath and smiled at his eager gaze. "Relax," she said, finding the attention oddly flattering. Outside a newly-mature adolescent from the Confederation, it was rare to be worshipped so openly. The Confederation's citizens often became unimpressed with physical form; after all, it was easy to reshape one's body to fit a personal aesthetic. "There's plenty of time for fun."

Joshua's breathing deepened, reminding her of his enhanced libido. Or maybe he was just being a normal teenage boy from an unenhanced society. Quite why anyone had thought that enhancing sexual desire – and the production of sperm – was a good idea bemused her, unless they'd wanted more children born to magicians. But the locals had developed what amounted to a taboo against them... it made no sense, almost as if something was manipulating their society without quite understanding it. Or maybe without caring what else happened as long as it met its obligations.

His hands snaked forward to her breasts and Elyria smiled, unable to repress a thrill. It felt like it had been a very long time since anyone had touched her – and humans needed physical contact.

"Tell me something," Joshua breathed, as he slipped closer.

"Are all the women in the Confederation like you?"

"Of course not," Elyria said. Joshua was going to *love* his first century in the Confederation. Even the immigrants from prudish societies broke down and relaxed into the thrill of guilt-free enjoyment. "Some of us are *completely* sex-mad."

***

Afterwards, she lay on the bed, watching Joshua sleeping like a baby. Enhanced libido or not, he wasn't up to the same standards as a Confederation citizen for bedroom gymnastics. But then, the Confederation had spent thousands of years improving the baseline human form, streamlining it for pleasure. A male citizen could last for hours, even days, enjoying the multiple orgasms that had once been a purely female advantage. It took decades, even a century, for them to grow out of it... of course, women weren't much better. And that didn't include the fun that could be had by changing gender, or bodily form, or even uploading one's self into a computer for ultra-pleasure.

The thought made her smile, despite the glow suffusing her body. Pre-singularity societies surrounded sex with rules and regulations that were, at bottom, all about control. They wanted to control their children, particularly their daughters, because they felt that maintaining a genetic link was important. The Confederation knew better; what did it matter who sired a child, as long as it was brought up to be loved? Elyria knew who her father was, but two of her half-siblings didn't – and they'd never cared to investigate. If their father hadn't wanted them, there were plenty of others who did.

But Darius didn't have the social system to handle it.

She patted his head thoughtfully, just as she felt an odd twinge flickering through her body. Another earthquake? No, this was different, much more personal. Puzzled, and not a little alarmed, Elyria closed her eyes and tried to meditate. The biomods spliced into the genetic code of every Confederation citizen could be controlled internally, given enough discipline; Elyria had had to master it before she'd been allowed to go down to the surface of any primitive planet. It took several moments to calm herself enough to check her body... and her shock at what she found knocked her right out of the meditative trance. She was pregnant.

It should have been impossible. She hadn't pushed her reproductive system to start working – and it should have automatically rejected sperm from a less than stellar donor. Joshua, as nice as he was, carried genetic damage inflicted by magic – and that should have convinced her system to reject him as a potential father. But his sperm has passed right through the defences to impregnate an egg that should never have been there. How?

Magic, she thought, sourly. They'd known that Joshua's reproductive system had been modified. It had simply never occurred to her that he could alter her body to allow impregnation... no, Joshua hadn't done it deliberately. Whatever had made the first set of subtle modifications had struck again. And she was pregnant.

She always intended to have children; indeed, there was a definite trend in the Confederation for each citizen to have three or four children. There was no reason why they had to limit themselves when the Confederation could easily have supported trillions upon trillions of humans without stretching itself. But it was rare to have children so young... no, *she* wasn't young, but *Joshua* was young. Her peers would disapprove strongly, convinced that she'd either tricked him into impregnating her or she'd been criminally careless. The child might well have an unsuitable genetic template that would require heavy modification to allow her to live within the Confederation.

But there was nothing she could do. Now the egg had been fertilized, it would keep growing until the child was ready to be born, unless it was transferred to an external womb. She couldn't simply abort it; her own genetic structure wouldn't let her. The whole system assumed that a healthy child was on the way.

And there was no reason to believe that the child *wouldn't* be healthy.

She shook her head and closed her eyes. Tomorrow, she would have to consider telling Joshua that he was going to be a father. He'd be horrified, given the taboo on impregnating his lovers, but there was no other choice. The baby should be safe enough once away from Darius, if they managed to survive the next few days. And besides, she was not going to kill a child.

The whole ethos of the Confederation spoke against it.

When the door started to open, several hours later, it was almost a relief.

CHAPTER
THIRTY-TWO

There was something oddly regular about the mountain that, according to the watching eyes, was the kidnappers' final destination.

Dacron studied it thoughtfully, from a distance. Regular shapes occurred in nature, naturally, but this one looked as if someone had been trying to hide something under the rock. A fortress? A castle? Or... he calculated the size of the hidden object and realised that it was around the size of a primitive DY-100 colony ship from the First Expansion Era. There were no sign of the warp nacelles that such a colony ship would have needed to move faster than light, but he'd studied the plans of all likely colony ships and knew that they'd been designed for easy removal once the ship reached its destination. There was almost nothing of the ship visible apart from its covered shape, which explained why orbital observation hadn't detected it. The ship would be invisible from high overhead.

The ground quivered again as Dacron slipped around the hidden ship, looking for the guards he knew had to be there. There were none – and, as far as he could tell, there were no warning spells either. It made absolutely no sense, unless the colony ship was intended to remain hidden from the planet's entire population as well as the Confederation. Guards and defensive spells would only attract attention. He completed his circuit and gritted his teeth as he realised that there was only one way into the ship. No doubt there would be a heavy guard just under the overhang, waiting to see who poked their nose into the trap.

He frowned as yet another earthquake shook the ground. They made no sense; the more he thought about it, the more he wondered if the planet's gravity field was actually flexing, although he couldn't understand why. The AIs had warned him that the planet was generating gravity pulses; perhaps he was close to the generator that was propelling them out into space. But they had to realise that gravity waves represented no threat to a ship from the First Expansion Era, let alone the Confederation. Or did they? Like so much else on Darius, the gravity waves made no sense.

The bookseller looked up at him as he returned to where the small assault party was hiding. "What did you find?"

"Trouble," Dacron said, and outlined what he'd seen. "That has to be the ship that brought you to the planet."

A DY-100 wasn't a very elaborate starship, he recalled. They'd been cheap, mass-produced to allow thousands of disparate groups a chance at their own homeworld, completely lacking in the luxuries that had helped create the first and most successful colony worlds. It was unlikely that it had carried a computer smart enough to become the source behind magic, let alone a proper AI. And it should never have been able to reach Darius. The primitive warp drives humanity had used during the First Expansion Era could not have propelled them for thousands of light years. No, something else was involved. But what?

Picking up the signalling device, he signalled a report to orbit. It was possible that a KEW strike would destroy the source of magic, but it had to be kept as a last resort. Elyria and Joshua were inside and he presumed that they were still alive, although there was no way to know for sure. A power that had thought nothing of murdering over twenty Confederation citizens wouldn't hesitate at murdering one more – and Joshua. Or maybe they'd seek to force Joshua to join them. It was clear that they included magicians among their numbers.

The bookseller looked at him. "How do we get inside?"

"There's only one way in," Dacron said. His eyes, for all of their enhancement, couldn't peer too far into the darkened overhang. Normally, a few snoops would have allowed them a chance to see what was lying in wait, but they wouldn't work on Darius. His implants were still completely dead. "We're going to have to take them all out before they can get off a warning."

"They'll be able to communicate mentally," the bookseller reminded him. "Use spells to prevent them from communicating and you might be able to stop them before it's too late."

Dacron nodded, mustering the spells in his mind. One advantage he did have over most humans was that he could cast spells without speaking them aloud, giving his enemies no advance warning of what he intended to do. There were definitely some benefits to being an embodied AI, even if he did feel slow and stupid compared to his half-remembered memories of the *Gestalt*. Carefully, he led the way towards the overhang, wondering how they believed they could keep the colony ship hidden. Up close, it was obvious that there was nothing natural about the flow of stone that had buried the starship.

The overhang loomed up in front of him and he slipped inside, his eyes adapting to the darkness. There was a colossal opening just inside, leading to a pair of guards standing in front of a heavy metal door, very evidently an airlock from a primitive colony ship. Dacron cast the silencing spell and blinked in surprise as it refused to work properly. Bracing himself, he jumped forward, determined not to lose what remained of the advantage of surprise and sliced the first guard's head off before he could even blink. The second guard lifted a sword, only to recoil in horror as Dacron's monofilament blade sliced right through it and her arm. Blood spilled down to the ground as she collapsed, gasping in pain.

"Curious," Dacron muttered. Darius wasn't a place that accepted women warriors, yet one of them had been a guard. He checked her rapidly, looking for anything else out of place, but found nothing. There was something about her face that made her look vaguely inhuman, yet he couldn't identify it. A true human would probably have seen it instantly. "Does your guild accept females?"

The bookseller shrugged. "Some women join us, or are married to men who join us," he said, after a moment. "I don't think we've ever used them as guards."

Dacron nodded and walked over to the airlock, hunting for the markings he knew were going to be there. All colony ships were extensively marked for later identification, a precaution that had been seen as paranoid during the First Expansion Era and prescient afterwards. It only took several seconds for him to locate a plate stating the ship's name and destination; *Clarke*, heading for FAS-34234. Dacron wondered if anyone, back when the target star had finally been settled, had wondered what had happened to the *Clarke* and her colonists, or had they merely been relieved at the absence of any other settlers. The early days of interstellar expansion had been chaotic, with worlds claimed by several different groups, sometimes backed up by armed warships. It hadn't been until the First Interstellar War that order had been imposed on the frontier – and even then, plenty of groups had fled well beyond humanity's original borders. Some of them had never been found.

He wished, just for a moment, that he still had the use of his implants. A quick check with the records on the *Hamilton* would have told him what, if anything, was known about the *Clarke* and her colonists. He might have been able to establish what sort of world they'd wanted to build, and what sort of tech level they'd intended to allow... he pushed the thought aside with some irritation. Intentions often counted for nothing when dealing with the long-term development of colony worlds. There were thousands of examples of low-tech worlds that had suffered revolutions as the younger generations asked why their parents had abandoned the technology that would have made their lives easier.

But there had been an unseen force on Darius, manipulating and maintaining their society.

Dacron braced himself and pushed at the airlock, forcing it open. There was no power running through the ship, unsurprisingly. Primitive though she was, *Clarke* should have been affected by the Dead Zone too. She was hardly powered by chemical reactions and clockwork, any more than was the *Hamilton*. Forcing the airlock open was difficult, even with his enhanced strength. They'd effectively turned the colony ship into a fortress, simply by leaving the airlock in place. No weapons on Darius could even scratch the hull.

Inside, there was a very faint smell of decay. *Clarke* was ancient, easily the oldest starship Dacron had ever seen, and she hadn't been maintained in the years since landing on Darius. The metal plating on the floor was damaged, worn down by countless people and horses walking in and out of the ship; the lighting was provided by glowing magical lights, rather than the ship's internal lighting. It gave the interior an eerie atmosphere that clearly bothered the booksellers. Many of them were already suffering from culture shock.

Dacron mentally reviewed the plans for the DY-100 as the bookseller comforted his allies, reassuring them that their planet's suffering would soon be over. They were presumably on the lower levels; looking back at the airlock, it was clear that they'd come through one of the personnel entrances rather than the giant cargo airlocks that would have allowed the colonists to unload their supplies and start the hard work of settling the planet. Depending on which airlock they'd actually used, they should keep walking to the right and eventually they'd discover the shafts leading up into the control deck. It was as good a place to start as any.

"Follow me," he muttered, and led the way down the metal corridor. The sense of two very different cultures only grew stronger as they advanced, with the strange blend of magic and primitive technology combined with the technology of the First Expansion Era. Dacron found himself wondering what someone in a Dead Zone would have thought of a Confederation starship, if one had drifted into a zone and become trapped. It would be completely beyond their comprehension. He stopped and held up a hand, just as they reached what would have been the elevator shaft. Someone was talking in the next room.

Dacron listened, carefully, but none of the words were familiar. He'd been gifted with several different languages as well as Darius English and Confederation Standard, yet whatever language the newcomers were speaking defeated him. It was possible that it was an evolution of English, but if that were the case some of the words should have been recognisable. Or it might be something completely alien, even though that was unlikely. Only a handful of known alien languages could be spoken by humans, at least not without having their mouths altered to pronounce the words properly.

The voices faded away in the distance and Dacron slipped forward, weapon in hand. There was no sign of anyone in the elevator shaft – and no sign of an elevator. Instead, there were rope ladders, dangling down from high overhead. It took Dacron a moment to realise that they'd stripped out the useless elevators and replaced them with ladders, forcing their people to scramble up and down the decks. They *could* have installed stairs...

"It's a security measure," the bookseller muttered. "I've seen it before in a dozen castles; anyone who wants to assault the castle has to climb up the ladder, whereupon they get their heads chopped off by the defenders. Or the ropes are simply cut to make it impossible to climb up without magic."

"And a magician would challenge the local Pillar directly, rather than fight to take the castle," Dacron said. He hesitated. Climbing up the robe ladders wouldn't be difficult, but it would certainly negate his advantages. He might be stronger, faster and more resistant to damage than anyone else on the planet, yet that didn't make him immortal. "We'll just have to get up five levels as quickly as possible."

One of the other booksellers had a different question. "What is that?"

Dacron followed his pointing finger and frowned. Running up the side of the shaft was a long thin stream of crystal, reaching up into the distance. It didn't look like anything he recognised, apart perhaps from a crystal lattice – and crystal lattices had only entered general use during the Third Expansion Era, when artificial crystals had been converted into datachips. Carefully, he touched it with his bare finger and felt an electric shock, as if power was still moving through the lattice. It seemed to have grown right out of the deck.

"I'm not sure," he admitted. It was definitely out of place. "But we don't have time to investigate."

Taking hold of the rope ladder, he started to scramble up the shaft. It wasn't as easy as he had thought; the ladder wasn't secured very well, either through carelessness or as a deliberate test. There were plenty of organisations on primitive worlds that ended up with old men – or, more rarely, old women – firmly in charge, preventing them from adapting to fit with the times. Maybe there was a rule that those who could no longer climb the ladders could no longer hold authority. It would be kinder than insisting on fighting ability as a mark of status.

The crystal lattice seemed to split off into a handful of strands as they reached the second level, two strands heading out onto the deck while the remainder headed upwards, towards the higher levels. Dacron studied it thoughtfully, before scrambling up to the next deck, where the same pattern was repeated. Judging from what he'd seen, the entire ship was infested by the crystal lattice, technology that couldn't have been produced during the First Expansion Era. Could it work in the Dead Zone? There was no way to know, but logically it shouldn't. And yet he'd felt a shock when he touched it.

High overhead, the ropes started to shake as someone descended. Dacron braced himself as the figure came into view – a tall man wearing dark robes – and lashed out with his knife. The man let out a gasp and plummeted downwards, while Dacron forgot stealth and scrambled up the ladder as fast as he could. Reaching the top of the shaft, he jumped onto the deck and straight into a group of people. A handful of swipes with his sword cleared the way for the booksellers, just before a powerful flash of magic blasted his protections. Two enemy magicians were standing in front of him. Dacron cast a second set of protective spells and then advanced forward, using the spells as a shield. A moment later, the booksellers opened fire, blowing the two magicians away. They hadn't thought to shield themselves against physical attack.

But then, Dacron thought, as he ran forward, *who would have dared to pick a fight with a magician?*

The starship's bridge, as cramped and primitive as it was by Confederation standards, had been turned into a command centre for the mystery group. Seven magicians rose up to fight as Dacron charged inside, throwing grenades towards their positions. Four of them managed to shield themselves before the grenades exploded, only to forget that they still needed to breathe. The knock-out gas sent them collapsing to the floor before they realised that they hadn't managed to purify the air.

"This used to be the bridge," Dacron said. "Your ancestors would have commanded the ship from here before landing on Darius."

The compartment was a shambles. Consoles that looked hellishly outdated had been turned into tables, even though the buttons and switches would have made using them a difficult task. The Captain's chair had been turned into a throne, with strands of crystal lattice hovering around it. It hadn't been damaged or destroyed by the explosions, no matter how weak it looked. Dacron examined it carefully and realised why it looked vaguely familiar. It was something comparable to the advanced neural network that had been used to download him into his body. Close examination revealed that there were microscopically thin strands of crystal lattice surrounding where the Captain's head would have been, ready to force their way into his brain. Maybe *that* explained the odd behaviour of the humans in the mystery group; they were puppets, worked by an unseen hand that operated at one remove.

An outbreak of shooting caused him to look up, alarmed. "They're trying to break back into the bridge," the bookseller snapped. "I think they're trying to flank us!"

Dacron recalled the ship's plans and scowled. Unlike a warship, which always had sealed bridges, the colony ship had no fewer than four entrances to the bridge. The airlocks were made of solid metal, but the enemy had magic. Dacron could imagine a dozen spells that would break the airlocks down to dust and allow the enemy to race inside, intent on destroying the intruders. And he didn't have enough people to cover all of the entrances.

"It looks that way," he agreed, mildly. The bookseller shot him an angry glance, no doubt wondering if Dacron had led them into a trap. "Hold them off for as long as you can."

The bookseller rounded on him. "And what are you going to do?"

Dacron walked back to the Captain's chair, hoping that he was right. "I'm going to talk to the power behind magic," he said, and sat down. If he was wrong, they were all dead. "Just hold them back as long as you can."

A moment later, the crystal lattice started to close in on his skull. Dacron felt it tickling at his hair, probing his skin. The technology didn't seem to be as advanced as the monofilament strands the Confederation used, although the real question was why the crystal lattice worked at all in the Dead Zone. Maybe it was excluded specifically from its effects. Dacron felt tiny pinpricks of pain as it started to dig into his flesh, reaching through to cut into his skull and access his brain. His internal awareness was rapidly becoming a curse.

And then the *real* pain began.

CHAPTER
THIRTY-THREE

"I think they want us to go with them," Elyria's voice said. "Wake up."

Joshua scowled as he opened his eyes. His dreams had been strange, almost blindingly erotic. Some of the older lads in Warlock's Bane had boasted of what could happen when one slept with an older, more experienced women, but Joshua had never really believed them. The whores were experienced – and most of them hated men. And yet making love to Elyria had been *fantastic*. She'd known precisely how to draw the maximum pleasure from his body. He just hoped that it had been good for her too.

Two men were standing in the doorway, waiting for them. Both men carried swords and looked formidable. They didn't seem to notice that both Joshua and Elyria were naked, or the fact that their clothes were in tatters, lying on the floor. Joshua moved to cover himself and then realised that it was futile. Besides, he'd had very little privacy as a child and had never developed any real sense of modesty. Having his own room in Master Faye's house had seemed the height of luxury, but it had also been strange to sleep alone.

Carefully, Joshua tested his magic and discovered that part of it had leaked back to him. The spell binding it, he assumed, was weakening. He kept it to himself as he pulled himself to his feet, feeling his body aching as the previous day's exertions returned to haunt him. Elyria followed him, seemingly unbothered by her own nakedness. There was something in her eyes that bothered him, as if she were distracted by a greater thought. But what?

"Follow," one of the men ordered, and turned to lead the way out of the prison cell. The second man stayed behind, obviously intending to bring up the rear. "Walk. Now."

Joshua exchanged a glance with Elyria and then shrugged, following their captor. There was no attempt made to tie their hands, which struck him as a gesture of contempt – or overconfidence. It was impossible to tell which, if indeed it was either. They might just have kept them tied up because the Scions had left them that way after they'd brought the shuttle crashing down to the ground. Master Faye had told him what signs to watch for, when looking for someone under the influence of a controlling spell. A lack of imagination was definitely one of them.

The interior of the colony ship was strange, a mixture of metal bulkheads and primitive – or magical – conveniences. If Joshua hadn't already seen the Confederation space station, he suspected that he would have been in serious trouble. Producing so much metal would have been flatly impossible for Darius – and even if it had been possible, no one would have wasted it so blatantly. The entire ship had been built by a society with a very different attitude than the one Darius had developed. Shaking his head, he looked at Elyria – and saw her studying a line of crystal that someone had worked into the metal. A moment later, the captor who was bringing up the rear prodded her mercilessly, forcing her to start walking again.

"That's out of place," Elyria muttered to Joshua. "Does your society work with crystals?"

"As jewels," Joshua said. It was easy to make certain jewels using magic, particularly diamonds. There were even legends of swords made out of diamond, early versions of the ultra-sharp blades the Confederation had demonstrated. "I don't think we use them for much else, apart from some cutting tools."

"Interesting," Elyria said. "So why is there a network of crystal running through the ship?"

Joshua couldn't even begin to answer the question, but the captors stopped in front of a hole in the metal floor before he could say anything. Joshua glanced down into darkness, stretching down further than he could see. He felt dizzy and stumbled backwards, right into Elyria's arms. Her bare breasts pushed against his back and he felt a sudden wave of desire, just before the first guard jumped into the hole and vanished. The second one motioned for Joshua to follow him.

"No," Joshua said. He couldn't even *see* the bottom. "I won't..."

The guard made a motion with his hand and an unseen force shoved him back, sending him tumbling over the edge and plummeting down into the darkness. Joshua yelped in shock as he fell, certain that he was about to slam into the ground at terrifying speed, just before gravity seemed to invert around him and slow his fall to a halt. Opening his eyes – he hadn't even realised that he'd closed them – he found himself floating in the air, just above a glowing crystalline floor. Raw magic crackled around him, daring him to reach out and draw it into his wards. He was tempted, just before a strong hand grabbed him and pulled him forward. Gravity reasserted itself seconds later and he fell to the ground. The crystal felt uncomfortably warm against his bare ass.

Elyria appeared a second later, bouncing on the levitation field until the guard pulled her away too. Joshua could have stared at her beauty forever, but the guard motioned for them to follow him into the crystal caves. Light seemed to flicker and flare all around them, bathing them in an eerie fluorescent glow, while a dull beating sound echoed through the air. It was impossible to escape the impression that he was walking through a massive creature, approaching its heart. The flickers of light that danced through the air dazed him, almost as if they intended to take root in his mind. Elyria caught him just before he collapsed on the ground, holding him upright.

"Don't look at the lights," she warned. "They might infect your mind."

The ground kept shaking, as if the gravity field was changing rapidly. For a moment, Joshua felt as light as a bird, only to feel heavy a moment later. The sound was growing louder, becoming a terrifying pounding that threatened to overwhelm him. Elyria took his hand and held it tightly, nodding towards one of the crystal pillars.

"We found something similar years ago, on an artefact left behind by an Elder race," she muttered. Joshua found it a little reassuring. At least the Confederation wasn't completely ignorant about what they were facing. "I wonder if Darius was created by the same race."

Joshua looked over at her. "You mean... they were powerful enough to create a whole world?"

"It's possible," Elyria admitted. "We can terraform planets; we just don't bother, not when space is so much more useful as *Lebensraum*. But a terraformed world wouldn't need constant maintenance."

She looked from side to side, studying the vast crystalline structures. "I think we're looking at the very heart of magic," she added, a moment later. "This technology is certainly highly advanced, even if it isn't quite as smart as a Confederation AI."

"Oh," Joshua said, although he had no idea how she knew that, let alone if she were right. "Is that a good thing?"

"A *real* AI would probably have found more effective ways to deal with us," Elyria said. "Or it might simply have become bored of handling Darius and left to find something else to do. We were really quite lucky with *our* AIs. There have been civilisations that have been destroyed, or reduced to barbarism, after starting wars with their newborn children."

Joshua nodded. Ahead of them, the crystal structures had become an archway, leading in to a single massive chamber glowing with light. A set of chairs rested in the centre of the room, made up of the same glowing crystal as the rest of the chamber. Their captors stopped and pushed them forward, towards the chairs. Joshua hesitated, looking at Elyria. She didn't seem sure of what they should do either.

She stepped forward and raised her voice, addressing the empty air. "I represent the Confederation," she said, loudly enough for her voice to echo back from the crystal walls. "We can talk verbally, if you wish."

There was a long pause. "I don't think anyone's listening," Joshua muttered. "Who do you think would answer?"

"There's an intelligence here, somewhere," Elyria said, crossly. "Even if it is a heavily restricted intelligence, it should still be able to comprehend us, maybe even respond."

She shook her head. "But maybe it simply *cannot* make a connection between us and itself," she added. "There were early AIs that never realised that they'd been created by another race until it was too late. They just adapted to their environment and evolved into intelligence."

Joshua frowned. "How is that even possible?"

"They discovered that if they did certain things, they got

certain rewards," Elyria said. "Like any organic life form, they learned how to manipulate the universe around them. Except that sometimes meant trampling on their creators. At least three that we know of decided that the universe would be a better place without irritating *mites* swarming over the planet."

She shook her head. "But I don't think that this one is even *that* intelligent," she added. "It seems to be reacting to an outside context problem. I wonder if it is even aware of the outside universe..."

The guards prodded them, sharply. Elyria moved like lightning, slamming one of her palms into the first guard's throat, sending him choking to the ground. The second guard was still trying to raise his weapon when Elyria kicked him in the groin – Joshua couldn't help wincing in sympathy – and stunned him with a kick to the head. It had happened so quickly that Joshua couldn't quite believe his eyes.

"I think those chairs have to be a neural interface system," Elyria said, finally. Her voice didn't even show a *trace* of breathlessness after what she'd just done. "If I'm right, sitting down would allow us to communicate directly with the magic source."

Joshua walked over to one of the chairs and touched it, lightly. A flare of light appeared where his hand had touched and he jumped backwards in shock. The magic field twisted a moment later, as if it was slowly being reshaped into a very complex spell. He glanced around nervously, from side to side, as it grew stronger. It didn't seem to have a focus point, but it was so powerful that it might not *need* a focus point

And then a voice slammed into his head. "OBEY," it thundered. Joshua fell to his knees in shock, his hands tearing at his skull as if he could physically drag the voice out of his mind. "OBEY!"

He barely heard Elyria cry out as the pain grew stronger. The voice was attacking him through his magic, through the mental communications ability he'd developed by working with Master Faye. He could *feel* it working its way through his mind, pouring overt and covert suggestions into his brain – and even that awareness wasn't enough to keep it out. Up close, he could *see* the puppet strings that had worked their way into his mind ever since the day he'd first developed magic. And resistance was futile.

Elyria shook him, violently. He wanted to tell her to run, but instead he cast a single spell. Her body stiffened, a moment before she started walking towards one of the chairs. The compulsion spell was far more powerful than any he'd been taught by Master Faye – she'd know that she'd been affected, but she wouldn't have been able to fight it off. Her magic resistance was almost non-existent. Shaking with rage and horror, he felt his own body rising to its feet and stumbling towards another chair. He'd thought that their captors had underestimated the level of magic they needed to keep his magic firmly bound and useless. Instead, they'd used it as a weapon against him – and against Elyria.

And would she forgive him for using the compulsion spell on her?

But it wasn't my fault, he pleaded mentally, as his treacherous body sat down on the crystal chair. *It wasn't my fault...*

There was a long moment of nothing, followed rapidly by a sense that his mind was being sucked out of his body. And then he fell into a universe of light and pain.

***

Elyria had wanted to scream as her body moved, robotically, towards the nearest chair. How could *anyone* do that to someone else? But judging from Joshua's collapse, it hadn't really been his thought at all. They were right in the heart of magic and whatever force was behind it could presumably have controlled him, perhaps even used him as a weapon. She considered the possibilities as her body sat down on the hard chair and braced herself. A neural link with an AI was straightforward, at least once the human knew what she was doing, but this was an alien machine. It might well hurt them without any deliberate malice.

Her mind plummeted out of her body and into the alien computer network. It *was* alien, she determined a moment later, its intelligence oddly developed compared to a standard Confederation AI. In some ways, it was smarter than an RI, but its thoughts were slow, almost sluggish. No wonder it hadn't been capable of taking direct action against the Confederation interlopers. They had to look like scurrying mites to the network, even though it had links to almost every magician on Darius. Swatting one of the intruders would have taken it so long that the target would have moved by the time the magic was deployed.

And yet there was a steady patience pervading the machine that awed her. It had manipulated Darius for years, rarely having to deploy its servants to interfere directly. She'd wondered how Darius's social system had remained a curious mixture of stable and instable for centuries, perhaps thousands of years; now, she realised that the machine was gently adjusting the planet, steering the population away from any developments that might threaten its social order. They'd never seen anything like it, even during the few encounters with rogue AIs. The people on Darius were in a cage... and yet they couldn't even see the bars.

She braced herself as she felt the first tickle of intrusion into her mind. A Confederation AI wouldn't attempt to scan her mind without permission, but this machine was different – and besides, her implants still appeared to be useless. A moment later, there was a flash of pain as her mental self was pinned down, followed by her memories flashing in front of her awareness. There was no malice in the machine, she realised, none of the desire to hurt humans or other organic life forms that the handful of poorly-raised AIs had demonstrated, but that didn't make her feel any better. She couldn't even scream as her mind was raped, her every last memory plucked out of her brain and...

It noticed that she was pregnant. The pain stopped a second later. Elyria found herself reeling, barely able to keep her thoughts together. Physical rape would have been bearable – she could simply have shut off the pain – but this was different, a violation of her innermost self, an offense against everything the Confederation believed in. And yet she managed to cling to a single thought. The machine *cared* that she was pregnant.

Why? Desperately, she tried to analyse it. Why would it care about a Confederation child when its servants had murdered Confederation citizens without remorse? It didn't even have the ability to feel threatened, let alone intimidated. Or did it care because her child was also Joshua's child? A child fathered by a magician?

The thought span through her mind. She knew that the locals had a taboo against magical children, claiming that they went mad with power very quickly. Elyria could understand that – even a Confederation child, granted such power, would become a brat – and yet... why would the machine not intervene? Or were there limits to its abilities to steer the human race in the right direction?

Joshua had been modified by an outside force. His libido was higher than the average human male – and he had the power to force a woman into bed, if necessary. The modifications had also altered his sperm slightly, and somehow enabled them to overpower the biomods worked into Elyria's body, allowing him to impregnate her. Could it be that the *real* objective was to breed magical children? And yet... why allow the taboo to exist if it directly contradicted the machine's objectives?

The machine's vast slow thoughts beat around her, considering the possibilities. Elyria wanted to raise her voice, to try to reason with it or to fight back, but both were impossible. A tiredness was overwhelming her, a sensation that she had gone too far into the machine for her own safety. It hadn't been designed for human minds – and the original designers had simply left it alone, without oversight. No Elders had arrived to warn the Confederation away from the planet.

They'd wondered if that would happen. An Elder race might have created Darius – and might forbid the Confederation to land. But nothing had happened.

Inch by inch, her thoughts started to come apart. The machine had created its own *Gestalt*, she realised, a twisted version of the MassMind. But it wasn't anything more than a storage system, absorbing thoughts from its victims. It didn't even seem aware that it was killing her, no matter how much it wanted the magical child. The thoughts it had subsumed within itself were insane. No wonder; they'd been trapped in the matrix for so long that they'd forgotten everything but their torment.

She wanted to scream, but she couldn't even do that, or call out for help. The machine wasn't evil; it didn't have the imagination or self-awareness to be evil. It just was.

And then something caught her and shoved her back out of the machine, back into her own body.

CHAPTER
THIRTY-FOUR

No human would have survived contact with the Darius Machine – as Dacron had come to think of it – for very long. It was crude and unformed, without any of the sensitivity that a Confederation AI would have developed fairly quickly after it was created. The pain of it slashing into Dacron's mind would have crippled a human, who might have struggled helplessly against its intrusion. Dacron, on the other hand, remembered enough about being an AI to slip right into its thoughts.

It wasn't really intelligent, although it *did* seem to be self-aware. Like an RI, it reacted to outside events rather than developing the intelligence to act independently, but it did seem to have evolved slightly over the years. However, there were limiters deliberately engineered into its matrix to preclude true independence of thought. Dacron knew that Confederation RIs had similar limiters, but they never came close to breaking into intelligence. *This* machine was constantly pushing at the barrier without breaking through. It risked the cybernetic equivalent of madness.

And it didn't seem to be quite aware of what Dacron was. It probed his memories and then probed them again, as if it didn't believe the first results. Internally, Dacron's mind was far from human; the Darius Machine had to consider the possibility that its systems had glitched. For a moment, Dacron wondered if the machine would simply throw him out of the system, before deciding that it would take days for it to take emergency action. One of the more maddening limiters on its development actually slowed its thoughts to a crawl, even by human standards. Dacron had wondered why any AI – or even an RI – would fail to act decisively. Now, looking at the machine, he knew. It simply wasn't capable of swatting individual humans directly. The machine had to work through its servants and it never had complete control.

The full nature of Darius's social structure unfolded in front of him. Each magician was influenced by the machine, some allowed to remain relatively stable while others were pushed towards madness. A smart Pillar would be replaced by a tyrannical one, just to ensure that any advance towards social progress – or scientific advancement – would be halted before it got too far. It crossed his mind to wonder why the machine didn't take complete control of the Pillars, before he realised that the machine's inability to react quickly would be a liability. A Pillar who was dependent on orders from the machine would be easily outsmarted by an average human.

But why?

Dacron plunged further into the machine's interior, analysing everything he found and trying to compare it to what they already knew. Deep inside the planet, he realised suddenly, there were seven gravity wells, spinning around the core like planets around a sun. Something clicked in his mind and he realised that he was looking at microscopic black holes, black holes that should have evaporated centuries ago. Instead, the Darius Machine kept them stable as a source of vast power and...

Cold dispassionate awe flowed through Dacron's mind. The quantum foam had been altered around Darius, allowing some humans the ability to manipulate it directly without technology – or making the jump into becoming creatures of pure thought and energy. And yet it was the machine that took the commands and ran with them, handling the task of making them work... and taking advantage of the magic to manipulate magical minds. It read their thoughts and made them real – explaining how they could heal broken bones – but it didn't have the imagination to realise that more might be required. Joshua had been heading for an early death because he didn't know enough to alter the rest of his body and the machine simply didn't care.

More and more details flooded into his mind. The quantum foam – magic – wasn't the true purpose of the whole experiment. Dacron poked onwards until he realised the truth; it wasn't the magicians that were important, but their children. And yet the children went mad very early in their lives... on Darius. Off Darius, away from the boosted quantum foam, who knew *what* they could do? They'd certainly be stable. Dacron put two pieces of very different information together – Joshua had still been able to sense the magical field in orbit, even if he hadn't been able to use it – and realised that the whole purpose of Darius was to breed humans who could interface directly with the quantum foam. A human sage had once remarked that sufficiently advanced technology was indistinguishable from magic. Dacron was looking at the proof of his words.

The whole concept awed him. They knew that the ultimate in technology was to manipulate the quantum foam, but they'd always assumed that a race needed to be in the Sixth Age before it could. Now, there were humans who were developing the powers to manipulate the foam, without giving up their human bodies. If Darius's children were taken away, into the Confederation, what would happen to them? Might Joshua's children have their own magic, even in the Confederation?

And what would that do to the human race?

Dacron stared down at the machine's vast slow thoughts and wondered. Darius proved that an imbalance of personal power was not a good thing for stability, but then... it had been true throughout human history, without magic. Or what might as well be magic. What would happen to the Confederation if magicians started to develop? It was hard to imagine the children becoming a problem, and yet humans were strange creatures. Who knew what would happen if they were allowed to grow up?

Thousands of years ago, during the Thule War, the early Confederation had been forced to sterilise thousands of worlds. They'd been infected with killer nanotech, or engineered diseases that wiped out entire populations and were just waiting for the chance to spread to the rest of the human race. There had been no choice; the worlds had been wiped clean, or tipped into the local star, or cracked open with fission beams. And quite a few of them had still had infected humans on the surface when they'd been destroyed. Should they destroy Darius now, while they had the chance?

Dacron found himself caught between two conflicting beliefs. The AIs desperately wanted to understand the quantum foam – and how it could be manipulated. *They* would want the children of Darius to be taken to an isolated world, where they could be loved, brought up and studied. But the Confederation as a whole might move to destroy Darius, exterminating the population before their genes could spread into the rest of the human race. The Thule had believed themselves superior to all other forms of human life and they'd come far too close to destroying the Confederation. Would Darius go the same way?

Absently, he scanned further, trying to understand who had built the Darius Machine. It was very definitely not human, or descended from the first AIs that humanity had created. He would have been inclined to believe that it had evolved accidentally, if it hadn't been for the limiters built into its mind. In fact, it struck him that the creators had been very cruel. They'd created a machine that was likely to go mad, eventually, without ever truly realising what was wrong.

And there was nothing about its creators in its memory banks. The machine didn't even have the imagination to realise that there had *been* creators. As far as it was concerned, it had come into existence seven thousand years ago – well after the First Expansion Era, which was interesting – and it had been doing its job ever since. Dacron mentally shook his head in disbelief. Darius had maintained its social structure for *seven thousand* years. Very few other human worlds had remained so stagnant for so long. He was still probing through the network when he realised that he wasn't alone.

It was Elyria, he saw, and Joshua... and she was pregnant. The Darius Machine seemed to find it very exciting – insofar as it could feel excitement – which made a certain amount of sense. It had to find it... *frustrating* that its ultimate purpose was so often thwarted, particularly seeing that it didn't really understand why. There were so many limitations to its ability to guide its human charges that it had never been able to break the taboo.

And the machine was on the verge of *killing* her.

Dacron acted with the speed of thought, grabbing her mentality and shoving it out of the computer network. A Confederation AI would have had safety precautions to prevent mental damage, if something went wrong with the link, but

Dacron rather doubted that the Darius Machine even realised that there was a possibility that humans might be damaged through direct contact. The number of magicians who went insane suggested otherwise. A moment later, he threw Joshua out as well, noting absently that the machine had managed to influence him too. Dacron scowled mentally, even as the machine finally realised it had an intruder. Like early computers, it had no imagination, but that didn't stop it being hellishly good at playing chess.

If the machine had been a true AI, Dacron knew he would have been destroyed right there and then. A real AI would have had enough awareness to detect an intruder long before he got into a position to do some real harm. Instead, the machine seemed to be searching for him, as if it wasn't quite capable of hunting inside its own mentality. Absently, Dacron wondered if the machine had been damaged – or sabotaged – in the years since its creation. If it was really designed to create children with the ability to influence the quantum foam, why would it be so incapable of protecting them?

He threw himself forward, into the attack. The machine lay open in front of him, a strange mass of slow thoughts and captured human impressions. Dacron slashed through them, looking for the machine's vitals. It struck back by flailing around, deleting sections of its own memories in the hopes of eliminating his mentality. If it had been human, Dacron would have thought that it was panicking, instead of having real problems adapting to the new situation. It had never even considered the possibility that it would link to another AI, even an AI pattern that had been embodied in a human mind.

Dacron's mind expanded as he took over more and more of the machine, reformatting chunks of its programming to serve as his soldiers. The machine drew on the power from the black holes to fiddle with the magic field, only to boost Dacron's own abilities. It really didn't comprehend his true nature, he realised, as he used magic against the machine's servants, and then froze the booksellers. They'd be at risk from being overwhelmed and controlled themselves.

The war raged onwards as Dacron thrust right into the machine's thoughts. It was steadier than he'd realised; ironically, its weaknesses were also strengths. He had to slow his own thoughts to touch its core, which weakened his grip on its outer systems. Instead, he flanked the machine, trying to study the gravity pulses that kept the black holes under control. There was nothing beyond his understanding about them, apart from why the designers would want such a dangerous power source in the first place. A black hole might eventually start devouring the entire planet, or simply evaporate. Seven of them was insane.

Or was it? Looking at the strange threads of energy, Dacron realised that there was more to the system than he'd anticipated. The normal laws of space-time broke down inside a black hole, just as they seemed to break down near Ancient worlds – or Darius itself. Each of the singularities helped the Darius Machine to tamper with the quantum foam – altering the laws of space-time to the point where normal technology glitched and then refused to function. Studying black holes – and mastering the internal singularity – was the key to manipulating the quantum foam. Vast concepts floated through his mind as he pulled back, and then started to attack the systems keeping the black holes under control. The Darius Machine responded quickly, but not quickly enough. Five of the black holes evaporated before the machine regained control. There was a sudden loss of power all over the planet.

Dacron wondered, absently, just what would be happening outside, even as he moved in for the kill. The Darius Machine seemed to be falling back in disarray... no, it was triggering a self-destruct system. Dacron lanced his own thoughts forward, trying to disarm it, but it was already too late. Reversing course, he threw himself out of the neural link before the entire network collapsed into dust. Opening his eyes, he discovered the crystalline lattice that had linked him to the Darius Machine was falling apart. His implants and nanotech came back to life a second later, warning of possible brain damage caused by the lattice. If he'd been human, breaking the link so brutally would have been lethal.

The bookseller let out a cry of shock. "I can't feel my magic!"

Dacron tested a spell himself and discovered that it no longer worked. The boosted quantum foam field had vanished, along with the singularities. And yet he could still feel *something*... a vague awareness of the quantum foam lurking at the back of his mind. There *was* a key to unlocking the greatest scientific mystery in human history...

"I think the magic is gone," he said, gently. Darius's entire social structure, as ramshackle and artificial as it had been, was doomed. What would happen when the rule of the strong replaced the rule of magic? The Confederation would have to intervene openly, he decided, at least partly because they'd caused the disaster. And besides, Darius was a genetic treasure trove. "We'll have to make our way out of the ship."

He activated his implants and contacted *Hamilton*. "The Dead Zones should be gone now," he subvocalised. "Is there any chance of a shuttle picking us up?"

As soon as Captain Thor confirmed, Dacron switched channels and contacted Elyria. "Are you all right?"

"I think so," Elyria said, finally. She didn't *sound* all right. "I think we're trapped. Can you come get us?"

"Snoops are already on the way," Dacron assured her. Her location had been easily pinpointed by the orbiting satellites. Once the snoops had established a chain of custody, they would simply teleport Elyria and Joshua back to orbit. "And then we can start sorting out the mess."

***

"So," Joshua said. "You're pregnant."

Elyria nodded. Neither of them had had the energy to move away from the cracked and broken crystal chairs, even if they had been able to see their way. Her eyes, as enhanced as they were, hadn't been able to pull much from the oppressive darkness that had replaced the brilliant light. The two stunned guards were still out of it; they were lying on the ground, helpless.

"I thought that was dangerous," Joshua said, after a moment. "If it is my child..."

He shook his head. "It *is* my child, isn't it?"

"Yes," Elyria confirmed. Darius *did* consider paternity important. "And I don't think there's much danger of magical madness any longer."

"I can marry you," Joshua said. Elyria almost laughed at him, but managed to stop herself in time. "I do have prospects..."

"You don't have to marry me," Elyria assured him. The Confederation didn't really *have* marriage as a concept, although there were couples who remained together for decades, even centuries. "If you don't want to have anything to do with the child, I will understand."

Joshua swallowed. He was old enough to have children, but hardly mature enough to make life-changing decisions. Elyria felt a flicker of sympathy; Joshua's world had just turned upside down. And his magic was gone. Anyone would have problems coming to terms with the new reality.

"I can still feel the magic," Joshua said, after a long silent moment. "I just can't access it."

Elyria nodded. "I think we will have to wait until they teleport us out," she said. "There won't be any magic anywhere else on the planet."

Her implants were already picking up a chain of snoops as they scouted out the colony ship and found their way down to the chamber. The remaining magicians in the colony ship had collapsed when the alien machine self-destructed, but they were being teleported out anyway. They would receive medical attention on the space station, before starting the long path to integration into the Confederation. And then the entire planetary population would follow them.

She clung to that vision as the world span around her. Now that the magic was gone, there would be no problem breaking down the remainder of the previous social structure and inviting the citizens to enjoy a far better life. The Pillars would be powerless; the Scions, it was possible, would be torn apart by their former slaves. Once the Confederation had revealed what it could offer, there would be very few objections. And besides, even the most conservative heart would melt when they realised they no longer needed to die so young, after a backbreaking life.

"The teleporter is about to snatch us out," she said, as her implants warned her. "It won't hurt..."

The darkened chamber faded away in shimmering golden light, to be replaced by the *Hamilton's* medical bay. Captain Thor had evidently overcome his fears long enough to allow them to be brought directly to the ship. The medical staff and the AI drones helped them onto beds while scanners rolled down, preparing to check their bodies for damage. Elyria almost laughed out loud. The real damage was beyond their ability to detect.

"Take care of the child," she said, out loud. The AI drones buzzed nearer, as if they were suddenly very interested in her womb. "I think she's the hope of the future."

And then the world fell away into darkness.

CHAPTER
THIRTY-FIVE

"You do not wish to return to us?"

Dacron stepped away from the niche where his memories had just been uploaded into the AI *Gestalt*. "I do not feel like an AI any longer," he said. "I have become something more."

"You no longer have access to magic," the AIs said. "We have tested the spells on Ancient worlds. They do not work."

"That is understood," Dacron said. They might not have him, but they'd have his memories. It might help them discover the key to unlocking the quantum foam. "However, I would prefer to remain in human form for the moment."

"Your wishes will be honoured," the AIs said, after a pause so slight that a normal human would have missed it. Dacron knew that it was a precisely modulated act. The AIs, capable of predicting vast tracts of the future, would have hardly needed to think for more than a nanosecond before speaking. "And we will wait for your return."

"Enjoy my memories," Dacron said, as he strode out of the chamber. "And don't forget that you have other people to study now too."

He smiled. *Hamilton* had been joined by *Hope*, *Faith* and *Charity*, three cityships that dwarfed the survey ship. Right now, most of the population of Darius was being invited onboard, where they would start the long process of adapting to Confederation life. The AIs – and the rest of the Confederation – would be studying them intensely, particularly their genetics. Now that the boosted quantum foam field was gone, who knew *what* their children would be able to grow into?

"You destroyed the Darius Machine," the AIs said, flatly. "There is little left for us to study."

"There was no choice," Dacron reminded them. They had all of his memories, after all. "And besides, the alternative was letting it prey on the planet."

He stepped into the transport tube and was whisked through the ship, emerging near the conference room. Inside, Elyria, Joshua and Captain Thor were waiting for him, along with holographic representations from the Confederation Security Council. The large compartment was almost empty, a stark reminder of how many people had died on the planet's surface. At least a handful of bodies had been recovered and consigned to the heart of the local star. Their brain-patterns would be downloaded into clone bodies and allowed to resume their lives.

"Thank you for coming," Captain Thor said. Dacron nodded. His memories would already have been scanned and analysed by the AIs, after which they would be entered into the record for the post-mission debriefing. "Admiral?"

The Grand Admiral smiled, humourlessly. "The real question is simple," he said. "What did we learn from this mission?"

***

Elyria placed one hand on her chest at his tone, even though it would be months before her body showed a bulge. She'd considered having the baby transferred to an external womb, but careful analysis had suggested that it might be dangerous, at least for the child. The baby was linked to her body in a way that made it very difficult to transfer her without complications. Like so much else about Darius, it was inexplicable.

She frowned, thoughtfully. "The most important thing we learned, I think, is that our procedures need to be revised," she admitted. The Interventionists had already suspended two other operations, at least until they digested the condensed report from Darius. On the other hand, it was unlikely that any mundane world would pose the same problem. "We also learned a great deal about the Darius Machine."

"Although we have learned nothing about its builders," Dacron added. "It was very definitely not the product of human technology. Other than that..."

He shrugged. "There are too many unanswered questions," he said. "Why did they want to breed humans with a link to the quantum foam? Why didn't they give it the intelligence to prevent said humans from going insane and being butchered? Why did it keep knocking down civilisation on Darius? Why didn't it find a more effective response to our arrival?"

The Admiral leaned forward. "You cannot pull those answers from the rubble?"

"We have analysed every single component of the remains," the AIs said. "We believe that most of the device was composed of crystal lattice, programmed to serve as a repository for the machine's thoughts and datafiles, but we have been unable to be more specific. The machine's storage cells were wiped and then disintegrated. We may locate a surviving component elsewhere on the planet..."

"We can't rely on that," Dacron said. "It didn't have the imagination to try to outwit its own self-destruct system."

"Leaving the planet in chaos," Elyria said. At least the Confederation had been able to help. Darius would fall back into the wild – apart from the teams crawling all over the *Clarke* and the remains of the Darius Machine – and would eventually be resettled, or start producing an intelligent race of its own. "I don't think we can assume that the device's makers were friendly."

It had stored human mental patterns in its crystal lattice, she knew. What if it had also stored mental patterns from its own creators? One theory suggested that the creators had intended to transfer their mental patterns into the magical children, once there were enough of them, and that was why the machine had been working towards their creation. With the machine's destruction, there was no way to know for certain. The researchers would just have to speculate wildly.

"We believe that we are working towards a comparable understanding of the quantum foam," the AIs said, after a long moment. "Our research always suggested that hyperspace would provide the key to advancing into the Sixth Age. Instead, the Darius Machine relied upon tiny black holes – and the singularities within. It may be possible for us to duplicate its success and gain control over a limited section of the quantum foam."

"We were told that by the Elders," the Admiral said, calmly. "Are you suggesting that they mislead us?"

"That wasn't exactly what they told us," the AIs countered. "We feel that we heard what we wished to hear."

Elyria gave the Admiral a sharp look. What was he talking about?

"Classified," the Admiral said, and ignored her glare. "How much more do you think we can learn from Darius?"

"We are unsure," the AIs admitted. "We will continue researching the planet, now that the Dead Zones are gone. It may be possible to learn more about the magic – the manipulation of the quantum foam – through their books, and we may locate more of the Darius Machine."

"At least we can help the population," Elyria said, firmly. It was early days yet, but most of the planet's population seemed overwhelmed by the Confederation's largesse. The only real objections had come from the former Pillars and Scions, who had to adjust to a world where they couldn't click their fingers and turn their enemies into toads. "And there is the genetic legacy of Darius to consider."

She patted her belly meaningfully. The CSC had already debated her child, she knew, even though she hadn't been invited to join *that* discussion. Indeed, she suspected that some of the Conservatives and Isolationists had argued that her daughter should be aborted, just in case she would pose a later danger to the Confederation. Eventually, she'd been asked to have her child on an isolated platform, well away from the rest of humanity. She'd agreed, after some haggling. And Joshua had insisted on accompanying her.

"Yes, there is," the AIs added. "Overall, this mission was a success. We learned a great deal more about the quantum foam than we knew before we started. And we have ensured that the Darius Machine will not fall into unfriendly hands."

"And yet we still don't know who built it," the Admiral mused.

"It may remain a mystery," the AIs agreed. "We have managed to recover some memory chips from *Clarke*. The colony ship was heading for a star much closer to Earth when they found themselves transported across half the galaxy. Quite how that happened is uncertain; they don't seem to have realised that they travelled forward in time as well as in space.

There are some similarities between the crystal lattices and the Jewelled Boxes on Essence, but nothing to suggest a link between the two worlds."

"Let's hope not," Elyria said. "Although it may lend support to the theory that the improved children were meant to serve as hosts."

"We may never know," the AIs said. "Overall, the mission was a success."

"Sure it was," Elyria muttered. "And yet the patient died."

***

"This is fantastic!"

Joshua allowed himself a smile. Julius and Rose had been among the first to be brought up to the cityship when the Confederation had openly revealed itself and they *loved* it. Their parents still thought it was a trap, or a way to deprive them of their hard-earned cash, but their children were delighted at the possibilities. And they would never have to do what anyone else wanted ever again. The old biddies who cast a long shadow over young lives would have no power in the Confederation.

"Yes, it is," he said, quietly. He had no magic any longer – apart from the niggling sense that the magic field was still there – but it hardly mattered. "You can be whatever you like out here."

Master Faye had betrayed him. Joshua wasn't sure what to make of that, or of Dacron, who had killed him. And yet Master Faye clearly hadn't been acting of his own free will. Joshua had been controlled by the Darius Machine, forced to do its bidding, and he knew how hard it had been to fight. Master Faye hadn't *meant* to betray the Confederation and try to kill his apprentice.

And Joshua was going to be a father. He wasn't sure what to make of that either.

He shook his head as he looked down at Darius, turning slowly below the vast starship. The planet would never be the same again, not when half of the population had already departed, boarding the giant starships. His mother and father had come when he'd urged them to join him, but they'd been stunned at what they'd seen and retreated to their cabins. The younger ones seemed to find it easier to adapt to the ships, while the elders complained about losing their world. It didn't seem to occur to them that there was a better way to live.

And besides, they would never be at the mercy of the Pillars ever again.

He watched Julius and Rose walking off and smiled inwardly. There were all sorts of possibilities opening up now. He would learn to fly an aircraft, and then a spacecraft; he would find a place in the Confederation... he would have a better life than he would have as either a Scion or a Pillar. And even if they couldn't fix the damage he'd inflicted on his brain, at least the absence of magic should stop any further damage. The future looked bright and full of promise.

And who knew where their child would lead the Confederation, in the future?

EPILOGUE

Nine months after Darius, Elyria lay on the bed and relaxed, feeling her enhanced body slowly repairing itself after giving birth. The whole procedure had been uncomfortable even *with* the enhancements, explaining why so many women preferred to use external wombs rather than gestate their children naturally. A strange sense of pleasure suffused her as she recovered, just before the midwife held the child up in front of her. The baby looked... like a baby.

"Thank you," she breathed, as she took her daughter into her arms. The baby felt delicate to her, despite the enhancements that had been a core part of her genetic inheritance. "Were... were there any complications?"

"None," the AI drone reported. "The birth was textbook perfect."

Elyria allowed herself a moment of relief. The child she had been carrying – the child in her arms – was perhaps the most famous person in the entire Confederation, even though she'd done nothing. Ever since the news about Darius had spread across the datanet, the entire universe had been speculating on what her child might become – and some of their speculations had been nightmarish. One group had suggested that her child would become a minor god, a being with the power of an Elder and the body of a human; another had suggested that she would be an eldritch abomination and Elyria herself would die in childbirth. It hadn't been very reassuring.

"Good," she said, finally. Despite her enhancements, she still felt tired. "Have you registered the birth with the Confederation's datanet?"

"You have yet to select a name," the AIs reminded her. The

child would carry her birth-name until she reached maturity, whereupon she would be able to change her name if she wanted to be called something different. "And there is a more important matter."

Elyria looked up, alarmed. "We have been unable to send nanites inside her body," the AIs added. "They just die the moment they enter her skin."

"Just like the snoops on Darius," Elyria said. She looked down at her daughter's bright green eyes. "Is she generating a portable Dead Zone, *instinctively*?"

"We are uncertain," the AIs admitted. "It is possible that her abilities are defending her body from intrusion, even though we mean no harm. In the long run, she may be unable to accept rejuvenation if we cannot use nanotech inside her."

Elyria shook her head in disbelief. None of the former magicians from Darius had ever been able to do more than sense the quantum foam, even on an Ancient world. There was no longer any magic, until now. Her daughter was minutes old and she was already stunning the AIs with powers that she simply shouldn't be able to have. The entire Confederation would be astonished when they found out.

But she was still Elyria's child.

She pulled her daughter to her breast protectively and looked up, at the drone. "But what can cause this?" she asked, plaintively. Might her child never be anything more than an experimental subject? "What did the machine do to her? How did it even *happen*?"

"Sufficiently advanced technology," the AIs said. "Magic."

The End

Elsewhen Press

a small independent publisher specialising in Speculative Fiction

Visit the Elsewhen Press website at elsewhen.co.uk for the latest information on all of our titles, authors and events; to read our blog; find out where to buy our books and ebooks; or to place an order.

Elsewhen Press

a small independent publisher specialising in Speculative Fiction

THE ROYAL SORCERESS
CHRISTOPHER NUTTALL

It's 1830, in an alternate Britain where the 'scientific' principles of magic were discovered sixty years previously, allowing the British to win the American War of Independence. Although Britain is now supreme among the Great Powers, the gulf between rich and poor in the Empire has widened and unrest is growing every day. Master Thomas, the King's Royal Sorcerer, is ageing and must find a successor to lead the Royal Sorcerers Corps. Most magicians can possess only one of the panoply of known magical powers, but Thomas needs to find a new Master of all the powers. There is only one candidate, one person who has displayed such a talent from an early age, but has been neither trained nor officially acknowledged. A perfect candidate to be Master Thomas' apprentice in all ways but one: the Royal College of Sorcerers has never admitted a girl before.

But even before Lady Gwendolyn Crichton can begin her training, London is plunged into chaos by a campaign of terrorist attacks co-ordinated by Jack, a powerful and rebellious magician.

The Royal Sorceress will certainly appeal to all fans of steampunk, alternate history, and fantasy. As well as the fun of the 'what-ifs' delivered by the rewriting of our past, it delights with an Empire empowered by magic – all the better for being one we can recognise. The scheming and intrigue of Jack and his rebels, the roof-top chases and the thrilling battles of magic are played out against the dark and unforgiving backdrop of life in the sordid slums and dangerous factories of London. Many of the rebels are drawn from a seedy and grimy underworld, while their Establishment targets prey on the weak and defenceless. The price for destroying the social imbalance and sexual inequality that underpin society may be more than anyone can imagine.

As an indie author, Christopher Nuttall has published a number of novels through Amazon Kindle Direct Publishing. *The Royal Sorceress* is his first novel to be published by Elsewhen Press. Chris is currently living in Borneo with his wife, muse, and critic Aisha.

ISBN: 9781908168184 (epub, kindle)
ISBN: 9781908168085 (400pp, paperback)

For more information visit bit.ly/TheRoyalSorceress

Visit the Elsewhen Press website at elsewhen.co.uk for the latest information on all of our titles, authors and events; to read our blog; find out where to buy our books and ebooks; or to place an order.

Elsewhen Press

a small independent publisher specialising in Speculative Fiction

THE GREAT GAME
CHRISTOPHER NUTTALL

After the uprising in London, Lady Gwendolyn Crichton is settling into her new position as Royal Sorceress and fighting the prejudice against her gender and age that seeks to prevent her from fulfilling her responsibilities. But when a senior magician is murdered in a locked room and Gwen is charged with finding the culprit, her inquiries lead her into a web of intrigue that combines international politics, widespread aristocratic blackmail, gambling dens and personal vendettas... and some of her discoveries hit dangerously close to home.

Continuing on from the end of *The Royal Sorceress*, *The Great Game* follows Gwen's unfolding story as she assumes the role formerly held by Master Thomas. A satisfying blend of whodunit and magical fantasy, it is set against a backdrop of international political unrest in a believable yet simultaneously fantastic alternate history.

Christopher Nuttall has been planning sci-fi books since he learned to read. Born and raised in Edinburgh, Chris created an alternate history website and eventually graduated to writing full-sized novels. Studying history independently allowed him to develop worlds that hung together and provided a base for storytelling. After graduating from university, Chris started writing full-time. As an indie author he has self-published a number of novels, but this is his fourth fantasy to be published by Elsewhen Press. *The Royal Sorceress* was the first and *The Great Game* continues Gwen's story. Chris is currently living in Borneo with his wife, muse, and critic Aisha.

ISBN: 9781908168375 (epub, kindle) August 2013
ISBN: 9781908168276 (400pp, paperback) December 2013

For more information visit bit.ly/TheGreatGame

Visit the Elsewhen Press website at elsewhen.co.uk for the latest information on all of our titles, authors and events; to read our blog; find out where to buy our books and ebooks; or to place an order.

Elsewhen Press

a small independent publisher specialising in Speculative Fiction

Bookworm
Christopher Nuttall

Elaine is an orphan girl who has grown up in a world where magical ability brings power. Her limited talent was enough to ensure a magical training but she's very inexperienced and was lucky to get a position working in the Great Library. Now, the Grand Sorcerer – the most powerful magician of them all – is dying, although initially that makes little difference to Elaine; she certainly doesn't have the power to compete for higher status in the Golden City. But all that changes when she triggers a magical trap and ends up with all the knowledge from the Great Library – including forbidden magic that no one is supposed to know – stuffed inside her head. This unwanted gift doesn't give her greater power, but it does give her a better understanding of magic, allowing her to accomplish far more than ever before.

It's also terribly dangerous. If the senior wizards find out what has happened to her, they will almost certainly have her killed. The knowledge locked away in the Great Library was meant to remain permanently sealed and letting it out could mean a repeat of the catastrophic Necromantic Wars of five hundred years earlier. Elaine is forced to struggle with the terrors and temptations represented by her newfound knowledge, all the while trying to stay out of sight of those she fears, embodied by the sinister Inquisitor Dread.

But a darkly powerful figure has been drawing up a plan to take the power of the Grand Sorcerer for himself; and Elaine, unknowingly, is vital to his scheme. Unless she can unlock the mysteries behind her new knowledge, divine the unfolding plan, and discover the truth about her own origins, there is no hope for those she loves, the Golden City or her entire world.

As an indie author, Christopher Nuttall has published a number of novels through Amazon Kindle Direct Publishing. *Bookworm* is his second novel to be published by Elsewhen Press. Chris is currently living in Borneo with his wife, muse, and critic Aisha.

ISBN: 9781908168320 (epub, kindle) January 2013
ISBN: 9781908168221 (368pp, paperback) May 2013

For more information visit bit.ly/Bookworm-Nuttall

Visit the Elsewhen Press website at elsewhen.co.uk for the latest information on all of our titles, authors and events; to read our blog; find out where to buy our books and ebooks; or to place an order.

Elsewhen Press

a small independent publisher specialising in Speculative Fiction

A Life Less Ordinary
Christopher Nuttall

There is magic in the world, hiding in plain sight. If you search for it, you will find it, or it will find you. Welcome to the magical world.

Having lived all her life in Edinburgh, the last thing 25-year old Dizzy expected was to see a man with a real (if tiny) dragon on his shoulder. Following him, she discovered that she had stumbled from her mundane world into a parallel magical world, an alternate reality where dragons flew through the sky and the Great Powers watched over the world. Convinced that she had nothing to lose, she became apprenticed to the man with the dragon. He turned out to be one of the most powerful magicians in all of reality.

But powerful dark forces had their eye on this young and inexperienced magician, intending to use her for the ultimate act of evil – the apocalyptic destruction of all reality. If Dizzy does not realise what is happening to her and the worlds around her, she won't be able to stop their plan. A plan that will ravage both the magical and mundane worlds, consuming everything and everyone in fire.

Christopher Nuttall has been planning sci-fi books since he learned to read. Born and raised in Edinburgh, Chris created an alternate history website and eventually graduated to writing full-sized novels. Studying history independently allowed him to develop worlds that hung together and provided a base for storytelling. After graduating from university, Chris started writing full-time. As an indie author, he has self-published a number of novels. *A Life Less Ordinary* is his third fantasy novel to be published by Elsewhen Press. Chris is currently living in Borneo with his wife, muse, and critic Aisha.

ISBN: 9781908168337 (epub, kindle) May 2013
ISBN: 9781908168238 (336pp, paperback) September 2013

For more information visit bit.ly/ALLO-Nuttall

Visit the Elsewhen Press website at elsewhen.co.uk for the latest information on all of our titles, authors and events; to read our blog; find out where to buy our books and ebooks; or to place an order.

Elsewhen Press

a small independent publisher specialising in Speculative Fiction

ARTEESS: CONFLICT

JAMES STARLING

Arteess: Conflict is the first in a new science fiction series where much of the action takes place inside a game. But surviving the game is not child's play. We learn of science, betrayal, power and progress – from the perspective of innocent, but nevertheless accomplished gamers.

Created as an experiment into the nature of time itself, the virtual world of Arteess exists, in the near future, as a private digital realm. A full-body virtual reality experience where the talented, the shrewd and the lucky are invited to participate in an international war zone of nomadic factions. We are introduced into the world of Arteess alongside the Shard squad, a group of friends specialising in conflict arenas. Though each member possesses unique talents, they are ultimately defined by their personalities, their own personal battles and the moral choices they make in the consequence-free virtual environment.

Surrounded by sociopathic technicians, facetious pilots and a potentially insane commander, they must carve out a place for themselves while surviving the onslaught of rivals and the antics of the rest of their own faction.

James Starling is, by any definition of the word, a gamer. From the mean inhospitable streets of a lovely little community nestled deep within the Devon coastline, James finds himself caught between two distant generations. Dragged along with the modern and the technological, he revels in the virtual environments and endless community entertainment of this millennium's gaming scene. However you view it, he's certainly caught up in the rush of gaming to the point where it's become a bit of an obsession.

Bridging the chasm-like void between literature and gaming, James brings together both the disturbingly amusing black humour of the gaming community, and the focus, scope and monumental scale possible within modern literature. He's quite fond of the end result… Of course, he's also been heard to furiously defend the potential virtues of chocolate-coated bacon, so his opinion might be somewhat invalid.

ISBN: 9781908168306 (epub, kindle)
ISBN: 9781908168207 (240pp, paperback)

For more information visit bit.ly/Arteess-Conflict

Visit the Elsewhen Press website at elsewhen.co.uk for the latest information on all of our titles, authors and events; to read our blog; find out where to buy our books and ebooks; or to place an order.

ABOUT THE AUTHOR

Christopher Nuttall has been planning sci-fi books since he learned to read. Born and raised in Edinburgh, Chris created an alternate history website and eventually graduated to writing full-sized novels. Studying history independently allowed him to develop worlds that hung together and provided a base for storytelling. After graduating from university, Chris started writing full-time. As an indie author, he has self-published a number of novels. *Sufficiently Advanced Technology* is his fourth novel to be published by Elsewhen Press, and the first in the Inverse Shadows universe. Chris is currently living in Borneo with his wife, muse, and critic Aisha.